PART TWO
BLOOD UNION
BLOOD GRACE BOOK VI

VELA ROTH

FIVE THORNS PRESS

ISBN 978-1-957040-18-9 (Ebook)
ISBN 978-1-957040-19-6 (Paperback)
ISBN 978-1-957040-20-2 (Hardcover)

Edited by Brittany Cicirello, Suncroft Editing

Cover art by Patcas Illustration
www.instagram.com/patcas_illustration

Book design by Vela Roth

Map by Vela Roth using Inkarnate
inkarnate.com

Published by Five Thorns Press
www.fivethorns.com

·t www.velaroth.com

CONTENTS

Content Note ix

Map of the Empire x

Map of Tenebra.. xi

69 Days Until Notian Winter Solstice................................ 1

    An Uncertain Compass... 3

    Nyakimbi 16

    Real Training... 29

68 Days Until Notian Winter Solstice.............................. 37

    The Golden Shield 39

    The Ancestors' Keeping.. 52

    Hesperines Errant 60

    On the Verge 66

67 Days Until Notian Winter Solstice.............................. 83

    The Face of the Enemy.. 85

    Forces of Nature 89

    Forgotten in the Maaqul 102

    Battle Arts 108

66 Days Until Notian Winter Solstice............................ 127

    A Free Service 129

    Pray Later 135

    Alone... 140

    Noon Watch 144

65 Days Until Notian Winter Solstice............................ 155

    Doernchen... 157

    Grace Union 160

64 Days Until Notian Winter Solstice...................................... 165

    Whispers in the Desert 167

    Peanut 175

    Mweya's Wings... 188

    The Braid.. 193

63 Days Until Notian Winter Solstice...................................... 199

    Sunburn.. 201

    Standstill 210

    Lonesome 213

    Lullaby.. 220

62 Days Until Notian Winter Solstice...................................... 229

    The Favor of the Moons 231

61 Days Until Notian Winter Solstice...................................... 241

    Oasis 243

    A Taste for Danger 251

60 Days Until Notian Winter Solstice...................................... 259

    Shadow and Sunshine 261

    Into the Ruins 274

    The Hidden Blade 284

    Seven Secrets.. 294

    Warpath.. 302

59 Days Until Notian Winter Solstice...................................... 315

    The Only Cord.. 317

    Obelisks.. 322

    The Cause 325

    Mirage.. 331

    Shattered Hope 337

58 Days Until Notian Winter Solstice...................................... 351

    The Best Intuition 353

    Lost and Found... 365

57 Days Until Notian Winter Solstice...................................... 371

    Mind Games... 373

    A Lesson in Diplomacy.. 378

    Court of Kings 391

    A Blessed Match 396

54 Days Until Notian Winter Solstice.............................. 403
   The Face of Death.. 405
   Work of Art... 407
53 Days Until Notian Winter Solstice.............................. 427
   Ancestors 429
   Final Test.. 448
52 Days Until Notian Winter Solstice.............................. 451
   Arcane Mystery.. 453
51 Days Until Notian Winter Solstice.............................. 469
   Medallion of Office... 471
   The Way Forward 475
   The Cassia Grove.. 486
   Winding Journey 504
   Ancient Blood 510
Glossary 515
About the Author.. 535

Marvelous word witches of the coven,
this half is for you, too.
Without you, I would never have
survived all 340,473 words!

CONTENT NOTE

BLOOD UNION Part Two portrays fantasy violence and characters healing from trauma. The heroine experiences flashbacks of her father's emotional abuse in "Ancestors" (53 Days Until Notian Winter Solstice). "The Cassia Grove" (51 Days Until Notian Winter Solstice) mentions pregnancy loss.

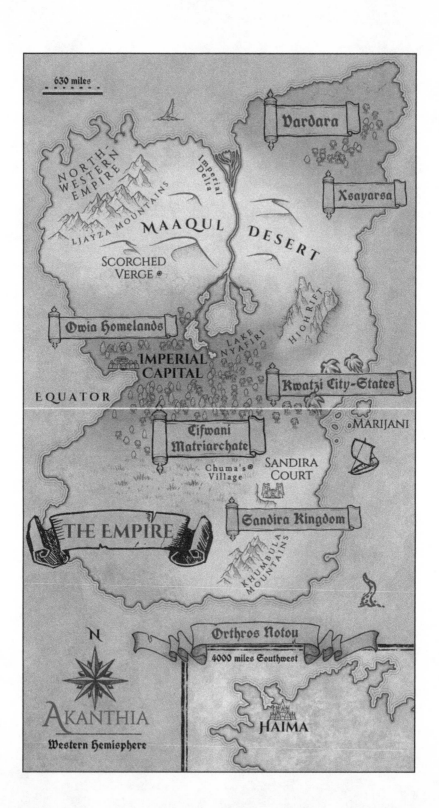

630 miles

Vardara

Xsayarsa

NORTH-
WESTERN
EMPIRE

Imperial
Delta

LJAYZA MOUNTAINS

MAAQUL

DESERT

SCORCHED
VERGE

Owia Homelands

HIGHRIFT

LAKE
NYAFIRI

IMPERIAL
CAPITAL

Kwatzi City-States

EQUATOR

MARIJANI

Cifwani
Matriarchate

Chuma's
Village

SANDIRA
COURT

THE EMPIRE

Sandira Kingdom

KHUMBULA
MOUNTAINS

N

Orthros Notou

4000 miles Southwest

AKANTHIA

HAIMA

Western Hemisphere

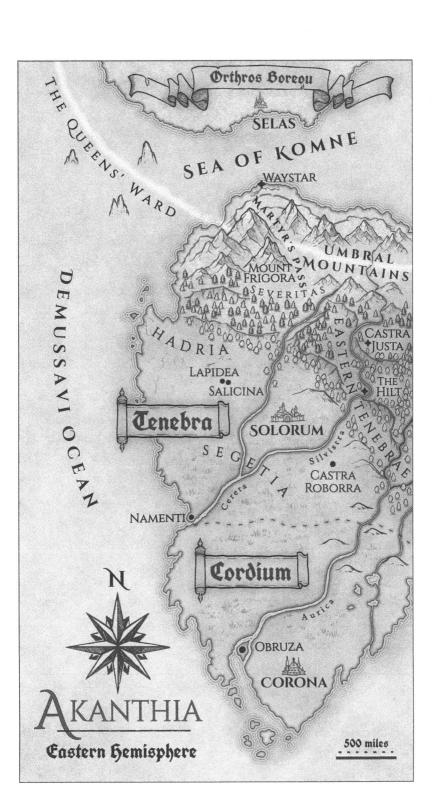

Orthros Boreou

SELAS

SEA OF KOMNE

THE QUEENS' WARD

WAYSTAR

MARTYR'S PASS

UMBRAL MOUNTAINS

MOUNT FRIGORA

SEVERITAS

HADRIA

EASTERN TENEBRAE

CASTRA JUSTA

LAPIDEA

SALICINA

THE HILT

DEMUSSAVI OCEAN

Tenebra

SOLORUM

SEGETIA

Silvistra

CASTRA ROBORRA

Cerera

NAMENTI

Cordium

Aurica

N

OBRUZA

CORONA

AKANTHIA

Eastern Hemisphere

500 miles

$\mathscr{E}$≈69≈$\mathscr{E}$

days until

NOTIAN WINTER SOLSTICE

36th Night of the Month of Annassa
1,596th Year In Sanctuary (IS)

AN UNCERTAIN COMPASS

L IO CRUMPLED THE SHREDS of Cassia's arrest warrant in his hands. When he had brought her here to the Empire to rescue her sister, he had never imagined she would be in as much danger as Solia. Despite his protection, his Grace was now a fugitive in the land of their allies.

His magic welled out of him, and he obliterated the warrant with a vicious spell. The resulting flash of light, brighter than the dying campfire, illuminated the dark, deserted veld around them. "We must get you out of this kingdom as soon as possible."

Cassia slid her small, strong hand into his larger one, and the destructive magic hovering at his fingertips banked at her touch. "If we cross the border to a different state within the Empire, will that help me avoid arrest?"

Their guide, if one could call a shapeshifting mercenary of dubious motivations such, was still wincing and rubbing his eyes in the wake of the glaring spell. Lio might or might not have aimed it in his direction.

This man who went by the cryptic name of Monsoon had once served as a guard for the Sandira King. The very king who now wanted to throw Cassia in prison. Even if Monsoon had apparently helped Cassia escape, Lio would never trust him.

Monsoon squinted at them and snapped the massive eagle wings he sported even in his human form. "I hope you two feel refreshed after your fun around the campfire because we're leaving now. Only bring what you can't live without."

"That doesn't answer my question," Cassia said.

"We don't have time for questions." Monsoon scowled.

As if the man's displeasure was a deadly threat, Knight cowered. Lio could scarcely believe the liegehound was on his belly instead of lashing out in defense of Cassia. "What have you done to our dog?"

Monsoon sighed. "He knows a more powerful predator when he meets one."

Cassia knelt by Knight and put an arm around his shaggy neck. "Stop frightening him."

Monsoon looked to the sky as if begging his ancestors for patience. But then his massive, ever-present magic eased off, a relief even to Lio's keen auric senses. Lio could still sense the vastness of Monsoon's power, but it seemed less aggressive somehow.

Monsoon's shifter magic felt much more powerful than that of the other royal guards. His abilities must have been valuable to his king. How had he lost that status and ended up with a mercenary's fortune blade strapped to his arm?

At last, Knight crept to his feet, although he still pressed himself against Cassia. Her calf-length travel robe and loose Imperial trousers were already covered by the dog's anxious shedding. She stroked his head while he watched Monsoon warily. "There, there, dearest. This inconsiderate fellow knows we'll dock his pay if he isn't kind to you."

"Mweya's Wings," Monsoon swore. "Kicking puppies is not on my list of deeds as a mercenary."

Judging by the scars on his arms, he had not been so kind to his human enemies. Lio gave Knight a comforting pat. "How precisely did you get on the gold roster of the Empire's most accomplished mercenaries?"

"By being the best at what I do." Monsoon said it like a fact, not a boast.

Lio cared nothing for the man's skill. It was a travesty that Monsoon was the only person in the sunbound Empire who could guide them to Ukocha.

For a renowned fire mage, sword master, and mercenary commander, Ukocha was certainly elusive. But she was also the woman who had aided Solia years before.

Lio would have stepped Cassia to safety that very moment, if he did not understand his Grace's need to follow their only lead on her sister.

Lio began rifling through their travel packs, tossing unnecessary items into their nearby trunks, and returned to Cassia's original question. "The surrounding kingdoms have complex alliances and rivalries with the Sandira King. If one state finds a fugitive from another within their borders, they'll call in the Imperial authorities to mediate and make a decision about extradition."

Cassia joined him, sorting through their trunks for what they did need and filling the space he had made in their packs. "We cannot afford attention from those authorities, either."

Monsoon crossed his arms. "There are no authorities that will turn a blind eye to a human from Tenebra setting foot here. Your presence is illegal everywhere in the Empire."

"She is no more a Tenebran than I am," said Lio. "Our ancestors may have been born there, but by blood and Will, we are citizens of Orthros."

Monsoon pointed at Lio. "You have fangs."

"So will I, soon enough," Cassia protested.

But there was no arguing with Monsoon's prejudice against so-called shadowlanders from Tenebra, nor his king's determination to arrest Cassia due to her origins and a barrage of false charges.

Lio gritted his teeth. "The Sandira King is known for getting his way."

Monsoon reached into the leather bandolier he wore across his chest and pulled out some jerky. It smelled like preserved snake. Disgusting. "Things aren't convenient for us mortals like they are for you, silkfoot. When tens of thousands of people live within spitting distance of each other, someone has to keep order, and that someone is the king. Lives depend on him getting his way."

"Cassia's safety currently depends on him not getting his way, so pardon me if I feel less than enthusiastic about his methods of governance at the moment."

"I never said he was perfect." Monsoon shrugged between bites of snake jerky. "We still need to get out of Sandira lands as soon as possible. As soon as he discovers she's no longer in the city, he'll widen the search."

Cassia's aura sparked with her temper. "Isn't he busy receiving some sort of state visitor? That famous brother of his—this Prince Tendeso everyone is gossiping about? The king should be too occupied planning feasts to chase some little shadowlander."

Monsoon gave a humorless laugh. "The business of the kingdom does not stop for Prince Tendeso, I assure you. We can expect search parties out here by dawn."

"I'll keep us veiled at all times," Lio said.

"That won't be enough." Now Monsoon looked a little smug. "Veil spells hide nothing from the ancestors."

Lio let the lid of his trunk slam shut. "The king is so determined to find Cassia that he would consult the ancestors to find her?"

"Why do you think I went to the trouble of flying her out here? It would have made her too easy to find if I had spirit walked. Our form of magical travel here in the Empire requires treading through the realm of the ancestors."

Lio could have predicted Cassia's reaction to all of this, even if their bond hadn't allowed him to sense her emotions. He felt her horror as a chill shivering through her aura.

"Your king can do that?" she demanded. "Simply ask the dead where I am, and they will find me for him?"

"Show some respect," Monsoon snapped. "Our clans have lived and died here for generations, earning the wisdom of the land. The ancestors deserve reverence. And you would do well not to give them reason to want you found and punished."

Regret swept through Cassia then. "Forgive me. Of course you are right. I am only a guest here, perhaps an unwanted one at that, and I should behave as such. I should not let my irreverence toward my own mortal kin make me insensitive toward yours."

"You shouldn't be irreverent to your own ancestors, either," said Monsoon.

"You don't know the man who sired me. I make a point to be as irreverent toward him and his rotting forefathers as possible. However, I would gladly pay my respects to the ancestors of the Sandira people, if there is any way I can beg their pardon for my offensive words."

"They'll decide for themselves." There was a bitter edge to Monsoon's smile. "They saw what you did yesterday, they hear your words today, and they know better than you what you'll do tomorrow. All you can do is accept the surprises they throw at you."

"It sounds like you speak from experience," Lio said.

Monsoon didn't elaborate. "The ancestors won't simply draw a map for the king where 'X' marks the fugitive. They aren't at our beck and call. If they decide to intervene, they might give the diviners signs to interpret or send the king a dream. We don't want to wait around to find out."

"How are we traveling to your contact?" Lio asked.

The mercenary pulled out another piece of jerky. "Unfortunately for you—and even more so for me—we really don't want to shorten our time together by smuggling Freckles here through any spirit gates. Illicit gate travel with a wanted fugitive will just decorate her arrest warrant. Skill and coin aren't the only reasons I am on the gold roster. We have a code of conduct, unlike the sellswords of Tenebra. Let's try to keep the law breaking to a minimum from now on, shall we?"

This man had kidnapped Cassia mere hours ago. Monsoon might have a moral compass, but Lio found it difficult to assess which direction it pointed. "I will step us where Cassia needs to go."

She looked up at him. "No, Lio. We talked about this. Stepping past the border authorities is illegal as well."

"My only concern right now is keeping you safe."

"I won't have your reputation in the Empire destroyed for my sake. You're already risking it by aiding me while I'm a fugitive."

"As if my reputation matters when you need me."

"Ah, love," said Monsoon. "How entertaining to watch you digging yourself in deeper, silkfoot. But in this case, I suppose I must agree with you. Stepping is the least of the evils, and if you get caught, the Empire will handle a Hesperine with care."

"Hesperines don't get caught," Lio said.

"That too." Monsoon polished off his last piece of dessicated snake. Lio had lost track of how many the man had eaten. "You've been to the Cifwani Matriarchate, I assume?"

"Of course," Lio replied in surprise. "The people who live there are present-day descendants of the ancient culture from which our Queen Soteira hails. Like many Hesperines, I have learned her language, so I can communicate with the Cifwani somewhat, although I am not fluent in their modern dialect."

"So you can step us there."

"Where specifically?"

"Anywhere. The place we're headed is out of the way, and I can't provide a focus to help you step directly there. But at least you can step us out of Sandira lands in a hurry. After that, you, Cassia, and the fur rug can wait in a safe location while I fly to our destination. After I reach my contact, you can step to me. Flying will be faster, and I'll enjoy a solo flight much more than traipsing cross country with you lovebirds."

Lio would also enjoy the man being as far from Cassia as possible. "We'll need to think about the safest way to get provisions while we wait for you."

Monsoon pointed at the tent. "Didn't you find my stash? There's enough wildebeest jerky in there to last a week."

"Are there any edible plants in the area?" Cassia asked. "I could forage if you tell me more about what grows here."

"Do I look like a botanist?" the man retorted.

"You seem like an experienced traveler," Cassia said. "I thought perhaps you would know something about the local flora."

"I'm from the city. I buy anything that isn't meat. I can tell you how to kill, skin, and smoke any animal in the Empire, though."

Cassia swallowed. "I am of no use on a hunt. Knight is, however. I'll see to it he catches his own food."

Monsoon raised an eyebrow at Lio. "Well, at least your provisions are taken care of."

Lio put a protective arm around her. "It is also my responsibility to make sure Cassia is provided for." He looked at her. "Eat the meat."

Monsoon rolled his eyes. "When you're a fugitive from Sandira justice in the wilderness, it's no time to indulge vegetarian whims."

"It's not a whim," she said. "It's preparation for my transformation into a Hesperine. I'm not sure I *can* eat meat anymore."

Monsoon shrugged. "Then you'll be hungry until we reach my contact."

"We can get supplies there?" Lio asked.

"Yes. It's a farm. You bleeding hearts from Orthros will love it. Plants. Milk. Happy animals."

"Until then..." Lio levitated the wallet of jerky from the tent to his hand and held it out to Cassia. "If I can stand to touch it, you can stand to eat it."

Her distraught expression was entirely endearing. "Will you work a cleaning spell on my mouth afterward?"

"Certainly."

Monsoon let out an angry huff. "That is an injustice to some excellent meat."

Cassia waved a hand at the wallet. "Then you eat it, since you've decimated your supply while we've been packing."

"Don't tempt me. You have no idea how much energy flying takes." He laughed and flexed his fingers. Talons arced out from where his fingernails had been. "These weren't made for hunting vegetables."

The predators chasing Cassia worried Lio only slightly more than the one helping them flee.

He tucked the meat stash into her pack and glanced at the Light Moon just rising over the horizon. "It's already past midnight, and the Cifwani Matriarchate is northwest of us."

Cassia's face fell. "So, closer to the equator, which means we'll have fewer hours of night after we step there?"

Each step they took northward made him feel cheated. He hated the thought of every minute she must spend in sunlight, without him, with the mercenary.

Monsoon cast one last glance around the campsite, then gave a nod. "You aren't bad at traveling light, for a couple of silkfoots from Orthros."

"This isn't my first joust." Lio refrained from saying that being a good traveler was requisite for his career as an ambassador.

Right now, it didn't matter what service he was in. It only mattered that he could be of use on their journey.

Cassia gave Monsoon a look of mock astonishment. "You just called me a silkfoot instead of a shadowlander. It's about time. I insist on the correct insult."

"Don't let it go to your head." Monsoon knelt and checked to make sure the fire was completely out.

Lio hoisted his and Cassia's traveling packs onto his back. She eyed them with a frown.

"It only makes sense for me to carry them." Lio didn't point out that he was a Hesperine and wouldn't get tired, and they would make better time if he carried everything. "You'll have your hands full managing Knight."

She pressed her lips together, but didn't protest that Knight was obedient and easy to manage. Lio was grateful. He knew his excuse was thin, but he didn't want to draw any more attention than necessary to the sensitive subject of her mortality.

Monsoon ambled closer to them. "Ever stepped a shapeshifter before?"

"I haven't had the pleasure." Lio gave the man a humorless smile.

"Well, the gods of luck are smiling upon you tonight. My magic is tied to the land of my ancestors and doesn't care for being dragged off. You're about to feel like a bird trying to fly with a ball and chain around your ankles." He narrowed his eyes at Lio. "But you're powerful enough. At least you can use enough magic to make it more comfortable for both of us. I'm not acclimated to your affinity, though. Best put your hand on my shoulder."

Lio did so. "You have a very thorough understanding of the magical principles of Hesperine stepping," Lio observed.

"Not my first joust, either. Try to aim for a deserted location."

"No, I thought I would drop us in the middle of the Queen Mother's royal seat and shoot some lightworks into the sky over our heads for good measure."

"Does a silkfoot like you even know any unpopulated areas to focus on?"

"How about a watering hole on the savanna a day's ride from the main road?"

Monsoon sighed. "That will do."

Cassia looked at Lio with curiosity. "Sometime you must tell me all about riding to a watering hole on the savanna."

Lio smiled. "I'll turn it into a bedtime story for Zoe."

Monsoon gave them one of his piercing glances, which reminded Lio that the man could shift his eyes into those of an eagle. "Don't tell me you have a fanged lovechild waiting for you back in Orthros. That really is impossible, right?"

"Right." Cassia's eyes glinted with amusement. "When we start our family, we'll adopt children like Zoe. She's Lio's eight-year-old sister."

"Ah." Monsoon's frown became less severe.

Hearing Cassia talk about their future children softened Lio's mood. He ignored Monsoon and covered all of them in his most thorough veil spells, then focused on their destination.

Stepping with Cassia had become almost as easy as stepping himself. His magic was in her veins, her blood in his. He brought Knight's familiar, recalcitrant weight into his concentration, along with the small distractions of clothing and packs and the potent magical artifacts in Cassia's satchel.

Then he cautiously applied his Will to Monsoon's aura.

Lio's teeth ached. His ears roared. With his head spinning, he stepped them as quickly and forcefully as possible to get the worst of it over. His stomach turned over twice before their new surroundings manifested.

Lio worked his jaw. "Your analogy was lacking. It felt more like being caught in a whirlwind."

"Oh?" Monsoon snorted. "My old Hesperine friend would be amused by that."

Lio pried his hand from the man's shoulder with relief.

Monsoon lifted his foot, observing the horse dung on the bottom of his sandal. "He'd also mock your aim."

With a start, Lio realized they were in the middle of the main road. "This was open savanna last time I was here."

"And when was that?" Monsoon asked.

"Forty-three years ago." Lio winced.

Monsoon looked from him to Cassia. "She can't be older than twenty-two. Cradle-robber."

"On the contrary," Lio replied, "by Hesperine standards, I am barely of age."

"I'm a little old for him, in fact," Cassia said.

Monsoon got off the road with the help of his wings. Lio levitated himself and Cassia to join him amid the low scrub, while Knight crashed into the underbrush after them and began sniffing the unfamiliar terrain.

Monsoon had found a stick and was cleaning the bottom of his sandal. Lio should offer him a cleaning spell, but didn't.

Night insects creaked around them, and the scent of grasses and distant rain drifted across the open land. Thunder rolled at the edges of the sky, the encore of the rainy season drawing to a close here, even as it began in the coastal city-states they had left behind.

Cassia gazed across the grassland dotted with low bushes and small thorny acacia trees. "It's so beautiful. This is where Annassa Soteira came from?"

"Not exactly. But the people who live here in the present day share her heritage."

Cassia smiled. "That makes it feel like we're a little less far from home."

"Don't get too comfortable," Monsoon warned.

Lio followed the man's gaze. Still some distance away, a group of mortals approached along the road.

"Wings," Monsoon said.

Lio's Hesperine eyes revealed the same truth. A small contingent of winged men with spears marched alongside a group of female warriors. The women were armed with iron axes and outfitted in light barkcloth armor that emanated magic.

"Bleeding thorns," Lio swore. "Those are Sandira guards with Cifwani warriors. What are they doing here?"

"Do the Sandira and Cifwani make any regular patrols together?" There was little hope in Cassia's tone.

"No," Monsoon said. "That appears to be a search party. I do believe the Cifwani are already helping the Sandira hunt for you."

Cassia's hands tightened on the strap of her gardening satchel. "How is that possible? I thought it would take mediation for them to decide to work together."

"Apparently they've made an exception," said Monsoon. "Lucky you."

She shook her head. "How did they beat us here? How many people in the Empire can spirit walk like you, Monsoon?"

"Anyone with enough magic, but only within their ancestral lands."

"So the Cifwani and Sandira can simply spirit walk and meet each other at the border. Perfect."

Lio strengthened his veils, for all the good it would do. "The Cifwani can consult their diviners as easily as the Sandira. The ancestors could peer through my veils at any time."

"Let's get farther from the road," said Cassia.

They sought shelter on a low rise where a line of bushes would conceal them while they observed the road. Not that foliage would deter ancestors who could see through veils. But it would give them some cover from the mortals the ancestors might send their way.

Monsoon stretched out on his belly to watch the riders. "The best tactic now is to not stay in one place for very long."

Lio crouched behind a thorn bush, keeping an arm around Cassia's shoulders. "We have to step directly to your contact."

"I told you, I can't provide you with a focus."

"Yes, you can."

"Lio." The urgency in Cassia's tone told him she knew what he was about to suggest. "Are you sure?"

"Needs must." He hadn't planned to reveal his affinity for thelemancy to Monsoon, to preserve the advantage of surprise in case he ever needed to use his magic against the man. But right now, he needed to use it to get Cassia to safety.

Not for the first time, he wished finding Solia was as simple as stepping to her. Using Cassia's memories as a focus, if he could have taken them directly to her sister, none of this danger would have befallen his Grace. But whatever concealing magic kept her safely hidden here in the Empire also prevented him from locating her.

Monsoon muttered a string of words that sounded like curses. "If I had something you could use to step to my contact, I would show it to you. I don't want to lie here and wait for the guards any more than you do."

"Give me directions."

"If that worked, my old friend would have tried it long ago."

"I take it he's not a mind mage."

"Oh, *gods*." Monsoon's shoulders shook. Then his laughter escaped him, the laughter of a man who'd had enough. "That arrest warrant accused her of 'manipulating a Hesperine guest.'"

"I told you the charges are outrageous," Cassia said.

The mercenary covered his face. "I could be relaxing over a flask of ora, but instead I'm lying in the mud next to a couple of overdressed fugitives because some bureaucrat thinks a little girl from Tenebra can outsmart a Hesperine thelemancer."

"Outsmart me, certainly," Lio said, "but she would never manipulate me."

"You're a lovesick fool."

"Well, I won't deny that."

"I will," Cassia said indignantly. "Except for the love."

Monsoon rolled to a sitting position, his humor disappearing. He looked at Lio with a warning in his gaze. "Don't think I'll let you parade through my mind."

"Of course not." Lio set aside his distaste for the man. No matter who Monsoon was, his Will was as sacred as every person's, and Lio would not trespass upon it. "I've trusted you with the knowledge of my affinity. Now I hope you'll trust me to use it with honor. All I ask is that you envision our destination strongly in your thoughts. How it smells. What the air tastes like. The personality of your contact. If you project those powerfully enough, I should be able to sense them without even applying my power to your mind."

"Oh, wonderful. Not any garden variety thelemancer. A powerful one."

Lio might as well put all his playing pieces on the board. "One of the three most powerful in Orthros."

"What were you doing slumming in the traders' camps around the Sandira Court?"

"Trying to be alone with Cassia."

"Not exactly the kind of getaway we had planned," she said grimly.

On the stretch of road below their hiding place, the riders finally drew near. Lio stopped breathing and heard Cassia and Monsoon hold their breath as well. They all waited in silence to see if the riders would pass.

The Cifwani and Sandira warriors left the road, dismounted, and began to organize a search.

"I'm stepping Cassia away," Lio said. "We can go to your contact together, or Cassia and I can go where I take us and leave you to fly after us and your payment."

Monsoon pointed at Lio. "You Hesperines have more conscience than common sense. You may listen to my thoughts. Listen. That is all. Don't imagine you can sniff around for what I know. My contacts won't talk to you. You need me."

Lio gave a nod. "You have my gratitude."

"If you wanted to raid my mind, you wouldn't have asked politely first. Get on with it."

Lio let his magic sweep up from within him to reveal the thoughts perched on the surface of Monsoon's mind. Lio was surprised to see a young girl's smiling face. She looked about Zoe's age.

Monsoon remembered her in loving detail. Her button nose, the short cloud of curly black hair around her head, the way the sunlight shone on her round auburn cheeks. Her aura came through his thoughts. She was brave and loving, protected and beloved.

Monsoon's care for her made a powerful focus. The guards' approaching footsteps faded from Lio's hearing as he stepped them all to the promise of safety.

NYAKIMBI

HEY ARRIVED IN THE gloom under a copse of trees, and Lio's night vision revealed that they were at the edge of a small village. "Did I get us close?" he asked.

"Yes," came Monsoon's grudging answer. "This way."

Monsoon was apparently capable of navigating in the darkness, but Cassia tripped over a rock with a frustrated grunt. Lio caught her under her elbow and lifted his other hand to his mouth. Pricking his thumb on one fang, he conjured a small spell light from a drop of his blood. She murmured her thanks.

Monsoon huffed. "Your goddess made you a powerful thelemancer, then threw in some light magic as an afterthought, too?"

"Blinding an attacker with a flare of light is much faster than bringing down his mental defenses," Lio pointed out.

"Huh. I suppose it is. Not as satisfying as knuckles to the nose, though."

"I save that for war mages."

Monsoon laughed. Lio didn't think the mercenary realized it was no jest. Lio could still remember the sensation of the bones crunching against his knuckles when he had hurled his fist at Chrysanthos. That had wiped the smug expression off the Cordian fire mage's supercilious face.

Lio could understand why his father had spent seven centuries as a Hesperine errant in Tenebra, battling their people's mortal enemies to protect the innocent and vent his own frustrations. Lio felt the need to break someone's nose at the moment, and there were no Cordian war mages at hand whom he could maim in good conscience.

He bit his tongue as he and Cassia followed Monsoon out from under the trees and into an open area surrounded by a circle of houses. The tidy round homes had mud walls and thatched roofs, and Lio could hear the peaceful breathing of the mortals sleeping within. This was most likely a community of farmers who rose and rested with the sun.

But for a seemingly humble village, there was certainly a great deal of magic protecting it.

"We'll be safe here," Monsoon said.

"Yes," Lio confirmed. "This whole village is draped in powerful protections of various affinities. How interesting."

Monsoon offered no explanation. He paused, and his own magic swept over the trees and across the ground, as if he too were checking the village's defenses. Knight whined, but didn't go into hiding behind Cassia this time.

The spells did not prevent Monsoon from leading them toward the largest home in the circle. The door was hung with artfully carved wooden symbols and female figurines. They had great presence, although Lio could not identify the magic they held. Ancestral power, he thought.

"This must be the village matriarch's home," Lio said to Cassia. "The rest of the residents are most likely her sisters and their families."

A pace from the door, Monsoon turned to them and planted a hand on Lio's chest to halt him.

The man waved a hand at Cassia. "You'll never find your way back here, so you aren't a threat."

Cassia must have decided this was not the time to protest that she should not be underestimated as a threat.

Monsoon fixed Lio with his eagle stare. "But you can step back here any time. I expect you not to abuse the privilege."

Lio looked calmly into the man's murderous gaze. "I have only the purest intentions, I assure you."

"Don't expect me to let you off easy because you're a Hesperine with overwrought principles." Monsoon gave his chest a little shove. "Think about that little sister of yours. Now think about what you would do to me if I harmed a hair on her head."

Lio let his fangs show. "This is not inspiring my purer intentions."

"Then you understand. If you bring misfortune upon the people you're about to meet, or even set foot here again without their invitation, my intentions will be anything but pure. What you would do to me for hurting your family? I'll do it to you. In your sleep. Then I'll turn you over to some friends of mine who are just as powerful as I am and let them have a go at you."

He gave his wings a snap, then approached the door.

Cassia, her aura bristling, slid her hand into Lio's. Nothing riled her like being dismissed. Nothing made him seethe like having his honor questioned.

Monsoon called quietly through the door in Cifwani. Lio thought he understood something about birds and flames. Code words? From within, there came the sounds of sleepy bodies shuffling. The door swung open, and firelight spilled out into the night.

"Monsoon!" cried the silhouette of a girl. Lio recognized her aura from Monsoon's memories. She threw herself into the man's arms.

He swung her around. "Hello, *nyakimbi*."

Lio didn't understand what Monsoon called her, perhaps an endearment or kinship term. What was clear was that the mercenary adored her.

Then again, Lio reminded himself, Chrysanthos doted on his young nephew. That didn't change the fact that he was a murderous war mage.

Listening closely, Lio was able to make out most of what Monsoon and the girl said to each other.

"I can't believe you're here!" she cried, laughing.

He set her down and held her at arm's length. "Mweya's Wings, look at you, so strong and pretty. You grew up while I blinked."

She was perhaps five years older than she had been in Monsoon's memories. The girl he remembered as all knees and elbows now bloomed with new confidence, her carefree spirit brighter than ever. Despite her rumpled headwrap, crooked cotton dress, and bare feet, the sleepy girl had presence.

"You wouldn't be so surprised if you came around more often," she scolded, beaming. "You have to promise me you'll take me flying while you're here. It's been ages."

"Of course I will."

"Oh, I'm so glad you've come back. You even brought friends!"

"They're clients."

Despite Monsoon's clear distinction, she beckoned to Lio and Cassia. As they came nearer, curiosity lit the girl's aura. "Monsoon, is she—"

"A client," he repeated.

Worry hung over Lio. Any citizen of the Empire could turn Cassia over to the authorities. Even this sweet girl. And if she didn't, she could face dreadful consequences for aiding a fugitive, especially a shadowlander.

But the girl beckoned again, bidding them welcome in Cifwani-accented Divine. As they entered her warm, firelit home, she appeared unfazed.

Until she had a good look at Cassia. Her eyes widened.

Lio held Cassia closer, her body strung with tension against his. They shouldn't have come here.

Then the girl's face lit up. "You're—"

Monsoon put a finger to his lips.

The girl danced in place, covering her mouth with one hand, shining with excitement. But when she spoke again, she suddenly sounded very grown up. "I am Chuma, the daughter of the house. You are my welcome guests."

The tall, broad man waiting for them further inside did not appear so enthusiastic. Wearing a waist wrap of animal skins, he crossed his brawny arms over his bare chest. Lio got the distinct impression they had disturbed a sleeping papa bear.

"This is my father, Mumba." Chuma tugged on his hand. "*Tata,* look who's here!"

"Monsoon." The layers of emotion in Mumba were not unfriendly, but he didn't smile.

"I'm sorry to intrude." Monsoon sounded sincere.

"Nonsense," Mumba responded. "You know you're always welcome here. But it's been a long time."

"I know." The mercenary's regret was genuine, too.

Lio bowed to Chuma's father. "I am Lio, and this is my intended, Newgift Cassia. We're both from Orthros."

"I see," Mumba rumbled.

The man must see many strange things coming in and out of his door, to be so calm when such an unusual party as the three of them appeared in his home in the hours after midnight.

"Is Chuma's mother home?" Monsoon asked.

"Ipika has gone to market," Mumba answered.

"Any idea when she'll be home?"

"It's a long journey."

Anxiety rose in Chuma's aura, but she kept smiling. "Allow me to invite you to join us at her fire."

The family's ancestral hearth burned gently in the center of their home, throwing warm light upon the whitewashed mud walls and sending comforting aromas up through the flue in the thatch. The fire was surrounded by votive wood figures, small dishes of food and drink, and other fragrant offerings.

There was no luxurious finery here, but the prosperity of Chuma's family was evident in the beautiful craftsmanship Cifwani artisans were known for. The furniture and dishes were carved in striking designs by the woodworkers. Ironsmiths had forged the tools and utensils to last. The floor mats and room dividers were made of red-brown barkcloth embroidered in tan raffia thread and painted with black geometric patterns.

But their greatest wealth was their family. Lio sensed the powerful bonds of love that ran between Mumba and Chuma and beyond their home to their clan in the neighboring homes. An undertone of worry bespoke their concern for her absent mother, Ipika.

But as they all pulled up stools around the fire, Chuma smiled at Cassia, her gaze bright with curiosity. "Coffee?"

"Please," Cassia replied gratefully.

"Do you need something to drink?" Chuma asked Lio.

"Thank you for your hospitality, but no." He put a hand on Cassia's arm.

At moments like this, it grated on him that he and Cassia were still unavowed and thus not permitted to call one another "Grace" in front of anyone but immediate family. But Hesperines had long since trusted their Imperial allies with knowledge of the sacred bond between Graces who Craved each other for all time. Chuma nodded in understanding, as if this were all quite natural.

While she led the rituals of hospitality, her father remained an intimidating presence at the fireside, a silent reminder that she was well defended. As they all drank coffee, Chuma and her father caught Monsoon up on news of friends, relatives, animals, and crops. No one said a word about why the mercenary had brought Lio and Cassia here.

Chuma never left the two of them out of the conversation for long. She peppered them with questions about all their travels and Orthros. They spoke of their time on the island of Marijani as if Cassia weren't a fugitive. No one mentioned Tenebra.

It was an altogether pleasant interlude that left Lio puzzled. Whatever understanding Monsoon had with this family, it remained unspoken.

When the shared pot was empty, Monsoon and Mumba wandered out of the house. Lio listened, but they didn't begin talking even after they were out of mortal earshot. Perhaps they were waiting to be out of Hesperine earshot, as well.

Chuma gathered a bundle of items from around the house for Lio and Cassia, then showed them behind a room divider. She gave the sleeping mat a fretful frown. "It's not our way to make guests sleep on the floor, but all our beds are too short for you, Lio."

He shook his head. "Think nothing of it. I much prefer a sleeping mat to dangling feet."

She giggled. "I thought so. I'm sorry, though."

Cassia accepted the blankets and other niceties from her. "Please don't trouble yourself. You've already done so much for us."

"Your visit is the most exciting thing that's happened in years!" Chuma pointed at Knight, who took the opportunity to lick her hand. She giggled again. "Is he really a war dog?"

Cassia petted his back. "Well, he's more of a family dog these days. But he has fought bravely in the past, and saved my life more than once."

"Oh, that's just like all the stories about liegehounds that I've heard." Chuma sighed. "I can just imagine your adventures! I can't even try to sleep at a time like this. I'm going to get a head start on the chores before dawn. But first I'll let you two get some rest. Please tell me if you need anything."

Cassia hesitated. "Well, we would be very grateful if you could help us send a few letters home."

Chuma gave her a knowing grin. "Preferably without the Imperial Mail Administration noticing you two sent it?"

"We wouldn't want to put you in a difficult position."

"Your family will worry if they don't hear from you, I'm sure. Give your letters to me first thing in the morning. I'll make sure some messages from me to Orthros go out with the village mail. No one at the Imperial Mail Administration cares what I send and receive. Your family can send their replies to me, too."

"Thank you so much for everything," Cassia said.

Lio bowed to her. "You have our gratitude for offering us Sanctuary. To Hesperines, that is a sacred act. We will always honor what you have done for us."

Chuma smiled warmly, inclining her head, then went back to the fireside, humming to herself.

In the relative privacy behind the room divider, sudden homesickness overcame Lio. He wished to be sitting at the end of Zoe's bed, telling her a bedtime story and illustrating it with illusions, with Cassia and Knight tucked next to her. But he was grateful for the refuge Chuma's home gave them.

Cassia took a seat on the sleeping mat, frowning as she did when her thoughts were busy. Knight lay down on one side of her, leaving the other side for Lio. The evidence of their alliance roused a quiet laugh from him. He gave the dog an affectionate rub before joining Cassia. When he raised his arm in invitation, that pulled her out of her reverie.

She slid into his embrace, resting her head on his chest. "I am not the first visitor of Tenebran origin who has stayed here."

He ran a hand down her hair, simply grateful she was not apart from him in this moment. "They've had Hesperine guests, too, although that is less remarkable. Many of our Imperial allies speak the Divine Tongue. Knowing the language of Orthros is useful, even in out-of-the-way places like this."

"What a change. No one looks twice at your fangs here, but I am an object of terror."

"Now you know how I feel when I'm in Tenebra. I wish you didn't have to experience it."

"No, most of the people I've met here have been so kind. Even the guards only see me as a criminal, not a monster." She snorted. "They simply want to arrest me, not set me on fire."

His arm pulled her closer on reflex. "No one is going to arrest you."

"I hope we don't drag this lovely family into our troubles."

"Monsoon is so protective of them. He would never have brought us here if he believed we were a threat to Chuma. Notice how very uninformative everyone is, though, despite being so talkative."

"Indeed. My greatest respect for their perception—and circumspection. Can you hear what Monsoon and her father are saying to each other?"

"They took a walk…out of my Hesperine hearing."

"Well, well."

Lio frowned. "Everyone is very anxious about her mother. I hope nothing happened on her trip to market."

"Perhaps she has hired Monsoon for protection in the past, like the traders at the Sandira Court."

"And if she is friends with one gold roster mercenary, then why not another? I believe she is Monsoon's contact, and he brought us here hoping she could give him word of Ukocha's whereabouts."

"We came so close," Cassia said. "If Ipika had been here, we might have met someone who has seen Ukocha—the last person we know of who saw my sister. It seems the harder we search, the more people there are between us and the truth."

Lio kissed her head. "It's been so many years. Solia's path has surely been a winding one."

"I still cannot imagine what twists on that path would cause her to need the aid of a mercenary like Ukocha. But the same could be said of Chuma's mother. Why would a simple farm wife need the best mercenaries to protect her goods? Does it have anything to do with why her family took it in stride when I, a shadowlander, walked through their door?"

"Either way, we can trust Chuma. It's safe to leave the rest of our unanswered questions for now. Let's write those letters, shall we?"

"Yes, and you haven't read the most recent ones that reached us from Orthros. Monsoon smuggled these out of the city with our belongings." Cassia pulled a few scrolls from her gardening satchel and handed them to him.

His homesickness only intensified as he read the letters from home. The one from their Trial brothers was very informative, however.

Dear Lio and Cassia,

First the famous privateer Captain Ziara, then Ukocha! Solia kept exalted company. Both of them are Victors of Souls.

Do you know what the acacia on Ziara's flag means? Every eight years, the Empress hosts the Battle of Souls, the most prestigious tournament in her lands. The winner receives an acacia branch from her hand and the right to display that symbol for the rest of their lives.

Hesperines never get to attend because the tournament is held during the day at the height of summer, but we did hear about it the year Ukocha won. Do you remember, Lio?

We went a little too far reading the account of the duels aloud. It was right after Ritual, and Xandra almost threw up before she cast a veil over her ears so she couldn't hear the descriptions of the burn wounds. We stopped following the Battle after that, because making anyone puke the Queens' blood just seems wrong.

When you find Ukocha, you must introduce us. The whole circle is coming over with your parents after the vote. We'll ward Xandra's ears if necessary.

See you then,
Mak and Lyros

Cassia sighed. "Well, meeting everyone for a nice family meal in the midst of our travels is out of the question now. Let us decide how to explain everything to Uncle Argyros. He can tell the other elders."

It took them some time and debate to write Uncle Argyros a suitably detailed account of the day's events.

"Don't say that," Lio protested at intervals. "You're too hard on yourself."

"I want him to know how much I regret what happened, even if I am striving not to feel guilty about it."

Lio was having trouble keeping his fangs sheathed. "It is the guards who should regret this catastrophe."

"But this letter is my chance to defend my future in the diplomatic service. Whatever the guards did, I must make my case for my medallion."

"It is the diplomatic service's opportunity to come to your aid. I will add some paragraphs of my own to defend you."

Uncle, I am certain you and the other elders will see that Cassia is in no way to blame for what has happened. It is unthinkable for our Imperial allies to issue a perfunctory arrest warrant against any citizen of Orthros, without even consulting our representatives. Worse still, the charges are insults and lies. Worst of all, the target is Cassia.

She came here with every expectation of safety and welcome, but the Sandira King sent his guards to terrorize her. He has no cause for complaint that she has written a record of her past fears on his warriors in bruises and liegehound bites.

Any mind healer should attest that her reaction was not willful malice, but self defense arising from her sensitivity to unjust—

She rested her hand on his to still his quill. "You must save that for your part at the end, my Grace, for I know any defense from you will take pages, not paragraphs. But first, please write what I want to say to Uncle Argyros, without the filter of your love."

"Very well. I will write what you dictate, but as for that filter, it is impossible to remove."

I am prepared to take any steps necessary to make amends for my trans-gression against our allies. Please advise us, as the Queens' Master Diplo-mat, on the proper course of action and your desired approach to resolving this debacle.

As my mentor, please counsel me how I can demonstrate to you that I am still suited to this service. I know a diplomat must be able to keep a level head in any situation, even when surprising dangers arise. If I am not able to do that at the current time, I feel sure I will be in future, once I am a Hesperine.

Dear uncle, have I lost my chance at the medallion I would be so proud to receive from you?

By the time they had both had their say, their letter no longer resem-bled family correspondence, but a thick dispatch from a remote embassy. Especially after Lio placed a veiled blood seal on it to prevent prying eyes. Their short letter to Zoe looked quite cheerful by comparison and con-tained as comforting a version of the truth as possible.

Dear Zoe flower,

We have met someone who can help us find Ukocha! But we had to leave with him quickly so we would not miss our chance to get his help.

We are now traveling with him to search for her. We are on the road and not sure where we'll stop.

That means we are unsure when or where Mama and Papa can bring you to see us. We are so sorry, Zoe flower. We know how much you wanted to meet us in the Empire for midnight meal, and we would never want to make you sad. We wish we could see you right away.

While we are moving around so much, we shall send all our news through Uncle Argyros. If you have any questions about where we are, ask him.

We hope you're having fun with courier lessons!

Love,

Lio and Cassia

"Now let us write Mak and Lyros our most candid account of what has happened," Lio suggested. "It will make us feel better to confide in our Trial brothers."

A smile tugged at Cassia's mouth. "I suppose you're right."

I wish we had all been there to see Cassia use the Stand's fighting moves against the guards. You two would have been proud, I'm sure. This may be the first time in history anyone has used a liegehound and the Hesperine battle arts together in a real skirmish.

Cassia snatched the quill from him and scrawled the next part herself.

No, I do not wish you were there. It was not how I should use my training. Do not tell Nike.

Lio stole the writing instrument back from her.

You should most certainly tell Nike that her trainee did her proud. And while you're at it, tell my father and Rudhira too. The Blood Errant are sure to be entertained by her exploits.

By the time they were done, she dissolved into weary laughter. She leaned into his side. "I wonder if they're making any progress with the vote. I'm sure there are times when Mak and Lyros wish they could use the Stand's fighting moves to win partisans, instead of persuading them to support us."

Of all times for him and Cassia to be away, when their Trial circle was defending their political position before Orthros's government. "But their support makes a powerful statement, without them saying a word. With them representing Orthros's warriors, Kia stoking the rebellious intellectuals, and Nodora's influence in artistic circles, I think Xandra will have many partisans behind her when she casts her royal vote."

"But I'm sorry we cannot be there to help."

Lio grimaced. "I know. Our Trial circle needs our political abilities right now. But Solia needs our protection."

"Yes. If only the vote hadn't prevented them from coming with us. She could certainly use their protection, too."

"We've done all we can for one night." Lio coaxed, "Why don't you get some sleep now?"

"Well, would it be silly of me to write one more note?"

"To Dakk?"

"Are you by chance a mind reader?"

Lio chuckled.

"I know he's just a university student I spent a few days touring the Sun Market with."

"But I know you were sorry we had to disappear from Marijani without telling him we were leaving." Lio handed her the quill. "I also know that making friends easily is still new to you."

"You're right. I never trusted anyone for so long."

"I'm glad that's changing for you, my rose."

She placed a kiss at the corner of his mouth and took the quill. "I suppose if I address it to him and send it to the university, there's a chance they'll deliver it to the right dormitory."

Dear Dakk,

This is Cassia from the Sun Market. The one who speaks Tradewinds with the accent of a lost goat, remember?

I know we planned to meet at the Sun Market again. I hope you can accept my apology for never arriving that day. Lio and I got a lead about my sister and had to leave in haste by night.

If your studies ever bring you to Orthros, we must all have coffee on the docks.

Jua's blessings upon you.

- Cassia

"Well," she said, "I shall give our letters to Chuma in the morning."

"Now you can sleep."

"But you'll be awake for a little while longer. I don't want to waste our time together."

"I gather that things start very early around here. You'll need to be awake during the day with our human hosts. You should get some rest while you can."

"I only just got accustomed to being nocturnal," she grumbled.

"I'm sorry your rhythms have been so disrupted." Lio nuzzled her temple. "I can use a little mind magic to help you fall asleep, if you like."

"If you use your mind magic on me, sleep is not the kind of rhythm I'll be thinking about." Despite her protests, within moments, her eyes slid shut. "Are you casting a spell after all?"

"No," he answered. "I'm cuddling you."

"Oh. Works like a charm."

"Sleep," he whispered. "We're safe here."

As she drifted off, Lio thanked the Goddess this night had ended with his Grace once again safe in his arms.

But what would tomorrow bring?

REAL TRAINING

"CAN WE GO FOR one more lap, Uncle Mak?" Bosko jogged in place, his sandaled feet bouncing up and down on the snow-dusted roof.

Mak gave his nephew a playful salute. "Spoken like a future Steward in Hippolyta's Stand."

That made a rare smile appear on Bosko's often-sullen face. As usual, he had belted his play robe in imitation of Stand regalia. The boy Slumbered in his speires, the ceremonial hair ties each trainee received.

Mak had never met a suckling with their heart set on serving in Orthros's army, which most pacifist Hesperines eschewed. At least, not since he and Lyros had belted their play robes and slept in their speires.

Mak swallowed a chuckle. "I'm sure we can go for one more round before Zoe wonders where we are."

They started another jog around the base of the grand dome of House Argyros. Their bloodline's home held a place of honor here in Haima, in one of the districts near the summit of the city. But Bosko had no eyes for the beautiful view below them, ignoring the spires, colorful tiled domes, and pointed archways of Orthros Notou's capital.

"How soon do I get to start real training?" he asked, for what seemed the thousandth time.

"This is real training," Mak reminded him. "Anything that builds your strength, endurance, or flexibility makes you a better warrior."

"But when do I get to learn my first fighting moves?"

"The battle arts don't start with fighting moves. They start with you."

Bosko's expression was so serious as he took in Mak's advice. Mak still wasn't used to having someone in his life who hung on his every word. A new and rather daunting responsibility, that.

He went on, "Your warding spells aren't what protect Orthros. Spells and fighting moves are only the tools we use. The protection is actually you."

"We don't use weapons...so our best weapon is us?"

Mak's conscience performed a fighting move, grabbing him in a Mortal Vice and threatening to squeeze the life out of him. When he had started his secret smithing efforts, he had not considered what sort of example he might one day set for suckling trainees. He hadn't thought that far ahead...as usual.

"Well," Mak said, "I don't think the Goddess would like us to be weapons. We're guardians. Think of us as shields, like the Chalice of Stars."

Bosko's eyes lit up. "Aunt Nike's shield! Did you know that when she was a Hesperine errant Abroad, she defeated eight bloodless undead with one blow from the Chalice of Stars? Or maybe it was twelve... All the Blood Errant were there. Uncle Apollon smashed their bones, and Methu cut their heads clean off. Then Rudhira used his magic to break the necromancer's spell over them so they would never rise again."

Mak shouldn't be grinning at the suckling's fascination with the violence, but he and Lyros had grown up with these same stories of the Blood Errant's feats. "It's all true."

"Have you ever seen her shield?" Bosko asked.

"No," Mak answered honestly. "You know the Blood Errant aren't allowed to bring their weapons with them when they come home from Abroad."

"Where did Aunt Nike's shield come from?" Bosko asked. "Is it the same place Rudhira got his two-hander Thorn, and Great Uncle Apollon got the Hammer of the Sun? And Methu got *both* his curved swords? What happened to the Fangs when he was captured by the war mages?"

"No one knows," Mak answered.

Except him, the younger brother cheeky enough to find his way into Nike's hidden forge in her absence. He had discovered that she had crafted the Blood Errant's famous arms herself, in spite of Orthros's ban on weapons. It had inspired him to draw up his own weapon designs.

Mak longed to study the Chalice, but Nike kept insisting he be patient. She ignored his pleas, which probably sounded remarkably like Bosko did at the moment. She seemed to think the single Fang of Methu's that now hung in the forge was enough of a temptation to Mak.

Suddenly Mak understood how Nike felt whenever she tried to talk him out of following her down the path of weapon smithing. He hated the thought of Bosko knowing about it, much less attempting such a thing.

But Mak was not a suckling. He was a Steward of full rank in the Stand, who had seen heart hunters and necromancers attack Orthros on his watch.

The Stand's calling was to bear the burden of violence for their peaceful people. Mak would not shy away from that, even when it came to weapons. His duty was also to uphold the law, but in this case, the law needed to change.

He and Bosko rounded the dome to where the rooftop widened into a broad terrace and Father's fruit trees grew in artfully positioned pots. Lyros sat at a table with Zoe, chalks and paints spread out before them. At this sight of his Grace with their little cousin, Mak stopped thinking about weapons and smiled.

"Bosko," Zoe called, "do you want to come draw with me?"

Bosko made a show of hesitation, but the truth was he would give Zoe his time, toys, or the robes off his back anytime she asked. The two of them still looked out for one another after everything they had endured together in their mortal childhoods. He looked at Mak. "Did we do enough laps for tonight?"

"Of course." Mak clapped Bosko on the shoulder. "We already went for two more laps than usual. That was a good training session. You did well."

Bosko's pride filled the Blood Union. This was the best part of having someone who took your word as law. It was easy to build them up.

The downside was, if you failed them, it would hurt both of you so much more.

Bosko flopped down into the chair next to Zoe, while Lyros passed him some sheets of blank paper and a fresh stick of drawing charcoal. Above Lyros's left eyebrow, there was a smudge of bright pink chalk on his olive skin.

Lyros glanced up, and his green eyes brightened with amusement.

I have a stupid grin on my face, don't I? Mak asked him through their Grace Union.

I am very fond of that particular grin, Lyros answered. *It usually means you're about to kiss me.*

Mak strolled over and dropped a kiss on Lyros's lips. "You have a bit of chalk on your forehead."

"Oh. Here?" Lyros rubbed his forehead over his right eyebrow. Now he had blue chalk on that side.

Mak managed not to laugh aloud, but it was no use when his Grace could feel his amusement through their Union. Lyros gave him a scolding look that made Mak want to kiss him again.

"No, Lyros, your *other* eyebrow," Zoe said helpfully.

Mak gently rubbed at the chalk on his Grace's forehead. "Right here."

Lyros's gaze softened under Mak's touch. "Thank you."

Zoe giggled. "Now you have chalk on you, too, Mak."

Mak scratched his nose with his pink, chalky fingers, putting on an absent expression. "Where?"

More giggles overtook Zoe. "Now it's everywhere!"

Mak pulled a face, and both the sucklings burst out laughing.

"I'll fix it for you, Uncle Mak," Bosko offered, clearly determined to be the hero who saved the warriors' dignity. The boy scrunched his nose in concentration.

Mak felt the tingle of the suckling's clumsy cleaning spell. *Do I still have my eyebrows?* he asked Lyros.

Lyros examined Mak's face. "Nicely done, Bosko. You didn't miss a spot." *And your eyebrows are intact,* he confirmed silently, while he patiently let Bosko cast a spell on his face, as well.

"Did you see Lyros's drawing?" Zoe asked Mak.

Mak plucked the colorful sketch off the table and wiggled his intact eyebrows at his Grace. Lyros stuck his tongue out and snatched it back.

How did you get saddled with art duty? Mak wondered.

Zoe wanted to color. Lyros set the drawing away from him. *How could I tell her no? At least she's a kind critic with no idea that I, the scion of Orthros's greatest bloodline of painters and sculptors, inherited the artistic skill of a clumsy Tenebran macer.*

Mak stood behind Lyros's chair, resting his hands on his Grace's shoulders. He tilted his head at the drawing. *Is this a flower or a dying squid?*

Your face after our next match in the ring.

Ooh, challenge accepted.

You know I jest, my Grace. I would never do anything to ruin your handsome face.

Hazard of the profession. You've landed a punch on me plenty of times.

But I healed you with my blood afterward.

And how I enjoyed it.

While Zoe was concentrating on her drawing, one of her caprine familiars bounced out from under the table. The little goat vaulted off an empty chair and landed in the middle of the papers. Zoe leapt to her feet and grabbed Moonbeam before the kid could nibble her artwork, but not before her hoof kicked over a coffee cup, which spilled its dregs on Lyros's drawing.

Thank the Goddess, Lyros said. *Saves me from having to destroy it myself.*

Zoe gasped, her entire aura distraught. "Oh no! I'm so sorry."

"It's perfectly all right, Zoe." Lyros tugged on one of her braids. "I like yours better, in any case."

Trying not to laugh, Mak picked up Moonbeam in one arm and plucked her sister Aurora off the floor. He took a seat and held them both in his lap to keep them out of trouble.

"I'll help you make a new drawing." Zoe offered her prized purple chalk to Lyros. "You can use the purple chalk."

"I would never use up your favorite color," Lyros said in dismay.

He was saved from another drawing ordeal when an aura entered the courtyard below. Zoe darted up and scurried to the railing, peering down at the newcomer below. "Ajia!"

Lyros smiled. "Is this your friend from courier training you've told us so much about?"

Zoe gave one of her shy smiles. "Yes. She became a courier last season but has already beat her speed record three times! She helps us new students."

Ajia stepped into sight on the roof beside Zoe. The tall, lean girl smoothed a hand over the rows of her deep brown braids. "Look, my parents gave me privateer beads too!"

Zoe grinned and held out her own pigtail braids, where the colorful privateer beads Lio and Cassia had sent her were woven into her light brown hair. "We match!"

Ajia held out a scroll to Zoe. "When I saw this come in, I snatched it before anyone else could deliver it."

"A letter from Lio and Cassia!" Zoe all but squealed.

Bosko ran his fingers through his hair, his own privateer beads clinking. His cool expression didn't disguise the spark in his aura. He was looking forward to Cassia and Lio's latest missive too.

"Now I need to make another delivery." Ajia sighed. "You'll have to tell me all about their letter later."

"Can you come back after midnight meal?" Zoe asked. "Bosko and I are going to play privateers at my papa's workshop. Papa said we could invite friends, and he would hang up sheets to be our sails!"

Ajia grinned. "I'll bring my jewelry box for the treasure hunt."

She stepped off to her next assignment, and Zoe raced back over to the table to open the long-awaited scroll.

Tension Mak had been ignoring now unwound from his shoulders. *It's high time they sent us another letter.*

I was concerned, too, Lyros agreed. "Why don't you read it aloud, Zoe?"

"Will you help me sound out the hard words?"

"Of course."

Dear Zoe flower,

We keep finding new clues about Ukocha that take us from place to place in search of her. We have to move quickly and are not sure where we will stop.

That means we are unsure when or where Mama and Papa can bring you to see us. We are so sorry, Zoe flower. We know how much you wanted to meet us in the Empire for midnight meal, and we would never want to make you sad. We wish we could see you right away.

While we are moving around so much, we will not be able to send or receive letters as often. Do not worry about us. We will buy you presents everywhere we stop and come home with many bedtime stories to tell you.

We hope you're having fun with courier lessons!

Love,

Lio and Cassia

Zoe's face had fallen, her disappointment sinking through the Union. Mak scowled at the letter. *Lio and Cassia never disappoint Zoe.*

Unless they have a very good reason, Lyros agreed.

Or a very bad one. What could make it that difficult for them to exchange letters? And how long are we to let that last before we go find them?

I'm sure there's an explanation.

"Where's the rest of the mail?" Mak asked. "Lio and Cassia usually send letters to all of us."

"If there were more, Ajia would have brought them," Zoe said.

Mak exchanged another glance with Lyros.

Now I'm worried, Mak said. *It's obvious they've given Zoe the suckling version of what's happening. They should have sent a real explanation to us. What clues about Ukocha? Where are they headed?*

"I'm sure we'll get more letters later," Lyros said aloud.

Mak crossed his arms. *I'm not sure at all. We should have received a long letter demanding every detail about our progress on swaying the vote.*

Not that Mak had looked forward to telling Lio and Cassia what an uphill battle it was. But he had wanted their advice. He felt more self-assured facing an army of heart hunters than he did standing before Orthros's government. But he had to change that, if he had any hope of changing the laws against weapons.

They needed Lio and Cassia here. And it was starting to look as if they needed Mak and Lyros wherever they were.

How had their diplomats ended up in rugged territory, while the warriors were here at home trying to fix politics?

"Everything is backwards," Mak muttered.

Lyros slid his hand into Mak's. "If they're on the move, perhaps they weren't able to mail all their letters in the same place. Our letters are likely to come in a separate delivery. Even the excellent Imperial mail service can be slow in remote areas."

"Good point," Mak admitted.

Stand down, my Grace, said Lyros. *Let's wait and see what we hear.*

Mak knew he had a tendency to leap into action without enough consideration. Sometimes being a decisive person was a strength.

Other times, it just got him—and people he cared about—into

trouble. Such as the time he, Lyros, and Lio had jumped off the highest cliff in Orthros. Had that leap into action awoken their levitation abilities early, as planned? No. It had landed them in the Healing Sanctuary for a lengthy and painful healing process, and an even lengthier and more painful reckoning with their parents. Especially his father, who had guessed, correctly, that the entire disaster had been Mak's idea.

The Goddess had known what she was doing when she matched Mak to Lyros, who thought things through before acting.

Very well. Mak sighed. *You're right.*

But if they didn't hear something soon, Mak might just have to take up a sword. Figuratively, of course.

68

days until

NOTIAN WINTER SOLSTICE

37 Annassa, 1597 IS

THE GOLDEN SHIELD

HE HOUSE AND THE village outside came alive at the crack of dawn. Cassia peeled open her eyes and tried to clear her groggy mind. Lio was beside her. She was safe.

Oh. She was a fugitive in three sister states of the Empire. Safe was a relative term. Her future as a diplomat might be ruined, and she still didn't know where Solia was.

But Chuma had offered them Sanctuary for now. They could wait out Lio's Dawn Slumber, then continue after nightfall to...wherever Monsoon intended to lead them.

Cassia gave Knight a vigorous rub. "Come along, darling. Time to get up and make ourselves useful."

She found Chuma and Mumba eating a hasty breakfast by the fire. Chuma took the letters from Cassia, then pressed a bowl into her hands. Cassia's efforts to learn Tradewinds, the language of commerce in the Empire, proved fruitful. Between her basic vocabulary and Chuma's knowledge of Divine, their conversation flowed as they mixed the two languages.

"You don't have to work," Chuma protested.

Cassia copied her hosts and dug into the thick, mealy porridge with her fingers. She discovered that the warm, filling dish was made from cassava, which she had eaten in Orthros. "I'm a gardener back home. I haven't had a hoe in my hand in weeks. I would love to help."

"But you're our guest."

"Would it dishonor your hospitality if I helped with the farm? I would be glad to do something to honor our bond of gratitude." Cassia lowered her voice and leaned closer to Chuma. "Besides, it would give us time to talk."

That brought a spark of mischief to Chuma's eyes. "Well, it is harvest time. I'll admit we need all the help we can get."

With work to occupy her, Cassia would be better able to face missing Lio all day. Even so, she couldn't have made herself leave his side if not for the knowledge that here, he slept under magical protections. With that reassurance, she accompanied Chuma's family out of the house with Knight at her heels.

Cassia spotted Monsoon perched atop the house. He was busy repairing thatch that appeared the worse for wear after the rainy season. A stick of jerky was poking out of his mouth, of course. Despite his humble task, there was no mistaking him for a farmer. Not with the scars of past battles decorating his arms.

She noted that a number of the young women strolled by rather slowly on their way out of the village. Apparently they thought Monsoon's face was handsome even with the perpetual scowl. Then again, they didn't look at his face for long. The sun gleamed on his deep brown skin, sweaty from his labor. They seemed preoccupied with the eyeful that the muscular, shirtless mercenary and his wings offered them.

Cassia recalled struggling to escape his iron grasp as he flew off with her, and she suppressed a shudder.

He exchanged good mornings with Chuma and her family, and Mumba seemed warmer toward him than he had been the night before. Monsoon ignored Cassia altogether. Well, that was a relief. She was perfectly happy to ignore him as well.

Cassia accompanied Chuma and her relatives out to the well-kept gardens and fields that surrounded the village. Their crops were nestled in cleared areas between small copses of acacias. The southern hemisphere's autumn had gifted them a good day for fieldwork, the air cool and not too damp.

Knight ran happily alongside Cassia, excited to be in the open. To ensure peace among the canines, she encouraged him to stay at the border of the field, on the opposite side from the farm dogs keeping watch for vermin and wild animals.

"Have you ever harvested pearl millet before?" Chuma asked Cassia.

"The closest I've come to millet is eating it in Orthros. Hesperines love Imperial foods. I'm glad for this chance to learn more about its cultivation."

Chuma handed Cassia a curved metal blade with a wooden handle and a large, empty sack. Together they waded into the tall, green-gold stalks of millet. They could easily see Chuma's father over the crops, but she and Cassia were so short that they disappeared into the field. They shared a conspiratorial smile.

As Chuma showed her how to cut the pale yellow heads of millet from their stalks, Cassia felt better than she had in days. The scent of ripe grain around her, the rustle of the plants, the feeling of the soil under her feet, all gave her a respite from her worries.

The voices around her were pleasant, too. Mumba was a steady man and a kind father. Chuma got along well with her aunts, uncles, and cousins. Everyone teased each other and sang as they worked. Although Cassia didn't know the words, she had heard the melody of the ancient reaping song at home, where the traditions of Queen Soteira's clan had become part of Orthros's arts and rituals. But Cassia had never seen a human family like this, much less spent time with one.

Cassia and Chuma fell into a rhythm of harvesting side by side. Their bags grew heavier. In the shelter of the millet stalks, they enjoyed some female talk.

"Cassia, can it really be true that men own all the farms in Tenebra?"

"Well, the noblemen do. Common men just work their lords' farms. Noblewomen can own land, but only if their husband dies and leaves it to them, or their father dies and they have no brothers. I'm afraid everyday women don't own much of anything."

Chuma shook her head. "How can one person own the land? Our farms don't belong to my mother, even though she's the matriarch. They belong to our clan."

"I can understand that. Everything Lio and I have belongs to our bloodline."

Chuma nodded. "My mother is rather like the firstblood in one of your Hesperine bloodlines. She's the head of our lineage, so she takes care of the land for our ancestors and our descendants."

"In her absence, you have a great deal of responsibility, I imagine."

"Well, my aunts make most of the decisions right now. I'm learning, though, since I'm my mother's heir."

Some of the light had gone out of Chuma's eyes. Although she sounded enthusiastic about her responsibilities, all this talk of her mother seemed to bring her worries to the surface.

Cassia respected Chuma's secrets—she herself was one of them now. But perhaps the girl would be willing to tell her more. "Does your mother travel often?"

"She's always on the road."

"It must be difficult for you to miss her all the time."

"I understand how important her journeys are. I have to think about what's best for everyone."

"I can already tell that you will be a great matriarch one day."

"I hope so." Chuma paused to wipe her brow. Her hand went to the bracelet she wore, as if on instinct. She ran her fingers over the beads and the wooden phial that hung from it. "But sometimes it's hard to decide what to do when someone needs help. Or they might, but you're not sure."

Cassia hesitated. "Is the trip to market dangerous?"

Cassia's question seemed to strike a chord. Out came Chuma's confession of the fears left unspoken around the fire. "She was supposed to be home already."

Cassia lowered her scythe. "Is she out there alone?"

At that, Chuma seemed to relax. "No. I worry too much."

Cassia soon found herself telling Chuma all about Solia. If there was anyone she could trust with the truth, it was Chuma, who had offered her Sanctuary.

"I never had a sister," Chuma said, "but I have all my female cousins, my aunts, my mother, and her friends. You only had Solia. I'll ask my ancestors to help you rescue her."

Despite the fresh air, Cassia's eyes stung, and her throat ached. Her enemies would not be the only ones asking the ancestors to intervene. "Once again, you have my gratitude, Chuma."

Chuma nodded, her mask of cheer slipping to reveal a deeply unhappy girl underneath.

For a moment, Cassia imagined what it might have been like to have her mother in her life. The mystery who was Thalia filled in with imaginings of everything a mother could be.

A celebrant at her Gift Night. A Grace-mother at her and Lio's avowal. A grandmother holding their child in her arms.

Cassia had never gotten to look forward to any of those things. Her mother had spent her life trapped in prostitution and died the concubine of a tyrant king.

But Chuma was close to her mother. Life had taught her to want that. How much worse must it be for her, now that she feared it would be taken away?

Cassia put a hand on Chuma's arm. "Lio and I will ask Hespera to light your mother's way home."

"Thank you, Cassia. I'm sorry you had to be without your sister while she was here spending all these years with other people."

"She was safer here, despite everything. That gives me hope."

"Don't worry. You've hired the right person to help you."

"Well, we hired Monsoon to help us find someone who has information on my sister. I haven't told him it's Solia we're truly looking for."

Chuma blinked at her. "You haven't talked to him about her at all?"

Cassia hesitated to speak ill of the mercenary in front of Chuma. She tried to be diplomatic. "He does not seem fond of shadowlanders."

Chuma shook her head. "Cassia, Monsoon is the last person who would bear ill will toward someone from Tenebra. He feels the same way about you as my family does. Why do you think he speaks Vulgus and brought you here?"

Cassia lowered her harvesting blade again. Chuma made an excellent point. Why would Monsoon learn the language of Tenebra if he hated people from that kingdom? Perhaps Cassia had not thought that through. "When I met him, he seemed so angry at my presence."

Chuma looked sad. "He's angry all the time because of the misfortunes in his life."

Like falling from that lofty nest he'd fledged in? "Not all the time. Not when he's with you."

Chuma grinned. "I love him like a big brother. I've known him all my life."

Cassia tried to match the mercenary who had flown off with her, threatening to drop her to her death, with Chuma's description of a big brother. Cassia simply couldn't see Monsoon from Chuma's rosy perspective. "He hasn't told me much about himself."

"You can trust him," Chuma told her. "With everything."

Cassia had no doubt Chuma could trust Monsoon that way. But Cassia and Lio were not on the apparently short list of people Monsoon gave a vulture's tail about.

At least he didn't hate shadowlanders as she had believed. It seemed he was also in the business of abetting fugitives from Tenebra. Somehow Cassia doubted he had the altruistic motivations she saw in Chuma's family. He was surely in it for the money. People would pay a high price to avoid deportation.

The man himself chose that moment to swoop down and land in front of Chuma. He took her scythe from her hand. "Enough work. Time to fly."

Her face lit up. "You don't have to ask me twice."

One of her little cousins came running between the millet stalks. Although Cassia couldn't understand what the boy said in Cifwani, she knew the tone of a begging child.

Monsoon rested his hands on his knees and bent to the boy's eye level, saying something placating.

"Guests first." Chuma waved Cassia forward.

Monsoon's smile disappeared, and Cassia could see the sudden tension in his body.

Did he really think she would describe the conditions of her flight with him and destroy his image in the children's eyes? Whatever their differences, she would not tarnish their pure bonds with him.

Besides, she suspected that if she told the story of how Monsoon had kidnapped her to keep her from getting arrested, Chuma would be greatly entertained, and her appreciation for Monsoon would only increase. He was more secure in her good opinion than he realized, Cassia thought.

She put on a gracious smile. "I've already had the pleasure of flying with Monsoon. You go ahead."

"Lucky you! Isn't it marvelous?" Chuma sighed. "I wish I had wings."

"An unforgettable experience, to be sure." Cassia thought Uncle Argyros would have been proud of her tact.

Monsoon acknowledged her words with a nod, and the smile he gave Chuma was more relaxed. "Who's first?"

She picked up her little cousin and put him in Monsoon's arms. He bounced the boy, and the child's face lit with an enormous smile. Who knew the vulture had so much mother hen in him?

"Not too long," Chuma said in Divine, which the boy must not be able to understand. "He'll get scared long before he admits it."

Monsoon's eyes crinkled. "He'll brave it out until he gets sick on my wings, will he?"

Chuma shook her head and tossed up a hand. "Boys."

"I seem to recall a little girl who was sick on my wings the first time I took her flying."

"Don't tell Cassia that story!" Chuma squealed. "Tell her how you got your fortune name."

"Fortune name?" Cassia asked.

Chuma nodded. "It's tradition among mercenaries. They name each other after what they hope to avoid, in order to ward off that evil. Your comrades bring you good fortune every time they call you your least favorite thing."

"Let me guess," Cassia said. "Flying in the rain is miserable?"

Monsoon sighed. "It was the beginning of the rainy season, and a sudden monsoon struck, one of the worst this village has seen in a generation. Chuma's mother was late coming home."

Cassia glanced at Chuma.

The girl's good cheer had faded somewhat. "Everyone was very worried because I was due to be born anytime. So Monsoon flew for hours in the pouring rains, searching everywhere for my mother."

"I found her trapped by the flood waters. The only way to reach her was to fly." The mercenary smiled faintly.

"He brought her home safely," Chuma finished, "and received the eternal gratitude of our clan. He's been known as Monsoon ever since."

"It will be your turn to fly next." He tweaked her chin and took off.

Several minutes later, he returned with an excited, spooked, and very happy little boy. After Chuma made over the child, he ran off toward her cousins, presumably to tell them all about his adventure.

Chuma set down her millet sack and held out her arms to Monsoon. "You can stay in the air with me as long as you want."

Monsoon arranged his arms around Chuma much more carefully than he had with Cassia. Then again, Cassia had been trying to gouge him in the eye. He took flight gracefully, and Chuma let out a delighted laugh.

Monsoon laughed with her. Chuma had that effect on people, Cassia could see. No one could mope in the girl's presence, not even the surly mercenary.

While they were gone, Cassia continued working with Chuma's clan in the millet fields. She was grateful for their trust. They were allowing her to help them with the crops their families depended on. She didn't take that lightly.

When Monsoon returned with Chuma a full hour later, she was wind-blown and exhilarated, and he actually looked cheerful. But once Chuma rejoined Cassia, he didn't linger. He muttered something about thatch and made himself scarce.

Chuma stood on tiptoe and peered through the field, glancing at her father, then her aunts. "I know I shouldn't shirk anymore, but you didn't get to fly today. I want to make it up to you."

"Oh, there's no need." Cassia wished she could explain that she didn't miss the flying one bit.

"You'll love this, I promise. Come with me. We'll be back before any-one notices."

Chuma's mischief was infectious. Quietly, Cassia called Knight to her side, and they sneaked off through one of the areas of unharvested millet. Leaving their sacks at the edge of the field, they went into the line of trees that bordered the farm.

Cassia hadn't asked Lio how far the protections on the village extended. She pushed her worries away. Chuma knew her home's defenses and Cassia's situation. She wouldn't suggest they go anywhere dangerous. Besides, they had Knight with them.

"Almost there." Chuma smiled over her shoulder.

The copse thinned into grassland. There in the open stood one of the most majestic trees Cassia had ever beheld. Its trunk had to be as tall as a dozen grown men standing on each other's shoulders, and its branches spread out like a canopy. It was vivid evidence of life in the harsh conditions of the savanna.

"What is it?" Cassia's voice came out hushed.

"A thorny acacia tree," Chuma said quietly.

"Oh," Cassia marveled. "I've seen little acacias in greenhouses in Orthros, but never one like this. How fortunate I am to get to behold it. Can we go closer?"

Chuma grinned. "We can climb it."

Cassia laughed. She could scarcely remember the last time she had climbed a tree for the joy of it. "Show me."

They raced across the grass and under the shelter of the huge acacia. Chuma circled the thick trunk, running her hands over the twisted ridges in its bark. To Cassia, the tree looked as if a goddess had braided its trunk together.

"Here they are." Chuma pointed to a series of handholds carved into the side of the tree, which led up its tall, straight trunk to the cradle of branches overhead.

"I can only imagine how long ago someone carved these."

"Actually, they are much newer than the tree." Chuma slipped her fingers into one groove. "My father carved them for my mother so she could reach the top. She showed them to me. She says I should marry the one who will lift me up, even when that means helping me higher than he can reach."

Cassia tilted her head back, lifting her face to the dappled sun and shade filtering down through the tree. "You father is a good man. There aren't any like him where I came from."

"Is that why you ran away with a Hesperine?"

"Most certainly."

Chuma showed Cassia her bracelet. "My parents made this for me from the acacia tree. To remind me."

Cassia studied the carved wooden beads, each bearing a different design of swirling lines and geometric shapes. The phial gave off a faint whisper of magic that seemed familiar. So much love, captured in one small masterpiece. "Truly beautiful."

The thunder of hoofbeats interrupted their conversation. On instinct, Cassia tensed. It sounded like a group of riders was approaching the village from across the savanna.

Chuma pressed her body against the trunk and peered around the tree. Suddenly she yanked herself back and gave Cassia a push. "Hurry. Up. Hide in the branches."

"Chuma, I thought there were wards."

"There are. But I have to let *them* inside our protections. I'll explain later." Her gaze fell to Knight. "They mustn't see a liegehound here!"

No time for questions. Cassia dropped to her knees and held Knight's face, looking into his eyes. There were no words in the liegehound training tongue that would make him run away and leave her to face danger alone.

But there was a way to make him run toward someone else he wanted to protect. A command she had devised the night a war mage had almost caught her with Lio.

"You know where home is, no matter where we are. *Loma hoor!*" Cassia told Knight. *Home. Silence.*

And he was off, running through the tall grass back toward Lio.

"Climb fast," Chuma said, "but watch out for thorns."

Cassia grabbed the first handhold on the trunk and started upward. The climb was a blur of her pounding heart and the sweat in her eyes. She made it into the safety of the branches just as the hoofbeats drew near under the tree.

A sharp, hooked thorn dangled in front of her eye. The tree sported many of the defensive spines amongst its leaves. Cassia leaned and wriggled, trying to avoid gouging herself or shaking the branches. She managed to wedge herself in the crook of two thick, gnarled limbs without losing any skin.

Through the leaves shielding her, she could see Chuma standing alone before four mounted soldiers. Cassia had never beheld anything like their shining company. They rode perfectly matched golden horses. From head to toe, they were covered in golden armor. They all wore the same woman's face embossed on their golden helmets.

The soldier in the lead dismounted from her steed and approached Chuma. The girl stood there with every appearance of calm. Only Cassia could see the knife hidden against the back of her arm. Where had that come from? She held it deliberately, with the grip of someone who knew how to use it.

The soldier did not draw her sword. It was eerie, hearing the woman's voice echo through metal and emerge from lips frozen forever in gold. The warrior spoke in a tongue Cassia didn't recognize, but she knew the tone of interrogation.

Chuma held her ground. She answered with innocent calm.

Cassia pressed her sweating brow to her sleeve. She felt a sharp pain on her wrist and glanced at it.

Her motion had caught her skin on one of the thorns. It was already bleeding. She pressed her mouth to the cut.

She froze at the sight of the blood shivering on a leaf, right over the golden soldier's head.

If one drop fell and caught an observant warrior's eye, Cassia would betray Chuma.

She inched her hand toward the leaf. Her balance faltered, and she went still. A shiver moved through the foliage, although not a breath of wind cooled the heat on the back of her neck.

The soldier interrogating Chuma raised her head. Her helmet angled in Cassia's direction.

Cassia thought her pulse would burst from her veins. Could the soldier see her?

The blank golden face turned to Chuma again, and the metallic voice continued speaking. Cassia let a great sigh escape her in tiny, measured breaths. She closed her hand over the bloodstained leaf, capturing the droplets.

The golden warrior got back on her horse, and her glorious, terrifying company rode away. Chuma sat down at the base of the tree as if she were just a farm girl stealing a break from the labors of the harvest.

The hoofbeats had stopped echoing in Cassia's ears when Chuma got to her feet. She slipped around the back of the tree again and motioned for Cassia to come down.

Cassia made it to the ground with several more nicks from the thorns. "Are you all right?"

"No." Chuma's sweet face was clouded with anger. "How dare they come here making demands like that?"

"Who are they?"

"The Golden Shield—Her Imperial Majesty's personal guard."

"Why are they here?" Cassia made herself ask, although she feared she already knew the answer.

"The Empress sent them to look for you."

Cassia stared at Chuma. "You just stood between me and a line of the Empress's guard."

Chuma's hand tightened on her dagger. "I am my mother's daughter. No one threatens my friends, least of all on my ancestors' land."

Cassia's limbs unfroze, and she pulled the girl into her arms. Chuma smelled like hearth smoke and fresh grain and had a fierce embrace.

A shadow fell over them, and Cassia sprang back.

Chuma put a hand on her arm. "It's Monsoon. Thank the ancestors."

Cassia could not bring herself to feel thankful for Monsoon at the moment.

He landed in front of them, his eyes flashing. "The Golden Shield is searching the village. Do you know what this means?"

"There's only one place for me to hide." Cassia steeled herself. "Will you do it?"

He let out a short breath, as if relieved. "I thought you'd argue."

Cassia touched a hand to Chuma's shoulder. "I will do whatever I must to make sure they never know Chuma's clan has harbored me."

Monsoon met Cassia's gaze and gave a nod. "I'll keep you in the air until they're gone."

He stepped behind her and crossed his arms over her torso. Panic made her stomach twist. He wasn't her captor this time. But the moment their feet left the ground, he would be in control. Again, she would leave Lio's side, powerless to protect him or herself.

"I'll make sure Knight stays hidden," Chuma promised.

Cassia had to go with Monsoon. For the girl who had just stood between her and the might of the Empire. For Lio, who would face less suspicion without a shadowlander at his side. "Stay safe."

Chuma nodded, her hand flexing on her dagger.

Wind ruffled Cassia's hair, and Monsoon's wings beat powerfully around her, stirring the grass. A smooth, mighty current of air swept under them and lifted them aloft.

They glided in a circle around the perimeter of Chuma's farm. The sun shone down on the fields, highlighting each set of brilliant armor below. The Golden Shield strafed the fields in precise, ruthless patterns, leaving the precious crop untouched, leaving a shadowlander nowhere to hide.

"Try to relax your body," Monsoon said in her ear. "It will make this less uncomfortable for you."

Relax? The Golden Shield might find Lio at any moment. Cassia was at the mercy of a stranger. She had to tolerate having her whole body pressed against a male she didn't know, and he was not Mak or Lyros or anyone she felt safe touching.

The wind changed. There was something almost soothing about how it carried them. Cassia realized Monsoon had gentled his hold, too.

"Imagine you're Chuma," he said. "You're like a little sister to me. I'm loyal to your kin. I'll never let anyone hurt you."

When he said it like that, she could almost believe he meant it. She tried to think how Chuma must feel when she was up here with him, and it did help. "At least this time I'm confident you won't drop me. It wouldn't do for the Golden Shield to find my body on Chuma's land."

His chest vibrated with laughter.

As the ground dropped farther away, Cassia gritted her teeth on a scream. Chuma's village shrank to a collection of miniature houses below. But Cassia didn't feel safer. Now she couldn't see when the soldiers would search the houses. She wouldn't know if they found Lio.

Her Grace was down there without her. She was, again, a helpless human at the mercy of magical and political forces she could not control.

THE ANCESTORS' KEEPING

SOME INNER WARNING JOLTED Lio's mind awake. He fought the paralysis of the Dawn Slumber, but his limbs refused to obey.

Cassia's fears had stalked his dreams. How much of that was real? Where was she?

The scent of her blood hit his nose.

His tongue wouldn't work, but his mind shouted her name. *Cassia.*

Monsoon cursed somewhere nearby. "Is he trying to give every mage from here to the capital a migraine?"

Then Cassia's voice, thank the Goddess. "I'm right here. Try to wake up. We have to leave."

His eyes flew open. His gaze fixed on a crimson droplet on the tip of her finger.

She waved it under his nose, patting his face with her other hand. "I'm sorry to startle you, my love. We don't have time to let the Slumber wear off slowly."

He breathed. "What happened?"

"The Golden Shield was here."

His fangs sliced his lip as they unsheathed. He sat up, his muscles fighting him. "The Empress's guard?"

"It seems I'm wanted all over the Empire now." The ghosts of her hopes haunted her eyes for a moment before she put on her mask of resolve. "I have our packs ready. Can you wait for the Drink?"

"Of course." He dragged himself off the sleeping mat against his body's screaming protests. His protective instincts somehow woke his leaden arm enough to wrap it around Cassia and hold her against him.

Chuma, Mumba, and Monsoon stood by the hearth. Lio knew the look of a council of war. One that had begun while he Slumbered, unable to lift a finger to help.

By the end of Cassia's hasty account of the day, his magic was spoiling for a battle that was already over.

She had yet to budge from his hold, her other hand in Knight's ruff. "Thank the Goddess your veils held. I feared the ancestors would reveal you to the Golden Shield."

"We can't stay here any longer," Monsoon said. "The Golden Shield has access to every kind of magic you can imagine. They're capable of anything."

Cassia should have been here, safe under Lio's veils, not once again dependent on Monsoon's dubious aid. Only Lio's respect for Chuma kept him from having it out with the man then and there.

Monsoon paced, his feathers on end. "Nowhere in the Empire is safe for you now. The Golden Shield are the best soldiers in human history, and every door is open to them. Nothing is secret from them. Every citizen is expected to give them the same obedience as they would the Empress herself."

Cassia betrayed no sign of fear. She was fully armored in her determination. "We should focus on what this new threat tells us about my mysterious enemies. How did the Golden Shield know to look for me here?"

"I wish I knew." Monsoon's voice was low and dangerous. "I would have a word with whoever brought them down on this family."

"No one in our village betrayed us." Mumba spoke with complete confidence.

"Of course not!" Chuma said. "Everyone here is our clan. We're loyal to each other. We all bear responsibility for each other's actions. No one could betray one of us without betraying themselves."

"The information came from outside," Lio agreed. "From the same source as the lies someone is whispering in the ears of the merchant governors of Marijani, the Sandira King, and the Cifwani Matriarchs whose soldiers are searching with his guards."

Cassia nodded. "Chuma, did the Golden Shield have the same warrant, or a new one with more charges?"

Chuma shrugged. "They didn't present a warrant at all."

"They don't need one," Monsoon said. "They are a walking warrant."

"Could the Empress's administration send them without her involvement?" Cassia asked.

Lio shook his head. "The Golden Shield are under her personal command. No one else has the authority to deploy them, and it is said their loyalty is absolute."

"They're incorruptible," said Mumba.

"Is anyone truly incorruptible?" Cassia replied.

"Once a woman dons the face of the guard," Monsoon explained, "who she was before is erased from history and record. No one can know her name or her past. Her entire family goes to live under the Empress's protection so they cannot be used against her."

As much as Lio wished there were any other explanation, the truth was clear. The most powerful human monarch in the known world wanted his Grace arrested. "Our unseen enemy has the ear of the Empress herself."

"Why would finding me be so important to her that she would send her best soldiers?"

"Because she believes you're the worst threat."

"The Queens have given me their protection. Whose word would have more sway with her than theirs?"

Monsoon crossed his arms. "If you're willing to consider going back to Orthros, now would be the time."

Cassia gripped Lio's hand and met his gaze.

How he wanted to sweep her back into the safety of the Queens' ward. But he knew she would never agree. Not when Solia's fate hung in the balance.

"We cannot," he acknowledged.

Her gratitude flowed into him. "The truth is, Monsoon, the person we're looking for is my sister."

He sighed. "That was obvious all along."

Chagrin tinged Cassia's aura, and Lio winced. Apparently the mercenary had seen through her tale more easily than they had predicted.

"Well," she said, "then I hope you understand that I will not leave the Empire without her. Whoever doesn't want shadowlanders here, I won't let them drive me away from her. We cannot let my nameless enemy win."

Goddess, help me keep them both safe. "Unless we receive a summons back to Orthros, we will remain. But we must get another letter home to warn our family of what else has happened."

Chuma shook her head. "Your earlier letters went out before the soldiers arrived, so they should reach Orthros safely. But now that the Golden Shield was here, I imagine they'll be watching mail from my village from now on. You should wait until you leave the Matriarchate before you try sending anything else."

"We must lose my pursuers," Cassia said. "We cannot lead them to my sister. Without Orthros's protection, she would face even greater danger from someone bent on catching shadowlanders."

"She does have Orthros's protection," Lio promised. "Whoever your enemy is, they have made themselves the enemy of our bloodline and all Hesperines. I will protect you both."

It was a bold claim, he knew, when today Cassia's safety had depended on the kindness of strangers.

Lio bowed to Chuma. "As long as our bloodline endures, we will have a bond of gratitude with your clan."

Cassia took her hands. "How can we ever honor what you have done for us?"

"Find my mother," Chuma bade them. "When you asked me if she was traveling alone, I told you no. What I didn't say is that the Ashes are with her."

The pieces fell into place. Ipika was not only Monsoon's contact, she was the Ashes' latest client. "Is that the long contract that has kept the Ashes away? The reason no one in the Empire has seen them in some time? Your mother has been gone that long?"

Chuma's dread weighed on the Blood Union. That empathic awareness all Hesperines treasured and suffered now revealed to Lio the full depths of the girl's fear for her mother.

"They've never been this late." Chuma's voice wavered.

"But if the Ashes are with her," Cassia said, "that means she has the best protection."

Chuma wrapped her arms around herself. "Anything bad enough to delay the Ashes is *bad*."

Mumba put one powerful arm around his daughter's slim shoulders.

She appeared to come to a decision, suddenly looking older than her young years. "There's something else I will tell you as well."

Monsoon startled, his wings rustling. Mumba frowned.

"They need to know, and it's my place to explain." Chuma's tone was kind, but firm.

Monsoon and her father looked worried, but didn't stop her.

She paused, clearly thinking over her words. "You see, there's a way to protect secrets with magic. Two people can share their secrets with each other's ancestors."

"The Ancestors' Keeping," Lio said. "It's one of the few ways to prevent a thelemancer from finding information in your thoughts."

Chuma nodded. "As long as the ancestors keep the secrets, no one can take the knowledge from you or the other person, not through interrogation or even mind magic. The protection is even stronger if more people and their ancestors participate."

"Such a powerful advantage must come at a cost," Cassia surmised.

"A great cost," Lio confirmed. "The bond gives the other person's ancestors power over you. When they or any mage of their clan casts a spell that draws on ancestral magic, you are uniquely vulnerable to its effects."

Cassia shuddered. "Knowing the ancestors of the Sandira King and Cifwani Matriarchs might be looking for me even now, I can imagine the dangers. That is a monumental amount of trust to place in anyone."

"The Ancestors' Keeping has another effect, too," Chuma went on. "The only way to reveal the secret is if all the participants come together and willingly reverse the spell."

Cassia frowned. "It seems that could cause a great deal of trouble, depending on the situation."

Chuma gave her a speaking look. "I was so young that my mother used her matriarchal power to take the secret from me, so I wouldn't have to be part of the spell. I can't tell you the secret. To find the information you came looking for, you'll need to ask the Ashes—and my mother."

"Chuma," Cassia breathed, "you know—knew—something about my sister? Your mother does, as well?"

"All of them have to tell you together. If you go with Monsoon to find my mother and the Ashes, you will find your answers as well. Will you do it?"

Hespera's Mercy. The very truths he and Cassia sought were locked behind one of the few spells in existence that could resist his powerful affinity. His magic boiled in him, still restless from her close call, useless in his veins.

Chuma was the key to their quest. And she would always be the person who had offered them Sanctuary, the small warrior who had shielded Cassia from the ranks of the Golden Shield.

How had his Grace's fate come to rest on the shoulders of the girl before them? Scant mortal years ago, Chuma had been a child as young as Zoe. Hesperines saved children. They didn't expect children to save them.

Lio did not trust Monsoon, but when it came to Chuma, they were in complete agreement. No harm must ever come to her.

Lio squeezed Cassia's hand, and she squeezed back. That was all the consultation necessary.

"Of course we'll do it," Cassia told Chuma.

"We won't rest until your mother is safe," Lio promised.

Chuma let out a sigh of relief. "You can try to step to her. Let me give you a focus."

Monsoon started forward. "He will not use his thelemancy on you."

Lio held up his hands. "That's out of the question. Chuma, do you have any charms your mother enchanted? Something that carries her magic could give me an adequate impression of her."

She gave him a straight look. "Now isn't the time for adequate. What would be ideal?"

Lio hesitated. Monsoon glared daggers at him, and Mumba's aura rumbled with concern.

Chuma held up a hand before any of them could protest. "Lio is a blood mage. Blood would serve best."

Mumba rested a broad, cautioning hand on his daughter's shoulder. A muscle in Monsoon's jaw twitched as he watched Lio with those predatory eyes of his.

Lio addressed Chuma, for it truly was her decision. "Yes, your mother's presence will be very powerful in your blood. But giving that to anyone for spell casting is no less of a risk than joining in the Ancestor's Keeping, especially considering the importance of blood magic in your people's rituals. I would never ask that of you."

"You have not asked," Chuma said. "I have decided. I will do this for my mother."

Her father hesitated for a long moment, but at last placed a kiss on her forehead. She touched a hand to Monsoon's arm again. With a sigh, he stepped out from between her and Lio.

Chuma pulled her bracelet off her wrist and held it out to Lio. "This acacia vial holds my blood. This is the amulet I use in rituals."

Reverently, he took the talisman from her. As soon as the smooth wood touched his palm, the magic within made his skin tingle. The Gift in his blood could still help his Grace and her young protector. "Orthros's power will not fail you."

Chuma smiled at him, then put her arms around Cassia and held on for a long moment.

"We will bring your mother back to you," Cassia told her fiercely.

Chuma pulled back and turned to embrace Monsoon. "I wish you could stay longer, but it's more important for you to go."

"I'll keep my promise to take you flying when we return."

"I'm so glad you came. Now that you're going after them, I know everything will be all right."

He gave her a crooked smile. "An extra pair of hands can't hurt."

"A pair of wings *always* helps. Just like when you got your fortune name."

Mumba clasped Monsoon's arm. "It may have been a long time, but your timing now is right."

Doubt and regret swirled in Monsoon, but he sounded completely confident. "We will bring everyone home."

The worry had lifted from Chuma's aura, replaced with reassurance.

"Come now, Chuma." Her father guided her toward the door. "We should let them discuss their plans."

"We can help them plan," she protested.

"We should keep watch outside while they step away under Lio's veils."

"You're right," she relented. "The Golden Shield is probably still spying on the village."

For a man without Blood Union, Mumba was certainly intuitive. He knew there were things that needed to be said, which none of them wished to discuss within Chuma's hearing.

"Be safe," were her parting words as she and her father left the house. Lio rounded on Monsoon.

The mercenary tossed up a hand. "Ah, here it comes."

"I thought we had an understanding," Lio hissed. "Cassia stays at my side while I Slumber!"

Cassia put a hand on his chest. "I asked him to hide me, Lio."

His gaze went to her, his heart constricting. "My veils held. You could have trusted them."

"We didn't know if the Golden Shield had a way to see through them. It took all my Will to leave you here, but I was afraid of what would happen to Chuma's clan if the soldiers found me. Can you forgive me?"

He pulled her into his arms, feeling the powerful pulse of her lifeblood inside her ephemeral mortal body. "There's nothing to forgive."

"They could have interrogated you," she said into his chest. "Your reputation in the Empire may already be destroyed. You might lose your medallion before I even get mine."

"You're safe. That's what matters."

Lio might still be an ambassador in good standing in the eyes of Orthros's diplomatic service, but his medallion was already long gone. All he had now was the lump of fulgurite he carried in his pocket. The twisted glass had been forged by Eudias's lightning magic during the battle in which Lio had saved the young apprentice.

Rose House had crumbled around them. The stained glass window Lio had crafted had shattered. And he had lost his medallion in the chaos.

In that duel, Lio and Cassia had faced the Collector. One of the Old Masters, the most ancient necromancers in history, who possessed unimaginable power. And for that victory, he had this warped trophy.

The fulgurite was his constant reminder that there were enemies too powerful to fight with words. When his Grace's life was at stake, diplomacy meant nothing.

HESPERINES ERRANT

HE EMPRESS NOW COUNTED Cassia among her enemies, and the only people who could help her and Lio find Solia were missing and most likely in grave danger. And yet, Chuma's revelation gave them hope.

Cassia focused on the quiet but powerful feeling as she held Lio, willing her emotions to sink into him and become his own. "We have every reason to feel encouraged by what Chuma has revealed to us."

After a moment, he relaxed in her arms. "You're right. We're getting closer. Ipika and her family give Sanctuary to shadowlanders. Ukocha was protecting Solia. Ukocha and the Ashes must have enlisted Ipika's aid to keep Solia hidden in the Empire, or perhaps smuggle her somewhere."

"To help Solia with her plan, whatever it might be. It must have brought her to this very house at some point."

"It had to be when Chuma was old enough to form clear memories of her, since her mother went to such lengths to keep what she knows secret."

Cassia eyed Monsoon. "Chuma assures me that you are as involved as her mother in harboring shadowlanders. Did you ever meet my sister?"

"I'm not one of the Ashes." There was more anger than usual in his tone. "I can't tell you anything."

"Do I detect professional rivalry?" Cassia prodded. Perhaps he was jealous that Ipika had hired Ukocha instead of him, a friend of the family.

"Some contracts require a band of mercenaries like the Ashes. Some call for a single expert like me. For the record, escorting a couple of nosy silkfoots around is beneath my skills, but Chuma wouldn't be happy with me if I left you to the hyenas."

Cassia narrowed her eyes at him. "You've clearly spent a great deal of time with her family. You really knew nothing of Solia's time here?"

"I know how priceless information about your sister is to you. Don't you imagine I would charge you through the nose for anything I knew?"

"Yes, unless you were unable to reveal the secret."

"That spell doesn't work with only one person, and I fight alone."

"Indeed," Lio said, "I find it hard to envision you making yourself vulnerable to another clan's ancestral magic. That would require things like trust and cooperation."

If Monsoon trusted anyone, it was Chuma's family. But Cassia still agreed with Lio. Monsoon would never tolerate a spell that would give him a weakness. It was not in his character to allow anything to give others an advantage over him. She knew the type. She had been that type herself once.

Chuma had said his anger stemmed from his misfortunes in life. Cassia had to admit, she understood that too. There had been times when she had hurt others because of her own pain.

Lio looked down his nose at Monsoon. "I dare say Chuma's innocent ancestors would spit your seedy secrets right back out again."

"Of course," Monsoon returned, "I wouldn't want to inflict all the skeletons in my past on her virtuous foremothers."

Cassia knew there was truth to that, as well. He would never want anything he had done to affect Chuma.

Monsoon sighed. "One secret I know is where Chuma's mother was headed on her travels. When we step to her, there's no telling what situation we'll land in. First we need to step to a place where we can resupply and prepare."

"Fair enough." Lio placed Chuma's bracelet in Cassia's hands. "I think you should be the one to safeguard this until we're ready to use it."

"I shall keep it with Solia's heirlooms." She tucked it safely in her gardening satchel with the ivy pendant.

"Where are we headed?" Lio asked Monsoon.

"Ever been to the Scorched Verge, silkfoot?"

Lio took a step toward the mercenary. "There is only one reason to go to the Scorched Verge."

"That's right. It's the starting point for all expeditions into the Maaqul Desert."

"What in the Goddess's name is Chuma's mother doing in the Maaqul?"

"Good deeds for fools. So we get to retrace her and the Ashes' path the hard way and hope we find them before something worse does."

"I've only heard stories about deserts," said Cassia. "I take it they're not as exciting as Zoe's storybooks make them out to be."

Lio pinched the bridge of his nose. "Deserts are the opposite of Orthros. Sand instead of snow. Brutal heat instead of cold. The Maaqul is the largest desert in the world, full of hazardous ruins, undocumented magical phenomena, and temperamental beings."

"How close can you get us?" Monsoon asked.

Lio tossed up a hand. "I've been to the Scorched Verge."

"You have?" Cassia asked in surprise. "It sounds…sunny."

"Mak and Lyros thought it would be good training to spend some time in the Maaqul. I thought it would be interesting to interview the Azarqi nomads about their diplomatic relations. Father arrived and preempted the undertaking."

Cassia raised her brows at him. "How long was this after you three ended up in the Healing Sanctuary from jumping off Wisdom's Precipice?"

"Several years, but our cliff diving was fresh enough in Mother's mind. Father did not take kindly to us giving her nightmares about us losing our way in the desert, befuddled by too much sunlight."

"This place is so dangerous that the Lion of Orthros didn't want you to go there? Your parents let you go to Tenebra where you might get immolated for heresy, but not the desert?"

"I'm older now," he said dryly, "and I have a few duels with war mages and necromancers under my belt."

But a desert sun was an enemy they had yet to face. "The sun exposure you've endured since our arrival in the Empire has already affected your Dawn Slumber. I see how much longer it takes you to awaken, even after nightfall. You sleep through twilight, which never happened in Orthros."

Lio put a gentle, reassuring hand on her back, but she knew him too well to miss the tension in him. He was dreading that sun as much as she was.

"Lio, how long is it possible for a Hesperine to Slumber after too much sunlight?"

He rubbed both her arms. "We will endeavor not to test it and find out. We'll have to find some shelter from the sun during the day."

He didn't need to test it, she knew. Her scholarly Grace would have already read precise mathematical calculations about such things in a scroll somewhere. He simply didn't want to worry her by telling her. She would have pressed him, but Monsoon preempted her.

"If it was just me," the mercenary said, "I would fly. You two make logistics complicated."

"If you would prefer not to have our help," Lio said, "you can leave us here."

"Don't fancy getting your toes hot, silkfoot?"

"I've dueled fire mages from Cordium, so the heat doesn't bother me. But my first responsibility is to keep Cassia safe, which means not subjecting her to the desert."

She knew his words were motivated by love, but they slid under her skin like the sharpest thorns. He might as well have called her a fragile human.

"I've walked through fire," she reminded him. "I can walk through the sunbound desert, too."

He brushed her hair back from her face. "This is different."

"You're not getting out of this so easily," Monsoon protested. "Don't expect the Ashes' help if you aren't willing to lift a finger for them in return."

"I agreed to go without complaint," Cassia snapped. "You're the one who first expressed uncertainty about our company."

"I'm adding a guide's fee to what you owe me when this is over. Someone showing you across the desert doesn't come cheap. Camels and supplies don't, either."

"The cost will not be an obstacle," Cassia said. "We can fund an expedition."

"Cassia—" Lio protested.

"If the information we need about my sister is in the Maaqul, that's where we have to go."

"When I finally get to meet her, I want to be able to tell her I've done everything in my power to keep you safe."

"You have." She took his hand. "I know your first responsibility is to protect me, but we are Hesperines errant, Lio. I may not have the fangs yet, but I have the heart. We cannot turn our back on someone in need. We promised Chuma we'd help her mother."

Lio's jaw clenched, but the way he sighed, she knew he agreed with her.

"Our biggest problem is him." Monsoon pointed at Knight.

Cassia ran a hand helplessly over his thick fur. "He is equipped for the harshest conditions—cold conditions. He can survive in the snow for days and kill something four times bigger and more magical than him. But heat? That is a problem."

Cassia's heart sank further. But what mattered right now was saving Chuma's mother and getting answers about Solia, not her feelings.

"The two of you could go," she made herself say. "Lio, you can step and levitate, and you can fly, Monsoon. Find me a place to hide, and I'll stay where Knight and I won't slow you down."

"No." Lio said only one word, but it spoke volumes.

Her heart pounded with frustration. "We may not have a choice."

He pulled her to her feet. "I can't believe you even suggested it."

"You know I don't suggest it lightly. I would never subject you to a separation willingly, especially in a place where the sun will make you even more vulnerable. But with your power, the two of you could go to them and bring them back before your Craving or the sun have time to interfere."

"After what happened at the Sandira Court, you and I stay together."

"We're all going," Monsoon cut in. "What the Ashes need is reinforcements, and we have no idea what threats have prevented their return. We won't leave a single weapon behind, including the dog."

Lio's battle with his conscience was written in every line of his body. She knew it was a difficult debate for him. She stood there, her human body feeling like a piece of baggage attached to her.

"I need you," Monsoon gritted. "I can't spirit walk in the Maaqul. No one can. It doesn't belong to humans, not even the nomads who make it their home. Ancestral magic doesn't work predictably. But Hesperine magic does. Even my wings aren't as fast as stepping. Getting to Chuma's mother quickly enough could mean the difference between life and death. And so could me not fighting alone."

A moment of silence ensued. That was quite an admission coming from the solitary mercenary.

Monsoon grimaced. "If it means getting Chuma's mother back to her, I'll drag you across the desert. A Hesperine, a war dog, and a strategist will be assets in this."

Cassia shouldn't have been so mollified. Strategist might be the nicest thing Monsoon had said about her. Her human body was a disadvantage, but if he thought her mind might be of use in the desert, then she could rely on her inner resources as she always had.

But Lio pulled Cassia aside, his veils wrapping tight around them. "Cassia...there are so many dangers. Thirst. Heatstroke. Poisonous snakes and insects. Getting lost. Not to mention whatever enemy we're headed toward, which is powerful enough to test the Empire's best mercenaries."

"I'm so sorry, Lio. I know what this does to you. After I promised not to put you through anything difficult again."

"You are not putting me through this."

That was true. She had not chosen any of this. But their search for her sister had brought it upon them. Guilt hissed within her, poisonous as one of those snakes he feared.

If he had issued an ultimatum, she would have protested. But Lio never insisted on his way. He always asked. "If the danger becomes too great, please let me step you to safety. Please leave with me without hesitation. Hesitation at a moment like that could cost...everything."

His plea went straight to her heart. "I won't hesitate."

He rested his face on her hair. "Thank you."

Cassia could not deny the truth. She *was* a fragile human.

ON THE VERGE

L IO STOOD AT THE edge of the Azarqi nomads' camp, keeping his veils over Cassia, Knight, and Monsoon while they assessed their surroundings.

In the decades since he had last been there, the Scorched Verge had prevailed, always changing and yet never changing. The town of tents was busy with life, clinging to the edge of the desert like a bright-plumed bird one wingbeat away from plummeting to the sand. He couldn't say if this was the same location where he and his Trial brothers had been before. He had stepped to the enduring people.

Beyond the vibrant tents and glowing campfires, the dunes, painted indigo by the night with undertones of soft gold, stretched as far as even his Hesperine eyes could see, and farther still.

"It's cold!" Cassia pulled her cloak out of her pack, while Knight plopped his warm, furry self on her feet.

"The land doesn't hold the heat here," Lio explained. "It's hot by day, but chills quickly at night. Another reason it's so dangerous."

"I've grown used to the dryness, at least, from living in Orthros." Cassia gazed out across the expanse beyond the camp. "'Orthros has two hearts, one of roses in the snow, one of thorns in the desert...'"

The quote from a poem by Prometheus gave Lio comfort he had not known he needed. Lio's loved ones who had been close to Methu often found it painful to read his writings, but Lio cherished the great warrior poet's words. As Cassia knew.

What would the Midnight Champion of the Blood Errant do when facing a trek across the Maaqul with a beloved human in need of protection?

He would charge ahead. But first, he would make sure said human was ready.

Lio pulled Cassia's cloak around her, only to discover she was shivering. He touched a hand to her cheek. It alarmed him to already feel the beginnings of a Craving fever on her skin. "Is there anywhere to rest before we start into the desert?"

"I shall manage," Cassia said.

He had been flat on his back all day while she brought in the harvest, hid from the Golden Shield, and endured another flight with Monsoon. He knew she must be physically exhausted. "Have you eaten?"

"Your favorite question. Yes, Chuma's family fed me again before you woke."

Even so, her Craving demanded care. Lio could wait, but he would take the blame for the delay if it would convince Cassia to let him give her what she needed. "I need a drink."

She leaned closer to him. "Yes, we need to stop for that."

Monsoon didn't argue. "I want both of you in good condition before we start in. A rushed venture into the Maaqul is a deadly one, and it won't help Chuma's mother if the desert kills us before we get to her. We'll take tonight to prepare. I have friends here who will sell us supplies and put us up for the night. They can get your letters out, too."

"Thank you," Cassia said, "although I'm sorry to endanger more good people."

"They'll find you boring compared to the dangers they live with out here. But let's try to get to their tent without giving every person in the Verge reason to gossip that a shadowlander has been here."

Cassia pulled out her map, so Lio pricked his finger to raise a small light for her. She held the paper near the glow of his spell. "We are back in the northern hemisphere, I see. On the other side of the continent from the Cifwani Matriarchate and the Sandira Kingdom. Surely the Golden Shield won't know to look for me here."

He put his hands on her shoulders. "We should still take precautions. I'll place a veil over you and Knight to encourage observers to look elsewhere."

She pursed her lips. "Like you did at the dance back in Tenebra, when none of the court noticed proper Lady Cassia chatting with a heretic?"

The memory brought a smile to his face. That had been the night when they had first sworn their Oath to always speak honestly with each other. "Precisely. You won't be invisible, and you'll look like yourself, but no one will give you a first glance, much less a second one."

"Well, it worked so well before." A smile tugged at her mouth, too. "We managed to sneak into the woods quite effectively. I suppose we can use the same magic to escape into the desert."

Cassia stood patiently while Lio concentrated on his spell. When he was finished, he glanced at Monsoon. "What do you think?"

His brows shot up as his gaze drifted away. "That…actually works. Even I feel the urge to look elsewhere and forget about you."

"You'd best not, if you want your pay," said Cassia.

"Not to worry," Lio replied. "I'll make very sure our guide doesn't lose us."

Monsoon looked up at Lio. "You're too tall to lose track of. Silk-foot eyesore."

With that, he turned and led the way into the camp. The Verge was still lively after dusk. People hurried to complete their business by night, when they had respite from the heat of the day. It wasn't difficult to blend in with the traders and scholars from various parts of the Empire who were doing business with the Azarqi caravaners.

Cassia glanced at Lio. "When we were in the Sandira city, you mentioned that you know the nomads' language."

Lio nodded. "We won't have to take Monsoon's word for translations."

"Excellent. I dare say you researched the Azarqi, Sir Scholar, in preparation for your canceled expedition."

"Their politics, diplomacy, and economy are fascinating. They command all trade across the Maaqul, the overland routes that link the Silklands and the Imperial capital. They navigate this sea of sand as effectively as the Empress's privateers rule the waves. And yet their culture is much less influenced by the Empire as a whole."

As Monsoon led them past a corral of camels, Cassia's aura twinkled with curious delight. "Lio, what are those?"

Monsoon eyed the beasts with evident distaste. "You've never seen a camel? Lucky you."

"I only just began my education in Orthros. These are the creatures called camels you two were talking about earlier?"

Lio drew to a halt near the drowsing beasts. "They're meaner than Orthros warmbloods and almost as smart. They are the best mount for deserts."

"Do we need one?" Cassia asked hopefully.

Lio swallowed a chuckle. "Not when you have me."

She tilted her head. "I don't expect you to carry me all the way across the desert."

"I would gladly do so, if called upon. But that's not necessary. I will step you anywhere you need to go, my rose. No camels required."

"And I will fly out of range of those things." Monsoon stood a safe distance away.

"Are they really so ill-tempered?" Cassia asked him.

"Try cleaning camel spit off your feathers."

Cassia raised a brow. "You must tell that story around the campfire."

"No."

Lio took Cassia a little closer to have a better look at the small herd. One sleepy camel raised her head and blinked her long eyelashes at them.

"They're so tall," Cassia marveled, "even lying down."

"Riding one is rather like being in a boat," Lio said. "They have a swaying gait because they pick up both feet on one side at the same time."

"How does one ride on a hump like that? They must have special saddles."

"Watch out," Lio warned, "they really do—"

Cassia looked dubiously at the wad of camel spit that had landed on the front of her robes. Lio provided her with a handkerchief and a cleaning spell.

Knight was sniffing the air madly, standing between his lady and the strange beasts, but did not growl.

"Knight thinks they're prey, not predators," Cassia mused, "but prey with hooves that hit hard."

The camel lipped Lio's sleeve affectionately, leaving behind a bit of a mess. He gave the creature a placating pat on her neck. "They like Hesperines, though."

Cassia covered her mouth with one hand. "All animals like Hesperines, to be sure. But I think this one is sweet on you."

The camel batted her eyelashes at him again and gave him another slobbery nuzzle, this time in his hair.

Goddess, it was good to hear Cassia's laughter. He would tolerate camel spit for that any night. "Shall I promise you and Zoe a camel ride when we all come to the Empire together?"

"Oh, yes, please."

"Enough sightseeing." Monsoon turned and moved on.

They followed him to the center of the camp, where there was a large, gabled tent of red skins adorned with tassels. Just inside, a campfire burned brightly. The family gathered around it had the medium brown complexion of the Azarqi and wore the blue fabrics for which their people were renowned. A group of men drank tea on one side of the fire, while the women were busy trading on the other. The lady at the heart of the activity wore flowing, deep blue robes that covered her hair and body.

"She looks powerful," Cassia observed.

Lio nodded. "Her robes indicate she is the senior woman of the camp, who decides where they travel and when."

"Her hands are blue. Is that a mark of status?"

"Actually that's common among the Azarqi. Their precious indigo dye stains their skin."

"Beautiful."

The lady was indeed beautiful, with the challenges of life in the Maaqul written on her weathered face. Her silver jewelry showed her success in the face of such adversity. As she changed money for her customers, the rings on her fingers glinted, and her bracelets clinked more musically than her coin. Who knew how many riches had crossed her blue palms over the years?

"Azarqi women own their family's tents," Lio explained. "The men own the camels."

Cassia's aura glittered with interest. "Oh, how fascinating. That would certainly give a woman power."

"She can divorce a man by simply taking her tents."

"Leaving him and his camels to fend for themselves in the desert?" Cassia chuckled, her grin wicked.

"Precisely."

"Oh, I can think of some Tenebran women who would have loved to do such a thing to the louts they were married to."

"Women hold great influence here, as they do everywhere in the Empire. But this woman is even more powerful. To hold such a position of authority over the Scorched Verge, the most influential Azarqi outpost, means her status is noble or even royal in the complex and ever-shifting politics of the nomads. Her tent is her palace, her people wear her treasury on their wrists and earlobes, and her trade agreements are her alliances."

"She exercises the power of life and death over her subjects," Cassia said in understanding, "every time she makes a judgment about which direction they should travel to find the next oasis in the desert."

"The man who shares her fire will be her husband."

"His blue turban does have the air of a crown."

The royal blue turban wrapped around his head and face covered all but his eyes. Although his expression was hidden, his aura shone with fatherly warmth as he stood and welcomed Monsoon in Azarqi. "The winds have brought you back to us."

"So they have," the mercenary answered in the same language, returning the man's embrace.

The queen's last customer departed. Lio and Cassia gave her a respectful bow, but when she beckoned to Monsoon, he bent to receive a pat on the cheek from her.

She clicked her tongue at him. "Monsoon. After all this time. You have let us miss you for too long."

"I am grateful for your welcome," he replied.

She arched a brow. "You sound surprised."

Chagrin filled his aura. "I respect your daughter's reasons for objecting to my presence."

"As do I. And she would respect why you are welcome in my tent. Sit, join us for our meal."

Did Monsoon count an Azarqi princess among his past lovers? If so, Lio had no trouble imagining why she might have tossed the insufferable man out of her tent long ago.

The queen gave Lio and Cassia a gracious smile. "Friends of our friends are always welcome here."

"You won't need your veil spells," Monsoon added.

Hesitating, Lio exchanged a glance with Cassia. He sensed that she was as hesitant as he to trust yet another family with the secret of her origins, as well as endanger them with that knowledge.

"The Azarqi place greater value on your deeds than where you come from," Monsoon informed them.

Interest lit the queen's gaze. "The desert cares nothing for where a person's ancestors walked."

"It's all right, Lio," Cassia relented.

He gave a nod and altered his veils so only those around this fire would be able to see Cassia.

The queen looked her over, no judgment in her gaze. "We will prepare a bowl without meat for our guests from Orthros."

A red acacia log was placed on the flames. Although Lio had to dodge a flurry of sparks, he appreciated the gesture, which signaled they were welcome guests. Monsoon joined the queen's husband by the fire. Lio and Cassia took a seat where the two sides of the gathering met, him on the men's side and her on the women's.

Knight, irrespective of such distinctions, positioned himself nearer the ladies. Clever fellow, he knew where he was most likely to get attention. A girl in braids immediately obliged him with pets and scratches. She struck up a conversation with Cassia in Tradewinds that revealed she was the queen's youngest daughter.

The queen's husband began the ceremony of brewing tea, which Lio had certainly read about, but had yet to experience in person. Lio found the process even more loving and elaborate than Uncle Argyros's most devoted attentions to brewing coffee.

"We must drink all three rounds," Lio advised Cassia. "If we didn't, it would be a terribly insulting refusal of hospitality, not to mention ruin all our chances of trading with the Azarqi—for goods or information."

"I would never want to dishonor such a kind family," she replied, "and with no coffee in sight, I am in desperate need of tea."

"You'll like it. It's strong."

The king raised the teapot high, pouring the rich liquid into tiny glass cups resting on the sand. Then he tossed the contents of the cups back into the sugary depths of the pot. He repeated this step again and again, until Lio lost count, mesmerized. The poetic practice was both art and tradition, a simple yet complex ritual that seemed to create an island of comfort in the harsh desert. An unexpected contentment settled into Lio as he watched.

At last the king handed Lio and Cassia one cup each. The tea had the perfect amount of froth. Lio sipped it, and the bitter strength of the brew enlivened his sensitive Hesperine tongue more than a jolt of magic.

Cassia raised her cup to the king. "Competes with Orthros coffee," she told him in Tradewinds, then used a couple of Azarqi words she must have already picked up. "Thank you."

His veil hid his mouth, but his eyes lit and crinkled with an unmistakable smile.

The second round of tea, brewed from the same leaves, was rich and sweet. The third round was nearly all sugar, and Lio had to admit, it was very pleasing to a Hesperine's sweet tooth.

As a Hesperine, Lio had to admire the Azarqi royals' self-sufficiency, as much as the rich traditions surrounding everything they did. By the time everyone had finished their tea, one of the queen's older daughters had cooked their meal. She filled bowls from the pot at the fire and set multiple spoons in each one.

Monsoon had the privilege of eating from the men's communal bowl, which smelled strongly of roasted goat. Lio kept his expression polite, for he knew it was an honor for the Azarqi to bring out their goat meat for guests. Thankfully, he and Cassia received the promised bowl without meat, and he bowed in thanks to the queen once again.

"Thank you for the meal," Cassia said, once again mixing the Azarqi term for 'thank you' with simple Tradewinds. "I eat Imperial food in Orthros, but not this."

"This is not Imperial food," the queen stated without rancor. "It is Azarqi."

Cassia appeared puzzled.

"The Azarqi culture is very independent," Lio said. "They are citizens, but bow to no one."

The Azarqi queen nodded, clearly pleased with his assessment. "The inscriptions on the tent poles withstand the winds, while the Empress's papers turn to dust."

Lio translated the idiom into Divine for Cassia, adding, "A woman carves or burns designs into the posts of her tents, often the writings of her ancestors. The Azarqi have their own alphabet."

"You have great scholars." Cassia tried the food. "And great cooks."

The daughter who had prepared the meal grinned. "We have to be inventive out here. But at the end of a long day, bread from the sand oven tastes like heaven."

"How does a sand oven work?" Cassia asked.

"You make a hole in the hot embers of the fire and put the dough in." The daughter motioned with her hands near the fire to demonstrate. "Then when it's ready, we break it up and mix it with camel's milk and crushed gourds."

The youngest girl licked her spoon. "Tonight there's lots of butter in my sister's recipe."

Conversation continued to ebb and flow around the fire. Some time later, Cassia gave Lio a look. "You've still only eaten three bites."

"Three bites ensures I do not insult our hosts, but I don't need food. You do."

"You expect me to eat both our portions, don't you?"

"It will do you good. It's very nourishing for desert travel."

She shook her head at him.

He brushed a strand of hair back from her neck, letting the tips of his fingers glide lightly over her skin. "You'll need your strength. I'll eat later."

"That does motivate me."

"I hoped it would."

To his relief, Cassia ate without further protest. Not at all to his surprise, she also observed the conversations around them with a perceptive gaze.

"Can you read lips in Tradewinds yet?" he asked with great interest.

"Alas, no." When she lowered her voice, he placed a subtle veil over their conversation. "But I can tell that the words we're hearing from Monsoon and the queen's husband are not what they're actually saying to one another."

"An Azarqi sound spell? Are they discussing personal matters, do you think?"

"Or business. Surely if anyone knows why the Ashes and Ipika went into the desert, it is the royal family of the Scorched Verge."

"You think they are also contacts of Monsoon's?"

"Shall we test his assertion that contacts will only reveal information to him?"

"Certainly."

Cassia struck up another conversation with the women, while Lio joined the men's discussion. He learned much about the politics between camel drivers and goat herders, but nothing about the Ashes. At length he turned back to Cassia to see if she had made more progress. He found her in discussion with the women about whether Azarqi girls could become warriors.

"Of course we can," the youngest exclaimed. "Our eldest sister can best anyone in a fight."

The middle daughter grinned. "But you should have seen how many times our sister won against Monsoon in a sparring match."

Lio laughed harder than he should at the girl's revelation. The idea of the princess not only throwing Monsoon out of her tent, but humbling the champion of the Court of Claws in battle was a fine mental image.

"We've seen Monsoon fight," said Cassia. "He is very skilled. Your sister must be amazing."

"She is," the girl said. "I wish I could be just like her."

Her mother reached over and stroked her braids. "You should wish to be just as you are, my little song."

The girl smiled at that. "And she should wish to be as she is."

Her mother nodded in approval.

"I'll be glad when she gets home, though," the girl said.

Lio wondered if Zoe was at home with that same despondent expression on her face. She was far less accustomed to her loved ones wandering, unlike this girl and her nomadic people.

The queen patted her youngest daughter's hand. "Let us play some music, hmm?"

The girl's expression lightened. The queen took out her imzad, the prized musical instrument of Azarqi women, and began to stroke its single string with her bow. Her daughters picked up their own instruments and joined her. The tones of the instruments rose, lamenting and yet resilient, as the woman sang an ancient ballad about an Azarqi princess who battled a jinn.

Cassia was clearly enjoying the music, and Lio quietly translated some of the lyrics for her. But the sheen of sweat on her brow and the increasing coldness of her hands worried him more and more.

He didn't realize his protectiveness had affected his fangs until, between songs, the queen cast him an astute glance. She gestured to him and Cassia. "While my eldest daughter is traveling, she does not have need of her tent. You may stay there tonight."

Lio gave her another bow. "We are honored."

The middle daughter showed them away from the fire. With gestures of hospitality, the Azarqi women had effectively stopped Lio and Cassia's questions. That convinced Lio that they knew more than they had said, and that the queen's daughters would make excellent politicians like their mother one day.

But right now, his Grace's Craving threatened, and he could not bring himself to be much concerned about anything else.

At the door of the princess's tent, her sister took Lio and Cassia's letters, promising their correspondence would go out with the next caravan headed for the nearest spirit gate. Then she ushered them inside and spoke an incantation in Azarqi. Light flared to life on the tent poles, tracing the Azarqi script incised on the wood. Warm, diffuse spell light filled the tent, and the script ceased to glow.

Cassia looked around them at the richly decorated tent poles, the thick carpets that covered the sand, and the tasseled cushions scattered about. "Beautiful."

The young woman bade them good night and departed. Knight was guarding the door, Lio was finally alone with Cassia, and she needed him.

"Did you learn anything useful from the Azarqi men?" she asked in between her hungry kisses on his neck.

Her teeth were too close to his throat. He knew he should stop her. They could not afford another close call like they'd had on Marijani.

He had felt her teeth break his skin. She had tasted his blood on her lips. Divine. Dangerous. An infuriating tease of her postponed Gift Night, when she would finally get to slake herself at his vein and transform into a Hesperine.

He let himself enjoy the feeling of her teeth on his neck. Just a moment longer. He tried to remember her question. "No, the men revealed nothing. Were the women forthcoming?"

"Only about currency exchange values. Kia would be proud of how much math I learned tonight."

He framed Cassia's feverish cheeks in his hands and covered her mouth with his. She sucked his tongue, her mind dragging on his magic. With a groan, he pulled her flush with him, grinding against her with each pulse of his power.

When her teeth scraped his tongue, he forced himself to break the kiss.

"Veils," she panted.

"No need. This tent is covered in Azarqi silence spells."

"Ah. Perfect for a princess's political secrets and noisy liaisons." Cassia cast a glance over her shoulder, her hands roaming down his chest. "Shall we forgo the bed?"

"I admit, I would feel like a rather bad guest if I did what I want to do with you on the Azarqi princess's bed."

"Which she may or may not have shared with Monsoon."

"Precisely. Although…" He took another breath, making sure he was not simply distracted by the scent of Cassia. "…none of the cushions are leather. How accommodating. I think it's possible the princess has entertained a Hesperine here."

"Excellent decision, tossing out the vulture and bringing in a Hesperine instead."

"Much worthier of her attentions, to be sure."

"The floor looks inviting. I'm remembering an excellent rug on the floor of a Hesperine fortress, which had a magnificent bloodstain on it when we were done with it."

"Don't remind me," he protested, but couldn't help laughing again at the memory. "It was the most embarrassing stain."

"It's good for you to be messy sometimes."

If only she knew just what a mess he had become since the battle with the Collector. She had an inkling. But even his Grace didn't know he had left his medallion in the rubble of the ruined building, along with many certainties about himself and his path as a diplomat. He had only recently realized it himself.

In this moment, though, the powerful certainty of the Craving drove away all doubt. He took her hips in his hands and spun her around, pulling her back against him. He bit her ear, then whispered in it, "I'll clean the messy stains off the princess's cushions after dinner."

He listened to her laughter and the spike in her pulse. She leaned her head back against him and began to open the high collar of her travel robe, one fastener at a time, a taunting warmth in her gaze.

Their quest, for the moment, was out there in the desert. They were here in the secret embrace of the tent. There was nothing they could do until tomorrow…except give each other what they needed.

He allowed himself the luxury of watching her slowly expose her throat. He let her watch his fangs lengthen and felt a shiver go through her at the sight.

She slid her robe down off her shoulders. The spell light illumined her freckles, and he gave into the urge to kiss his way across them to the sensitive place where her neck and shoulder met. She let her hands fall, and her robe slid open, revealing her small breasts.

He cupped them in his hands, and she let out a soft sound as he touched her cool skin with his warm palms. Her nipples pebbled. He massaged her, enjoying how the soft, slight rounds of her breasts fit in his hands.

He murmured in her ear again. "I like it when you eat properly."

"They're still negligible. But I suppose that's a step up from nonexistent."

"They were perfect before. But I like this perfect version of them, too."

"Glasstongue, you earn your epithet in bed most of all."

He ran his tongue down her neck again.

Her voice came out breathy. "Well, Orthros is a safe place to have breasts for the first time in my life. No uncouth Tenebran courtiers to make me regret they're there."

"I would blind any such man. These are not regrettable in the least, my rose."

He teased her nipples between his thumbs and forefingers, tugging and caressing the way he knew it pleased her every time. She pressed her hips back against him, as if on reflex, teasing him with the instinctive motion.

The way her aura drank his magic sent rushes of pleasure through his body. He had never imagined it would be possible for a mortal to draw on a Hesperine's magic like this. But their bond was deepening, woven of Grace Union and the mind ward they had cast together within the hallowed halls of her Will.

Magic and pleasure were powerful surrogates for his blood, keeping her Craving at bay. He let her feast on his power and devoted all his physical attention to her breasts.

"Ohh." Her fingers tightened on his forearms. "Are you trying to make me climax just by touching my breasts?"

"Is it working?"

She moaned. "You wicked Hesperine."

He grinned against her neck. "Would it be cheating if I used my mind magic as well?"

"I don't care if it is cheating. I want it."

He slid his power into her mind, and like a river into its natural bed, his thelemancy flowed into her along the paths of the mind ward. Their motivation for the costly magic had been to shield her thoughts from enemy thelemancers. But he had to admit, its erotic benefits were the sweetest reward for what they had endured to create the irreversible spell.

She tossed her head back, her throat tempting him. But for the moment, what he craved was the sensation of her feeding on him, the sight of her enjoying him.

He dove, swift and deep, into the regions of her mind that governed her body's pleasure. Her knees buckled. He held her up with levitation. With his thelemancy so deep in her mind, he could have pushed her over the edge in a heartbeat. But he gave her the barest touches there, little caresses to enhance his hands' worship of her breasts. Measuring his magic, he let the spell of physical touch hold sway.

When he let her come apart at last, her soft gasps filled the tent, and her pleasure cried out through their Blood Union. The vicarious release left him hard and aching, his fangs heavy in his mouth.

She heaved a sigh of satisfaction, her hand reaching up to tangle in his hair. "I will never regret my breasts."

"Good. I'd like you to enjoy them as much as I do."

"Enjoy me now, my Grace."

He levitated her down to the carpets, and she let out another gasp. With her on her belly, he let his weight sink gently down over her. Her heart sped up again, and the musk of her fresh arousal met his nose.

"Shall I enjoy you like this?" he asked.

"Yes," she answered, in her husky bedchamber voice.

With a touch of Will, he used magic to lift her hips and pull one of the tasseled cushions under her. Just high enough to give him the right angle. Goddess, she fit perfectly under him.

Kneeling back, he pushed her travel robe up over her hips and tugged her trousers down. Off. He wanted them off. He ran his hands along her short, slender legs.

He couldn't resist placing a gentle bite on one spray of freckles on one of her buttocks. That made her laugh.

"Sunbathing naked in the Empire suits you, my rose." He slid his pale fingers over her dusky olive skin and watched a shiver travel through the muscles of her thigh.

She stretched, glancing over her shoulder at him with her secret smile. Cup and thorns, she was a feast.

Straddling her legs, he slipped his fingers between her thighs. Her krana was wet from her release and tense with her hunger. He took his rhabdos in hand and fitted himself to her.

So tight from this angle. She uttered his name, as if in surprise at the new sensation. He pressed into her with a groan. He needed to bite.

Bracing his hands on the carpet, he sank his fangs into her throat. Her thundering heart made her blood rush into his mouth, spiced with her primal enjoyment. The rhythm of her pulse in his ears urged him on.

And then her voice. "You're so hungry. You were caring for me and got—so hungry—"

She was right. He had not even realized. His own Craving was as far gone as hers.

He pinned her to the cushion with his hips, setting an intense pace to stoke the friction. Now she put the silence spells to the test, crying out with him, for him.

She had been taken from him last night. Today, she had been in danger. But now she was here, enfolded in his magic. Joined to his body. Sealed in his blood.

Her release gripped them fast. As her krana sucked at his rhabdos, he sucked hard at her vein, tension gathering in his back. He didn't want to miss a single choice swallow of her release, the richest course of the feast.

He kept pumping into her until she climaxed again and gave him a second course. With her pleasure at its richest, he sank still further into her mind. She cried out again, her thoughts unfurling to pull him closer. Her hips tilted up, allowing him deeper inside her.

He drove into her once more. Perfection. He let himself lose control, let his own pleasure crash through the uninhibited reaches of her mind. Then neither of their minds held any more room for thought, and their Union consumed them.

He took a breath at last, scenting her blood and satisfaction. The ripples of her climax still trembled in her channel. He relaxed over her, fulfilled.

When he had withdrawn from her vein and healed the bite with his tongue, he rested his cheek on her skin. No more fever.

She traced a finger over the rug before her, where a bloodstain to rival the one at Waystar painted the fine Azarqi carpet.

"I won't regret that," he said, "so long as you do not regret your breasts."

She laughed, the sensation doing pleasant things where they were still joined. Her body would need care, now that they had worked it so hard to care for her Craving.

He would carry her on one of these tasseled cushions all the way across the desert, if he thought she would let him. But she wouldn't.

He brushed her tangled hair away from her neck and placed a kiss on the traces of blood on her skin. Tomorrow, he must accept that his mortal Grace would face the dangers of the Maaqul. But tonight, he could treat her like royalty.

67

days until

NOTIAN WINTER SOLSTICE

38 Annassa, 1597 IS

THE FACE OF THE ENEMY

"I T'S BARELY SUNDOWN, AND we silkfoots are ready to go. I dare
        Monsoon to complain." Cassia set her pack at the front of the
        tent next to Knight and gave him a pat.

Lio tightened one last buckle on his pack. "I can scarcely believe how
early I escaped the Slumber. My head is clearer than it's been in days. The
light-blocking enchantments the Azarqi use on their tents are excellent."

"What an advantage for humans and Hesperines. And dogs. Knight
seems none the worse for wear, thanks to spending the heat of the day in here."

"A light mage could learn so much from the Azarqi. I wonder if there
is any Hesperine scholarly literature on the caravaners' magical special-
izations for withstanding the heat and sun. I would be surprised if there
isn't, considering how their adaptations to their homeland would be of
such relevance to our nocturnal existence."

Cassia smiled. "Your head is much clearer, Sir Scholar."

"I credit our respite in the privacy of the tent, not only the tent itself."
He smiled, his fangs so well tamed, he looked more divine than heretical.

She was about to take one more taste of that beautiful mouth of his
when Knight backed away from the door, bumping into her. The front
flap snapped open.

A chill draft of dry air burst inside, along with Monsoon. "The Golden
Shield are already here."

"Bleeding thorns," Cassia swore.

Lio pulled her into his arms. "Let them come. This time, I'm awake."

"Yes," she said, although her heart raced. "They'll find that looking for
me after dark is a mistake."

"They have no fear of Hesperines," Monsoon said. "Stay here. I'll ready our supplies. We'll leave the Verge under the cover of veils as soon as possible."

With that, the mercenary was already gone from the tent.

Cassia felt Lio's veil spells thickening over their hiding place, like a heartbeat that grew stronger with every pulse. She straightened her shoulders and rested her hands on his chest so they wouldn't shake.

"You're safe here." His voice and his magic soothed her senses. "My veils held last time. They will hold again now. Why don't we sit down?"

She felt much better on her feet. "Would it be wise to step into the desert and wait there for Monsoon to meet us with the supplies?"

"We cannot," said Lio. "Not without permission."

"You did say you weren't worried about violating the Empire's policies anymore."

"True, but violating the Desert Accord is something else."

"I think you'd best explain it to me."

While the Golden Shield were somewhere outside, sweeping through the camp, Lio and Cassia sat down together in the shelter of their tent. She called Knight to her side, and he pressed himself against her.

Her tongue dry, she asked calmly, "Is the Desert Accord the reason you came here to study Azarqi diplomacy?"

"Yes." Lio's voice was steady, his arms around her steadier still. "It's one of the most important treaties in the Empire's history, which secured peace between jinn and humans and ended the Thousand Fires War."

Beyond the tent, where the campfire burned, voices rose.

"Jinn?" Cassia asked. "There are other non-humans besides Hesperines?"

"Unlike us, they were never human. They're immortal beings endowed with powerful magic drawn from elements of nature, but who simultaneously have a connection with the spirit phase."

Footsteps sounded outside. Not the soft treads of the Azarqi. The march of soldiers.

"So are the jinn enemies or friends?" Cassia whispered.

"Neither." Lio spoke at a normal volume, reminding her they were hidden. "They are neutral under the terms of the Desert Accord, which state that jinn shall do no harm to humans who enter the desert, and humans shall walk there with respect for the jinn."

A debate began outside. Cassia recognized the voice of the Azarqi queen…and the metallic echo of a Golden Shield speaking through her mask.

Lio's arms wrapped closer around her. "The jinn are not ruled by the Empress. The Desert Accord ensures their independence and places limits on what humans are allowed to do in their territory. We will need to enter the desert on foot and present ourselves to the jinn. Once we secure their approval, I will step us to Chuma's mother."

Escape. So easy, and yet so difficult. They could step into the desert at this very moment. They could step all the way back to Orthros right now.

But not without consequences that would tear through all these interconnected peoples.

The curtained doorway of the tent flew open once again, letting in a flare of firelight. A soldier stood silhouetted against it for an instant before she prowled forward.

Lio stroked Cassia's hair, his body tight with tension against hers. The thunder of her heart seemed loud enough to give her away.

She made herself look at her beautiful enemy. A crest of silk spilled from the top of the soldier's helmet. She wore a smooth, rounded breastplate that resembled pure gold, but she moved with impossible lightness. A wrap of brilliant fabric stopped at her knees, and sandals adorned her feet.

Every other inch of her skin was covered in lustrous gold, as if the metal had been forged onto her body. What Cassia had taken for armor was pure magic.

At her waist, she wore a long, curving sword with a filigreed handle and a deadly edge.

Cassia felt magic rise inside the tent, human magic. The hairs on the back of her neck stood up, and a headache began behind her eyes. She felt Lio grow tenser.

Then the Golden Shield turned on her heel and left the tent.

Cassia sagged with relief against Lio.

His thelemancy slipped softly into her mind, and her headache abated. "She was sensing for human minds. But you're all right."

Cassia felt suddenly ill. "She was a mind mage?"

"I don't know. Her armor has spells all over it—wards, theramantic protections. I couldn't sense her emotions or her affinity. But when her spell moved over you, I felt it."

"But she couldn't sense me."

"I promised you my veils would hold."

Cassia let out a breath. "I'm glad we didn't have to test the mind ward for the first time tonight."

He pulled her head against his chest. "So am I."

Silence stretched between them as they waited for the Golden Shield to finish their search of the Azarqi camp. Cassia lost track of how much of the night passed, wasted, while they waited for the all clear.

But she had to admit, after such a close call, she wanted nothing more than to sit in Lio's arms for a while.

At last Monsoon ducked into the tent again, this time through the back entrance. "Ready."

"Are the Golden Shield still here?" Lio asked.

Monsoon smirked. "Enjoying the hospitality of my very distracting friends while we make our exit."

"I wish we had time to thank them," said Cassia.

"You'll get your chance," Monsoon replied, but offered no further explanation.

The supplies awaited them behind the tent. Cassia's heart sank at the sight of the extra packs. "Are you certain we shouldn't bring a camel?"

Lio made a low, braying sound and slung the luggage onto his back.

Cassia pressed her lips together, but a laugh escaped her. Even so, she held stubbornly to her pack from Orthros and her gardening satchel.

"I take it back," Monsoon said. "She's definitely guilty of befuddling a Hesperine's wits. Just keep them about you while we make our escape, will you?"

Lio took Cassia's hand, and they followed Monsoon through the camp, keeping the tents between them and the campfires. The shadows of robed Azarqi and armored soldiers played on the walls of hide.

Once the tents were behind them, the dunes lay ahead.

FORCES OF NATURE

A COOLING WIND BLEW ACROSS the Maaqul, bringing with it a thousand smells. Lio's Hesperine senses revealed to him a secret he suspected the nomads already knew.

The desert was not desolate at all. Life hid in its pockets and struggled forth from its cracks. A tiny lizard slithered out of a crevasse in the rocks. A bird rode a dry wind overhead. Night insects chirped. Laced with the scents of dust and rock, there was the pungent snap of spiny plants and the distant promise of water at some oasis he could not see.

What a beautiful and terrible challenge stood between them and the truth.

He had to get his Grace—his oh, so human Grace—across this.

Standing beside him, she licked her dry lips and slipped her hand in his. "Humans live here. I'm certain we can manage one journey through it."

Her aura was full of determination, with no trace of fear, a small but mighty match for the harsh environment looming before her. He couldn't help smiling as he squeezed her hand.

She was less afraid than he was.

He had already voiced his fears to her. He wouldn't say more and risk eroding a speck of that inner strength she so beautifully displayed at the moment.

"I love you," he said.

Her face and aura softened. "I love you too. Try not to worry."

"I can also try to make the moons reverse their orbits."

Monsoon led them from the embrace of the camp, and they followed him out across the sand.

"How do we request an audience with the jinn?" Cassia asked.

"So you know a thing or two about desert diplomacy?" Monsoon called over his shoulder. "The last thing we need is ignorant foreigners making trouble with the jinn."

Cassia gave his back a cutting smile. "Tenebran girls aren't allowed powerful things like books, but now that I have access to Orthros's libraries and scholars, I am making myself dangerously educated."

"And she's the quickest study at every symposium." Lio knew Cassia was still frustrated by her progress toward literacy, but she could listen to a botany lecture once and remember it without taking a single note.

"In this case," Monsoon replied, "all that book learning in your marble towers might actually help you. The single most important survival skill in the Maaqul is complying with the Desert Accord."

They were headed into a negotiation, and Lio didn't even have an ambassador's medallion to wield. All he had was a lump of warped glass. His fingers pressed against the cool, rough formations of the fulgurite in his pocket. He had never imagined he might arrive before the jinn as a supplicant with so little bargaining power.

"The most important term of the Accord," he explained to Cassia, "is that we must not take anything that isn't ours. We can't leave the desert with anything except what we brought with us."

"Don't even slip a pebble in your pocket," Monsoon instructed.

"If their magic comes from nature," Cassia reasoned, "I can understand why even a rock would be important to them. But what about the nomads who live here? Aren't the Azarqi allowed to use the natural resources of the desert?"

"They have a special arrangement with the jinn," Monsoon explained. "Think of them as the jinn's neighbors. But we are guests from afar, and we may only use what we need to survive."

"So we could forage for food, but not set up a gold mine?" she asked.

"Right," Monsoon answered. "If you visited someone's home, you would eat with them, but you wouldn't walk out with their furniture, would you? Don't dishonor the jinn's hospitality."

"So." Cassia shared a glance with Lio. "Our desert journey will begin with peace talks. We're very good at those."

"Oh?" Monsoon cast a glance over his shoulder. "How were your peace talks with the Sandira royal guard?"

At the twinge in Cassia's aura, Lio wanted to make the man regret prodding her wounds. Alas, Monsoon would be of no help to Ipika if Lio turned his mind to jelly.

The mercenary pointed ahead. "As soon as we're out of sight of the Verge, we officially leave human lands. The jinn will find us."

Lio looked at the hike ahead of them. "Perhaps we should have brought a camel after all."

Without slowing, Cassia mounted the first low dune. "I'll be fine. It would be a waste to hire a camel just for this part of the journey, when we'll be stepping the rest of the time."

"Nothing that ensures your well-being is ever a waste," Lio said.

"I can walk this far," she reassured him.

He sighed. "Very well, my intrepid explorer."

The Azarqi music faded behind them. Soon the loudest sound in his hearing was their footsteps. Knight took to roaming back and forth, ahead and behind, sniffing his lady's surroundings without ever straying too far out of her reach.

The footprints of three people and one hound made a lonely trail, marking their path out of civilization and into the expanse. But only for an instant. A wind swept along the ground, covering the evidence of their passage with sand.

Lio raised his brows. "It usually takes longer than that for a natural desert wind to erase a trail."

"My magic isn't only useful in the air," Monsoon said.

Lio eyed the mercenary's supplies, which were distributed into multiple smaller satchels that he wore across his chest and around his waist. "I was wondering how you fly with so much weight."

"It's a combination of physical and magical effort. Wings and wind. Even carrying enough supplies to keep a couple of silkfoots comfortable, I can fight from the air."

An hour passed, and the most dangerous thing that happened was that Knight scared a small snake out of a bush and into a hole.

"Can you still see the nomads' fires?" Monsoon asked Cassia.

She drew to a halt, not too winded as yet. "Ah, you and Lio can see farther than those of us without enhanced sight. The treaty is based on human sight?"

Monsoon gave a nod. "The Azarqi were the main negotiators for the Accord. We have them to thank for peace with the jinn."

Cassia looked back the way they had come. "No. The fires aren't visible to me any longer."

"We'll stop here and wait." Monsoon took a measured sip from his waterskin.

Lio halted beside Cassia. "How shall we proceed when they arrive?"

"Let them tell you," Monsoon advised.

"Should I drop my veils?"

The mercenary paused to consider. "I think they're more likely to respect a display of power—as long as it's polite. It's unwise to be too brazen, but equally foolish to be a boot licker."

Cassia arched a brow. "Do jinn have boots?"

Lio and Monsoon both chuckled at that. Who knew she would take it upon herself to be the one who brought much-needed lightheartedness into the moment?

Lio scratched his chin. "I'm not sure they have feet."

"They're called the Hidden for a reason," Monsoon said. "They respect secrets, too. Keep your veils."

Silence prevailed. Lio listened to their hearts beating in the night.

And then the jinn were there.

Lio started. He hadn't sensed them coming. He hadn't felt them arrive. One moment, they were utterly concealed from him. The next, they surrounded him, his Grace and their guide.

Lio had seen illustrations in books, but no portrayal in ink on a page could capture the reality of them. They hovered over the ground, their garments rustling in a wind Lio couldn't feel on his own skin. He could smell a sandstorm, although the night was still.

Their bodies were humanoid, shrouded in robes that shifted like the sand. Large, clawed hands and muscular forearms could be seen where their sleeves ended. It was disorienting to gaze too long at their faces, where human eyes and mouths dwelt amid the horns and hair of beasts.

There was no trace of their emotions in the Blood Union. They were of earth and sky. The elements, not blood, flowed within their other-worldly bodies.

It was disorienting to behold sentient beings whose emotions were out of his reach. They were more opaque to his auric senses than ancient elders wrapped in the deepest of veils.

But their magic was astonishing. They were like twelve suns hovering just below the horizon, their power immense and looming and great enough to fell him.

For the first time in his life, Lio confronted beings with power to rival Hesperines. Here in their domain, it was likely they would best him in any magical confrontation. He must make sure he never needed to test that theory.

Monsoon bowed, and Lio and Cassia did the same. Lio felt the urge to place himself between his Grace and the powerful beings, but that was impossible when they were surrounded. He wrapped an arm around her.

Knight whined and flattened his ears, his lips peeled back. Cassia gave him a firm command, and he stayed close to her. But his whole body was tense, as if he was ready to attack at a moment's notice.

A jinn with a golden mane spoke in a voice like cliffs rising from the earth. "Hesperine."

The single word was so layered, it was at once a greeting and an acknowledgment of Lio's power, but also suggested disdain.

Cassia sucked in a breath and whispered to Lio. "Did you understand that?"

"I heard him say 'Hesperine' in Divine."

"I heard him speak the old Tenebran garden tongue. How can that be?"

"I wish I knew," Lio said in astonishment.

"Honored guardians of the Accord," Monsoon addressed the jinn, "I return once again to your domain in the company of two who rely on my guidance. I am here to walk as lightly as I did before."

The jinn's rumble might have been a laugh. "We remember you, warrior on wing. It is not your footsteps that concern us."

The corner of Monsoon's mouth lifted. "Once again I find myself called upon to search for my own kind in your lands. I fly only for that purpose."

"Take care what else you do in the name of your cause."

Monsoon bowed again. Lio had to wonder what had transpired on his previous journeys in this desert.

Lio felt the moment when the jinn's attention focused on him. The being's eye sockets were hollow, and he could see into them as if into windows. He beheld a sky that was a bright blue of day, where a flock of birds swirled. A wave of vertigo swept through him.

He bowed his head to break eye contact, as much as to show respect.

"What is your purpose here?" the jinn asked him.

"To ensure the safety and well-being of the mortals."

"And should their safety and my people's interests be at odds?"

"I am not the first Hesperine to tread here. I hope your previous meetings with my people have demonstrated our goodwill. We are known to walk in lands both hostile and friendly, and in every case, find a way to be harmless against the most harmful odds."

"You do not specify which our domain is—hostile or friendly. A wise dance, fellow immortal."

"Allow me to convey my people's admiration for your accord with the mortals of these lands. After our own centuries of negotiation with humans, we appreciate what you have accomplished."

"Can you, who walk outside nature, pretend to know our deeds?"

"I can respect what I do not know."

Then the jinn beside the first speaker turned its feathered head toward Cassia and gazed at her with a predator's green eyes. Lio could not hear what the being said to her, but he could tell it was speaking because of the way Cassia paid attention.

His protective instincts and all his magic strained within him. Monsoon sent him a warning glance, but he did not need the man to tell him to keep his power locked down under veils and his self control.

Cassia was quite equal to any negotiation with jinn. She would speak for herself with wisdom and skill. He just couldn't help wanting to protect her from the powerful, unpredictable immortals.

"I am sorry," Cassia said in Divine. "I cannot understand you."

"Woe is she who does not understand the tongue of her ancestors," the jinn replied in kind.

She gave a deep nod. "I bow before your knowledge. I stand amazed that you can speak the old garden tongue of Tenebra. How is it you have learned the language of the Lustra, once spoken by the sorceresses of the wilds?"

The dark feathers atop the jinn's head rustled. "The sands carry words. I can learn the fate of an entire people from a drop of water. This world is vast, but sand and water know no borders."

"Do you mean soil and water from Tenebra actually reach here, on the winds or ocean currents?"

"So too have you breathed the dust of the desert when you did not know it. Nature knows everything. Woe, that the passage of its lessons to you have been broken."

"My elders are living ancestors whose blood and teachings will soon run in my veins."

"The earth is in your bones. You cannot change your marrow."

Cassia's aura snapped with protest, but she spoke evenly. "Good intentions are a universal language. Allow me to assure you of mine."

"A sandstorm has no ill intent, and yet it wipes humans from the face of the earth." Its ancient eyes stayed focused on her, hard as emeralds.

Its scrutiny tightened the tension in Lio's limbs and made it ever more difficult to keep his magic calm.

"I am hardly a force of nature," Cassia said with a demure smile.

"Do you wish to be?"

"Yes." She hesitated. "But I have not succeeded in becoming one yet."

Lio begged to differ, watching her face a jinn.

"Why are you here, foreign vine?" the feathered immortal asked.

"To find answers," Cassia answered.

"The desert holds all truths. Are you prepared to meet those you do not seek?"

"I am not afraid."

"Then you will most likely survive," the jinn stated. "Take what does not belong here at no cost. Take what is yours with no penalty. But if you take that which is of the desert, you must give of yourself."

Her voice calm, Cassia continued, "We come seeking those who do not belong here. But if we ask you for knowledge of where they are, it would come at a cost?"

Monsoon stiffened. Now it was Lio's turn to give him a warning glance. They should trust whatever Cassia had in mind.

"Our knowledge is of the desert," said the green-eyed jinn.

"And everything that occurs within it, I am sure," she replied. "If you told us where to find the mortals we seek, all of us who do not belong here would depart much sooner and cease to trouble you."

A third jinn formed words, although not from its snarling jaws. It had the head of a jackal, which swiveled toward Cassia, while its voice echoed from everywhere and nowhere. "The desert will rid us of them soon enough, if they are not found."

Hesperines and jinn might have immortality and power in common, but there Lio's sense of connection with the beings ended. Its inhuman uncaring about Chuma's mother and the Ashes dying in this desert chilled his blood.

"I will not take what is of the desert," was Cassia's answer, "but the desert will not take what is mine."

Emptiness chased her words. They were once more the only ones there. The jinn were gone.

She looked to Monsoon, her profile set with even more determination. "Was that permission?"

He raised his brows. "If I didn't know better, I'd say they were impressed."

Lio lifted her hand to his mouth. Was it possible to fall deeper in love with her? Yes. Yes, it was. "I am certainly impressed, my rose."

She gave him her arch smile and squeezed his hand. "They wouldn't tell us where Ipika and the Ashes are. That means they also won't tell the Golden Shield where we are."

"The jinn are not ruled by the Empress," Lio confirmed. "The Golden Shield's mandate has little power here."

Cassia faced the dunes that were both their Sanctuary and their crucible. "Onward, then."

Monsoon unrolled a map and spread it out on the ground between the three of them. They all crouched around it.

He pointed out an unmarked location. "My Azarqi friends informed me that their home is located here at the moment. That is our starting point in the Scorched Verge." He traced his finger over the various regions delineated on the map. "The Maaqul is not actually one desert, but many. Each region has distinctive geographical features, wildlife, and dangers."

Monsoon proceeded to give them a lesson in desert survival and outline what actions should be taken in various possible crises that could occur. There was none of his usual rancor in his tone. His words were factual, his bearing confident. "The desert is dangerous, but when traversed with wisdom and respect, it need not be deadly."

Who was this capable leader, and what had he done with the bitter mercenary Lio and Cassia had met at the Sandira Court?

Lio was loath to admit it, but in life or death situations, this was exactly the sort of man you wanted on your side.

Monsoon rolled up his map. "You can rely on me to guide you safely, if I can rely on you to heed me."

"Understood," said Cassia.

Lio nodded. "We defer to your expertise."

Monsoon got to his feet and stowed his map. "All right. Let's try to step to Chuma's mother now."

Lio stood, helping Cassia up. "Is there anything you can tell us about the situation we're stepping into? I know Chuma and her family have good reasons for their secrecy, but as you've said, preparation could mean the difference between victory or defeat."

Monsoon grimaced, looking out across the desert. After a moment, he appeared to come to a decision. "Be ready to fight. Humans with weapons or magic, possibly both. I don't know how many."

Cup and thorns. They had to contend with jinn, the elements, and any number of mortal attackers. They could only pray Ipika stood a chance out here, thanks to the Ashes.

"Would you consider letting me step first?" Lio asked. "If I go ahead under veils, I can assess the situation, then come back for the two of you."

"Lio is right," Cassia agreed, although she didn't sound happy. "With Ipika's life at stake, this is no time for charging in blind. We must use strategy and surprise to our advantage."

Monsoon held up a hand in acquiescence. "If you're willing to let Cassia stay here with me, I have no grounds to protest sending you ahead to Chuma's mother."

"Ipika and I are resourceful enough to withstand exchanging protectors for the time being," Cassia said dryly.

They gathered around each other in a circle. Cassia reached into her gardening satchel and carefully withdrew Chuma's bracelet.

When Lio held out his hand for it, Monsoon caught his wrist in a merciless grip.

"I am a Hesperine," Lio reminded him. "We do not use blood magic to harm innocent young women or our Imperial allies."

"That doesn't make blood magic less dangerous." The man fixed Lio with a look. Lio knew that look well. If he saw himself in a mirror while thinking of the people who had hurt Zoe in the past, that expression would be staring back at him.

Lio's argument was clearly the wrong approach with Monsoon. Hesperine principles and diplomatic relations between Orthros and the Empire were not powerful enough to reassure such a deep need to protect. What would? Something more personal, Lio hoped.

"Back in Tenebra," Lio said, "there was a mage hunting children, seeking to punish them for their parents' heresy. My little sister Zoe was one of those orphans."

Monsoon spoke with obvious reluctance. "In Tenebra, isn't the punishment for heresy...immolation?"

"Yes. We invited the mage to swallow his own fire spell."

Cassia put a hand over Monsoon's and Lio's. "I shed my blood for that casting. That is how Hesperines use human blood sacrifices."

"I respect your hesitation, Monsoon. Blood magic is very dangerous. But not to you and yours."

Monsoon's expression didn't change, but he released Lio's wrist.

Lio took Chuma's bracelet from Cassia with careful hands. Within the acacia vial, the small amount of her blood hummed with powerful life force. He fixed his Will on Chuma's signature written in her blood. He considered the layers of her that felt like her father and tuned them out. What remained was a blend of her unique self and her mother's legacy.

He focused on those aspects of her and sought to bring himself closer to them. A sense of direction came to him, and he stepped.

He found himself on a stony outcropping. Cliffs rose behind him, and a jagged rock face dropped away before him, descending to the open desert. The ledge was littered with the remnants of a destroyed campsite: tents, bedrolls, cooking supplies.

The stones at his feet were stained with blood. So much blood.

He murmured a prayer to the Goddess and opened his senses. He felt no one in distress nearby. In fact, he couldn't feel a human presence as far as the Blood Union and his mind magic could reach.

But traces of arcane power lingered around him. Scorch marks scored the outcropping and the cliffs behind Lio. He put a hand to one, then yanked his fingers back. Fire magic.

Lio flexed his hand, waiting for the burn to subside. Hesperines were highly vulnerable to fire, it was true, but for mere spell residue to sting so, the caster had to be powerful indeed.

Ukocha had been here.

Torn between reluctance and urgency, he stepped back to Cassia and Monsoon.

"Did you find her?" Monsoon asked.

"I'm afraid not. Come see for yourself."

He stepped Monsoon, Cassia, and Knight to the bloodstained site.

Angry words streamed from Monsoon's mouth, curses in more languages than Lio could identify. "How much of this is Chuma's mother's blood?"

Lio grimaced. "All of it."

Monsoon crouched by the dark stain on the ground, his wings perfectly still, the wind dead. "Not fresh."

"It's been here for days," Lio confirmed.

Cassia's gaze roamed the grisly evidence, her aura cold with denial. "Lio, can a human survive losing that much?"

"It would be a very close call, but she could still be alive."

Cassia collected herself and spoke calmly. "There are no bodies. There's still hope."

"Focus on her blood this time," Monsoon commanded. "Try taking us directly to her."

"Of course." Thinking of Chuma's hope and trust, Lio let her mother's blood open up a path for his senses.

That path abruptly ended.

"There's no time to waste." Monsoon's voice rose.

"I'm trying." Lio knelt at the pool of dried blood.

Cassia stood close by, her hand on his shoulder. He dragged his fang across his palm. The generous libation splashed onto the rock. He felt a jolt, and flashes of the woman's emotions flurried through his senses. Pain. Grim determination. Anger. Cassia's grip tightened.

It should have been easy. With such a clear sense of the woman, he should have been able to step to her without thinking. But no matter how much he Willed it, he couldn't reach her.

"I'm so sorry." He clutched Chuma's bracelet in his hand. "I can't."

"What do you mean, you can't?" Monsoon demanded.

"I am unable."

"Are you all right?" Cassia knelt beside him, turning his face toward her.

"My power is unaffected. I should be able to do this. I can't explain it. What I'm experiencing should be impossible."

"Is it like when you tried to step to Solia? It makes sense that Ipika might hide herself with magic."

"This feels different. It's not as if she's hidden. It's as if…there's simply no way to follow her."

Monsoon's voice was dangerous. "Does that mean she is already—"

Lio shook his head. "If she were no longer living, I would still be able to step to her remains."

Monsoon gripped the hilt of his sword, scanning the ledge. "This is a defensive position. Cliffs at their back, difficult climb, good view of anyone approaching. How could they have been ambushed?" Monsoon put a hand to the scorch marks. "Ukocha's magic did this. The Ashes put up a fight. So why did only one person shed blood?"

"And where is everyone now?" Cassia wondered.

The unspoken fear hung between them all. Had Ipika's enemies, whoever they were, taken her and the Ashes prisoner?

Or disposed of their bodies somewhere else?

Lio did not want to acknowledge it aloud, but a fire mage of Ukocha's power would be well-nigh impossible to capture alive. A person like her would surely go down fighting.

Had he and Cassia come all this way, only to be too late? Had Ipika and Ukocha died on this ledge, along with the truth about Solia?

"This is impossible," Lio said again. "What power could prevent me from reaching Ipika?"

"A jinn?" Cassia ventured quietly.

Lio shook his head. "That would be in violation of the Desert Accord. I'm sure they have the power, but they wouldn't."

Cassia hesitated, then sighed. "Even if Ipika broke the Accord?"

Monsoon made a slashing motion with his hand. "Out of the question. She's too honorable."

Lio rose to his feet. "Whoever attacked her and the Ashes, perhaps they left a trail of some kind, magical or physical."

It was so little go on. Lio braced himself for an angry outburst from Monsoon at his failure.

But the man didn't waste time on that. "I search on wing, you search on foot." He pointed at Knight. "Track her."

Cassia nodded, calling Knight to her side.

Without another word, Monsoon raced toward the edge of the cliff and hurled himself into the open air. His wings spread, caught, and lifted him over the desert.

Lio bowed his head, staring at the blood. All his mighty Hesperine power had just proved to be useless for saving the mortals who needed him.

FORGOTTEN IN THE MAAQUL

WHEN LIO'S STEPS BEGAN to drag behind her, Cassia knew dawn was approaching. She came to a halt on the rocky semblance of a trail they followed between two jagged rock faces. Knight sat down at her feet, his ears drooping.

"It's time to stop," she announced.

Lio came up behind her and rubbed her arms. "Let's just search around that bend, and then we'll call a halt."

"Lio, we have to make camp."

"I'm sorry, I know you must be exhausted, but—"

"No." She shook her head. "I would gladly push myself farther."

It was true that she was shivering and she couldn't feel her feet and her tongue felt dead. But she didn't ask for the waterskin again. She hadn't complained about a sunbound thing, even after hiking through the cliffs all night. She refused to be weak.

Cassia turned to Lio. "The sun will rise soon."

His jaw clenched, and he looked away, his eyes veiled under his lashes.

Cassia brushed a smear of desert dust off his cheek and pulled his arms around her. "We've done everything we can for one night. We've roamed all over this mountain. Knight hasn't caught a whiff of Ipika's scent, and you haven't felt a hint of her presence. We need to find out if Monsoon has discovered anything, then make a new plan."

"So much for Hesperines rescuing mortals in distress."

"I feel terrible, too. All I can see in my mind is her blood." Her breath hitched. "I know what it's like not to have a mother. And to lose the person who raised you."

"Chuma will not lose her mother. We will find her."

"Yes." Cassia forced the word out, bolstering her conviction. "Yes, we will."

He offered her Chuma's bloodstained bracelet. He hadn't let it out of his hand all night. "You should put this back in your satchel to keep it safe."

Cassia took it from him, but she slid it around her wrist instead. She would wear their promise to Chuma until they fulfilled it.

Lio lifted a hand and hailed Monsoon, who was flying within sight above them. "He signaled his agreement. We must stop for the night."

"I hate dawn."

"So do I."

Cassia and Lio found a place where a rock overhang would offer shelter from the day's heat. Monsoon landed just outside.

The three of them and Knight had made an excellent company of hunters that night. Their abilities complimented each other. Cassia wondered if a shapeshifter, a Hesperine, and a woman with a liegehound had ever combined their unique skills.

"I'll search until it's too hot," Monsoon said. "You two prepare for dawn."

"I can search past dawn as well," Cassia offered. She couldn't. But she would.

Monsoon shook his head. "It's all right if you're asleep by the time I get back. I want you both in good condition for tomorrow night."

"And what condition will you be in if you fly longer?" Cassia asked him.

"I can't stop." His smile was sad.

"I understand," Lio said.

"I will not leave Cassia alone here long. And I'll keep your earlier remarks in mind."

"I appreciate that," Lio replied.

"Which remarks?" asked Cassia.

"All the things he threatened to do to me if I harmed you in his Slumber."

Cassia raised a brow at him. "You should keep in mind what I did to you the first time you so rudely flew off with me."

Monsoon's lip twitched. "I admit, you're a menace to a man's instep."

"I told you, the Stand trained me in self defense. Your foot is still sore, isn't it?"

He snorted and turned to go. "Get some sleep. But stay ready to leave at a moment's notice. Just in case."

"Monsoon," Lio called after him.

The mercenary paused just outside the overhang, his wings halfway unfurled. "Yes?"

"I have every confidence in you," Lio said.

"That's nice to hear, silkfoot." With a graceful leap, he took to the air.

Lio began setting up their light-blocking tents. Monsoon had left all his packs behind when he had flown off at the ambush site, but Lio had carried those all night without complaint. His only complaints had been at himself.

With a sigh, Cassia stepped just outside and gathered what brush and spindly twigs she could find. In a sheltered spot under the overhang, she arranged her kindling and fuel inside a circle of stones. When she took out her fire charm, she rubbed a thumb over the enchanted moonstone, thinking of home and her Trial sisters. This had been a thoughtful gift from Xandra.

She placed the charm at the center of the kindling and smeared her blood on it. Easy to do, considering how many times the desert thorns had scratched her. As soon as she withdrew her hand, a lick of blue fire wavered inside the milky stone, then darted over its surface. Finally, the small flames caught the kindling and rose into a gentle orange campfire.

Her exhausted hound curled up next to her. She reached into her robes for her little wooden flute, Nodora's gift before their journey. The notes it played, which only dogs could hear, had a variety of benefits. Cassia had kept it in her pocket all night, in case Knight's tracking took him out of earshot of her voice and she needed to call him.

Now she blew gently into it, trying to play soft tones that would soothe a distressed dog. Knight lay his head down on her knee and closed his eyes in apparent contentment.

Her hound was fast asleep when Lio came to sit next to her. She tucked the flute back into an inner pocket of her robes and took her Grace's hand.

He lifted her fingers to his mouth and, one by one, licked each cut and scrape until they healed. She was too exhausted to properly appreciate how erotic the moment could have been. But she relaxed a little more with each of his gentle ministrations.

"Now I understand what our Trial circle was talking about," she said.

Lio frowned. "When? About what?"

"Often, about you. To quote Lyros, 'If a human guest you've never met finds a bug in her shoe on the other side of the city in a guest house you've never set foot in, it's always your fault.'"

Lio huffed. "He told you about that?"

"Oh, our Trial brothers tell me everything about you. And may I also remind you I'm on excellent terms with Xandra? As your former sweetheart, she feels honor bound to turn over all your secrets to your Grace."

"Oh, thorns."

"So I happen to know that prior to when you and I met, you had a reputation for apologizing too much and blaming yourself for things that weren't your fault. Everyone thought your adventures with me had cured you of your self-flagellation, but apparently not."

"This isn't a bug in someone's shoe," he said quietly.

"Of course not," Cassia said. "But it is something that's not your fault."

Lio stared into the night beyond the fire. "My uncle once told me to focus on the ones we can save. I suppose that's a lesson I haven't learned yet."

Feeling powerless to save someone's life was enough to make anyone be unfair to themselves...or fall back into old habits.

Like Cassia's old habit of making sure she didn't need anyone. Her iron rules of self-reliance. Self-defense.

She poked at the fire with a dry stick, a scowl coming to her face as she realized the truth. During their trek, she had been so determined to prove she wasn't a weak mortal that she had forgotten one of the most important Hesperine principles. Gratitude. She had scarcely said the words "thank you" to Lio all night.

One of her hands drifted into Knight's ruff, as if her dog could be an antidote to the difficulty of admitting she was wrong.

She scooted closer to Lio. "Well, Monsoon was lucky to have your help tonight, although he won't admit it. You carried all our supplies while he was off flying."

"My Hesperine strength was useful for something. Huzzah."

"Lio." She touched his face, turning him to look at her. "I couldn't have gotten through this night without you. You stepped Knight and me over impassable terrain, and never once did I fear getting lost, because you're with me."

He kissed her forehead. "Thank you, Cassia."

"I'm trying to thank you."

"Hmm. Gratitude going both ways is powerful stuff."

She smiled and stroked his pale cheek, tracing a finger through the thick stubble of his beard. "So it is."

He pressed his lips tenderly to hers, and she could feel that she had made his anguish bearable.

He wrapped his arm around her. "How would I have known? I never could have predicted that magic preventing Hesperines from stepping would interfere with my ability to rescue Ipika."

Cassia rested her head against his shoulder. "There are so few kinds of magic that can do that. I know Gift Collectors and Aithourian war mages have specialized methods for making sure Hesperine prisoners don't escape, but I didn't think any of our Imperial allies had developed such spells."

"None that I'm aware of. Tenebra and Cordium are where Hesperines get captured and killed." He let out a humorless laugh. "The Empire is where we come on holiday."

"And it's not as if some elder Hesperine is out here using veils to hide from her own people."

"Indeed, Nike may be the only one on record who didn't want us to find her."

"I wish we knew what Ipika was doing here," Cassia said. "After the way her family helped us, I have a suspicion her activities could make her powerful enemies."

"Yes. If she makes a habit of helping fugitives, it certainly could."

"She's helping the innocent, though. I must not be the only one facing false accusations. Even here in the Empire, where governance is just, humans are imperfect and make errors."

"It does seem that Chuma's mother is a champion against injustice. I take Monsoon at his word that she would never violate the Desert Accord. I'm sure no jinn is hiding her from us."

"War mages and necromancers are out of the question, and we've ruled out Hesperines and jinn. What other possibilities are there?"

"A new kind of magic we don't understand," Lio answered, "or one so ancient, it has been forgotten in the Maaqul."

BATTLE ARTS

TORCHES LINED THE COURTYARD in front of Xandra's residence, reflecting on the long pool at the center. Mak doubted there had ever been this much fire in all of Haima, much less at House Annassa.

But tonight, the Queens' home was brightly lit by Hesperines' opposing element. Everyone who looked toward the summit of the city, where the royal residences crowned the capital, would see that the youngest princess was showing off her unusual affinity.

Xandra dusted her hands, putting out the last of the flames at her fingertips. "There. I think that makes a statement, don't you?"

"I hope my mother has to cast a light blocking spell over her eyes," Kia said with savage delight.

Xandra glanced up at the statue of Hespera, who sat her on her royal stool even higher than House Annassa, her stone braids flowing down around her. "Well, our heretical Goddess made a Hesperine fire mage for some reason. Tonight my torches shall be an emblem of her teachings that we should thumb our noses at authority."

"With songs of resistance!" On the musicians' dais nearby, Nodora adjusted a tuning peg on her lute. "This will be the event of the season. Orthros's youngbloods won't be able to stop talking about how they were treated to the latest entertainments in the excellent company of our people's youngest princess."

Xandra made a face at her. "I even pulled the larvae out of my hair for the occasion. I'd rather be in my greenhouse watching my baby silkworms destroy another batch of mulberry leaves, but here we are."

Kia checked one of the scrolls that adorned her sash. "Alas, my mother is guaranteed to pull princesses away from their worms, rain on festival parades, and curdle any milk within radius. Let us hope all our guests leave this event as angry as we are about her upcoming proposal to the Firstblood Circle—and determined to join us in opposing it when it comes to a vote."

Mak shook his head. "I still can't believe she wants to place more restrictions on Orthros's involvement in mortal affairs in Tenebra."

Kia's aura was sharp with bitterness. "Because a princess no one has seen in fifteen years is in line for a throne she probably doesn't want, and all the risk-averse traditionalists in Orthros are having improbable visions of Hesperines involving ourselves in a dynastic dispute in Tenebra, where we've been neutral in politics for sixteen hundred years."

Why did so many of their people like to overcomplicate things? "Solia will just want to come home to Orthros to become a Hesperine and be with Cassia. The elders have their underlinens in a twist over nothing. They're trying to threaten the Solstice Oath and make life harder for Hesperines errant Abroad for no good reason."

Nodora put an arm around Kia's shoulders, giving her a sympathetic squeeze. "Well, no matter what happens, the Solstice Oath will stand. That treaty isn't something Hypatia has the power to rescind. We have to keep reminding ourselves of that."

"But we need to build on it, not stop there," Kia said, in the tone that usually meant she was warming up to unleash a flurry of irrefutable logic. She was clearly ready for any debate with tonight's guests.

Do you feel ready? Lyros asked Mak.

Why yes, you look so handsome in your formal robes, I am ready. To tear them off of you.

Don't try to deflect, my Grace. Are you ready to do our part to persuade people to vote with us?

No. Not in the least. I'd rather punch someone in the face. The opponent should be someone I can beat to a pulp without remorse. But tonight we're up against Kia's mother. My own Ritual mother. I hate politics.

Lyros's shoulders shook with suppressed laughter. *Well, you can certainly work out your frustrations on my robes and me after all this is over.*

Veil hours can't get here soon enough.

Lyros ran a hand over the front of Mak's dark brown formal robe. *I enjoy seeing you in silks for a change, too.*

Mak hated politics, but he didn't mind dressing up for Lyros just to see that look in his eye.

As they awaited the arrival of the first guests, Xandra eyed the arched gateway and bounced on her feet, her anxiety sparking in the Union.

But an aura approaching from the direction of House Annassa. A very, very powerful one belonging to the last person they had expected to see here tonight.

"Oh, thorns," Xandra said.

Her eldest sister strolled through a side entrance to the courtyard from the direction of her own residence. Konstantina, Second Princess of Orthros, was dressed for a formal occasion in her ceremonial stripweave, the long coils of her hair heavy with moonstones. The torches gave her deep black skin a rich glow.

"Don't look so alarmed, Sister." Her gaze took in the silk banners and luminescent star moths hovering in the cedar trees. "I only came to admire the lights."

None of them would believe for a moment that Orthros's most brilliant political mastermind was here to compliment the party decorations.

It made Mak a bit queasy to think how easily Konstantina could win this match with a single move, if she decided to resume her efforts to isolate Orthros from Tenebra. Hypatia's proposal was bad enough, but Konstantina, as a royal, had the power to invoke the Departure and cut of Hesperines from Tenebra forever.

"Would you like a mince pie?" Xandra seemed to decide she wanted to take the high ground and play the proper hostess.

Konstantina strolled closer, smiling at Xandra. "No, thank you. Hypatia is sure to serve her own at the gathering she's holding tonight. I must admit, I am partial to her recipe, and not only because she is my dear friend."

Mak and Kia exchanged glances, and she shook her head. Clearly she had known nothing about her mother's party, either.

"Of course she would host a rival event," Kia muttered. "Somewhere for all the elders to be scandalized together…and scare more voters into supporting them."

"I promise to sound properly scandalized when I tell them about the torches." Amusement glittered in Konstantina's aura. "It really is an exclusive event. Under veils. Invitation only. And such elegant invitations, too. Hypatia did the calligraphy herself." Konstantina ran a scroll through her fingers. It was decorated with a complex geometric border in gold leaf and tied with a gold silk ribbon.

"All our people are welcome at my event," Xandra said. "My doors are open to everyone in Orthros who wishes to join us tonight."

"Except the elders who were politely warned not to interfere," Konstantina replied with a rueful tilt of her brow.

Xandra lifted her chin. "We are proud to have the support of many ancient Hesperines. But we know that Orthros's youngbloods need leaders who act independently. We establish our own positions. We don't merely parrot the opinions of our elders. That would make us seem no different from Hypatia's supporters."

"Do not mistake adherence to tradition for a lack of independent— or even innovative—thought," Konstantina warned with a smile. "Well, I really must be going now, or I shall miss the first course of pie. Enjoy your evening."

With that, she strolled out the gate to the boulevard that led down to the homes of the Elder Firstbloods.

"What was that all about?" Mak wondered. "Was she trying to be pleasant or insult us?"

Xandra sighed. "One can never tell with Konstantina."

"But one thing is certain," Lyros said. "Everything she does is part of her strategy."

Kia's aura was cold with anger. "How did my mother manage to plan such a lavish event under my nose? I've been paying close attention to everything that goes on in our House."

"She knows that," Mak said. "She must have gone to mighty complicated lengths to plan it in secret."

"Only for Konstantina to come boast of it," Lyros pointed out.

Nodora had joined them from the dais. "That invitation she was holding—I recognized it."

Xandra frowned at her. "What do you mean?"

"The gold leaf pattern was so distinct, I'm sure it was the same one I saw in my fathers' concert hall."

Lyros snapped his fingers. "There was one in my parents' studio, as well."

Mak crossed his arms. "I haven't seen one in House Argyros or House Komnena..."

"Or House Kassandra," Xandra added. "Hypatia wouldn't dare."

Mak grimaced. "But I did see plenty of them in the houses we've visited while calling on partisans."

Together, they recalled all their visits of the last several nights, comparing what they had seen. They soon had a clear impression of Hypatia's guest list.

Xandra's eyes widened. "Did Konstantina just reveal to us exactly whom Hypatia is courting for support?"

Lyros smiled. "Of course not. Your sister simply strolled through the opposition's event to assess her rivals...with an invitation in her hand, incidentally. What we do with our powers of observation is hardly her affair."

Xandra shook her head. "This is just like how she incidentally showed me the Firstblood Circle's schedule because I happen to be a royal with a vote...even though she never gives it to me, her youngest sister, ahead of time. If she hadn't warned us about Hypatia's measure in the first place, we would never have been able to organize an opposition at all."

"I won't say she's playing both sides," Lyros mused, "but she is keeping her promise to remain neutral in this vote."

Mak whistled. "Cassia truly convinced Konstantina to withhold judgment until after we see how the Tenebran succession turns out."

"We truly can avoid the Departure." Xandra looked around at all of them. "We have to hold on to that hope tonight and remember what we're fighting for."

Soon their fellow youngbloods began to step in from all over the city. They might not carry the same air of power as the ancients of their bloodlines, but their auras filled the courtyard with magic and anticipation even brighter than their fancy silk robes and the jewels in their hair.

Mak loved the moments when the stands over the arena filled with spectators before a fight. But the rising emotions in the courtyard made him feel like someone had strung a bow with his nerves.

Lyros's hand smoothed down his back. *You weren't this nervous before our first battle in Martyrs' Pass.*

Why would I be nervous about facing an army of heart hunters? I trained for that.

You're never nervous around these people when we drink with them on the docks.

Lyros was right. Many of tonight's guests were in their social circles or watched their matches in the arena. But knowing he had to talk them into a political position made them seem more intimidating than oncoming enemy liegehounds.

Mak felt even worse upon the arrival of Xandra's share, the human who was her current sweetheart and snack. Harkhuf Addaya Khemkare strolled in wearing the latest New Delta Imperial fashion, his white and gold robe setting off his dark, handsome features. He seemed perfectly comfortable at an immortal political event, even though he was a mortal guest. But as the Empress's cousin, he had probably mastered politics as he had learned to walk.

Seeing how Xandra's face lit up when Harkhuf kissed her cheek, Mak knew it was unfair for him to resent the fellow. Harkhuf made Xandra happy, he was a good friend to Cassia, and his only ulterior motive was getting high marks in his mind healing studies. But Mak hated feeling like this human was more useful to his Trial circle than he was.

"Did you finish writing your letters?" Xandra asked Harkhuf.

He sighed. "At last. I would never have forgiven myself if my correspondence had made me late to your party."

Xandra put on a pouting expression. "You must tell all those important mind healers in the Empress's court that it's impolite to keep a Hesperine princess waiting."

He laughed and gave her another kiss, a light one on the lips this time. "Alas, my mentors back home insist that I keep them abreast of everything I'm learning in Orthros."

"Well, at least they had the courtesy to send you here to study mind healing with my mother Soteira, so I can distract you after your lessons."

"But no more talk of theramancy theory tonight!" Harkhuf turned his light-spell-bright smile on Mak and Lyros. "Stewards, you see before you a mortal in need of rescue. Please save me from the scrolls, my friends. Tell me we can enjoy a match in the arena sometime this week."

It just added insult to injury that Harkhuf could hold his own in a fight and had the muscles to prove it.

"Of course," Lyros said with a casual smile. "How about tomorrow night?"

Mak clasped Harkhuf's wrist, resisting the urge to sprain it.

Let's try to save that for the arena, Lyros suggested.

Xandra wound her arm in Harkhuf's with that spark in her aura she only got around him. She wiggled her fingers at Mak, little flames dancing across her hand. "Time to go mingle, as we agreed. Remember, don't beat them over the head with our agenda. This is a party. Once we make sure everyone is having fun, then we can subtly insert a few political matters into the conversation."

Mak sighed. "Right. Into the fray, then."

Xandra drifted from one group of guests to the other while the initiate culinary crafters emerged from her residence bearing trays of drinks and delicacies. Nodora's human share, the handsome sitarist from the Empire who was her current romance, joined her on the dais with their musician friends. Kia's share was an Imperial mathematician she liked to do "research" with, as Mak liked to tease her. They drifted expertly from one young scholar to another, leaving lively discussions in their wake.

Mak followed Lyros's lead. They started with a son of one of Orthros's bloodlines of aromagi, gifted with an affinity for farming. Mak and Lyros often saw him at Hyacinth's Ambrosia, the favorite coffeehouse of male Hesperines looking to enjoy romantic evenings with each other. Mak tried to recall what the fellow grew in his greenhouses. Was it root vegetables of some kind?

Don't worry, Mak wanted to say, *I can break the nose of anyone who threatens your tubers.*

Lyros remembered the aromagus's name, asked after his familiar, and struck up a conversation on one of the few things they had in common— coffee. But Mak's eyes began to glaze over as they got deeper into the coffee supply chain.

Mak gathered that the aromagus was worried about how it would affect trade with the Empire, if Orthros aligned itself more closely with Tenebra. The fellow vented his fears that the Empress would restrict coffee exports to Orthros to keep the prized beans out of the hands of shadowlanders.

My father and Cassia have successfully grown the first coffee tree in Orthros. We are prepared for the Great Coffee Disaster, should the Empress suddenly hoard all the beans for herself.

He couldn't think of a more appropriate response, so while Lyros carried the day, Mak entertained himself with mental ripostes.

He hated this. His Grace was fighting a battle, and he was not helping.

Lyros even maneuvered them out of the conversation deftly, extricating them from the death grip of carrot prices with a few verbal parries.

When Mak spotted two new arrivals, he sighed in relief. "Alkaios and Nephalea are here to reinforce us. Thank the Goddess."

Lyros smiled. "Let's go strategize with them."

"And talk about the battle arts for five blessed minutes," Mak grumbled.

Nike's newgifts had only recently come to Orthros with her, both legends in their own right after their deeds Abroad, but tonight they looked quite at home in silks. Nephalea wore white lilies in her yellow hair, woven in with Alkaios's light brown Grace braid. But his nearly bald head certainly stood out in the crowd. His last run-in with fire mages had left him with only one lock of hair, the one entwined with Nephalea's braid and the ward that protected it.

As Mak and Lyros approached, frequently stopped by other Hesperines wishing to greet them, Mak heard Nephalea sigh. "Why do I have the feeling I shall be talking about clothes all night?"

Alkaios appeared bemused. "When you were mortal, no one could pry your spindle from your hands. But I don't think you've touched thread since you got your fangs."

She gave a graceful shrug. "I discovered that magic and fighting are more fun."

Alkaios shook his head. "You took comfort in your craft once. Are you certain you don't wish to accept Kassandra's offer of mentorship in spinning and weaving?"

Nephalea bit her lip. "I know what an honor it is for the Oracle to invite me to be one of her students. And as excellent a seamstress as Kadi is, she could use an extra pair of hands outfitting the Stand."

When Mak and Lyros reached them, Alkaios looked up from his Grace and smiled. "So sorry for arriving a few minutes late."

"Trying to make a quiet entrance to avoid your admirers?" Mak asked.

Nephalea ran a hand down her Grace's arm. "You notice he's veiled us to everyone but you."

Alkaios pulled her closer. "Perhaps I'm jealous of all the nice-looking young Hesperines who are enamored of you."

She gave him a light kiss. "And too modest to let your own devotees fawn over you."

"Did you hate the residence you toured tonight?" Mak asked hopefully. "Spiders in the attic? Perhaps a leak in the roof?"

Alkaios shook his head at the comments he and Nephalea had come to expect from Mak on this topic. "The house was quite lovely, I'm afraid. And if we did find a leak in a home built by a Hesperine lithomagus, we would suspect you had put it there to convince us not to move out of House Argyros."

"And you would be right," Mak said with an unabashed smile.

Nephalea tutted at him. "No need to resort to breaking things. We have yet to make a decision. And how would vandalism look on your service record?"

Not as bad as forging weapons. Mak had to work to keep his best comic smile on his face. "Well, if you wake from Slumber with your doors warded shut, just consider it a loving reminder from me. You're our Ritual tributaries, and you might as well be family. You're welcome to stay under Father's roof as long as you like, and all of us love having you there."

Alkaios snatched two goblets of wine from a passing tray and handed one to Nephalea, meanwhile raising a veil around them. "Half the residences we looked at this week don't actually interest us. But viewing them makes an excellent cover for courting our partisans."

Nephalea nodded. "The young Firstblood whose Trial sister fell in battle as a Hesperine errant is now seeking to pass her home onto a worthy bloodline."

Lyros shook his head. "He's had a rough century. Thank you for speaking with him. He didn't want to hear anything Mak and I had to say."

Mak sighed. "Since we've never gone errant, he felt we couldn't understand what he and his Trial sister endured."

Nephalea nodded. "He was much more open with us."

Alkaios looked thoughtful, resting a hand at his Grace's back. "He is disillusioned with our cause in Tenebra, for understandable reasons. In his position, it is easy to feel that his sister wasted her life for ungrateful mortals. He needed to be reminded why he was once inspired to fight."

Mak took a deep breath. "Did he say which way he plans to vote?"

Nephalea smiled. "Yes. He promised to vote against isolationism—because that's what his Trial sister would have wanted."

Mak and Lyros clasped Alkaios and Nephalea's wrists in thanks.

"Politics," Nephalea mused. "We remember how to do that, don't we, Alkaios?"

"Certainly, bluebird. We've done our fair share of attempting to negotiate between feuding nobles. Of course, that negotiation ended in us dropping a quantity of Hesperine magic on their heads during a siege, but the point stands."

"The Firstbloods are a friendly audience compared to our mortal families," Nephalea said. "It's refreshing to have rational discussions with Hesperines. The most entrenched traditionalists are still more broad-minded than any mortal."

"But eternally stubborn, too," Mak muttered. "There's the problem."

"Well, which stubborn immortal can we help with next?" Alkaios glanced around the gathering. "Thank you for inviting us to Xandra's event. We weren't certain a couple of hardened comrades of an ancient would be the right choice for your guest list."

"Well," Mak said, "you may have been on the battlefields of humanity when Lyros and I were still trainees. But you've been Hesperines for less time than anyone in our circle."

Lyros nodded. "You're some of the youngest immortals who have your own vote in the Firstblood Circle. That puts you in a unique position to set an example for other new bloodlines."

Mak cast a glance at a Hesperine in a blue mantle nearby. "You could start with her. She's a clothier who is reluctant for Tenebran linen and wool to affect Hesperine fashion."

Nephalea's eyes widened, but she squared her shoulders. "Anything for the cause."

Mak laughed. "Oh, I had you there for a moment."

She gave him a swat on the arm. "You *are* an impudent younger brother."

"Of course. It's my sacred duty." Mak knew Nephalea had parted with her own mortal brother on bittersweet terms, so he tried to make her feel like he was her honorary brother.

"No need to talk to the clothier," Lyros said with a chuckle. "Most of the textile crafters are willing to side with Xandra, since she supplies them with the most coveted raw silk. But there is another aromagus who could use some persuasion."

"Please," Mak begged. "I don't think I can survive another conversation about carrots."

"This one grows grains," Lyros reminded him.

"That's even worse. I won't be able to resist jesting about separating wheat from chaff, and then I'll offend someone."

"We're happy to talk with him," Alkaios offered. "Actually, planning our crops was one of my chief occupations as a mortal lord. I might be able to keep up with the fellow."

"Too modest," Nephalea said again. "Alkaios's good management was what protected all his people from the famines that frequently afflicted Tenebra in those days. He even devised his own types of grain by crossing different strains to improve their properties."

"That's impressive," Lyros said with admiration.

Mak just nodded and smiled.

"Do you think you'll choose an agricultural craft?" Lyros asked.

"We shall see," Alkaios answered. "Nephalea and I are glad to be settled in our service already and want to focus on our Stand duties, before committing to crafts or residences or anything else."

But they didn't have to ask Alkaios twice to go speak to the grain-growing aromagus, before Mak even had a chance to bring up the battle arts.

He sighed. "Who next?"

Lyros scanned the guests. "Lio would want us to talk with that initiate from the diplomatic service, the one who specializes in...what was it? Joint research between Hesperines and Imperials."

Mak groaned. "What are we supposed to say to his fellow scrollworm?"

Lyros frowned. "That's a good question. I wish the letter that came from Lio and Cassia today had answered our questions. It's unfortunate they only had time to write us about catching that ferry up the river."

Mak shifted on his feet, his senses prickling. That letter only increased his desire to punch something. But Lio and Cassia swore that all was well. There were no enemies for him to protect them from...or so they said.

All he could do for them was be here tonight and give it his best.

"All right," Mak said. "Let's find that scrollworm and hope he's read a few of our favorite military history books as part of his diplomatic education."

They were soon discussing ancient battles with the initiate over goblets of Starfrost Brew.

"Oh yes," the diplomat said, "I remember the debate over siege engines that took place during the Solstice Summit. I'm sure it comes as no surprise that I was there among the scholars that night. But I admit to some surprise that Ambassador Deukalion and Newgift Cassia are not here tonight."

"As I'm sure you've heard," Mak said, "they're traveling in the Empire before her Gifting."

Very few outside the Elder Firstbloods knew why, and Mak's father had been particularly careful not to apprise any of Orthros's diplomats to the Empire of Solia's illegal presence there. The whole situation could turn into a disastrous test of Orthros's alliance with the Empire, if not handled carefully.

"What an interesting time to go on a romantic holiday," the initiate diplomat said. "How courageously they positioned themselves at the fore-front of the Summit, when their future together was at stake. Now that Hypatia's measure threatens everything they worked for, one would think they would be at the center of resistance efforts. But I suppose they find each other too difficult to resist."

Mak's senses prickled with warning. The diplomat's tone was like a False Friend, the fighting move that made you think you knew where your opponent was positioned in the arena, only for them to sneak up behind you.

Lyros cut in smoothly, his tone unruffled. "They went through some difficult ordeals during the Summit. They've certainly earned their leave of absence, haven't they?"

"Oh yes, everyone in Orthros knows how hard Ambassador Deukalion works to earn everything. What a stellar rise in the diplomatic service. Not one to take advantage of his luck being the nephew of the Queens' Master Ambassador. Or use his position for personal gain."

Stand down, came Lyros's voice in Mak's mind, even as he bristled.

"What a happy outcome," the diplomat went on, "that Orthros's entire diplomatic policy rearranged itself to accommodate peace—and Ambassador Deukalion's love affair with Newgift Cassia. Now that they have secured their personal happiness, I am certain they will continue to selflessly serve our people. After they return from their extended romantic getaway."

Lyros slipped the dented goblet out of Mak's hand and twined his fingers in the other.

"Grace-Father takes the wellbeing of his diplomats to heart," Lyros said, "as I'm sure you've experienced for yourself, anytime you have come to him with a problem."

"Oh, to be sure. The door to his library is always open, even to those of us who have no blood ties to anyone of ancient status in Orthros, who are the first of our families to aspire to achieve greatness." The diplomat's emotions were veiled, but his smile didn't reach his eyes.

Mak envisioned his fist wiping the smile off the bloodless, corpse-feasting excuse for a Hesperine who dared insult his father and Trial brother.

Time to walk away, Lyros said.

Mak's pulse pounded with such fury that he didn't even hear Lyros's words as he excused them from the conversation.

Lyros stood up, his hand still clasped in Mak's. *Do I need to physically drag you out of here, or are you coming on your own two feet?*

Lyros started moving, and Mak made himself follow the tug of his Grace's hand.

The crowd milled past. Lyros's veils swept around them, and the next thing Mak knew, Lyros had stepped them to an empty room inside Xandra's residence.

Lyros put both his hands on Mak's shoulders. "All right. Cool off before I toss your handsome ass into the polar ocean."

"Bleeding thorns," Mak snarled, "that self-absorbed little maggot—"

"I know. But breaking him into tiny pieces won't actually defend Lio and your father's honor. It will only add fuel to his fire."

"How can you be so calm?"

"I'm not calm." Lyros's green eyes gleamed with fury. "But I'll find it much more satisfying to slowly corner him than to give him the satisfaction of disrupting Xandra's party with a brawl."

Through the pounding in his head, Mak realized that Lyros probably could have outmaneuvered their opponent. They might be in the courtyard with their Trial sisters right now, constructing a way to disprove the diplomat's insinuations and discredit him before the other guests.

If Lyros hadn't had to retreat to help Mak tame his temper.

Mak rubbed his face. "Goddess, I'm sorry."

Lyros pulled Mak closer and rested their foreheads together. "Never apologize. The way you defend people you love is one of my favorite things about you."

"I'm sorry you had to keep me in check tonight."

"I hope I'm always the one who has to do that. Taming your temper is also one of my favorite things."

Mak knew it was true, but he also knew he had just made a mistake. An avoidable failure that had sent them retreating while their enemy prevailed.

"I'm going to fix this," Mak swore.

"We will. But this one seems a difficult case. His jealousy of Lio clouds his judgment, and his preoccupation with his own status makes him imagine your father makes distinctions based on rank. It will take time to win him over."

"No, I'm going to fix it now."

"What do you have in mind?"

What could Mak do? He had no eloquent arguments like Lio, nor secret insight into this diplomat's weaknesses like Cassia might.

How could he possibly make this person see how much Lio and Cassia had sacrificed for everyone? How could he stop the diplomat from poisoning others' opinions and remind everyone of what Lio and Cassia had done?

"I need to go to House Argyros for a moment."

"I'll come with you," Lyros said.

"No." Mak gave him a kiss, then pulled back. "I have to make this right."

With a step, Mak stormed into his father's library. The elders gathered around the coffee table gave him startled looks, their auras filling with concern.

His parents were sharing a pot of coffee with Lio's. On Aunt Komnena and Uncle Apollon's other side, Kassandra relaxed while she rolled a wad of yarn into a ball. Across the table, Rudhira and Nike were locked in a match of Prince and Diplomat, many of their playing pieces already fallen to the sides of the game board.

"Oh," Mak said. "I didn't realize you all were having an event, too."

Nike winked at him. "Our hotbed of sedition predates your own, you know."

Mak had never doubted that, but he hadn't realized his father's library had ever been the scene of it.

"What's wrong, Mak?" his father asked.

"I have a favor to ask." Mak cleared his throat. "Two, actually. One of you, and one of Kassandra." He gave a slight bow in the Oracle's direction.

"Anything to assist you bright young things," Kassandra said. "Your efforts are a sight for world-weary eyes."

Mak took a deep breath. "I know it's a great deal to ask, but may we display the Akron's Torch at Xandra's residence tonight?"

Rudhira and Nike exchanged speaking glances.

Mak turned to Uncle Apollon. "If Lio were here tonight, he might have brought it with him. I want it to be there, as a reminder of everything he has done."

"It is Kassandra's decision, of course," said Apollon, "but I know Lio would appreciate that very much."

"It's an excellent idea," Komnena approved.

There was a gleam in Mak's mother's eyes. "The Akron's most sacred relic in the hands of my son." She folded her hands on the table in front of her. Hands that had killed Aithouros and countless other Mages of Anthros. "My, what poetic justice."

Kassandra smiled and set aside her ball of yarn. Then she reached under the table for the long silk box at her feet. The one she usually kept under her loom at her residence.

"You foresaw my request?" Mak asked.

Wonderful. She had probably also seen him almost lose his temper with the diplomat. And every version of that situation in which he had actually lost it and thrown the worm into the pool. Or dropped him off the summit of Haima. Or encased his feet in adamas and left him at the bottom of the sea where no one could hear him whining.

Kassandra looked at him, her eyes twinkling, and laughed. "I thought it was a possibility. Of all the different ways this night might have proceeded, this was the outcome I was hoping to see in reality. I do love it when my favorite version of the future comes to pass."

She opened the lid, and golden light spilled out. Even though Mak had seen the Torch before, he couldn't help staring at the controversial artifact with a shiver. The pillar of engraved gold topped with spell light had been the most sacred treasure in the Hagion of Anthros, the war mages' greatest temple. Until Methu, the first bloodborn, had stolen it. How fitting that Lio, the eighth bloodborn, had brandished Methu's prize before the First-blood Circle the night he and Cassia had stopped the Departure.

Mak looked at his father. "We must display a symbol of peace as well. Father, could you spare a treaty?"

"Not just any treaty," he guessed.

Mak nodded. "The Solstice Oath."

"Come with me."

He led Mak to the stairs that spiraled around the library, and they ascended to the gallery that ringed the dome. They walked in and out of beautifully colored light that streamed in through the half-moon stained glass windows.

His father halted before the alcove that housed the most valued documents entrusted to the Queens' Master Ambassador. The display was inlaid with stylized patterns of moonflowers in silver and white. The ancient scrolls hovered on the power of levitation enchantments, dripping with wards and illuminated by lavish spell lights.

Mak always knew the documents were here, but never gave much thought to the scrolls themselves. Only to the deeds of his loved ones who had risked their lives for these pieces of paper.

The scroll at the center was sixteen hundred years old, and the Mage King and Changing Queen of Tenebra had placed their seal on it with their own hands. Their mingled magics glowed gold and green beside the Queens' blood seal.

The scroll beside them was new, but smeared with ash and stained with wine. The recent treaty between the Hesperines and the free lords of Tenebra had almost not survived the Solstice Summit. He could see Cassia's handprint where she had rescued it during the battle with the Collector.

"Cassia needs to be with us in spirit, as well," he said.

His father rested a hand on his shoulder. "You are making us very proud tonight. And every night."

Mak's throat squeezed. He had never imagined they would be having this conversation over treaty documents. He wished his father's words were true.

"What happened tonight that made you so angry?" his father asked.

Mak could tell him. Explain all about the bitter initiate trying to climb in his diplomatic service. He probably already knew that youngblood's name, personality, and the subject of his initiation treatise. He would tell Mak exactly how to handle him.

But Mak wasn't sure he had the skills or temperament to carry out his father's advice…and if he did, he wouldn't be fixing his own mess. "It's all right. I'll handle it."

"I'm sorry tonight is turning out to be so difficult."

"I knew it would be. I'm no good at saying things without saying them or buttering up people I don't like."

"That is why your circle needs you. You are honest, and you act with conviction."

"My candidness only creates problems in a situation like this."

"None of the Hesperines at Xandra's party will look to a Steward for innuendo or flattery."

"Then what are we there for?" Mak muttered. "Standing around and looking intimidating?"

His father chuckled. "No. Your mother is excellent at that, and you certainly inherited her talent. I love watching her intimidate people. But I would say your role tonight is something at which you in particular excel. You are better at it than anyone in our family, in fact."

"I can't imagine what."

"Making people feel safe," his father said. "Why do you think Thenie prefers to sleep on your lap? You exude an aura of security."

"I do?" Mak frowned. "Somehow I don't think the Hesperines at Xandra's party are as receptive as my three-year-old niece."

"You are asking them to take a great risk, and the future of our people is uncertain. It will reassure the more skittish partisans that a new generation of the stand intends to protect Orthros through it all. Besides, not everyone responds to pretty speeches. They will relate better to your straightforward approach."

Mak hoped that was true, and that there were more of them than there were of the conniving, ambitious types. "Thank you, Father."

His father clasped his wrist. "I'll be proud of you, regardless of what happens tonight."

Mak gripped his father's wrist in return. He had fought hard for that assurance. Now he had to make sure he could end the night proud of himself.

Mak stepped back to the party with the scroll in his hand and the silk box tucked under his arm. A ripple moved through the attendees as he forged his way through. By the time he reached the head of the gathering, the guests had parted to let him walk between two rows of onlookers.

He set the silk box at his feet. He probably should make a speech. Lio or Cassia would think of something properly poetic and dramatic to say to stir the crowds' hearts. All that came to Mak's mind was *if you say another less than admiring thing about my cousin and Grace-cousin, I will knock out your teeth.*

Exude security, he reminded himself. Candid. Straightforward.

Despite his father's excellent advice, his words stuck in his throat as if he were wrapped in a Mortal Vice.

So in absolute silence, he did the only thing he knew to do. He acted.

He extended his hand, palm out, and with a push of levitation, set the treaty to hovering over the pool. When he tore away the veil spells concealing it, the crowd gasped.

Then he flipped the lid of Kassandra's box open a little too hard and seized the Akron's torch. It felt like nails on a slate and grinding teeth and magefire burning into his ear canals. Bleeding thorns, how in the Goddess's name had Lio held this thing long enough to walk through the Firstblood Circle with it?

Mak tossed it out over the water, and it righted itself to hover next to the treaty.

Lyros slid an arm around his waist. *That was the most glorious fighting move I've ever seen.*

Mak resisted the urge to shake his hand. It was numb, and his skin was blistered.

I'll heal it, Lyros promised. *Slowly. When we're alone.*

Mak hadn't managed to say a word, but at least his Grace was proud of him.

Lio and Cassia would be too, Lyros told him.

Absolute silence reigned over the party.

Kia broke into applause. Nodora and Xandra started clapping, too, and Alkaios and Nephalea were the first to follow. The applause overtook the crowd.

The young diplomat looked around him, his eyes narrow, his mouth puckered. Not a pair of hands was still. He had no allies left.

All the seditious youngbloods of Orthros were applauding Lio and Cassia's triumphs, even if Mak could not claim to have won a victory of his own. Yet.

66

days until

NOTIAN WINTER SOLSTICE

39 Annassa, 1597 IS

A FREE SERVICE

BY THE TIME MONSOON returned, waves of heat rippled outside the overhang. He landed heavily and joined Cassia in the deep shade under the cool stone. She sat by the now-cold firepit with Knight stretched out and panting beside her.

"I could see that fire from the air," Monsoon said. "Please tell me it wasn't visible to any enemies who might be lurking in the area."

She gestured to the tent where Lio Slumbered. "Lio veiled our campsite so that only you can find it. Here."

She offered Monsoon a waterskin and some jerky. He took both and sank down on the other side of the fire pit.

It was clear his search had been unsuccessful. She doubted he wanted comforting words. No, he wanted results. So did she, which was why she had been thinking back over Mak and Lyros's recent letters. "I've been considering our strategy. Lio's and my friends in the Stand sent us information on tactical search patterns. We could adapt them to searching from the air and on foot."

He paused. "That's a good idea. Thank you for everything you two tried today. You did your best."

That was a great deal of praise coming from him. "We won't fail Chuma."

Silence fell between them. Monsoon sipped his water and gnawed on the jerky. Cassia returned her attention to the book she was trying to read.

She'd left most of her books in their trunks in the veld. But the traveler's language primer Kia had given her was tiny enough to slip in a pocket. She applied herself to memorizing useful phrases in the major Imperial languages.

Her headache grew sharper, and the text swam before her eyes. She cursed inwardly and kept trying, but she couldn't find the word she was looking for.

She hesitated a moment longer, but finally said, "What does *nyakimbi* mean? If you don't mind me asking."

Monsoon was quiet for a moment, and she wasn't sure he would answer, but then he did. "It means 'little sister' in my language. Chuma isn't my sister by birth, but she and her family are like kin to me."

"I understand. All my family in Orthros are like that. Something more powerful than birth connects us."

"You came out here to find the Ashes, not Chuma's mother." Monsoon's eyes were piercing, as if he were trying to puzzle her out.

"I know what loss feels like," Cassia tried to explain. "We *will* find Chuma's mother."

His gaze fell, and silence returned. Cassia looked down at her dictionary again, reading and re-reading the word for sister in multiple languages.

Monsoon spoke again after a while. "Why don't you like speaking Vulgus?"

"It reminds me of my old life, which is over."

"You were so happy to leave Tenebra?"

"In the words of one of the greatest officers in the Imperial army—who is now a Hesperine—Tenebra is a dreary little cesspit."

"Didn't you leave anything behind there? Family?"

"No."

"There's nothing and no one worth remembering?"

She thought of Perita. Callen. Ben, too. "I'll never forget the few people I called friends. But they're happy there, and I'm happy in Orthros. We all made the right choice."

He sighed. "I can understand that."

Cassia raised an eyebrow. "You don't still believe that all I wanted from the Hesperines was a free trip to the Empire?"

"I don't know," he said with exaggerated hesitation. "They do fall for sad stories so easily."

"My sob story isn't what Lio fell for," Cassia said pertly.

"If you really didn't know your sister was alive, then I suppose you would have had fewer reasons to stay."

"I had no idea she survived until…about an hour before Lio was to transform me into a Hesperine, actually."

Monsoon gave a low whistle.

Cassia traced a finger in the grit on the floor of the cave. "I should have gone through with it. Then I could have been more powerful when I came to find her. I would have the strength to protect her. And I'd be so much more help to Chuma and her family."

"Becoming a Hesperine is an extreme approach to protecting your family and friends."

"I've fought to protect them before. I know how much strength it takes."

"Is that why you're studying combat? You intend to become a warrior?"

"Not professionally, no. But I've had enough close calls to understand how valuable it is to know some basic fighting moves." She thought of the greenhouses at home that Apollon, Lio, and Mak planned to build for her. Apollon had promised to work on the foundations in her and Lio's absence, while Mak forged the iron. Perhaps by the time she and Lio returned, it would be ready for his glass. "I'm a gardener."

For some reason, that made a rather genuine smile appear on Monsoon's face. "I have no trouble imagining that."

Well, he was better at judging a person's profession than Dakk. His silly theories had involved gentle hands and animal healing.

"So you ended up in Orthros," Monsoon mused, "and Solia ended up here. What an unusual pair of Tenebran sisters you make."

"You have no idea."

"How did you meet the silkfoot?" Monsoon pointed at the tent.

Cassia smiled. "I went looking for a Hesperine."

"Isn't that rather unusual for a Tenebran woman?"

"Oh, yes, and even more so for one whose father would kill her if he knew."

"Well, he sounds like a controlling bastard."

"Actually, I'm the bastard. My sister's mother was his wife. After he got my mother killed, my sister raised me. Until I was seven. After that, I believed our father murdered her."

Monsoon sat frozen. Not a single feather on his wings twitched. "I'm sorry."

"Thank you."

"Wasn't there someone to take care of you after you lost her?"

"I had no one to rely on but myself." She rubbed her hound's head. "And Knight, of course. But the only people who ever showed me any kindness were the Hesperines."

Her tone must have come out harsher than she intended, for Monsoon paused. "You aren't paying me to ask questions you don't want to answer. Listening is an optional, complimentary service."

"You offer a number of free services, it appears. I don't get the idea Chuma and her family are paying you for this."

"That's not a free service. That is…what is it you silkfoots say? Honoring a bond of gratitude."

"I can see that." She looked up the word for goat. "I would do anything for my Hesperine family."

"I'm trying to imagine you, the dog, and your nocturnal sorcerer wrapped around the finger of a little girl with fangs, and it's not difficult to envision."

Cassia laughed. "I'm not ashamed to admit it. We dote on Zoe."

Having finished his jerky, Monsoon dusted off his hands and capped his waterskin.

Cassia tilted her head. "I'm trying to imagine a scarred mercenary in a bad mood wrapped around a girl's finger, but I've already beheld it with my own eyes."

"Not ashamed to admit it," he said.

The different words for love took up an entire page, Cassia discovered.

Before she knew it, she had told Monsoon her whole story. How her sister's memory had brought her and Lio together, and all that had happened since. It was easy to leave out everything to do with the king and politics. In fact, it was a relief to simply talk about the personal aspects of her experiences.

Cassia swallowed hard, the emotions still so close to the surface. "I never imagined such a thing could be possible, but it's real. Solia didn't die. She escaped the shadowlands and came to the Empire."

"It does happen," Monsoon said. "Shadowlanders are extraordinarily rare here, but there are more of them than most citizens realize. They're just very good at not drawing attention to themselves."

"I can only imagine what Solia has been doing all these years. Living like a fugitive, I suppose."

"Are you angry she never came back for you?"

"Of course not. I don't see how she could have reached me. Staying away from our father is the best possible thing she could have done. Staying alive is the best thing she could have done. Now we have a chance to see each other again, thanks to the Hesperines."

"So you intend to ask your sister to return to Orthros with you."

"Lio's family is waiting to welcome her with the same love they have shown me. We would both be safe there. We could make up for all the lost years." She cleared her aching throat. "She belongs with our bloodline."

Monsoon draped an arm over his knee. "Have you considered the possibility that she might want something different for you two?"

The mere thought felt like a fist closing around Cassia's heart. But Kassandra had suggested the very same. The Hesperine oracle had told Cassia that she must offer Solia more than Orthros. "Free Will is sacred to Hespera. She must choose Orthros for herself. I will ask her what she wishes to do. But I want with every fiber of my being for her to tell me she never plans to set foot in Tenebra again."

"What if she wanted to stay here?"

"If she became a Hesperine, she could spend as much time in the Empire as she wished, without fear."

"And if she had a life here that she didn't want to leave behind for fangs?"

"Perhaps with Orthros's influence, we could get her a pardon from the Empress and permission for her to remain."

"Do you have any idea how difficult that is?"

"I know it doesn't appear so, due to my arrest warrant, but Lio and I actually specialize in that sort of thing."

Securing a pardon from the Empress for the Tenebran family member of a citizen of Orthros was a task for a Hesperine diplomat.

Just not one who was a fugitive herself.

Cassia said no more about her or Lio's careers. She didn't want to think about how far she had fallen or how she had endangered his position. "I admit, this is not my finest hour. But if my sister wants to live here, I will move the sun and moons to make it possible. I'll do anything for us to have the lives we thought we lost."

"Even if she wants to stay human? And you become a Hesperine?"

Cassia looked away. "I cannot think so far ahead."

"You haven't gotten her back yet," Monsoon said with remarkable sympathy in his voice. "Of course you aren't ready to face the prospect of losing her again."

"But I will get her back. And I will be so grateful for that moment."

When he said nothing more, she thought it might be an opening to ask some questions of her own. "What about you, Monsoon? Do you have any family?"

He crossed his arms over his chest and looked at the sky. "Yes."

She waited, but that was all he said.

She had given him the invitation to speak of them. He knew she would listen in return. She deemed it best not to prod the private mercenary. She thought they had gained some ground…and she found she wanted to keep it.

PRAY LATER

KNIGHT'S SNARL JOLTED CASSIA awake. With a gasp, she sat up in the confined darkness of the tent, where Lio lay in Slumber beside her.

She lunged for the tent flap, but couldn't get it open. Knight was outside, blocking the exit.

He was standing between her and danger. But until she knew what that danger was, she was of no use against it.

Nike's voice came to her mind. *The most underestimated opponent is the most dangerous.*

Cassia wormed her fingers into the gap of the flap and pried it open just enough to peer out.

Monsoon stood silhouetted against the daylight, his wings spread, his sword and fortune blade drawn. Before him, the outline of a robed figure moved in a lightning-fast attack.

"*Ckabaar!*" Cassia cried.

Knight sprang into the duel. He and Monsoon and the attacker were a whirl of fur and feathers and cloth, in and out of Cassia's line of sight. She couldn't see enough to command Knight.

She crept out and crouched with her back to the tent.

There wasn't one attacker. At least ten robed warriors assaulted the entrance to the overhang.

One had already made it past Monsoon and Knight. The attacker spotted Cassia and closed in, sword at the ready.

"*Dockk!*"

Knight released his current opponent and came toward her with blood and fabric in his mouth. Just as the attacker's sword came within range of Cassia, Knight lunged from the side.

The warrior screamed as they went down, pinned beneath the weight of a liegehound. Knight's jaws went for their neck. Cassia told herself to look away.

She was still watching when the attacker vanished.

They had chosen a magical escape instead of death. Was she relieved or more afraid? She was unsure.

Fight first, Nike had taught her. *Say your prayers later.*

Cassia took hold of a rock the size of her fist. Under duress from two warriors with swords, Monsoon was backing farther and farther out of the overhang. Toward more drawn weapons.

Cassia hurled the stone at the nearest attacker. Her aim was miserable, but it bounced off their lower body and fetched their attention.

The attacker hurled a small blade at Knight and raced toward her.

She shouted the command for Knight to leap. His powerful haunches propelled him into the air, high enough to reach a levitating Hesperine, and the dagger sailed beneath his paws.

Cassia threw another rock. The warrior caught it in their hand. But then they had to turn to face her oncoming hound.

She called for Knight to leap again.

The attacker was smart. They ducked. But as soon as Knight sailed over their head, he spun and barreled into their back.

The warrior hit the ground face first. Knight was upon them, snarling. Before her hound's bite landed, that attacker disappeared as well.

Cassia looked to the fight outside the overhang. Monsoon was not surrounded. He was nowhere in sight.

One of the attackers was suddenly yanked heavenward, screaming. A moment later, they fell from the sky onto one of their comrades, and both went down in a tangle of robes and drawn swords. There was a ripple in the air, like heat rising from the ground. Then they too vanished.

The six remaining attackers retreated to the cover of the overhang. Three drew bows, taking aim as Monsoon's shadow swept past.

The other three did not turn their attention to the sky. But Cassia was ready for them.

She backed away from the cold fire pit, liegehound commands rolling off her tongue. Knight took down one attacker before they made it halfway to her. As they vanished, the blood they left behind splashed across the rock. Knight started on the next, leaving only the third for Cassia to deal with.

The warrior's height and broad shoulders made her think he was a man, although the robes shielded him from head to toe, except for his eyes. The attire of any wise traveler in the Maaqul, but not the vibrant blue of the Azarqi who had welcomed her around their fires. He wore colors that blended into the desert. He could have been anyone.

In that moment, he was her enemy, and she was all that stood between him and Lio.

The warrior fixed a hard gaze on her. Was she looking into the eyes of someone who had spilled Ipika's blood?

As he drew nearer, she froze and put on a frightened expression. Nearer. He rasped something in Tradewinds, and she couldn't understand most of it, but she caught "come," "quiet," and "mercy."

Was he telling her he would grant her a swift death if she surrendered? She pretended to cower.

Waste no advantage. She would never forget Nike's words. *You can turn even that which you fear into your strength.*

When he was close enough to reach for her hair, she threw her handful of firepit ash right into his eyes.

He recoiled, hissing, and tried to wipe his face. It was too late. He never saw Knight attack.

Her hound barreled into the man and trapped him flat on his back.

"*Baatat!*" Cassia ordered her hound to hold his prey. They needed one for questioning.

Knight shouted barks in the man's face, saliva flying from his jaws. When the warrior tried to lift his sword, Knight locked his jaws on the man's forearm. He cried out in pain and called out a word Cassia didn't know.

When Knight didn't relent, the man yelled again. This time, Cassia understood "peace."

"*Het baatat.*"

Knight let go of the warrior's arm and settled for crouching on his chest, growling into his face while he wheezed.

The archers at the entrance were gone, their own arrows peppering the ground where they had made their stand. It appeared Monsoon had sent their own missiles right back at them.

One more body fell from the sky with a sickening scream. A hand's breadth from the ground and certain death, the attacker disappeared.

Monsoon landed at the entrance and stepped gracefully over the arrows, sheathing his sword. He was breathing hard, and sweat slicked his skin in the heat, but he didn't have a scratch on him.

He came to her side and put a steady hand on her shoulder. "All right?"

She nodded, her pulse still pounding. "One surrendered."

"Well done."

He didn't even follow the praise with an insult.

She hid her shaking hands in the folds of her travel robes and focused on what they needed to do. Question their captive.

She spoke in Vulgus, the only tongue she was sure the attacker didn't understand. "He might be able to tell us where Ipika is."

"Oh, he'll serve up what he knows on a platter by the time I'm done with him." Monsoon stalked toward the prisoner.

"We have to interrogate him in a way that won't cause him to flee."

Monsoon stood over the prisoner. "Call off your hound."

"You said people can't spirit walk in the Maaqul," Cassia persisted. "How are they disappearing? How can we stop him from escaping?"

Monsoon gave Knight a look. Her dog backed away, his fur on end, and pressed himself against her legs.

Her mind raced, seeking an approach before Monsoon did anything rash. When escape and death were the man's options, why had he chosen surrender? "Do you think he's more frightened of his allies than us?"

"Not for long." Monsoon kicked the man's sword out of his reach.

The weapon skidded to a halt at Cassia's feet, and she noticed something she hadn't been concerned about during the battle. The blade wasn't metal. It appeared to be made of some kind of reddish desert stone.

Monsoon stepped on the man's injured arm, and a growl of pain emerged from the captive's hidden mouth. Monsoon's foot pinned the man's wrist, exposing his palm.

Fury clouded Monsoon's face, but no surprise.

"You know who they are," Cassia said.

She looked closer at the man's hand. A design was tattooed in red-black ink on the brown skin of his palm. It resembled broken pieces of something arranged in a circle.

Monsoon said something to the man in a language Cassia had never heard. But his murderous tone was easy to understand.

How far would he go to protect those he loved?

How far would Cassia watch him go without stopping him?

Her inner battle was too costly a distraction. She didn't catch the flicker of movement as quickly as she might have. By the time she called out to warn Monsoon, the captive had already drawn the sliver of a blade from his sleeve and thrown it.

It sliced through the air. Too fast. There was nothing she could do to stop it from hitting Monsoon.

When the shiv landed in her left arm, Cassia realized the captive had aimed for her.

Pain seared her flesh. She felt dust in her eyes. Then everything around her vanished in a ripple of desert heat.

ALONE

THE VOICES WEREN'T WHISPERS this time, but Cassia recognized them from the spirit gates. They were a chorus now, one she still could not understand. But she was sure they were telling her everything would be all right.

Then momentum tore her from their embrace and cast her down. When her vision cleared, she found herself lying on flat, sandy ground.

She had landed on her wound. With a snarl of pain, she picked herself up off the sun-hot dirt and cradled her injured arm.

There was no one to hear her. She was alone.

As far as she could see in any direction, desert. Not a cliff or mountain to orient her. Not a speck of green prying its way out of the dry ground. Just clear and deceptively beautiful blue sky above. Russet sand all around, scattered with gravel and stones.

Cassia felt like the only living creature on the vast surface of the world.

She tried to ignore the pain in her arm and gather her thoughts. How had she gotten here? It hadn't felt like stepping or traversal. She had heard the voices from the spirit gates. But no one could spirit walk in the Maaqul.

It had happened when the blade hit her. She looked at her left arm, where the small dagger was buried hilt deep. Was it still working magic on her? Would freeing herself from it somehow put her back where she belonged?

She closed her hand around the hilt and yanked the blade from her flesh. Her angry cry echoed across the desert.

She was still here. She cast the knife away and pressed her hand to the blood blooming on her sleeve. Her head swimming, she grit her teeth and knelt on the ground to take deep breaths.

The heat rose in waves around her, and the sun beat down. She didn't have long before this became dangerous.

A different kind of danger than an avalanche, but she had survived that. Knight had pulled her from underneath the snow. Would he be able to track her out here?

A thought struck her, and she patted frantically at her robes with her good hand. Yes, there. The dog flute was still in her pocket.

She put it to her lips and blew with all her might. "Knight?" she called, in between each silent note. *"Dockk!"*

When she was out of breath, she had to admit it to herself. Wherever she had landed, she was too far away from Knight for him to hear even an enchanted flute crafted with blood magic by a Hesperine.

Had she disappeared without a trace, like Chuma's mother?

She had seen Monsoon's map. The Maaqul was the size of countries. She could be anywhere.

But Lio could always find her.

He was safe. She and Knight had defended him during the skirmish. Now all she had to do was keep her wits about her and hold out until her Grace woke at dusk.

She must do something about her wound first. At least she had the clothes on her back. She had been sleeping in her light cotton travel robe and trousers, with her scarf around her shoulders. She thought carefully about what part of her garments she could sacrifice for bandages, and which part she could fashion into a scarf to prevent sunburn.

She eyed the hated knife where it had fallen. Such a small thing, barely longer than her hand, with a rough, carved hilt and a sharp-hewn edge. Dust clung to her blood on the stone blade.

She needed a knife out here.

She rolled up her left sleeve and balled it around her wound, bending her elbow to hold the fabric in place and apply pressure. With her good arm, she wrapped her scarf around her head and face to shield her from the sun.

She reached for the knife, but with her hand hovering above it, she hesitated. She didn't want to touch it. And yet, no magic had surprised her when she pulled it out.

Gingerly, she picked up the shiv. Nothing happened.

After a lot of wrestling, cursing, and bleeding, she managed to bandage her arm without fainting. She put her head between her knees and breathed.

She should stay where she was. Wandering aimlessly would only waste her strength and make her harder to find, with no guarantee she would find shelter or water. She had no choice but to rest and wait for nightfall.

Her gaze fell on the only irregularity in the forbidding landscape, a little ripple in the earth. She tucked herself in the dip in the sand, such as it was, and spread her scarf over her upper body like a tent, keeping her clothes between herself and the hot sand.

The day passed in a haze of heat and thirst. She thought of snowy nights in Orthros and feeling safe with Lio in their residence.

Her mind kept circling back to the skirmish. She analyzed the attackers' actions, her decisions. Who were they and what did Monsoon know about them? Had she done the best she could?

Whatever tricks the captive still had up his sleeve, she was confident they would be short lived in the face on Monsoon's wrath. The captive himself might be short lived. Or perhaps Monsoon would leave some of him for when Lio woke and found his Grace separated from him yet again. Hespera forgive her, but she could find no pity for the man.

At last the punishing sunlight faded on the other side of her scarf. She uncovered her face. Dusk painted the horizon red, then blue. The first star appeared overhead.

Lio should be awake by now.

The coolness of night set in, and constellations came alive in the sky. Still her Grace did not come for her.

Cassia put a hand to her mouth, fighting down panic.

Lio was all right. He had to be all right. The dagger in her arm had been the captive's last revenge. Monsoon and Knight had been there to fight off any attack.

But her fear for her Grace knew no reason. His name flew from her lips and screamed across the desert, reverberating in her thoughts.

The mind ward within her pulsed, as if answering to his name.

She gasped a breath and sagged with relief. The ward was still intact within her. It endured, and so did Lio.

He was alive. Her Grace was alive.

But what had befallen him that kept him from stepping to her?

No, no. Nothing had happened to him. Something had happened to her—the same fate Ipika had met, perhaps. Lio couldn't step to either of them.

Cassia rose to her feet and hurled the knife as far from her as she could.

She felt a new and strange kind of fear. There was no enemy to fight. There was no threat to avoid.

She was lost.

"Hello, fear," she said hoarsely. "I see you're wearing a new face, but I know you. And you're no match for me. I have a ward."

Lio had told her he could use the mind ward to track her. Even if he couldn't step to her, he would be able to locate her. He didn't thirst for water, and he could levitate and cross the terrain much more easily than a human. He had protection from the sun and the strength of a Hesperine.

She wanted to stay in one place to make it easier for him to find her. But she would have to risk searching for water, shelter, and food.

It would be all right. No matter where she wandered, he would find her.

She picked a random direction and began to walk, knowing Lio would follow her path.

Nothing could keep them apart. Not the mandates of kings and mages, not the border of Orthros and Tenebra, not even an untold expanse of desert.

NOON WATCH

L 10.
Her voice cried out to him. But he couldn't answer.

Weight. So heavy. Pressing him into the ground. Grinding him into dust.

Heat. Rising from beneath him. Bearing down on him. Under his skin.

Sun. The sun had done this to him. Too much daylight. The burn of it lingered in his veins. How? The tent…where was the tent?

Lio tried to move. Agony speared his upper body and shot through his veins. A chest wound.

Alarm sent a surge of energy through his limbs. His toes tingled. His fingers twitched. Finally, his eyes came open.

A sword protruded from his chest, pinning him to the ground. Lio stared at the uncanny blade hewn of stone the same color as the desert sands.

His head seemed to float, and a vivid memory ran through his mind. He and Kia, as small sucklings and intrepid readers, had sneaked into the veiled section of her mother's library. With the fascination of children who had never been exposed to violence, they had read the scroll that detailed the five ways a Hesperine could die.

Starvation, exsanguination, decapitation, immolation. And excardiation—removal of the heart.

The desert couldn't kill a Hesperine. But if Lio's heart was damaged, he was in trouble.

The muscles in his neck woke, and he was able to turn his head. There was nothing around him but sand the color of a painted sunset. The Blood Union felt deserted.

What had happened to Cassia?

Lio reached within, feeling for the current of their Grace Union. His fragmented senses fumbled, but there. There she was, a strong vine twined deep within him.

She was alive.

Another aura rose in his awareness, drawing near. Powerful, ancient, immortal, as familiar as the stars. A fellow Hesperine.

He entered Lio's line of sight. Deep brown skin. White fighting robes. An impossible thought formed in Lio's mind.

Prometheus.

Had the Goddess sent the Midnight Champion to bring Lio to her Sanctuary?

The immortal halted over him and looked down, hands on his hips.

The face above Lio did not match the statue of Methu he had seen all his life. This Hesperine was not the fallen bloodborn descending from the Goddess's stars.

The warrior had a broad, strong face framed by a massive cloud of hair. The rest of him was massive, too. His aura was larger than life. He was every inch a Hesperine hero. Perhaps he was no harbinger of the end, but Lio's salvation.

"Good morning, sunshine," he boomed.

If Lio hadn't been awake, he was now. He thought that voice could rouse a sleeping youngblood as effectively as a magical Night Call.

Lio pulled air into his mangled chest. The sword had missed his lungs, then. "By the Goddess, I am glad to see you. You have my gratitude."

"If you can be that polite right out of the Dawn Slumber with a sword sticking through your chest, you're definitely a morning person!"

He was a hero indeed, to bring the ghost of a smile to Lio's face while he was wondering just how close to his heart that sword was. Hespera had sent someone with kindness and a sense of humor.

The Hesperine knelt at his side and looked at his chest. "I'm Karege. What's your name, youngblood?"

"Lio."

"This blade has a rude way of making introductions, but I'm pleased to meet you all the same. There's nothing a sword can do that surprises me. I have five hundred years of combat experience, and I know my battle wounds."

Lio barely felt Karege's careful hands. The warrior peeled back the torn fabric around the blade and examined the wound.

Lio reached for Cassia again, Willing her to feel him. *I will survive this, my Grace. I will get up off this sand, and I will come to you.*

"Good news," Karege said. "It missed your heart. Looks like it slid neatly between a couple of ribs."

Lio let his head fall back and closed his eyes, his thoughts drifting up to the night sky as inarticulate prayers of gratitude.

"Hm," Karege went on, "whoever did this to you knows their battle wounds, too. They were precise. For someone who didn't want to kill you, they certainly made a statement. This is a mean way of getting a Hesperine out of the way."

"It should be safe to take it out, yes?"

"Safe, yes. Comfortable, no. Sorry I'm not a healer. My only affinities are the Gift and my fists." He held them up. "Fortunately those will do to get this thing out of your way."

No sense in delaying the inevitable. The sooner they got it out so Lio's Gift could go to work on the wound, the better. "I'm ready."

"There's something you should know first." Karege pointed to his left arm.

His fighting robe was missing a sleeve. Lio frowned at the bandage around the warrior's bicep. Hesperines didn't use bandages. They healed too fast to need them.

"I've had this for several nights," Karege explained. "It's from a dagger like the sword in you. It's healing, but not like any wound I've ever had before."

"You're saying I'm going to have a hole in my chest for several nights."

"Seems like it. So when I take this out, I want you to lie still while I get the bleeding under control and give you a Ritual drink."

"Your body is already struggling to heal. I can't take your blood."

"Your wound is more of a liability than mine. The sooner I get you on your feet, the better we can help each other. You're not going to be difficult, are you?"

"No," Lio deferred to the elder veteran. "Thank you."

"Good. Now then. I'm going to cut some bandages off your travel robes. I'll send the textile artists in Orthros an apology note later."

Thinking of Kassandra receiving such a note from Karege, Lio chuckled, then regretted it. "My Ritual mother collects decorative lanterns. You can send her one of those."

"I'll pick her up one of those sparkly little mosaic ones they sell in the capital."

Lio was surprised to hear a dagger slicing through the fabric at his knees. Karege carried a blade? It made short work of the seams without jostling Lio very much. The warrior soon had a quantity of bandages laid out.

Karege leaned over Lio. "Think of a place full of happy sucklings and playing animals."

Lio's lips twitched. "My little sister's goat barn."

"Ah." Karege smiled. "Now imagine yourself there and ignore me for a moment."

Lio was immortal. And contrary to Monsoon's accusations, he was not a flimsy silkfoot. But he had to admit, he would be very grateful at the moment if a mind mage was capable of rendering himself unconscious.

His meditation on Zoe's goat barn lasted for an instant, before Karege pulled the blade and a scream of pain out of Lio.

That was the last thing Lio remembered before he regained consciousness to find his chest bandaged and Karege's wrist under his nose. He had passed out. With an overdose of sunlight, a hole in his chest, and unquenched Craving for his Grace's blood, he couldn't spare the energy to nurse wounded pride.

"Well done," Karege said in a bracing tone.

Lio grimaced. "It didn't hurt this much when I jumped off a cliff as a newblood."

Karege laughed. "Trying to get your levitation early, were you? I'm sure that was a less painful adventure. These infernal stone blades hurt worse than any of the battle wounds I've had. There's something wrong about them."

"I would like to think so. I am usually better than this at coping with pain." Living with the Craving for half a year had acquainted Lio with physical suffering in ways he had never imagined before he had been separated from Cassia.

"Here, see if my blood helps."

Lio's fangs were already unsheathed out of pure survival instinct. He accepted the offered gift of Karege's vein and partook of five hundred years of might. Karege's strength and vitality charged into Lio's blood, sustaining and vibrant.

When Lio released Karege's wrist, he was relieved to see the bite marks heal with the rapid power of the Gift. It seemed that only Karege's dagger wound wasn't healing, and the rest of his body's ability to recover was not compromised.

"You have my gratitude," Lio said once again.

"Being lost in the desert together does tend to forge a bond of gratitude. I'm sure you'll have plenty of chances to honor it while we're out here."

Karege helped him sit up. The pain in his chest was bearable now. Barely. He took an experimental breath, then stopped when pain stabbed through him again.

He wouldn't be taking any breaths at all for the next several nights, except a shallow one when he had something to say. "I don't know how I got here."

"The same way I did, I imagine, although I've had several nights to get my bearings since. Let me guess. Some bloodless vulture moved you in your sleep, and you woke up here with no idea where you are—or whether your companions are safe."

"I have to get to her."

"You won't have much luck stepping, I'm sorry to tell you. I've tried. I can't step a stone's throw away, much less to my friends."

"That's impossible," Lio said.

"Probably one of the strangest things that has happened to me in my career as a Hesperine errant in the Empire, and I've seen some *strange* things. Try to think of it as an adventure."

Lio was very glad for Karege's magnanimous aura at the moment. His good nature filling the Blood Union kept Lio from the brink of despair.

He knew it was futile, but even so, he tried to step to Cassia.

Oh, Goddess. He couldn't step. Not even to his Grace.

He levitated to his feet, his chest wound tearing at him with the motion. He slammed a blast of thelemancy across the desert, sending the sword flying. Her mind was out of his range.

"Bleeding thorns, youngblood!" Karege shouted.

Lio sank back down onto the sand.

Karege knelt beside him, brow furrowed with sympathy. "Just who did you leave behind?"

"If we're lost for very long, my symptoms will make her importance to me very clear."

"Hespera's Mercy. Well, what's her name, then?"

"Cassia."

"Has she got her fangs?"

"Not yet."

Cassia was still human. She could die in so many more ways than he could.

Lio gazed out toward the horizon. Even the farthest range of his thelemancy was like a speck of sand in the vast Maaqul.

It was time to discover the mind ward's true range.

Lio levitated to his feet again. The blood he'd lost was drying on the sand. Let it be a libation to Hespera.

I swear to you, My Goddess, I will find her.

Lio was alive. And while he was alive, he had the power to help Cassia.

Lio let his power flood the imperceptible veins of their Grace Union. He fixed all his senses on his awareness of her. She was his second heartbeat, pulsing under his skin, even while she was far away. She was a soft mortal breath in his mind.

Lio closed his eyes, shutting out the desert and the pain. He let levitation lift him, hovering in the dry night air.

He reached deep into his and Cassia's inner world, the bastion of glass they had spun from thelemancy and Will. He turned to her.

He opened his eyes. His body had turned northeast.

"I can sense where she is," Lio announced in triumph. "I know what direction to go in to search for her."

Karege let out a whoop. "Well, you have some mind mage tricks up your sleeve, to be sure. Onward, then. Goddess willing, we'll find my companions along the way."

Lio let his feet touch the sand again. "Who were you traveling with? And to what do I owe the good fortune of encountering you out here, Karege?"

"I'm here on a contract." The warrior touched the blade strapped to his uninjured arm.

The knife Karege had been using was a fortune blade. What a strange sight on the arm of a Hesperine's fighting robe. "You're a mercenary?"

Karege had a good laugh. "I love the look on Hesperines' faces when I tell them that. Why should serving in the Stand or getting killed by mages in Tenebra be the only things a Hesperine warrior can do? Border patrol is boring, and I like being alive. Why shouldn't I earn some gold while I'm at it? I know most Hesperines don't have much use for coin, but I'm not most Hesperines."

"I can see that." Lio smiled. "The Goddess gives us freedom to choose our own paths for a reason."

"I like you already. You don't take after the stuffy elders. So what brings you and your sweetheart to such an unlikely place for a romantic getaway?"

"Cassia and I and our guide are here to find the Ashes. Is it possible you're one of them?" What were the odds of meeting any other mercenaries in this forsaken place?

Karege laughed again. "Things aren't as bad as they seem, sunshine. You've found First Blade Ukocha's longest-serving comrade."

"Well, you found me." Lio moved his arm gingerly to give Karege a wrist clasp. "I had no idea one of the Ashes is a Hesperine."

"I advertise, but only my skill. I like for the elders to leave me in peace to enjoy my work. And my money."

How astonishing that Hesperines had played a role in both Cassia and Solia's lives. Hespera, in her mysterious workings, had kept her shadow of protection over both the sisters. "Thank the Goddess. Karege, I am here with Cassia—Solia's sister. If you have been with Ukocha for so long, you must have met Solia."

Karege's brows rose up into his cloud of hair. "Your sweetheart is a girl with freckles and a drooling guard dog?"

Lio grinned. "Oh, yes."

Karege whistled. "Well, this is getting interesting."

Lio was standing in front of someone who knew the truth.

And yet, the secret was still out of reach. "Chuma indicated that you will not be able to answer our questions about Solia unless we reunite her mother and all the Ashes."

"All I can say is that Chuma is a very smart girl."

"She gave us Sanctuary, although Cassia is a shadowlander. We have a great bond of gratitude with her. We promised her we would bring her mother home." Lio took another shallow breath, the pain flaring around his heart. "We found Ipika's blood on a cliffside ledge, but no trace of her. Have we already failed? Do you know what has befallen her?"

Karege's aura dimmed. "Whatever happened, it must have been during the day. Cowards attacking us while I Slumbered. My fortune name didn't do me any favors that day."

"What do you comrades call you, if I may ask?"

"Noon Watch, after the time of day no one wants a Hesperine to stand guard."

Lio grimaced. "I resent our uselessness in daylight hours."

"What's worse, I don't know how they got through my veils."

"And mine." Lio shook his head.

"You mentioned a guide. One of the Azarqi? It seems these unseen enemies can get through their magic, too."

"We had Azarqi supplies, but our guide is a Sandira mercenary by the name of Monsoon."

Karege laughed even harder this time. "Monsoon? You don't say."

"I imagine you have a professional acquaintance with him through Chuma's family."

Karege raised his eyebrows. "Oh, I know Monsoon."

"Or perhaps you have dueled with him in the Court of Claws," Lio revised his theory. He and Cassia had watched Monsoon fight in the elite sparring area at the Sandira Court, where he had humiliated every gold roster mercenary and royal guard who challenged him.

"You don't forget Monsoon." Karege squinted at Lio. "And he doesn't forget you, apparently. So he told you we're here with Ipika?"

"Yes, although he did not reveal the purpose of her journey. I have to wonder how Chuma's mother made enemies such as these."

Karege did not volunteer any further information. "Just remember, whoever did this didn't aim to kill, and all of us in the Ashes are veterans who know how to handle ourselves, even in the Maaqul."

"But what if Ipika was separated from the Ashes?" Lio's power rumbled in his veins again. "Cassia was separated from me."

"Ipika is a strong woman. And so is Cassia, I have no doubt."

"You're right. She is the strongest person I have ever known." His Grace had survived the king's court on her own. She was not a woman to be daunted, even by the Maaqul. "The mortals have a fighting chance."

"But they'll still be glad for the Hesperine errant cavalry to arrive. I've kept on the move ever since I landed out here, hoping to catch a hint of my comrades' auras in the Blood Union. That's how I sensed you."

"I can use my magic to increase the range of our senses."

"Yes," Karege said dryly, "judging by that thelemantic battle cry a moment ago, you've got the mind magic for it."

"Combining our power, we should be able to search much farther."

Lio was ready to speed off in Cassia's direction, but Karege levitated in front of him, arms crossed.

"Before we go," said the elder warrior, "some rules for the road. Nobody has anything to prove out here, youngblood, and the mortals' lives are at stake. If I'm better at something than you are, you listen to me. If you're better at something, I listen to you. If your Craving starts to get in your way, you tell me so I can take it into account. Understood?"

"Thank you, Karege."

"Sorry you're stuck with me for the time being. I know I'm not as pretty as your sweetheart."

"I apologize that I'm such poor company, especially after all your kindness." Lio gave a half-hearted smile. "What have you been drinking out here? I hope you can replenish yourself after your generosity to me."

"Snake blood. I find it quite invigorating."

Well, it seemed Lio would find out how snake blood compared to deer blood for coping with Craving. "My Trial sister's familiar is a serpent. She says their blood has properties that benefit the intellect."

"No wonder I'm such a clever fellow."

"You are an excellent person with whom to be lost in the desert."

"And so is a mind mage like yourself," Karege said. "You aren't just any scrollworm, if you're traipsing across the Maaqul with Monsoon, Cassia, and Knight. Have you seen combat?"

"Yes, but not in the Empire. Only in Tenebra." And Orthros, but Lio preferred not to remember that.

Karege whistled. "Errant in Tenebra already at your age? You may be a youngblood in years, but not in mettle. Ever fight anyone interesting?"

"The usual. A war mage from Cordium, warbands of heart hunters, a Gift Collector." He left out the Old Master.

Karege gave a delighted laugh. "Well, our journey will be much more interesting now that we can swap tales!"

"I'm sure you have many more than I."

"Let's get moving. You can tell me about your other skills on the way. Then I want to hear some war mage stories."

Lio and Cassia had survived those ordeals together. And now they had a powerful connection they had lacked then—the mind ward.

They would not let the Maaqul be the end of them.

65

days until

NOTIAN WINTER SOLSTICE

40 Annassa, 1597 IS

DOERNCHEN

AWN HAD ARRIVED, AND Cassia had found nothing resembling water or shelter. She had taken her time, rationed her strength, and hoped every step would bring her closer to…anything.

Every ache from the long night of searching berated her. Her few hours of sleep gathered in her sandy eyes and foggy head. Moving was the only thing that kept her from freezing.

She thought back over the battle. All the ways she wished it had gone differently taunted her like the mirages of water she saw on the horizon. If only she had dodged the knife. If only she'd had time to take even one sip of water before she'd been sent here.

When she realized she was not alone, she halted in her tracks.

It was the first life form she'd seen. A single, gray-green scrap of a plant rooted proudly in the sand, its little spines pointing threateningly in all directions like the claws of a hissing kitten.

She crouched beside it to rest. She touched her fingers to the tiny patch of shade beneath its twisted form.

"How do you even grow out here?" Her voice came out like the stones on the bottom of a riverbed long dry.

There had to be some kind of water from somewhere, if this plant could grow. Using the smudge of plant life as her landmark, she stood again and turned in a slow circle.

There. One more plant. Everything in her fixed on it.

Now she had a strategy. Follow the plants.

She knelt again, resting a moment longer by the first one. This little twist of thorns may have saved her life.

The jinn had chastised her for not knowing the old garden tongue, which had been spoken in Tenebra long before her time, although it might not seem so old to an immortal. But the jinn had been wrong. She knew a few words, mostly for plants. She had always listened to the wisdom of aging farmers and gardening grandmothers. They remembered the names once used by the sorceresses of the Lustra.

That was how Cassia had known the word for ivy, which was also the name of the Changing Queen from centuries ago, who had been one such sorceress with powerful nature magic. Ebah. Her name was the spell word that unlocked the secret passages inside the royal palace of Tenebra.

Now Cassia wracked her memories for anything that might apply to this little plant.

"*Doernchen,*" she dubbed it. Little thorn. As if she could somehow honor it with the title. Then in Divine, "Thank you."

She got to her feet and headed for the next plant.

When she reached that one, she spotted one more. And when she reached that one, there was another in the distance. There was always one more plant.

Until there were two more. Then three more. Then half a dozen, scattered around her like the whispers of a path.

When she stumbled into a whole patch of them, she laughed and turned in a circle.

From there on out, the way was covered in spiny plants spaced less than a pace apart. She began to see larger ones as tall as her ankles. She was soon navigating between thorn bushes as high as her knees.

She shielded her gaze from the sun and looked as far ahead as she could. No, it wasn't her sun-fevered brain. There was a pattern to those shrubs. They grew around...something.

She tried not to get her hopes up, but by the time she made it to the thicket, she was half running. When she saw what the thorns guarded, she fell to her knees.

She didn't know any names of any old garden goddesses. "Hespera," she rasped, "thank Ebah's ancestors for me."

Water. A little watering hole about as long as she was tall.

Life.

She dipped in her hands and scooped out the sandy, warm liquid, and it felt more wonderful than the clearest, coldest rosewater in Orthros.

She longed to guzzle it until her stomach ached. But mindful of Monsoon's instructions on desert survival, she didn't drink too much, too fast.

Her wound needed attention. It would have to wait. Cleaning it with sandy water seemed a bad idea, and she didn't have the strength to fight with her bandage right now.

She crawled under one of the bushes. Its thorns caught in her robes like welcoming fingers. She let herself collapse in the relative respite of the shade.

At twilight, desert birds joined her at the watering hole. The moons had not risen, but dusk and countless brilliant stars seemed to make wondrous colors appear in the plumage of the drab little birds.

They were so unafraid of her that she wondered if they had ever met a human before. They were magical, lovely messengers of how lost she was.

If she had learned anything from Hesperines, it was that the most wondrous and beautiful things were dangerous, and that power could be benevolent without being safe. The desert was no exception.

Cassia must respect and harness its power, or it would destroy her.

She had to decide what to do. Stay here by the water? Or move onward and hope to find food and shelter?

She could survive for quite a while by the watering hole. Water alone could keep her alive for some time. But she doubted the thorn bushes would provide much in the way of sustenance.

One of the birds hovered before her face, darting back and forth with rapid little wingbeats. One tiny bead of an eye gazed at her, all curiosity.

That's when she realized. She had seen them arrive here. Where had they come from? Somewhere that could sustain life.

She watched them roost among the thorns. Come morning, they would return to wherever they went during the day.

And she would follow.

GRACE UNION

"I CAN'T SEE A LIVING creature in this direction," Karege said.

Lio shook his head, his gaze on the opposite horizon. "There's no one in this direction, either."

Levitating this far off the ground, they had a good view of the surrounding desert with their keen Hesperine eyes. If anything were moving out there, they would have spotted it.

But the ephemeral beacon of the mind ward was like a distant light winking at him, promising his harbor was not unreachable.

In the meantime, he must try not to imagine what Cassia was enduring while she battled the forces of the Maaqul alone. The agony of her distance was so much worse than the constant pain in his chest.

He could feel his flesh pulling and throbbing as it knit sluggishly back together. He had never imagined that healing could be such an unpleasant process. Physical and magical exertion increased his pain. He actually felt tired, as if weariness radiated through his body with his discolored veins.

But whatever poison the sword had spread into his blood, it didn't inhibit his ability to sense Cassia via the mind ward. His other symptoms were irrelevant.

He analyzed his sense of distance again, then ran through some calculations of Hesperine levitation speed in his mind. "It should take us six nights to get to her...if nothing slows us down."

"Ha!" Karege patted his fist against his palm. "I'd like to see anyone or anything try to slow down the two of us."

"It's a good sign that our mysterious attackers have not tried. That encourages me that they haven't gone hunting for the mortals, either."

"Indeed, they seem content to scatter us to the four winds and leave us out here to dry up and blow away. Ha. When they picked a fight with us, they had no idea what they were getting themselves into."

"You're right," Lio agreed. "That greater horn viper the Ashes once beheaded was much more frightening than a lot of humans with rock swords."

"And you've fought hundreds of heart hunters at once. A few desert brigands are no match for you."

Lio was grateful for the storytelling that distracted them from their predicament. The Goddess had led Karege to Lio. If the two of them had landed within a reasonable distance of each other, it was not impossible that they might encounter the other Ashes as well.

"Shall we try listening again?" Lio suggested.

Karege nodded, and they paused in their flight so the rush of air wouldn't interfere with their ability to hear. The night air felt too cold on Lio's skin, sending a shiver through him. Ignoring the Craving chill, he shut his eyes and listened.

When one was a Hesperine, no place was truly quiet, except for private rooms in Orthros layered in spells. But it was quiet here. Few places in the world had ever met his ears with such absolute silence.

Not the scratch of a claw. Not the whisper of a jinn. Not the beat of a heart.

"Nothing," Lio whispered.

He heard the slight movement of air as Karege shook his head. "One more try with the Blood Union, then."

Lio let his auric senses expand and meet Karege's in the Union. Unruly with hunger, Lio's thelemancy raged to the surface. He enhanced their awareness with his power.

"I'll never get used to that," Karege rumbled. "It's a thrill for the Blood Union to feel keener and stretch farther, but..."

"You'd prefer a good, honest sparring match any night," Lio finished for him with a smile.

"Sorry."

Lio pushed their awareness out and out in ever wider circles. "It's all right. My cousin feels the same way. Alas, he's cursed with a mind mage for a father and sister and me for a Trial brother. He keeps our feet on the ground, to be sure."

Karege chuckled. "Sounds like my kind of Hesperine."

"You would get on famously with Mak and my Grace-cousin Lyros. They're both warriors."

"A new generation of warriors? Orthros has gotten much more interesting since I left."

"They're the ones who taught me the strategic search patterns we've been using out here."

Lio felt his awareness fading at the edges. He had reached the limit of his mind magic's geographical range.

But there were dimensions of Grace Union not bound by geography. He focused on Cassia's aura, trying to reach her despite the physical distance.

He savored the moment of connection. He had tried this often when they had been trapped on opposite sides of the border between Tenebra and Orthros. Even then, he had felt a faint awareness of her in his blood.

It was so different now. Their Grace Union had become ever more powerful the longer they had been together. The mind ward now anchored him to her.

"How is she?" Karege asked.

"Alive." Lio swallowed. "But weaker."

"Well," said Karege, "I've thought of something that might cheer you. Let us continue toward your sweetheart, and I'll tell you a different story this time."

"Gladly." Lio let his instincts pull him in the direction of the mind ward.

Karege levitated alongside him. "I can tell you a story about a friend of mine. Someone who traveled with us for a time. She…hmm, how shall I say this? She didn't grow up around Hesperines."

The significance in Karege's tone made Lio meet his gaze. Karege grinned and raised an eyebrow.

Could he be trying to skirt the bounds of the vow of secrecy? Was he devising a way to tell Lio something about Solia?

Lio dare not ask any questions that might prod the limits of the spell. "Go on."

"You should have seen her face the first time we met." Karege laughed. "She wondered what den of monsters she had fallen into. I think she saw her life flashing before her eyes."

Not the reaction of an Imperial. Karege must be talking about a shadowlander—Cassia's sister.

"I can imagine," Lio said.

As a young Tenebran woman, Solia must have come here with all the usual Tenebran prejudices against Lio's people. She would have believed that Hesperines were violent creatures who preyed on humans and lured them to their destruction. She must have been horrified to arrive in a strange land and discover it to be a place where Hesperines roamed free.

Unlike Cassia, she had never had an experience that had shown her the true character of Hesperines. Until Karege, perhaps. "Were you able to convince her she need not fear you?"

"Not at first. Our mutual friends weren't having much luck making things clear to her, either."

Lio's heart sank. He had been so focused on helping Cassia rescue her sister that he had scarcely thought of whether Solia harbored prejudices against Hesperines. But she must have, if she was frightened even in the face of Karege's kindness. "How could she spend time around someone like you and still believe our people are evil?"

"In the end, it was neither my charm, sense of humor, nor excellent musculature that changed her mind." Karege shook his head with a dramatic expression.

Lio's mouth twitched. "But something convinced her?"

"Chuma was barely two days old, and Ipika let me hold her."

"Your Hesperine-averse friend must have been beside herself if she believed the tales of terror about how Hesperines steal children and drink their blood."

"It was quite a shock to her when all I did to the babe was sing her a lullaby." Karege's expression softened. "I rocked Chuma till she giggled. Then she shocked everyone by falling asleep. It was the first time she'd given her mother a moment's peace." He laughed again, an affectionate grin on his face. "It's a good thing Hesperines can be so still. I cast a veil spell over the little mite's ears and didn't move for hours."

Lio smiled at the mental picture of the tiny girl in the Hesperine's powerful arms. He thought of the night when Cassia had persuaded the mages of Kyria to trust Hesperines with two dozen orphans. The night he had met Zoe. She had given him hope and purpose, even as he had to leave Cassia behind. "Children have a way of changing everything."

"So they do. When Chuma woke up from her nap in my arms, safe and happy, my Hesperine-averse friend finally saw matters differently. I think it confirmed everything for her when I helped the midwife change a diaper."

Lio tried not to laugh and disrupt his wound. Relief lifted his spirits. "So she understands our true nature? She trusts us?"

"Oh, yes. She grew quite accustomed to how many of us there are in these parts. She and I became great friends." Karege opened his mouth, as if to say something more, then shook his head.

"I understand." Lio smiled. "Thank you, Karege. You've given me a gift beyond value."

Lio was looking at the Hesperine who had taught Solia their people weren't evil. Thanks to Karege, when Lio and Cassia asked Solia for her blessing, he could expect her to say yes.

64

days until

NOTIAN WINTER SOLSTICE

41 Annassa, 1597 IS

WHISPERS IN THE DESERT

ASSIA GNAWED ON A stem she had dethorned, although it did nothing for the gnawing in her stomach. She had been following the bird all day, but there was nothing but barren desert within sight. Not even a suggestion of water anywhere within walking distance. Her only drink came from sucking on the scarf she had soaked before leaving the watering hole.

The little creature who was her guide darted back and forth across the sand. Sometimes it landed to peck at things of interest she couldn't see, giving her a rest. Then it would take off and flutter away, sending her into a run, lest she lose her only compass in the wilderness.

She pushed herself onward. She couldn't feel her left arm anymore, only a mess of pain there. The lethargy in her body was spreading, and with it, the fear. She was already growing weaker than she had bargained for.

Her foot caught on something, and she stumbled. Vertigo assailed her, and she fell. Hot pain shot through her arm. She landed hard and curled in on herself like a child in the womb.

She wasn't sure she could get up.

She had to get up. The bird was getting away. No, she *would* get up. In a moment.

She heard a rush of air in her ears. All she needed now was a wind to come up and make the dust blow.

No. It wasn't the wind. It was a whisper.

The fear crept closer. She was hearing the ancestors, nowhere near a spirit gate. Did that mean death drew near?

Where was the bird? She couldn't see it now.

This was not how she imagined meeting Hypnos would be. The whispers didn't sound like the god of death. They sounded like the promise of life.

Then a song joined them, trilling and bright. The bird. It landed before Cassia's face, hopping back and forth. Something inside Cassia took flight again.

She hauled herself to her feet and fled the voices, following the flutter of wings.

The hours wore on. Put one foot in front of the other. That was all she had to do. Cassia gave it all her strength. Nothing else mattered. Follow the bird. Rest when it stopped. Move when it flew.

Her body seemed to sink into the shining sand, while her head seemed to float up to the grains of the sky. Her thoughts circled like vultures. She ignored them.

Then a structure before her. Real or not?

Half a temple, rising from the sand as if lifted by a goddess's strength. Or sinking, never to be seen again?

The bird darted through the divine gateway. Cassia tripped on the steps and bumped down into darkness. She landed on her back. Bruised. No cracked head, though.

Blessed darkness.

Cassia heaved a breath. She smelled water and lamp oil and something succulent that made her mouth water.

Surely a dream.

No, she trusted the bird. Cassia crawled deeper in. The sounds of her movements echoed. A large stone chamber.

She came on her knees to the altar, where there was a stone brazier covered in carvings she could not understand, its embers long since gone to ash. The brilliance of sunset flooded down from above, setting the temple aglow in the vivid haze of the desert.

There in the pool of light was a well of water, as deep as Cassia could reach, its bottom a sparkling pile of gems and precious metals. She looked around her. Everywhere the light beamed into the temple, it illumined a tree covered in fat indigo fruits. Their fronds rustled in the breeze that caressed down through the skylights.

Cassia had not died and gone to Sanctuary, for Hespera's realm would be lit by the moons. This was real. A nameless goddess's sacred fruit and water were here for her taking.

"Goddess of the desert," she rasped. "I do not know your name. May Hespera honor our bond of gratitude."

Water, food, and being still restored much of Cassia's alertness. With her mind clearer, she realized she had a fever.

The temple held no remedy for her Craving. Her belly was full, but a deeper hunger clawed at her. No matter how much water she drank, she still felt thirsty. Sheltered inside from the heat of the day, she shivered with unnatural cold.

Even so, she hoped her Craving was the only reason for her fever. If it meant her wound had gone bad, that could kill her much faster.

Resting in a patch of sun beside the pool, she eyed the dust and crusted blood on her makeshift bandage. She would have to clean it. She couldn't avoid it much longer.

Mustering her strength, she dragged herself to the side of the pool. In the hoard below the surface, she spotted a gem-encrusted bowl. That would do for scooping water. Surely it would be no violation of the Accord if she used it here and didn't remove it from the temple.

Dreading the removal of the bandage, she gave into her need to feel clean everywhere else. She laughed a little at herself. Only she would be so determined for a scrub that she would manage it in these conditions. When she was at her worst, bathing was always her compulsion and comfort.

She eased out of her dusty, sweaty robes first, setting the dog flute safely aside. Using the lavish bowl so she wouldn't soil the pool, she poured water over her clothes and washed them out as best she could with only one good arm. She left them drying across the branches of a sun-dappled tree.

Then she washed all of herself except her wound. The trees' fronds were good for scrubbing. The bath left her feeling more like herself, but it exhausted her.

She wished she had managed to keep hold of her gardening satchel, not least because of the soap she kept there. She hated to think of their attacker pawing through the irreplaceable treasures inside. All he had left her with was his dagger and a bad arm.

She couldn't avoid it any longer. She must take off her bandage.

She refilled the bowl and used the stone knife to cut a fresh bandage off her robes, then laid out all her supplies on the smooth stone by the pool.

She stared at the mess on her arm. Everything she had endured had given her a strong tolerance for pain. A flesh wound was nothing compared to the ordeals she had faced. She was stronger than this.

Lifting the bowl, she doused her arm. She was glad she was alone, and no one could hear the humiliating sounds and filthy curses she uttered. It took some time to soak the bandage off and separate it from her skin. By the time she succeeded, her flesh had reopened and started bleeding again. Her head spun, and she shook all over, as if somehow the blood flowing out of her made her need Lio more.

She gritted her teeth and poured water over the bare wound. Spots danced in her vision. She bit her lip hard and tried to focus on the wound. It didn't smell wrong. But her veins were darkly visible all around it, as if some poison the color of the stone blade spread from the wound and through her blood.

She hurried to tie her fresh bandage around the wound. When it was over, she lay still by the pool for a long time, applying pressure to the injury.

She tried to think, to keep her mind busy so she wouldn't slip into sleep or unconsciousness. But she drifted, the warmth of the sun easing her beleaguered body. Her eyes slid closed.

The whispers sang her to sleep. She rested in their embrace. They were so familiar. If she only listened carefully enough, surely she would understand. They were her ancestors, after all.

Her human ancestors. The twisted branch that had produced the king. The rootless seeds that had left her mother with no harvest, casting her into the life of a concubine.

She fought them, trying to struggle out of their reach, to silence them.

She came to with her hands over her ears, her arm in agony. Gasping, she made herself sit up so she wouldn't slip away again.

She spoke to herself just to hear Divine, reciting the names of all the Ritual and elder firstbloods.

"Elder Firstblood Apollon," she said at last, "Gifted by Anastasios, who was Prismos of Hagia Boreia."

She rested her head on her knees, watching the sun glitter on the surface of the water and the pile of long-forgotten wealth beneath.

Generations of treasure lined the bottom. Gold and jewels, carvings of wood and charms of bone. Someone had once loved this goddess. Immeasurable riches, right at her fingertips.

Were these what foolish mortals came seeking in the Maaqul? Did the promise of wealth tempt humans to break the Desert Accord?

She tossed the bejeweled bowl back into the water. None of this interested her. She wanted something else the jinn had. Information.

The question was, did she have anything they wanted?

Cassia had no magic, no treasure, and had even been found deficient in wisdom by the jinn. But one thing she had was skill as a negotiator.

But how did one open negotiations with a jinn?

She didn't want to do it naked and cowering on the ground. She checked her robes and found them warm and dry from the sun. She clothed herself, careful not to disturb her new bandage, and considered her options.

With a sigh, she realized there was one treasure on her person she cared to keep. But if she would feel its loss, would that increase its value to the capricious immortals?

She twisted the gold and coral ring on her index finger. What would such a trinket mean to a jinn who possessed a desert full of riches?

It held even greater value than the gold and coral of which it was made. Captain Ziara, the queen of the Empress's privateers, had given Lio and Cassia these rings when they had done her a favor. But what did an alliance with a seafarer mean to the lords of the sands?

What did the ring mean to Cassia? Ziara's respect. Another victory she and Lio had achieved together. The feel of his hand in hers on the beach, the assurance that he was safe.

What use did the jinn have for respect, love, comfort? She had seen none of those things in their hollow eyes.

What had she seen? Power. The vast might of nature. The mysteries of the spirit.

Life. Death.

Those might be the only forces the jinn valued.

Her gaze fell to the dagger. Her only weapon. It was the one defense she had against death out here, the one tool she could use to fight for her life. It could mean the difference between perishing or surviving.

She picked it up and tossed it into the pool. It sank into the depths, dull amid the glittering array.

"A surprising choice, mortal." The jinn's voice drifted into the temple like the wind, rustling the trees. "Most humans take instead of sacrificing."

"The knife doesn't belong to me," Cassia said. "Nothing here does."

Now she could see the jinn. It hovered in one of the red-gold beams of the setting sun, as if its body was made of all the light of dusk. She didn't recognize its form, but when she met its gaze, she saw through its vivid green eyes to a lush garden that could never exist in the parched sands of the Maaqul. She thought it was the same jinn she had met when she had entered the desert, the one with the predatory eyes and the feathered head.

It spoke again, and this time, she recognized its voice from their previous encounter. "This temple belonged to humans once. Now they are gone, and the desert has reclaimed it."

"I beg your pardon for intruding here. I have eaten only what I needed to survive. Keep the blade with my gratitude."

"Jinn do not practice gratitude."

"Then I hope it pays a debt."

"We do not practice debts. We balance a scale beyond human comprehension."

"Will you read that scale for me then, immortal one, and tell me how I weigh in your eyes?"

"Yes. I will grant you a boon."

Cassia's breath caught. That seemed almost too easy. Was this a trap?

She thought carefully about her words. She didn't want to offend the jinn—or lose the offer of a boon—by questioning it. But she also didn't want to be a boot licker.

"May I ask if there is any additional cost to the boon you are offering?"

Something like laughter echoed through the chamber. "You are clever, too. No. We deem the knife worthy payment for the boon, for sacrificing your weapon could mean paying with your life."

Was that a prophecy? Did jinn have foresight? Or was this merely a heartless prediction after the jinn had watched many mortals before her lose their battle with the Maaqul?

It didn't matter. She had not expected a bargain with a jinn to come easily.

"Some things are more important than my own survival," Cassia said.

"Few humans who enter the desert weight their choices as you do."

"I will take my chances without the knife."

"Very well. By the Desert Accord, I cannot intervene in your situation. I cannot act. But ask me any question, and I shall give you information to guide your own actions—if you survive long enough to use it."

"If I ask you why Lio has not stepped to me, will that use my boon?"

"Yes and no, little mortal. The secrets of the desert come at a great cost, but the rules, I will teach you." The jinn extended a clawed, feathered finger toward the knife that now lay at the bottom of the pool. "Only the lithic edges give humans the power to move as the jinn do."

"Lio isn't human."

"He is not one of my kind."

"So the weapon sent him somewhere, too?"

"As you have learned, where you end up is not always predictable."

What were these strange weapons the jinn called 'lithic edges'? Should Cassia ask more about them? Would that give her an advantage?

"Ask me more than that," it warned, "and you will use your boon."

She could only ask for one thing. This was her sole chance to tap the wisdom of the immortals of the Maaqul and access their unfathomable secrets.

She could ask it where Lio was.

Her every instinct screamed that nothing was more important than her Grace. That she must do anything, sacrifice everything to find him.

But she heard Chuma say, *I have to think about what's best for everyone.*

Cassia must make the best, the wisest choice. Not just for herself. For all of them brought together and torn apart by this strange quest.

Cassia thought of Chuma waiting at home for her mother. Of how she herself would feel if she survived the desert and knew Ipika hadn't. She imagined telling Chuma she would never see her mother again.

She thought of her own words along this journey. *We are Hesperines errant, Lio. I may not have the fangs yet, but I have the heart.*

Would she let those be nothing more than words? Or would she act upon them and show she had the heart?

She knew what the right choice was. She knew it, and Lio would know it too.

She didn't need an almighty jinn to reunite her with her Grace. That was already within her mind mage's great power. She might not know Lio's location, but he knew hers.

They were partners, working together, even now.

She had faith in Lio to find her. Hespera had made him her Grace, and her his. The Goddess had written it in the laws of the world. They would find each other.

But oh, how it pained her not to ask for him in this moment. She had thought she had prepared herself for the cost of this boon, but she had been wrong. This price cut deep.

"Tell me where Chuma's mother is," Cassia requested.

"As you will," said the jinn.

It reached toward her with a clawed hand. Her every instinct screamed for her to shrink back, but she stood her ground.

The feathers on the back of its hand stood on end. Light like the sun glowed from its palm. It extended one finger and touched the tip of its claw to her chest.

Pain pricked her heart, and a bright flash erupted behind her eyelids. Her eyes squeezed shut, and she gritted her teeth. Still she did not scream or back away.

When the spots and tears on her vision faded, and she could see again, the jinn was gone.

But there was a new awareness within her. An inner guide. A compass as sure as the thorns in the desert.

PEANUT

LIO HUNG ONTO THE tattered threads of Cassia's emotions. "She is less afraid tonight. What could that mean?"

"Less afraid is good news." Karege's voice echoed in the Blood Union they shared through Lio's thelemancy.

Lio sustained the connection, holding their range at the farthest limit. The only life forms nearby were yellow dwarf bushes sprouting from the red sand. But Grace Union continued to bring him Cassia's emotions from afar.

A sense of hope lifted her. And yet, she grew weaker every night. He could sense her symptoms, vague echoes of the acute sensations in his own body. His chest burned and ached, as if the wound really had torn at his heart. He tried to feel encouraged, but the Craving played with his mind. He had survived it for half a year; it took him aback that he was struggling with it now, after only two nights. But his body was damaged and trying to heal, which made his need for his Grace's blood all the more severe.

Blood hunger conjured horrific imaginings of what she might be going through. A vivid mental image came to him of Cassia with a sword through her chest. He pushed the thought away with all his might.

"Do you sense any of your comrades?" he asked Karege to keep his mind where it belonged.

Karege sighed. "No, not a—wait. Wait!"

Karege's senses stretched. Lio poured more thelemancy into the Union, his thirsty power flowing in uneven pulses.

Karege gave a shout and levitated swiftly over the next line of bushes.

Lio glided after him, the motion sending an uncomfortable rush of air over the torn skin on his chest. "Who is it, Karege?"

"Don't you sense her?"

Lio searched again for any hint of a presence. "I don't—"

He stopped himself. There was definitely something. Not a person's presence, but an auric ripple of some kind. Familiar, touching the Union, in and out of sight.

Magic. Mind magic. No, mind healing. "A mind healer is signaling us?"

"It's Tuura!" Karege said in delight. "That rascal of a diviner."

They levitated onward for nearly an hour, tracking the other mage. The ground below them became uneven, scored with low ridges and little gullies. The fellow mind grew stronger and stronger, nearer.

The hint of magic strengthened into a powerful, feminine aura, rich with the affinity for theramancy. The Ashes' diviner was truly someone of stature in theramancy, the Imperial mind healing tradition.

At long last, their destination came into sight. A small lean-to in a ditch, fashioned out of a vibrant yellow robe.

Karege landed and knelt in front of the opening. "Peanut! By the ancestors, I am glad to see you."

"Noon Watch," came the woman's deep, affectionate voice. "You got my message."

Lio crouched beside Karege. "Your magical signal is the best thing we've heard in this silent tomb of a desert."

"Peanut, meet Lio. Lio, this is Tuura, diviner of the Ashes, spirit travel expert, master herbalist—and worst enemy of nefarious ground nuts."

Tuura rested on her side under the lean-to. Her brightly colored head wrap was slightly askew, her long tunic smeared with dust and blood, but her cheerful round face lit with a dimpled smile. "Hello, Lio. How pleasant to meet you in person, and not just through our magic."

"It is an honor, diviner." Lio smiled.

"I'm quite happy to see you, too."

"What happened?" Karege asked. "How did we get separated?"

A strong fragrance of astringent herbs wafted from her. It seemed she had managed to keep some of her magical supplies with her. A gnarled wooden staff rested at her side, along with her medicine bag and a waterskin.

She patted the flattened vessel. "I'd love to explain it to you over a drink, but I've recently run out of water. I don't suppose you two immortals can offer me anything other than your preferred beverage?"

Karege put his hands on his hips. "What sort of Hesperines would we be if we didn't take the needs of our mortal comrades into account? We scented water earlier tonight and made note of where it was, in case we found any of you thirsty. We'll head back there now."

"Ah, Karege, who needs the cavalry when they have you? Be a dear and help me up, would you?"

"Are you all right, Peanut?"

"I admit I may be just a little bit dizzy from rationing my provisions and some blood loss."

"Blood loss?" Karege roared.

"Just a shoulder wound. Nothing to worry about."

"It was a distress signal! Why didn't you say so? How bad is it? I can't smell blood past the herbs in your medicine bag!"

"You two look rather the worse for wear yourselves." She peered at Karege's arm with concern, then frowned deeply at Lio's chest wound.

"I'm in excellent condition," Karege declared, "and all that's wrong with Lio is being separated from his sweetheart. Fangs a bit on edge at the moment, you understand."

"I may be able to help. First, let us all patch each other up."

"I'm going to carry you." Karege reached inside the lean-to.

She tapped his chest with her staff, fending him off. "I can walk. Just lend me your good arm."

"Pretend we're competing in the holy goat race at the children's festival in Golden Ways and let me carry you."

Tuura's eyes twinkled. "I'm still surprised they let me enter with a Hesperine partner. It was an unfair advantage."

"I've never seen someone play the role of a holy goat with such shamanic dignity. The first place ribbon looked well on you."

Lio added this to his list of stories he wanted to tell Zoe when they made it out of this wretched desert.

Karege gathered the plump diviner into his arms with care and not a hint of how much his arm must hurt. She patted his cheek with a soft hand. Lio collected her yellow robe for her.

"Onward to the oasis!" Tuura said with cheerful enthusiasm.

Lio suspected that was her way of encouraging them to hurry. "Diviner, would you care for some pain relief on the way?"

"I advise you to save your magic," she replied.

Lio pursed his lips. "I believe my resources to be sufficient."

"We don't entirely understand the effects of these stone weapons. Spare your efforts for finding the others."

"As you Will."

They traveled back the way they had come, toward the water source they had smelled earlier. Tuura was mostly quiet on the way, although she listened intently as Karege and Lio caught her up on what had befallen the two of them.

"It's a good thing the ancestors sent you to Karege," she said.

"Is that why I ended up near a fellow Hesperine?" Lio asked.

"Did you think it was chance?" the diviner replied.

"I didn't know if the ancestors intervene on Hesperines' behalf."

"Of course they do!" Karege looked at him askance. "Just because we can't hear them when we go through the spirit gates doesn't mean they aren't aware of us. Do the stars in the sky sit still?"

Lio thought of the image of Prometheus he had seen in Karege for a brief moment. "No. No they don't."

By the time they reached the water, Lio did smell Tuura's blood, and her sweat gleamed on her deep brown skin. Karege made her comfortable beside the rivulet of water that ran through a fold between two sandy ridges. The little yellow bushes lined the lip of the oasis overhead, providing cover from the unruly dust dancing about on a midnight breeze.

Karege refilled Tuura's waterskin, helping her drink in small sips. Lio resorted to drinking some water. It wouldn't help his kind of thirst, but at least it soothed his Craving-parched throat for a moment.

"Much better," Tuura said. "Now all I need is a bandage and a shave, and I'll feel like myself again." She gave the stubble on her chin a scratch.

Tuura made Lio think of Nodora's Ritual mother, Matsu. She had also been born with a female spirit and a male body.

A sudden wave of homesickness hit Lio. How he wished he was back home at the Kitharan theater with Cassia and Nodora and their Trial circle, watching another of Matsu's triumphs on stage.

But he thanked the Goddess that he was with people like Karege and Tuura in the midst of this crisis.

Karege patted his fortune blade. "It won't be the first time we've had to shave the mercenary way. Lio, you wouldn't happen to have any fancy soap from Orthros hiding in your pockets, would you?"

Longing for his Grace stabbed at him again. "Cassia might, if she were here. She loves fancy soaps."

Tuura sighed. "Where's Hoyefe when you need him? He probably landed with his full mustache-grooming kit and a bottle of scent oil."

"Hoyefe?" Lio asked.

"Our light mage," Karege explained, "and professional interrogator. He's a very persuasive fellow. I don't know why. I'm always surprised people can even see to find him attractive, his vaingloriousness is so blinding."

Under Karege's cheerful ribbing of his absent comrade, Lio sensed the discordant worry within the two mercenaries. Their words were a way of keeping Hoyefe with them, to distract themselves from their fear about wherever he had landed.

Tuura rummaged in her medicine bag with one hand, keeping her other arm still. "Let's patch each other up. I don't like that your wounds aren't healing, and I'm not entirely sure whether my remedies will have an effect. Let's find out."

"The Gift will heal us eventually," Karege protested. "You should save the medicines for yourself and any of our mortal comrades who might need it."

"We need our Hesperines in good condition, too."

"Our magic is uninhibited," Lio said, "and we can tolerate the inconveniences of our wounds. Please reserve your remedies."

"Very well. If you two are determined to be stubborn."

"You know that once I dig my heels in," said Karege, "there's no arguing with me."

"But I argue all the same," Tuura replied, "and I usually win."

"Nonsense. I seem to recall I just won our most recent argument about carrying you."

"What about the ten arguments before that?"

Vela Roth

Karege made a noise of protest, but then said, "You are injured, diviner. It would be ignoble of me to argue with you further at a time like this."

Lio added another point to Tuura's score.

"Well," she said, "if you're not going to argue, make some bandages from my robe."

Karege frowned again. "You need your robe to provide shelter when the sun comes up."

Tuura shook her head. "If you sacrifice any more of your clothing for bandages, you'll have to run about the desert in your underlinens."

"Hesperines don't need armor *or* clothes to hold up in a fight."

"As entertaining as it always is to see you wrestle in your natural state, I think you'd best keep what's left of your fighting robe. Slumbering naked in the sun will just make you wake up grumpy."

Lio could only imagine the many adventures the two friends had shared. He had to wonder if they had ever considered becoming more than friends.

Lio glanced at his own tattered travel attire. "I can spare another part of my clothes. I shall have to risk offending Hoyefe's sense of fashion when we meet him."

Karege grinned. "Good idea. Let's tear that robe to fighting length. As long as you're traveling with the Ashes, you're an honorary warrior."

"Thank you, Karege." Lio felt much more like a warrior than a diplomat lately.

"Lio," asked Tuura, "do you know anything about alchemy?"

"I don't consider myself an alchemist," Lio said, "but I did practice it avocationally for a time."

Karege sighed.

Tuura patted his arm. "Karege is excellent when you need someone to carry you in the holy goat race, but the only person more useless than him at mixing things is Ukocha herself. You should have seen the time they tried to bake together. I'm surprised the death toll wasn't higher. You can be my extra pair of hands while I make a poultice."

Lio bowed to her. "I'm honored to assist, diviner. I did requisite service in the Healing Sanctuary with Annassa Soteira, so hopefully I will be of use to you."

"Did you, now?" Karege asked with interest.

"All mind mages do." Lio hadn't meant to draw attention to himself.

"But not always with one of the Queens." Karege squinted at Lio.

"Our Queens are generous with their time. So is my Grace-cousin, who serves as one of Annassa Soteira's apothecaries." Lio wished Javed was with them even now.

Lio held things for Tuura and followed her instructions as she mixed a poultice using her precious supplies, some water, and a flat stone he found for her nearby. The comforting scent of herbs wafted through their little Sanctuary in the desert, and her powerful theramancy filled the air, reminding Lio very much of home.

Lio borrowed Karege's fortune blade to modify his robe, handing over the knife and the fabric for the warrior to make bandages. The elder's cleaning spell left the fabric and his knife spotless.

"All right, Peanut," Karege said. "One thing I can do is apply the poultice."

"It's certainly not the first time you've patched me up." She smiled. "It's my left shoulder."

Karege carefully investigated the bloodstained area on one of her shoulders. His reaction made Lio's ears throb. "Those sneaking cowards shot you from behind!"

Tuura rubbed an ear with her good hand. "Unfortunately, the best I could do was break off the shaft. I couldn't reach to get the arrowhead out myself. I believe the stone is affecting my magic."

"What *are* these weapons?" Karege growled.

"I have a theory," Tuura said, "which I can explain much better once one of them is no longer attached to me."

Karege sat behind her and examined the wound further. "How about some of that pain relief now, Sunshine?"

"Might I?" Lio asked Tuura. "In truth, I have plenty of thelemancy."

"He once knocked out three hundred heart hunters in one fell swoop," Karege said.

"Is that so?" Tuura's brows rose. "Well, I suppose a moment of pain relief wouldn't set you back too much. Go right ahead."

Lio closed his eyes and concentrated on Tuura's mind. Once again, he found himself in awe of her bright, deep magical power. Careful to tread respectfully in such a great mind, he applied his thelemancy to ease her discomfort.

He heard the rustle of cloth, and the smells of blood and steel stung his nose as Karege worked. But not a whisper of pain from Tuura.

At last, she sighed. "Much better."

Lio bowed out of their joined minds and opened his eyes.

Tuura smiled at him. "I can tell you're from Orthros. You have a silk-glove approach. They trained you well."

"High praise from you, diviner. Thank you."

Her smile faded. "It goes against my grain as a healer to leave you with a wound of your own."

"My cure is out of reach for the time being. Please, what can you tell us about who attacked our two parties?"

Tuura sighed. "We were all getting some sleep in the heat of the day, except Hoyefe, who had taken watch. But I never heard him call an alarm. What woke me was the spirit tears."

Karege's brow furrowed. "Spirit tears?"

"That's the best way I can describe them. They're nothing like properly cast spirit gates. They're painful disruptions, as if someone tore right through to the ancestors' realm. By the time I got out of my tent with my staff in hand, the attackers had descended upon us. It was an ambush by warriors with shrouded faces, all armed with the stone weapons."

"How did the battle go?" Karege's aura was tight with tension.

"Hoyefe was nowhere to be seen," Tuura went on. "The rest of us fought hard, but they had the advantage of surprise. I managed to down one with my staff, but before I could deal him a blow that would render him unconscious for questioning, he disappeared."

"No one spirit walks in the Maaqul," Karege protested. "You've always said that it can't be done."

Tuura nodded. "No one's ancestors have a claim on the desert."

"Even Kella can only spirit walk in the Scorched Verge." Karege glanced at Lio. "She's Azarqi. Our second blade."

"The attacker didn't spirit walk," Tuura answered. "He opened a spirit tear. I saw the air ripple and felt the ancestors' nearness. He escaped through the opening, and then it closed behind him."

"What in all the martyrs' stars—?" Karege sputtered.

"It gets worse," Tuura said. "I owe you an apology, my friend. One of our attackers got past my guard and made it to where you were sleeping."

Karege's aura gentled. "Peanut, you're our diviner. We warriors are supposed to protect you in combat, not the other way around."

Tuura sniffed. "All the same, no member of the Ashes is useless in a fight. I did my best to defend you in your Slumber. But we were outnumbered. I saw him inflict the wound on your arm with his dagger. When the blade pierced your flesh, you disappeared through a spirit tear."

"That's how I ended up in the middle of nowhere? What happened to the others?"

"The arrow hit me right after that, and I was sent away as well. The last thing I saw, Ukocha was still raining fire upon them."

"You didn't see what happened to Ipika?" Lio asked.

Tuura shook her head, her eyes apologetic.

Lio swallowed, his mouth dry as sand again. "The same attackers must have ambushed Monsoon and Cassia while I slept. Even with Knight, they would be far outnumbered."

"Don't lose hope," Tuura said. "Everything I saw confirms what you and Karege concluded. The attackers were not striking to kill."

"Or to take prisoners," Karege pointed out.

That still meant his Grace was wounded and lost in the desert. He longed to gather her in his arms and ease her every hurt. Right before he found the attackers who had done this and showed them how Apollon's son delivered justice.

Karege patted his shoulder. "Try to put your fangs back in your head, youngblood."

Lio rubbed his mouth. What an impolite display to make in front of a respected diviner. "My apologies."

"We understand," Tuura assured him kindly.

Thinking with his fangs would not help Cassia at the moment. "Can you tell us more about these spirit tears and how they work? You said you have a theory?"

Tuura nodded. "Do you understand the general properties of the natural phase and the spirit phase?"

"Yes, diviner. Although I am not from the Empire, I was taught about ancestral magic by my loved ones of Imperial origin. The natural phase is the physical world, where we all have life. The spirit phase is the realm of the ancestors, whence our spirits come and to which they return. Hesperines' immortality is a union of flesh and spirit that binds us to the natural phase, making the physical world fluid to us. And yet because the Gift binds us here, we cannot hear the ancestors or cast ancestral magic."

Tuura nodded. "I'm glad this was part of your education. It's important for everyone to understand, no matter what part of the world you came from."

"Of course," Karege agreed. "We may not be able to use ancestral magic, but it still works on us. For instance, we can travel through spirit gates cast by someone else, even if we can't step through them."

"We can't step through spirit gates," Lio echoed in realization. "Could the spirit tears and our inability to step out here be connected somehow?"

Tuura's gaze became distant, and her magic swelled. "Now that the arrowhead is out, my magic is recovering. Based on what I'm sensing, I believe your inability to step has to do with where we landed after the stone weapons banished us. They sent us into…it's difficult to describe. The nature of the magical landscape is different here."

"It doesn't feel different to me," Karege said, "but then, my only magic is the Gift."

Lio shook his head. "I can't sense anything unusual either, even with my affinities."

"You two wouldn't sense it," Tuura replied. "You would have to be attuned to the spirit phase to be aware of it. This is the territory of ancestors not my own, and yet my ancestors feel somehow closer than ever before."

"So it has to do with where in the desert we are?" Lio asked. "Some kind of regional effect?"

Tuura looked thoughtful. "Or an effect radiating from something… or someone."

"Jinn magic?" Karege wanted to know.

"It feels akin to the jinn," the diviner answered, "but…bigger. Like the sky is to a storm."

"Who are these warriors?" Lio wondered. "Why send us to this place? What do they want?"

Tuura and Karege exchanged a look.

"We know this much," said Tuura. "The warriors who attacked us are known Accord breakers."

Lio sucked in a breath. "There are rogue mortals in the desert breaking the Accord with the jinn? Then there is more at stake here than Cassia and I understood."

"This could get more dangerous," Karege chose that moment to inform Lio.

"Could the stone weapons be jinn artifacts?" Lio wondered. "The Accord breakers might have stolen them."

"We don't know for certain," said Tuura, "but they're not like any human weapons I ever believed could exist."

Lio looked down at the discolored veins of his chest. There might be jinn magic in his blood even now. Cassia might be carrying the same kind of wound, and she didn't even have the Gift to mitigate its effects. "Diviner, you said the arrowhead was inhibiting your theramancy. What effect could such a wound have on Cassia? We believe her to be a mage, but we don't know her affinity yet."

"It's difficult to theorize," Tuura said, "but I must admit, even with the arrowhead out, I feel as if the stone left a mark on me of some kind."

The thought hurt worse than the sword that had torn Lio from Cassia.

Karege stroked his beard. "If the stone weapons send us all into the region where magic doesn't work right, perhaps we didn't land as far apart as we feared after all."

"And I can sense where the tears were," Tuura told them.

Karege's face lit up. "Well, of course you can, Peanut. That's our diviner, always coming to the rescue."

His words took the edge off the regrets in her aura. "I can detect the disruptions left behind in this unusual magical territory. If Lio lends his mind magic to extend my range, as he did for you with the Blood Union, I hope to pinpoint locations where our companions landed."

"Goddess bless," said Lio, "that gives us great hope, diviner. I am at your service."

Karege folded her robe into a pillow. "After you rest."

She let him put it behind her head. "I suppose I'll give these herbs some time to work on my wounds. Why don't I lie here and tell Lio a story while we wait for the Dawn Slumber to catch up to you two?"

"Rest," Karege repeated.

"But Lio and Cassia have come so far to hear the stories only we can tell them."

Lio should join Karege in encouraging Tuura to rest. But he couldn't bring himself to stop her, if this was another hint about Solia.

Tuura smiled fondly and began her tale the same way Karege had. "We had a friend who traveled with us for a while."

"A friend who didn't grow up around Hesperines?" Lio guessed.

Karege nodded with that significant look in his eyes again.

"She didn't grow up around the written word, either," said Tuura.

"I dare say she had not seen more than three books in her life." Or so Cassia had told Lio. Tenebran women were not given an education, unless they were temple mages.

"A very educated guess," Tuura approved. "Every time she saw me reading one of my scrolls, I could see the curiosity in her eyes. And yet she hesitated to ask."

"Why would she hesitate to seek an education when given the opportunity?"

"She was very focused on her other goals."

Was that the plan Ziara had mentioned? Perhaps her plan for how to get back to Cassia?

"She felt responsibility toward others," Tuura said. "I realized it would require some convincing for her to take better care of herself, especially her mind. So one day, I told her I needed an extra pair of hands on a trip to a trader."

"What kind of trader?" Lio asked.

"A scroll seller," Tuura explained. "One of my favorites, a supplier of rarities. But arcane texts are not all he trades in. He also has an eye for the most delightful epic poetry and children's storybooks."

Lio grinned. He began to understand Tuura's clever plan.

The diviner shared a conspiratorial smile with him. "While the trader and I were haggling, my friend couldn't resist nosing around his selection. I caught her looking through the illustrations, although she couldn't read a word of the Imperial dialects. I paid attention to which volumes intrigued her the most. Then I made sure he included them in the price."

"That was such a kindness."

"Oh, it was the best fun. When she saw that I had bought them all to bring with us on our travels, she could bear the frustration no longer. She begged me to teach her to read Imperial languages."

"Did you have time to teach her?"

"Oh yes, she became quite proficient. A fast learner, once she put her mind to something. From then on, whenever there was a bookshop or scroll trader where we stopped, she and I went on another treasure hunt. It was lovely to have someone to share my love of books."

"They weren't safe in the bookshops," Karege said. "We tried to hide their coin purses."

"Never come between a woman and the next volume in the series she's reading," Tuura scolded.

Karege sighed. "Alas, I learned that lesson the hard way."

"Thank you, Tuura," said Lio. "I'm so grateful to hear more about your friend."

These little pieces of Solia's life began to fit together. Lio was so glad to know she had not been alone. He could see how much her world had expanded after she had left Tenebra. She'd had the support of friends and the opportunity to improve her mind.

"Now then," said Tuura, "I think I'll take a little nap before I shave."

Lio fought at the exhaustion that dragged at him. The sun was coming for him again, and he would spend another day without Cassia.

But he could look forward to telling her about Solia's life here. Perhaps when they all returned to Orthros together, Lio would not be the only one helping Cassia learn to read Imperial languages.

To keep his bleaker imaginings at bay, he allowed himself to envision the two sisters, their heads together over a scroll in one of Orthros's beautiful libraries. Safe.

MWEYA'S WINGS

CASSIA KNEW WHERE SHE was headed. Night was falling. It was time to go.

The problem was that her hands shook. Her knees were weak. Impossible thirst burned in her throat. She felt utterly hollow, like a sandstorm that wanted to suck in everything around it.

"Lio survived the Craving for six months," she encouraged herself. "He even managed to not throw up in front of Zoe and to revolutionize Hesperine and Tenebran politics. I can walk across this sunbound, vulture's ass of a desert."

She looked up the steps that led out of the temple. They seemed as tall as Hypatia's Observatory, the highest tower in Orthros.

When a man's silhouette blocked out her view of the night sky, she stumbled backwards.

Had the attackers found her?

The figure spread his wings. Wings. She realized he was her ally too late to stop herself from falling.

Through the roar in her ears, she heard him swoop down. He caught her before she fell and eased her to the floor, leaning her against the nearest wall.

"Monsoon." Her lips cracked as she smiled.

"Are you all right?"

"I'm alive. And so are you." She shut her eyes. There was hope for everyone else, too.

He lifted her eyelids and felt her forehead. "You look like a siren's nectar addict in a back alley of the Moon Market. I've never seen heatstroke do this to a person."

"It's Craving." She frowned. "Lio has more practice holding up than I do."

"What? I didn't think humans got symptoms from it."

"We do. Although most humans I've talked to only had emotional effects, not physical ones like I get." She sighed. "It's getting worse."

"But you can't drink his blood to cure it."

"No."

"And yet you put off your Gifting."

"Yes."

"To find your sister."

She nodded and rested her head back against the wall. "But first we have to find Chuma's mother. I know where she is."

"You—what? How?"

"Bargained with a jinn. It gave me some kind of inner sense of direction. I can lead you to her."

"Mweya's Divine Wings." Monsoon sat back on his heels, his feathers ruffling. "A jinn offered you a boon, and you used it to find out where Chuma's mother is?"

"It didn't offer. I asked."

"You silkfoots are such sentimental fools." Despite his words, Monsoon had never been so gentle as he was now. He wrapped his wings around her shivering form.

"Oh," she said. "It's very warm under here."

"So I've been told." His wings wrapped closer around her. "I'm sorry, Cassia. I never should have let him wound you."

"Neither of us saw the knife."

"But I should have stopped him."

She knew the tone of a protector who wouldn't see reason about what he perceived to be his own failures. She had just never expected to hear it from Monsoon on her behalf. "It's not your fault."

"I should have warned you." He hesitated. "I've fought these men before. But back then, they never used anything like that knife. When you disappeared, it took me by surprise. I let myself be distracted an instant too long."

His anger when he had seen the tattoo made sense now. Questions beleaguered Cassia. Her Craving focused her hazy mind on one thought. "What happened to Lio?"

"I'm sorry, Cassia. I don't know. I didn't see anything before his knife cast me to the middle of nowhere."

Cassia blinked away the threat of tears. She knew Lio was alive. They would find him. "You're wounded too? Are you all right?"

"He got my foot."

"Your foot? Monsoon, how bad is it?" Many a warrior had lost his entire way of life to such an injury. Cassia looked at the bandage around Monsoon's foot, remembering the knee injury that had changed Callen's life forever.

It was the same foot she had bruised when he had first flown off with her. Ages ago, it now seemed, when she had thought him her enemy. Now his jests about his instep didn't seem funny at all.

"I'll live," he said.

Callen had also lived to never march in the army again, until Queen Soteira herself had rebuilt his knee with her magic. Cassia could not allow Monsoon to lose a career on the gold roster because of her contract. "When we make it out of this desert, the Hesperine healers will fix your foot for you. I'll make sure of it."

"It's all right, Cassia. My people's healers will be able to fully repair it. Sandira physicians blend ancestral shapeshifting and healing magic. They can alter the body in powerful ways."

Cassia breathed a sigh of relief. "What are you going to do until then?"

"Good thing I have wings," he said.

"Is that how you found me? You flew all the way here from—wherever you landed?"

"I had some help. When I was transported, I heard voices between one place and the next. I don't know how it's possible, but they must have been my ancestors. The stone weapons seem to be artifacts that open up fleeting passages through the spirit phase."

"Like small spirit gates."

"Yes, although these are unstable and temporary. It still gave my ancestors the opportunity to intervene."

"They told you where to find me?"

"Don't sound so apprehensive."

"Well, I've been worrying someone's ancestors would hunt me down. I didn't expect it to be yours, helping us."

"It's not as if they drew me a map. They gave me impressions, flashes of things that are symbolic to my people. It's a good thing for you I pay attention during religious rituals and understood they meant for me to fly south. Even so, it took me two days of searching before I spotted this temple and came to check if you'd found shelter here."

"You were lost in the desert with Chuma's mother missing, and you looked for me first?"

He shrugged.

"Apparently sentimentality isn't only a silkfoot characteristic." She gave his fortune blade a poke.

There was a smile in his voice. "So, what did you hear when the knife hit?"

Cassia thought of the whispers urging her to her feet when she thought she couldn't go on. Of the little bird, waiting patiently for her to get up. "I don't know."

"Fine, I won't pry. But considering they sent you to a ruin with water and food instead of skeletons and booby traps, I'd consider showing them more appreciation from now on."

"Hesperines can't hear their ancestors. If the attackers banished Lio using one of the stone weapons, he won't have any help."

"Just because he can't hear them doesn't mean they won't help."

Cassia tried to take comfort in that. "Do you suppose there are any animal spirits out here that would have some compassion for Knight?"

"I don't doubt it. Besides, Knight has the best survival instincts of all of us."

Her Craving didn't often listen to reason, but it was so unusual for Monsoon to say something comforting that she took it to heart.

"I can't be sure," Monsoon said, "but based on the geography, I think we could be in the same region of the Maaqul as where we were attacked. You and I landed within a few days' travel of each other. So our comrades could be scattered, but not at impossible distances. We should keep trying to find the others, starting with Ipika."

"I've fashioned a sling bag for the fruit from scraps of my robe, but I have no way to carry water."

"You're in luck. I had a waterskin on me when we were attacked."

"What about your map?"

"I have it, but it's useless. I can't tell where we might be. Neither this temple nor any other landmark I've seen out here matches anything on my map."

"Well, at least we have provisions. I'm afraid I may have to ask you to carry them."

"That won't be a problem."

"Walking could be a problem, but I'll do my best to be our feet if you'll be our wings."

He picked her up with such care, it didn't even hurt. "You're not going to walk, *nyakimbi*. I'm going to carry you."

The unexpected endearment made her throat dry and her eyes moist. "Thank you, Monsoon."

"You have my gratitude as well."

THE BRAID

THE HEAT OF THE forge rippled around Mak's creation, making the braid of metal seem to wave like real hair. He held his tongs steady, keeping the piece in the heat.

The length and thickness of his forearm, the adamas braid was his most ambitious piece yet, and just as likely to be a failure.

"Just a moment longer." Nike's aura vibrated with tension.

Mak had spent night after night hammering, bending, and weaving three cords of adamas into the shape of a vow. He had layered more metal and magic into it every time. He might be built like a bear, but this alloy had humbled his perception of his own physical strength. And although their mother's ancient warding magic flowed through his veins, he had learned what it meant to test his power.

Within a matter of moments, his latest labor to achieve perfect adamas could be ruined before his eyes.

"Do you feel it yet?" his sister asked.

"No. I'm still pushing my magic into it. It's not pulling."

"It will. If you've performed each step correctly, your magic will bond to the alloy and the enchantment will become self-sustaining."

She had repeated the instructions over and over. Mak kept trying, kept waiting for that moment when his adamas would take on a life of its own. Was he about to see another labor of love turn into a lump of useless metal?

"I've studied," he said through gritted teeth. "I've practiced. What will it take, Nike?"

"Why are you doing this, Mak?" Her voice echoed around them in the underground chamber, a secret within a secret under stone and wards and veils.

"Because I'm impulsive and stubborn. I don't know when to hold back—or give up."

"That is not what motivates you. You are a Steward of full rank in the Stand. You have a spotless service record. Our parents are proud of you, and you have a Grace waiting at home. Why are you risking all of that for adamas?"

Why was he doing this? Asking for his parents' ire, confirming his Grace's fears?

"You shaped this into a braid," Nike said. "Why? What promise are you making?"

"I made a promise to protect Orthros."

"You can do that with wards and fists. Why adamas?"

Geomagical heat bathed him in waves as frustration surged in him. It felt wrong to push that into the metal. That would not forge the right Union with his creation. He would not taint something meant to protect with the poison of anger.

But he was so angry. His family had nearly been assassinated, and he had not been there to defend them. The Collector had breached Orthros's defenses, and he had not been there to stand against him.

"I'm making a promise to myself," he said. "No one I love will be without my protection ever again. When I'm not within reach, my creations will be."

Mak's magic spun out of his control. The shadows of his warding power formed a dark whorl inside the forge, then spiraled into the braid.

He gasped, bracing his feet against the force of the connection. The braid glowed bright, nearly blinding. His heart pumped blood magic through his veins and into the alloy, infusing the adamas with part of himself.

Nike let out a sound of triumph. "Now take it out. Quickly."

He yanked the braid from the forge. As he plunged it into the nearby trough of glacial runoff, he raked his fangs across his wrist and splashed his blood into the water.

A wave of dizziness overcame him, but he stood steady as the steam hissed around him. His wrist healed. The forge quieted.

In the ensuing silence, he stood holding the tongs.

"It's safe to take it out now," said Nike.

With care, he lifted his creation from the icy water. The spell lights in the forge glistened on it, as if it were spun of moonstuff and starlight.

"It worked," Mak said in a hushed tone.

Nike's pale hand hovered over the shining metal, her eyes sliding shut. Her own warding magic rose in the Union, laced with her mind magic. Then her eyes snapped open again, and her ancient gray gaze fixed on Mak.

"Well done, Brother. You've just become the second smith in Orthros's history to master the secrets of adamas."

He heaved a breath. "We should test it. Just to be sure."

Nike smiled, but her aura was grim. She took a few steps backward and raised a ward before her. She became a vague silhouette behind the bulwark of her magic. The shadow ward looked as deep as the sky.

Mak knew that spell. It was a ward powerful enough to crack bones and steel.

He cast one more gaze at the braid, wondering if this was the last time he would ever see it in its perfect state. Then he pulled back his arm and threw.

He watched it hurtle toward the ward and collide. The clang was deafening. Then it was flying back toward him. He caught it in his hand, rocking on his feet with the force of it.

Not a scratch on it.

"Oh, Goddess. I did it."

Nike's sandals padded on the stone floor. Her hand came to rest on his shoulder. "Congratulations, Mak. I wish I could nominate you for your mastery for this."

He looked up from the braid. "Nominate me for mastery when I craft my first sword—and present it to the Queens with my petition for them to rescind the ban on weapons in Orthros."

"You have so much potential, Mak. So much skill. You could still turn this into something safer."

"Would something safer than the Fangs have availed Methu Abroad?"

"Our defiance endangered us." Her gaze drifted to where one of his two long-lost swords hung on the wall. She ran a hand along her tousled ginger braid, which hung to her ankles.

Mak hadn't seen her unbraid her hair since she had returned home from her near-century Abroad. While the rest of their family thought her missing in action, he was one of the few who knew the truth. She had been searching for Methu, refusing to believe that her Trial brother was dead.

"That's what your braid means, isn't it?" Mak guessed. "Your promise to find him."

"After he was captured, Rudhira and I braided our hair. His promise means something different from mine. But neither of us has surrendered the vows we made that night."

"Don't blame yourself for his fate, Nike. Blame the enemy. The fault lies with the war mages who took him captive, not with your creations."

"The Blood Errant's willingness to take risks led to his capture, and my weapons were one of those risks."

"To Hypnos with the Mage Orders' laws about not wielding spells and weapons. We aren't bound by any of their strictures, even if it does make them angrier when we defy them."

"But we are bound by the Queens' laws."

"And Hesperine laws change over the centuries. They must. The Queens are always saying we shouldn't stagnate."

"But we must not lose what makes us Hesperine."

"Hesperines have always been heretics." Mak held up his creation to catch the light. "Lio and Cassia have changed diplomacy forever. Kia is shaking up all our ideas, and Nodora is composing our future. Xandra is leading the way in politics. And have you read my Grace's initiation treatise? Lyros is brilliant. He'll change the Stand's strategy in ways we have yet to imagine. I am proud to be in the Eighth Trial Circle, and I will do my part. Who will reform our battle arts, if not the son of Hippolyta, the greatest of Hesperine warriors?"

"You are also the son of Argyros, our people's greatest peacemaker. That is our great challenge in this family, Mak. Learning to be both."

Mak looked down at the promise in his hand. He knew it could sever his new relationship with his father.

It had taken years for them to begin to understand each other. Mak had once learned to live without his father's approval. That had been before he had known how good it felt to have it.

But what if he must bend himself into unnatural shapes to keep it?

"He has accepted a revolution in diplomacy." Mak said. "Will he not accept me?"

Nike put a hand on his arm. "I broke his heart. You just put it back together. Are you sure you want to test him?"

"This new epoch is testing Orthros." Mak crossed to the wall where the Fang hung and placed his braid in the empty sword bracket beside it. "This is how I will answer."

63

days until

NOTIAN WINTER SOLSTICE

42 Annassa, 1597 IS

SUNBURN

"ARE WE STILL GOING the right direction?" Monsoon called over the wind.

"Turn a little to your right." Cassia shivered and tried not to look down. The Craving made it even harder not to vomit.

Numb with cold and miserable with Craving, her body sought the refuge of sleep. But it was impossible to rest in this situation. She drifted in a half state, somewhere between unconsciousness and waking. Until sunlight drove under her drooping eyelids.

In the middle of all the hardship they had faced, the world presented her with a sight of stunning beauty. They were flying into a desert sunrise more astonishing than any she had ever imagined. Brilliant golden sunlight broke over the horizon, streaking the sky with red, orange, and coral pink, lifting the blue of predawn into brilliant turquoise.

"Still sorry you're human?" Monsoon asked.

"I can reconcile myself to it at the moment."

They flew toward that breathtaking sun until it became too bright to look at.

Monsoon kept flying. Eventually, the sun no longer shone on Cassia's face, and she found herself in the shadow of his wings. It occurred to her the direct sunlight would become oppressive on his back soon.

He began a descent. She roused enough to notice something irregular visible below.

She squinted. "Are those more ruins?"

"Yes. Let's check if there's any water or food there, like at the temple."

She focused all her attention on controlling her stomach as he carried them down. He set her gently on soft sand with warm stone against her back, and the world stopped moving.

She must have fallen asleep, because she woke when a bitter smell assailed her nose. "Uuurrghh. What is that?"

"Something to wet your whistle."

She blinked and took in their surroundings. The ruins were a collection of rubble, marking where the walls of buildings had been. She could almost imagine the village that had once thrived here in some past that seemed impossible now. In the shelter of the skeletal walls, mangy, faded vines snaked across the ground, eating at what remained of the foundations. The tenacious things bore knotty little gourds protected by long spines.

The support behind her back was a broken pillar, perhaps leftover from whatever structure had once shaded the open area where she and Monsoon now sat. The village square? In its center was a stone well set deep in the ground.

She gasped. "Is there still water in it?"

"I'm afraid not, but there's some moisture in the fruit of the bitterblade vines." He held up a hollowed-out gourd filled with something mushy. "I thought it might be easier for you to take crushed, rather than solid."

She sniffed and nearly gagged. Then she noticed the sores on his fingers where one of the vines' spines had gotten to him. Gratitude welled in her, sudden and sharp.

If she wept and sincerely thanked him for all he had done, would such a display drive him back into his hardened mercenary armor?

She tried for a teasing tone. "Are you sure it's not poisonous?"

"Yes. But don't expect me to drink some to prove it to you."

"You have to drink something."

"If you must know, eagles don't need to drink. I can take bird form, catch anything that moves out here, and safely eat it raw to satisfy hunger and thirst."

"That's fascinating, actually. And convenient."

He gave her a shocked look. "You aren't going to lecture me about the poor little animals?"

She wrinkled her nose. "Not if you don't judge me for how much I wish this nasty gourd was a goblet full of Lio's blood."

"We have a bargain."

She accepted the gourd and took a sip of the horrifying stuff. It almost came right back up, and her hand shook so much she spilled some on her chin. "This is embarrassing."

"Can you hold it down?"

"If Lio could survive for half a year on deer blood, I can make myself drink gourd juice."

"He did?"

"He had to go back to Orthros without me at first. It nearly killed him. I will never allow that to happen again."

Monsoon's gaze dropped. "You two have been through some ordeals together. I imagine you didn't expect finding your sister to be one."

"No, we didn't."

He took the gourd from her and held it to her lips. She was glad he kept talking. Keeping her mind off what she was drinking helped.

"Are your memories of your sister hazy?" he asked. "You were very young when you were with her."

"I have many powerful memories of her. It's surprising how strong emotions can make us remember things with perfect clarity."

"What was she like?"

Cassia thought back, cracking open the tender feelings of that time. "When I was with her, she always made me feel as if everything was right in the world, even when I knew it wasn't. She always had an answer or words of comfort."

"She protected you."

"Always. She taught me what to wear and what to say to avoid criticism due to my birth. When people censured me anyway, she taught me to hold my head high. She taught me how to be a lady, and she set the example herself."

Monsoon listened with quiet attention. He truly was a good listener.

"She always seemed patient and calm," Cassia went on. "Looking back now, I often wonder just how afraid she was. She was young as well. She must have struggled and doubted herself. Realizing that now, it doesn't make her seem weaker. It makes me realize just how strong she was, to keep going despite how hard it was for her."

204 me Vela Roth

"What's your favorite memory of her?"

"Oh, I have so many." Cassia paused to think, turning the gilded recollections over in her mind. They did not hurt any less to touch now that she knew Solia had survived. But they hurt in a different way, with a breathless, hopeful ache rather than the anguish of mourning. One occurred to her, and she laughed. "It was the summer before...before she left. Tenebra is cold and rainy nearly all the time, but this was a rare sunny day. She promised me we would play outside. But then she had to go fulfill some duties for our father."

"Duties?"

"There was a religious ceremony, and she had to sit through the whole thing. I had to stay out of sight at home. When she got back, she was so flushed. It had been hot in the crowded temple. I thought she was ill, but now I think...she might have been angry."

A smile twitched across the grim mercenary's lips. "Had a temper, did she?"

"I never saw it, but I would not be surprised if she did. That day, I think she'd had all she could take of Father and responsibility and heat. She plucked me out of the care of my nurse and said we were going to lie down in her cool room. But when she got there and shut the door, her face lit up, and she told me we were sneaking out."

His smile widened.

"She took me by the hand and led me through the garden, and then we sneaked out into the woods. We went to a hidden pond so far out in the forest, no one would think to look for us there."

"Do you suppose she made a habit of sneaking out?"

"She did a lot of sneaking for self-protection. But perhaps she did it for self-preservation in another way. To keep from going mad when it all became too much. That time, she took me with her. It felt like we were in another world. The woods weren't some frightening place I wasn't allowed to go. For that afternoon, they were transformed into a magical kingdom— her kingdom. Nothing could hurt us while she ruled there."

Cassia closed her eyes, savoring the memory. "We played in the pond all afternoon. The sun was warm, the water was cool. There was no one to take me away from her or her away from me. It was perfect." She opened her eyes. "I didn't want to go home. She had to talk me into it. I wish I had gone more willingly, so she would only have had to talk herself into it, and not both of us."

Monsoon held the gourd for her to take another sip. "I think it helped her."

Cassia swallowed hard. "What?"

"Talking you into it. It would have been harder for her to do what she must, if she didn't have you to think of." He shrugged. "Or so I would think."

"I never thought of that. You're probably right."

"Anyone with one eye and half sense can see how much you love her. And I have very good eyes."

"And more sense than most people, I suspect."

"A mercenary who isn't sensible is a dead mercenary."

A silence passed between them, a rather comfortable one.

"I spend most of my time avoiding my brother," Monsoon said suddenly.

Cassia considered that. "Well, I can't point fingers, considering that I have done much worse things to my father than avoid him."

"No. My brother is a good man. I would die for him. I just...can't deal with him."

Cassia tried not to smile at his exasperated tone. "It sounds like you two have a complex past. I don't want to cross the veil—that is, pry into what is none of my affair."

"You don't have to say it. I know I should be grateful I have him."

"Would he talk to you if you tried?"

"He wishes I spent more time with him."

Cassia swallowed another sip from the gourd before deciding to speak her mind. "He's your brother, and he's within reach. Why don't you reach?"

Monsoon gave a nod. "I haven't seen my nephews and nieces in a long time, either. None of it is my brother's wife's fault."

"Uncle Monsoon," Cassia mused.

He snorted.

"You're good with children," she observed.

His response to that was a more eloquent snort.

"So your brother is a family man…what about you? Does the mercenary life leave any room for love?"

"Oh, it's a marvelous life of adventure." He flexed his bicep. "Men like me are in high demand."

She rolled her eyes. "Oh, I'm sure."

"In my line of work, the battles are great, the wine is better, but best of all…" He shook his head, smiling at the sky. "The women. Women with swords. Women with magic. Women who can give as good as they get."

"It sounds like you appreciate strong females." But Cassia found it difficult to imagine Monsoon having a woman in every sister state. After seeing him with Chuma, he struck her as a family man, too. "Anyone in particular?"

He was quiet for so long, she thought he would change the subject, or make another snide jest. Finally he said, "Sunburn."

"A fellow mercenary with a fortune name?"

"She could best anyone in the Empire with a sword, including me. Finest warrior I ever trained."

"You taught her how to fight with a sword?"

"I taught her a lot of things." There was a rather cocky glint in his eye.

She definitely didn't cross the veil about what that look implied. "So your fearsome reputation is not entirely true—you don't always fight alone."

His mask of bitterness descended, although it came with a smile. "I do now."

Cassia winced. "I'm sorry."

He gave her the last swallow from the gourd. His words were softer than any she'd heard from him. "It's not your fault."

She finished the sustenance he had worked so hard to give her. "Do you want to talk about what happened?"

He tossed the empty shell of the gourd away. "I can't."

In that simple admission, she heard complicated grief.

"Do you want to talk about…before that?"

"Seems I do," he murmured.

"What's your favorite memory of her?" Cassia arched a brow. "Of the ones you care to mention aloud."

She had never heard him laugh like that before. The smile that appeared on his face made all his ill humor disappear for an instant. Cassia finally saw for herself what Chuma had meant when she had said his anger came from pain and disappointment.

"There are too many to tell you." His eyes crinkled at the corners. "But a very memorable one was when she got her first sword of her very own. You should have seen how her face lit up. You'd think someone had given her a crown of gold and diamonds."

"The power to fight is better than jewels," Cassia agreed.

"And so is earning something on your own merit. She was so proud of that sword, and she felt beautiful wearing it. You could see it in the way she walked. She slept with it, took it to the bath…and kept it with her when she stayed in the sun for much too long." His chest shook with laughter. "There was only one place on her body that wasn't sunburned, in the shape of her blade. And that's how she got her name right after her sword."

Cassia and Monsoon burst out laughing together.

That laughter woke Cassia up, and her weary mind made the connection that should have been obvious all along.

There's not a man in the Empire who can best Ukocha with a sword.

All the mercenaries she and Lio had questioned agreed on that. No one had mentioned Ukocha's fortune name, but it was well known that for her, love would always come second to battle.

That must be why Monsoon knew so much about Ukocha, why he had connections with the same clients as she. He had trained her, loved her.

No wonder he hadn't wanted Cassia's contract. How it must grieve him that Ukocha had chosen the sword he had taught her to use over the love they might have shared. She was asking him to lead her toward the woman who had broken his heart.

"Thank you for doing this, Monsoon."

"Hand feeding you costs extra, by the way."

She laughed again. "So, is that why you became a mercenary? For the riches? Or was it for the wine and women?"

"Ha. Actually, it had to do with my brother. I'm the eldest, but it was decided that he would inherit everything. Oh, and marry the woman I had been betrothed to since childhood."

"Did you want your inheritance?"

"What?" He sat back. "Of course I did. I spent my whole life preparing to lead the family and fulfill my responsibilities."

That didn't entirely answer her question. "Did you love your betrothed very much?"

"We spent years expecting to be wed, planning our marriage and our lives together."

That didn't answer her question, either. "So, being a mercenary was your second choice?"

"I needed something to occupy me as far away from home as possible."

"And Sunburn?" Cassia asked. "Was she your second choice?"

He looked away, his gaze scraping over the surrounding ruins. "I wasn't her first choice, so the answer to that question doesn't matter."

Cassia couldn't find a reply to that. She was afraid anything she might say would only prod his wounds, but she wanted to offer him some comfort about life's disappointments. Her life had turned out nothing like she had expected—in marvelous ways.

If she could make it to Orthros…if she could find someone like Lio, in spite of the fate life had tried to dictate to her, surely a man like Monsoon could find happiness.

"If she's the right one for you," Cassia said, "you'll find your way back together. Every time."

His lip twisted. "Is that what the pretty Hesperine ballads say?"

"No. It's what I learn over and over again, every time Lio and I nearly die trying to stay together. When there is no way, love makes one."

To her surprise, his expression became thoughtful. "I suppose you did have to fight hard to stay with him, since he's a heretic where you come from. You must have given up a great deal to be with him."

"It didn't feel like a sacrifice. I've gained so much."

"Didn't you have some kind of inheritance?" he asked. "Wouldn't you have to forfeit it to leave with Lio?"

"My sister was the heir, because she was the legitimate daughter, as well as the eldest. There was a time when I thought I would have to take on her responsibilities. Thankfully that was not necessary, and I was able to leave it all behind to be with Lio."

He gave her a long look. "Did it ever bother you that your sister had a right to everything, and you didn't?"

"Not in the least. We all pinned our hopes on her becoming…head of the family. She deserved it. I wanted to follow her leadership."

"Who gets the inheritance now?"

"I arranged for someone else to receive it."

"Bastards can do that?"

Cassia gave him a humorless smile. "I was not particularly legal or straightforward about it. If all goes according to plan, my father will lose his influence, and another man will take his place."

"You're quite the rebel, wrecking your family legacy and running off with a Hesperine."

"I'm rather proud of it." She looked away. "I'm sure my sister doesn't want it anymore, and that we can let him have it and live our lives in peace."

"It's a lot to ask of anyone," he said quietly, "to give up what they were born to."

"I don't really understand how that feels," said Cassia. "I always hated what I was born to."

"You'll have to reckon with your ancestors, eventually."

"Not if I'm immortal."

STANDSTILL

MONSOON WOKE CASSIA AT intervals throughout the day to force her to drink what she could.

"Have you slept?" she asked.

"Enough," he answered.

"We don't have time for you to get ill with exhaustion."

"Point taken, *nyakimbi*."

They had found some shade by the wall of the ruin. Sitting beside her, he leaned his head back against the stone and spread his wings out. She pulled her scarf over her head once more and resigned herself to more rest.

The whisper of steel against leather startled her. She sat up so fast that her head spun.

Monsoon had drawn his sword. He was on his feet, his wings folded tightly against his back. As his piercing gaze scanned the deserted village, he held a finger to his lips.

Cassia felt around for anything she could use as a weapon. A broken piece of rock came to hand.

Mere paces away, a shape bolted out from behind a crumbling wall. It coursed toward Monsoon. Like a bolt of sunlight, like a piece of the desert come to life.

Cassia watched the creature out of myth draw near. A woman from the waist up, blending seamlessly into the body of a lioness.

Jinn were real. Hesperines were real. Leotaurs were myths. Craving had addled Cassia's wits.

"Standstill!" shouted Monsoon.

And then he dropped his sword.

He danced out of the leotaur's path at the last instant. She landed almost soundlessly and pirouetted to face him.

He held up his empty hands, flaring his wings.

Her paws approached him quietly, and he simply stood there. It occurred to Cassia that she knew nothing of how a leotaur chose her prey. Why wasn't she coming after the weakest of the flock—Cassia, who lay defenseless?

The leotaur halted in front of him. "Monsoon? What are *you* doing here, you carcass-licking buzzard?"

"It's lovely to see you, too."

The sight before Cassia began to make sense, and she realized the leotaur was no such thing.

She was a petite woman about Monsoon's age, wearing a long, blousy tunic and a scarf, both in shades of indigo. She rode a cat for a mount. The graceful feline had thick fur as golden as the sands of the Scorched Verge, with darker rings around her legs and tail. Cassia saw no reins. The woman and her mount moved fluidly together, a perfect and deadly partnership.

"I thought the only humans out here were Accord breakers," the woman snarled.

Monsoon smirked. "I thought you were a feral sand cat."

"I'll take that as a compliment."

"Considering our last conversation, I probably deserved the greeting you just gave me, even if I'm not an Accord breaker. But before we feed the past to your cat as a snack, hear me out."

"Not probably. Definitely. But right now, you're not worth the effort." She twirled a dagger in her hand, its silver-filigreed handle reflecting the sun. "No guarantees once we aren't lost in the desert anymore." She sheathed the dagger on her upper arm.

It was a fortune blade.

Cassia found her voice. "Are you one of the Ashes?"

The woman's sharp gaze trained on her. "Who's asking?"

"Cassia," Monsoon said.

The cat padded toward Cassia, its belly low to the ground. Its face filled her vision, and she shrank back against the pillar. Huge ears. A short nose.

Intelligent green-gold eyes. What strange things to notice, when she might soon see its fangs. Why wasn't Monsoon stopping it?

The cat lay down smoothly before Cassia, its rider resting a hand on its head.

The woman leaned forward and cupped Cassia's face in her indigo-stained palm. "You *are* Cassia."

A thousand questions stuck in Cassia's throat. *Did you know my sister? Did she talk about me? Where is she now?*

"I am Kella," the woman said, "Second Blade of the Ashes."

Tears blurred Cassia's vision. No, her eyes were dry. Her vision was blurring all on its own. She felt breathless, and her heart was racing, even though she was completely still.

"Cassia? Are you all right?"

Monsoon's voice faded into the distance and echoed strangely. Her head roared.

Of all times for the Craving to rob her of consciousness.

LONESOME

T HE MIND WARD GLITTERED on the edges of Lio's awareness. Every time he tried to pinpoint Cassia, she seemed to have risen on another horizon. His Grace was on the move. He felt like he was chasing a star across the Maaqul.

He gazed up at the low rise ahead and tried to discern whether they were heading toward or away from her.

Tuura halted to catch her breath at the foot of the hill. "The spirit tear residue I'm sensing is up there."

Karege stopped at her side. "Are you sure it's not an *open* spirit tear that's going to spew Accord breakers at us?"

"When have I ever made a mistake about something that important?"

"Never. It's just wishful thinking on my part. I'd love to get my hands on some of those bloodless vultures."

"So would I." Lio paused beside the mercenaries, letting his spell light hover over their heads. Standing still for a moment appeased the channel of pain running through his breastbone and out his back, but did nothing to ease his frustration. "It certainly feels deserted. If one of your companions were near the tear residue, we would surely sense their aura by now."

"Let us investigate in any case," said Tuura. "We may find clues about who landed here and where they went."

"Are you sure you won't let me carry you?" Karege asked.

"My feet in are in perfect working order, my friend."

"You're not feeling dizzy?"

"When have my poultices ever failed to work wonders?"

"Never. Just wishful thinking again. I love to reenact the holy goat race."

"Levitation isn't allowed in the race, but it is here, and it's faster."

Karege wrapped his hand around Tuura's staff and levitated the two of them up the rise. Lio followed, squinting at a faint gleam that shone from over the crest of the hill. What could that be? The moons weren't due up for another hour.

They reached the top of the rise, and Lio stared at the sight below.

In the distance, an oasis glowed like an enchanted jewel cupped in the sands of the desert. A pool of water shone bright turquoise in the dark night, and the trees were like luminescent emeralds.

"What could that be?" Lio wondered. "A jinn site?"

"Why would they allow us to see it?" Karege sounded suspicious.

"We should determine what it is," Tuura said. "Let's go closer. With caution."

The three of them levitated down the rise and across the valley below. It was a deceptively long distance. What appeared attainable across the open spaces of the desert proved to be far away, the closer you tried to get to it. They were only about a third of the way there when Lio became aware of an aura within range—a human one.

"That's no jinn!" Karege exclaimed. "That's a preening illusionist showing off for the rocks and sand."

Tuura made an exasperated sound, but her aura lit with relief. "Oh, Hoyefe!"

"Your light mage?" Lio blinked at the spectacle before them. A mortal illusionist had conjured all this? While trying to survive in the Maaqul?

When at last they neared the oasis, a graceful gateway of palms admitted them into the little paradise. Motes of light drifted in the air, escorting them along a pathway lined with a rainbow of night-blooming flowers. But Lio realized he couldn't hear the rustle of the palm fronds or smell the blossoms. He did smell real water, however.

At the center of the palm grove was the sparkling pool they had spotted from afar. A man lounged there with one arm around a buxom woman and his other around a strapping man, with nothing but the crystal-clear water for modesty.

"The Craving has been known to cause hallucinations," Lio said. "Could you two please verify what I should be seeing?"

"No one's delusions but Hoyefe's," Karege rumbled.

Lio couldn't judge, considering how many times he himself had conjured an illusion of Cassia to comfort him on lonely nights in Orthros.

He only sensed one human aura, which belonged to the man in the middle of the trio. Lio wondered how much of Hoyefe's appearance was an illusion, too. He wasn't sure how anyone could maintain fashionably clipped hair, a perfect goatee, and a complexion as smooth as a bronze statue while stranded in the desert.

"My friends!" exclaimed the only real person in the pool. "I hoped one of you would spot my signal."

"This isn't a signal," Karege said. "It's enough to put a jinn's eyes out."

"Why, thank you, Noon Watch. It had to be visible from a great distance to increase my chances of being found."

Karege shook his head. "No danger of you going unnoticed, Lonesome, that's for certain."

Hoyefe spread his arms wide. "Welcome to our very own pleasure palace in the desert. Come on in. The water is, well, water, and everything else is fine, courtesy of your favorite expert in the illusionary arts."

"Dear Hoyefe," said Tuura, "we are immensely relieved to discover you're alive and in top spell-casting form, but please stop wasting your strength this instant. We need your magic for later."

"You wound me, Peanut. What could be a more important use of magic than comforting a man in his final hours? If we're doomed to die, lost and starving in the Maaqul, we should go out surrounded by the sweetness of life. Place your orders, please, and I'll provide you with your very own dreams come true. Perhaps a virile young fellow for you, Tuura? Karege, how about a pretty armful with fangs? Who is our new friend there? Do you know his tastes?" Hoyefe looked Lio up and down. "On second thought, nevermind illusions. Is he available?"

"I'm taken," Lio replied, "and my Craving makes me very poor company."

The illusionist winced and made a sympathetic noise. "That's just an unfair way to go out, my dear fellow. You especially need an illusion. Describe your one and only, and I'll present you with a very comforting vision, I assure you."

Lio stalked forward. Karege's hand on his shoulder held him back, sending a surge of pain through his chest. "No one conjures illusions of Cassia but me."

Hoyefe sighed. "Lucky girl, your Cassia. That growling, fangy look is very fetching on your pretty face. Well met, my fellow light mage. I am Hoyefe of the Ashes, master fencer, visionary illusionist, and alumnus of Imperial University's School of Fine Arts. I am also a professional interrogator, if you enjoy that sort of thing."

Karege kept his hand on Lio's shoulder. "This is Lio. He came here with Monsoon to reinforce us."

"Monsoon has migrated back our way, has he?" Hoyefe frowned. "Wait a moment. Lio, did you say your most beloved vintage is named Cassia? The plot thickens."

"Put away your toys, Lonesome," Karege said. "We have work to do."

"Someone left his sense of fun in the Scorched Verge." Hoyefe rose from the water, striking a pose with his hands on his hips, while illusionary droplets of water cascaded from him.

Lio tried to tame his annoyance at the man. They must all depend on each other for survival and a fighting chance to rescue everyone. This was no time to let his emotions get the better of him, volatile as they were due to the Craving.

The oasis disappeared, along with Hoyefe's illusory paramours. The man stood before them with a few days' growth of beard, hair long enough to show his curls, and fashionable travel attire besmirched by dust.

He was no less an exhibitionist with his clothes on. He rested a hand on the hilt of his slim, elegant sword and put the other on the patch of bare chest revealed by the partly open collar of his tunic. "Ready to die for the cause when you are."

"No one is going to die," said Tuura. "Look at all this water."

Hoyefe's oasis pool was in truth a sandy watering hole. The broken remnants of pillars jutted from the water.

Lio ran a hand over the nearest column, unable to make out the time-worn carvings on the stone. "Who could have left these ruins behind? They look like the work of humans, not jinn."

"Whatever they were," said Karege, "they belong to the jinn now. Best not disturb anything but the water."

Hoyefe took a seat on the stub of a pillar, propping up his boots. "It takes much longer to die of hunger than thirst, but we'll still die if we don't find sustenance."

Tuura rummaged in her medicine bag and pulled out a sack of candied almonds. "You know I always keep a little something on hand to eat. We'll need to ration them, but I have enough treats to keep us alive for now."

"Bless you, diviner." Hoyefe kissed her hand and accepted the nuts. He put a single one in his mouth and savored it. "Mmm. No illusion, that."

"Neither is your bag of tricks, I hope." Tuura pointed at the light pack sitting beside him.

"No. I had my essentials on me while I was on watch, and they landed here with me." He rummaged in the bag, then straightened and offered Tuura a bar of soap with a smile.

She put it to her nose with a contented smile. "Definitely not an illusion."

"We cannot shave dry," Hoyefe declared, "not even in the Maaqul."

"Can you tell us what happened at the beginning of the ambush?" Karege asked.

Hoyefe was silent for a long moment, chewing on another nut. At last, "I was keeping watch and considering ideas for a new play—comedy or tragedy, I have yet to decide—when some craven, inexplicable magic sent me out here. I had no time to react. Clearly the perpetrators of the ambush were too frightened to face my sword. What befell you, my friends?"

After they compared stories with Hoyefe, Tuura looked him in the eye. "What injury banished you?"

"I barely noticed it, as you can see."

"It's what we can't see that worries me."

"I wouldn't have known such a little nick was the cause of all my troubles if you hadn't explained how the stone weapons work."

"Arrow?" she prompted. "Dagger?"

Hoyefe waved a hand. "It felt like a mere dart."

Karege rubbed his arm. "Too bad they didn't extend us the same courtesy."

Hoyefe smiled at Lio and rubbed his hands together. "So, we're going to meet Cassia."

Karege shared his grin. "We've been telling Lio as many tales as we can about a...certain old friend of ours. Do you think you could come up with something?"

Hoyefe's expression lit. "For any delicate dance around secrets, I am your man. I'm sure I can disclose some fond memories of our mysterious traveling companion."

Lio wasn't sure he wanted to know what story Hoyefe might tell about Solia. He knew the Craving was making him petty and illogical, but he was still bristling at the thought of the man adding an illusion of Cassia to the oasis harem.

Hoyefe sat back, stroking his beard. "She was a non-citizen, you see. That much I can tell you. Obscuring her status was always a bit tricky, especially in populated areas."

"She avoided impersonating a citizen," Karege said. "That's a serious crime."

Tuura nodded. "She was very patient about keeping her face covered if necessary. She could blend right in when it was sunny and everyone was wearing scarves."

"But where's the fun in that?" Hoyefe mused. "There were plenty of opportunities to get creative. We had the best fun disguising her, didn't we?"

Karege chuckled. "Remember the time I completely veiled her so we could take her with us into that dining hall full of administrators?"

"I'll never forget!" Hoyefe laughed. "The people at the next table kept staring at you, thinking you were guzzling two drinks at a time."

"They had to be wondering what possessed me to order double portions of food, when Hesperines don't need to eat."

Hoyefe flashed them a broad grin. "My favorite, though, was the time I used illusions to give her fangs. She made a very persuasive Hesperine."

Lio frowned. "Wouldn't mages realize she had a mortal aura and see through the illusion?"

"Possibly, but it worked a treat in a cave full of thick-headed outlaws. The sight of her brandishing her fangs to scare them was priceless."

What had Solia been doing in a cave full of outlaws? How many times had the Ashes rescued her from danger?

And how much more sympathy for his people had Hoyefe helped Solia build, giving her the chance to walk in a Hesperine's shoes?

This man had done much more with his magic than create silly fantasies. He had devoted his great power to keeping Cassia's sister safe. The cloak of secrecy he had kept around Solia had helped open her eyes.

Lio couldn't quite banish his anger, but he pushed it away. "You have my gratitude, Hoyefe."

"My pleasure, I assure you." He twirled his hand.

The four of them disappeared. All Lio could see was the sands of the Maaqul where his and his allies' bodies should be.

"My illusions are at your service." Hoyefe gave a wistful sigh. "How lovely that your mind ward enables you to fly to your lady like a homing pigeon on the wings of love. Don't worry about running into any Accord breakers. I won't let those tasteless louts ruin the happy ending of a good romantic drama."

LULLABY

Ａ WOMAN'S GENTLE SINGING EASED Cassia awake. The familiar lullaby blanketed her in the sense that she was safe and all was well.

Five hawthorns sharp in my winter garden
Red berries in the snow
Five hawthorns ripe with winter bounty
To guard my little ivy

Cassia lay there with her eyes closed, savoring the comfort.

Six betony in my bright spring garden
No trouble can trespass here
Six betony of royal purple
But none so fine as my little ivy

Memory returned to her, and she roused with a gasp. She opened her eyes, and firelight blinded her for a moment.

It was night. There was a damp cloth on her head and a warm blanket around her. No, those were feathers. Monsoon had draped his wing over her.

The cat napped across the fire. Beside her sat Kella.

She smiled at Cassia and sang the last verse, playing the tune of the old Tenebran lullaby on an Azarqi imzad.

Seven ivy vines in my bright spring garden
To tear down every wall
Seven ivy vines that built my fortress
Each as strong as my own

Cassia blinked the tears from her eyes. "Solia used to sing that to me. She said my mother sang it to me the day I was born."

Kella lowered her imzad, saying nothing, her reply surely locked behind the secret. But apparently an old song had slipped through the ancestral spell.

"Thank you," Cassia whispered.

"Back with us, *nyakimbi*?" Monsoon asked.

"I think so."

She smelled something cooking. Gourds were arranged over the fire, roasting on the twisted limbs of desert shrubs.

Kella rotated one of the sticks. "These will be ready soon."

"Don't protest," Monsoon said to Cassia. "You won't recognize the bitterblade after Kella is done with it."

They were talking about gourds. One of the people who knew what had happened to Solia was sitting right there across the fire, and all they could talk about was gourds.

"She hasn't killed you yet," Cassia observed.

"No, she decided I'm more useful alive. Especially since I brought you here." Monsoon adjusted the cloth on Cassia's forehead.

She frowned. "Did you soak this cloth in gourd juice? Will it rot my freckles off?"

"No, it's soaked in this." He put a hand behind her head and lifted her so she could drink from his waterskin.

Cool, pure liquid blessed her lips. "Water? How?"

"I woke up the well." Kella gave Cassia a little wave, and droplets of water played between her blue fingers.

A water mage. They were saved, truly.

Kella sat with one arm draped over her slumbering mount. Her deep blue scarf was around her shoulders now, revealing her black, looping braids and tawny face. Red war paint adorned her brow, and indigo stained her full lips.

She looked at Cassia with none of her earlier anger in her eyes. "Monsoon told me what you found out from the jinn. Thank you, Cassia."

"I have a bond of gratitude with Chuma that I need to honor many times over. What happened to Ipika? We saw the place where all of you defended her."

Kella described an ambush all too similar to the one that had caught Monsoon, Cassia, and Lio unawares. "One of the Accord breakers' arrows caught me in the shoulder. I was thrown out here before I saw what happened to Chuma's mother."

"Are you all right?" Monsoon asked.

"How kind of you to be so concerned all of a sudden. I was lucky. The head went straight through, so it was easy to get the shaft out. Just a flesh wound." Her mouth twisted. "I've had worse."

"I'm not sure luck had anything to do with it," Monsoon said. "They had very good aim, but they didn't aim to kill."

"Well," said Kella, "I won't be so courteous if we meet again. We should keep going toward Chuma's mother. Cassia, you'll be our compass. Monsoon will carry you. I'll keep us all alive."

"I've been demoted from mercenary to pack bird," Monsoon muttered.

"That's because I actually know how to survive in the Maaqul," Kella returned. "It's a good thing someone around here does."

"Cassia and I were doing fine before we found you."

"Before I found you," Kella corrected.

Cassia smiled innocently. "Kella, are you by chance an Azarqi princess who threw Monsoon out of your tent?"

"Mweya's Wings." He threw up a hand. "I thought you silkfoots didn't believe in crossing the veil."

"If I have to survive the desert with you two, I need to know what hazards I might face. Being caught between two former lovers with a grudge is a hazard of the highest order."

"She is an Azarqi princess." Monsoon sighed. "But that was never why I was in her tent."

Kella shot Monsoon a glare. "This buzzard was welcome once, as a friend. But now I'd happily throw him out of my desert because I have no respect for a man who doesn't stay loyal."

Cassia's brows rose. Could Kella's anger be on Ukocha's behalf? Monsoon had made it sound as if Ukocha had jilted him, not the other way around. But when things went badly between lovers, the two of them often saw things entirely differently. Kella would naturally take her first blade's side.

Monsoon's wing had gone tense. The firelight showed the harsh edges of his expression. "I'm here now, aren't I?"

Kella didn't look at him and spoke to Cassia instead. "I know why else you're here. I wish I could say more. I promise you, Cassia, I'll make sure you get what you came for, as well."

The lullaby was proof. "That promise means more to me than I can say."

"But we have to make sure you're in a fit state to hear what we Ashes can tell you, once we find everyone. Which is it," Kella asked, "siren's nectar or jinn breath?"

"I'm not an addict," Cassia said.

"I'm not judging," Kella replied. "Ancestors know it took me long enough to give up the opium. But your addiction counts as a hazard, too. We need to know."

Monsoon shook his head. "Cassia's bad habit is tall, fanged, and immortal. She's here with a Hesperine, and they've been apart for too long."

"Lio is a very good habit," Cassia protested.

Kella stared at them. "A Hesperine? Are you serious?"

"Apparently humans get symptoms too." Monsoon sighed.

"Well, love feels like caravanning through a sandstorm most of the time, but this is too much. No wonder Karege isn't interested in settling down."

"Who is Karege?" Cassia asked.

"My Hesperine comrade. Longest serving member of the Ashes, after our first blade."

Cassia clutched Monsoon's arm. "One of the Ashes is a Hesperine?"

"I suppose I neglected to mention that," he answered.

"Sunbind your secrets," Cassia said. "If the ancestors did intervene on Lio's behalf, he might land where there's another Hesperine."

"Even if they're not of the same bloodline?"

"All of us are of Hespera's blood."

Monsoon turned to Kella. "Any idea what's become of Karege?"

"No, but I know he'll use his keen senses and the Blood Union to look for us. Take heart, Cassia. Two Hesperines together will stand an even better chance of finding us."

Monsoon leaned forward. "Kella, as you so accurately pointed out, you know the desert better than any of us. Having been born here among the Azarqi, you've always been an asset to the Ashes."

"Flattery will get you nothing, except maybe my cat's claws in your wings."

"Regardless, we need your wisdom. You have every dune memorized."

"Not out here. Even my people don't come this far into the Maaqul. Only the jinn do."

"And the beasts. What animal spirits reign here? Which of them might show favor to a dog?"

Kella gave Monsoon a probing look.

Captain Ziara's words came back to Cassia. *There's no mistaking your freckles and the dog.*

"We need to find Knight," Cassia said. "He's a liegehound, you know—a war dog. He'll be an asset to us in battle."

"He won't fare too well out here, will he?" Kella asked.

Cassia thought of all the years when he had been her only friend. "He can survive a blizzard, but not a desert. And not separation from the human he's bonded to."

"I understand." Kella stroked her cat's chin. The feline rubbed Kella's hand with her head, one of her large ears flattening under Kella's palm. A mighty vibration sounded from that side of the fire.

Cassia had to smile. "That's quite a purr. What's her name?"

"This is Tilili. She's a greater sand cat. Her kind are native to the Maaqul."

"Really?" Cassia marveled. "Her fur is so thick, I'm surprised she's from a hot climate."

"That keeps her warm on cold desert nights."

Tilili rolled over onto her back and exposed the buff-colored fur on her belly. She looked at Kella with a slow blink.

Kella's mouth twitched. "See there? She's cooling herself off. Her belly fur dispels heat. Just don't pet it without permission."

"How can you tell if you have permission?" Cassia asked.

"You can't. You find out after the fact. If she flays you, that means you guessed wrong."

There must be mighty claws hiding in Tilili's paws, but none were in evidence at the moment.

Kella petted the mat of wiry black fur that covered Tilili's toes. "She can float over the dunes without burning her paws, and her footprints are all but invisible."

Cassia could only imagine how many stealthy kills Kella and Tilili had made together. "I didn't know it was possible to use a cat as a mount."

"Tilili and I spent a long time working on our partnership, with some help from a very wise Azarqi mage."

"I can tell she's a mighty protector, and a good friend."

Kella dared trail a finger through Tilili's belly fur. The cat blinked again, slowly. Her claws appeared, but only to flex gently.

"You've had Knight since you were seven, haven't you?" asked Kella. She knew that detail about Cassia's past, too. "Solia took me to the kennels to get him, so I would have him for protection."

"We'll start looking for him after we've eaten. On one condition."

Cassia was willing to agree to anything, if it meant getting Knight back. "Yes?"

"Don't ask me why I've never been to Orthros. Don't invite me to Orthros. Don't talk to me about all the miraculous things they can do in Orthros. Tilili and I have bigger snakes to snare."

"Of course," Cassia said, puzzled.

"Good." Kella reached into her saddlebag and pulled out a silver scroll case. "Tilili and I got transported together, so I landed with everything attached to my saddle."

A slow smile spread across Monsoon's face. "Oh, Kella. Tell me that's an ancient text full of the desert's secrets that only the Azarqi know."

"It's not a text, and it's mostly a record of what we don't know. But still, it's a map."

"A map?" Cassia raised her head for a better look, ignoring a wave of vertigo. "You have a map of this part of the desert?"

"Can you tell us where we are on the map I have?" Monsoon asked.

Kella shook her head. "This forsaken region won't be marked on yours. But my people's scholars record everything we learn from our travels, our mages' research, and our negotiations with the jinn. In preparation for the Ashes' contract here, I consulted with the scholar who possesses the only map of what we think we know about this region. He let me make a copy of the original in return for my promise that I will bring him my findings."

"You've outdone yourself this time, Standstill," said Monsoon.

Standstill. The fortune name of a nomad, to be sure.

Kella opened the scroll case. "Keep in mind, myth doesn't translate well into a map. We could seek a watering hole recorded here and find a pit of fire jinn instead. But..."

She unrolled the document in front of her and held it close to the firelight, favoring her left arm. "I thought I saw...yes, there it is. A wild dog boneyard that, according to stories, is haunted by the ancestral spirit from whom all Azarqi hunting hounds descend."

"How long will it take us to get there?" Cassia asked. "Assuming we don't run into any fire jinn."

"By tomorrow, perhaps."

"We should also check my inner directions against your map," Cassia suggested. "Perhaps that will give us an idea of where we're headed."

"We will. But first, eat."

Monsoon cut one of the roasted gourds into small bites with his fortune blade. Once again, he showed remarkable patience through the grueling exercise of coaxing food into Cassia.

Her dependence on him, and now Kella, would have made her scream with humiliation if the mercenaries hadn't been so sunbound kind about it all.

She couldn't wallow in the miseries of her humanity. They had work to do. The sooner she ate without vomiting, the sooner they could look for Knight, and the sooner they found Knight, the sooner they could keep looking for Ipika.

Finally they were ready to go. Cassia gazed across the ashes of the fire at one of its namesake mercenaries.

Kella set her light cloth saddle on Tilili's back. Then she ran a hand along the cat's spine to the base of her tail. Tilili stuck her rump in the air, stretching, and Kella took the opportunity to secure the girth under her belly.

Tilili flopped back down. Kella swung her thigh over the saddle and into a pocket-like fabric stirrup. Finally Cassia's addled mind understood. Both of Kella's legs had been amputated just above the knee.

The fear of what Kella lived with every day drove many to Orthros to seek healing, or even the Gift. Her fearlessness had taken her all across the Empire on Tilili's back.

If Cassia had learned anything since leaving Tenebra, it was that the right path took a different shape for every person.

"Thank you for this, Kella," Cassia said.

"You're welcome," she replied. "It's hard work, not killing Monsoon, but I know you're grateful to me for sparing his life."

"Ha, ha." He lifted Cassia in his arms.

"For the water," Cassia specified, "and the food and the map and especially, for being willing to scour the Maaqul for a lost hound. You have my gratitude."

Kella reached behind her and touched the base of Tilili's tail, and the cat rose to her feet again. "I honor bonds of loyalty, the way Hesperines honor bonds of gratitude. You and I have had a bond of loyalty for a long time, even before you knew it."

62

days until

NOTIAN WINTER SOLSTICE

43 Annassa, 1597 IS

THE FAVOR OF THE MOONS

ASSIA'S INNER COMPASS WAS a constant warning, after a night and a day of searching for the ancestral hounds' resting place.

"Still heading farther from Ipika?" Monsoon asked her again, raising his voice over the wind and his wingbeats.

She cleared her aching throat and called back, "Yes. But at least we haven't fallen into a pit of fire jinn."

She couldn't hear it, but she was sure he snorted.

Kella, racing along on Tilili below, suddenly raised a beckoning hand. They followed her over the next rise.

There was a wide, shallow depression in the sand, ringed by jagged rocks. The center was scattered with bones bleached by the desert sun.

"Finally," Monsoon called out. "That map isn't just deceptive. It's as tricky as a jinn in a bad temper."

"Can we land?" Cassia asked. "If Knight is nearby, he might smell me."

Monsoon descended to circle over the boneyard. He set them down at the edge beside Kella and Tilili. Resting his weight on his good foot, he let Cassia lean on his arm on that side.

She gazed across the dog spirit's grounds. Some bones were fresh, resting atop the sand. Teeth marks bespoke past fights and deadly injuries. Other skeletons were half-sunk into the earth, or just faint impressions beneath the ground. One creature's remains blurred into another, making it difficult to count how many had died here next to their kin through the ages. In death, they were all one great pack.

With the sense that she was disturbing a sacred quiet, Cassia called out, "Knight? Knight! *Dockk dockk!*"

Silence answered her.

Cassia's hopes sank as quickly as they had risen. "If he were nearby, he would have come running by now."

"Let's look around for any sign of him," Monsoon suggested.

"I'll circle around the outside," Kella said. "My cat's footsteps might anger the ancestors of her natural enemies."

"We'll search from the air." Monsoon picked Cassia up and took off again.

He criss-crossed the boneyard in low glides, carrying Cassia close enough to see the skeletons of the lean desert dogs. The Light Moon was generous with its glow tonight, making it possible to perceive details. In the very center of the boneyard, Hespera's Eye guided Cassia's gaze to the fresh tracks of a living dog. The unmistakable impressions of familiar, beloved paws.

"Knight was here!" she cried.

She and Monsoon followed his tracks, which led them to the other side of the boneyard. As they crossed out of the circle, Kella came around to join them, and Monsoon landed beside her again.

Cassia sank down before the faint impressions in the sand, following them with her gaze as they grew vaguer. "The trail is so hard to see."

"Tilili and I can still follow it," Kella assured her. "Ayur favors us tonight."

Cassia glanced at her. "Ayur?"

"My people's goddess of the moons." Kella pointed up at the white gibbous lighting their way. "Her silver brings prosperity and inspiration. But beware of her blood. She is also the goddess of creatures that hunt by night."

Cassia checked the horizon, but there was no sign of the Blood Moon's rise yet. "I hope she will shine kindly on Hespera's creatures tonight."

"You two follow us." Kella and Tilili stalked off across the silver-lit sands.

Monsoon helped Cassia up. "All right, back into the air."

"You've stopped asking me if I'm going to vomit. I must be getting better at this."

With a snap of his wings, Monsoon lifted them off again. "Watch out. You might even start to like it. Next thing I know, you'll be one of the squealing girls tugging at my feathers and begging me for a flight."

"I wouldn't dare impose. This journey has used up all my flying credits with you forever, I'm sure."

"Imagine," he griped with a smile in his voice, "using the power of my ancestors to find a lost pet."

"I'll pay you the largest bonus of your career for this," Cassia said, and she meant it.

"Eh. Just throw in a nice case of alcohol from Orthros, and we'll call it even."

"I can arrange that. Do you like mead? I'm friends with the royal beekeeper."

"Too sweet. I prefer hard liquor."

"Ah. Something from the Absinthikos, then. Lovers of fine spirits all drink there."

Cassia wondered how Xandra's bees were doing. Had Nodora been disappointed that Cassia and Lio had missed her concert? How were Zoe's lessons with Kia progressing?

Thoughts of home only deepened Cassia's gloom as half the night passed with no sign of Knight. When Monsoon landed so they could consult with Kella, Cassia made herself say it.

"We're spending time that could cost Chuma's mother."

Monsoon shook his head. "We need Knight if the Accord breakers stand between us and Ipika."

"But if we have to choose between Chuma's mother's life and..." Cassia's throat closed.

Knight should be enjoying his retirement in Orthros. Fighting heart hunters and the Collector should have been his final battles. He should be safe at home playing with Zoe.

Kella stroked Tilili's ears. "You owe Knight your loyalty, as surely as he owes you his. We keep searching."

"Thank you for understanding." A red gleam on the horizon drew Cassia's gaze. The Blood Moon was rising at last.

"Watch yourselves," Kella murmured. "A hound spirit's hunting grounds are not where you want to be under Ayur's Blood."

The red moon crept up from the desert sands and sliced into the dark indigo sky. It was a stunning vision, that orb of blood hovering on the horizon, vivid against the countless white stars.

Excited yips echoed through the night.

Kella drew her fortune blade. "Those are Maaqul hounds. A whole pack, by the sound of it."

"I thought you said this is where they died centuries ago," Monsoon returned, "not where they live now."

Kella shook her head, her gaze darting around. "Nothing like that can survive out here anymore. Not even sand cats inhabit this region."

The yips became a chorus of excited howls. If they didn't belong to living dogs, what could they mean? Cassia didn't follow that thought to its conclusion.

Kella spun Tilili toward the sounds. "They're on the hunt. But what is there for them to hunt?"

Monsoon snatched his fortune blade from his arm scabbard and wrapped Cassia's cold fingers around the grip. "Hang onto this. Just point it away from my wings."

"Thank you." In the absence of her spade, she had to admit, she was glad to have the enormous knife in hand. But she had the eerie feeling that whatever was out here couldn't be hurt by ordinary steel.

A ferocious bay split the air. Cassia would know that sound anywhere. "That's Knight!"

Kella was already setting off toward the sound. Monsoon snatched Cassia up and took flight after Kella.

"*Oedann*, Knight!" Cassia called. "I'm coming!"

They made it over the next dune, and Cassia beheld an impossible sight. A gazelle raced across the desolate landscape. Pale as the Light Moon, she pranced over the red sands with wild grace.

At her heels came the pack. The Blood Moon cast their hides and teeth in crimson light. The hounds, lean as skeletons, coursed after their prey, mingling and shifting, impossible to count. They lifted their slender snouts to the moon and howled.

In the midst of the beasts ran Knight. His heavy fur gleamed the same shade of crimson, and he moved with the pack as if of one mind with them. His broad jaws opened, and he joined their chorus.

"Knight!" Cassia called. "*Ckuundat! Dockk!*"

He paid her no heed, bounding toward the fleeing gazelle with single-minded ferocity.

Fear seized Cassia. What could cause Knight to ignore her commands? What could sever their bond?

Only death.

No, no, no.

Had they come all this way only to find his apparition?

"Monsoon," she cried, "take us lower."

"We don't want to get their attention," he protested.

"The gazelle is their prey. But I need to get closer." Her voice broke. "Please."

He muttered a curse, but relented and made a low pass over the pack. Cassia could hear the Azarqi dogs' panting breaths and see the muscles rippling in their backs. She reached out. Almost there. Almost.

Her hand passed through the blood-kissed forms of the spectral hounds. Their pointed ears were perked, their tales curling excitedly toward the moon. They didn't glance at her.

There was Knight in the center of the pack. She kept her hand out, holding her breath.

Her fingers raked over shaggy, dusty fur. She let out a laugh of relief.

Knight lifted his head and snapped at her fingers.

Monsoon gave his wings a heave and lifted them out of reach.

Her hand was unharmed, but hurt welled in Cassia. "That's impossible. He never growls or snaps at me, except when he's trying to protect me."

"Maybe he's warning you away."

"I won't give up on him."

"Ayur has challenged us," Kella called. "We stay with the Hunt to its end."

They tracked the trackers over the dunes and through the valleys under Ayur's Blood. Cassia called every command she knew in the training tongue, but Knight was consumed with the pack's quest to bring down that gazelle.

The fleet doe led them all on a chase as if it were a merry game to her, while the hounds heaved for their spectral breaths, Tilili lagged behind, and Monsoon's wings strained.

"Are you all right?" she asked him.

"No mangy dog spirits are going to out-hunt Mweya," he snarled back.

Kella leaned low over Tilili's neck, murmuring something in her ear.

The boneyard appeared so suddenly below that it took Cassia by surprise. The gazelle had led them back to where they'd begun.

The pack split, cascading around their ancestral grounds. The gazelle raced for the other side, aiming for the gap in the dogs that was rapidly narrowing before her.

The pack closed in, and she pivoted, darting away from the solid wall of fangs and howls.

It was too late. The pack converged. Blood like moonlight spattered across the bones of their ancestors. The white creature fell, a silent gleam in the midst of the hunters. A pall went through Cassia, and she looked away.

Kella halted on a dune overlooking the pack's kill. Monsoon landed, and Cassia found her feet, only to stumble. The other two caught her before she went tumbling down the hill and eased her to sit down on the sand. She was glad they avoided her injured arm. She couldn't feel it anymore, and that was just how she liked it.

Monsoon's chest labored as he caught his breath. "That was no natural creature."

"That was Ayur's Hunt." Kella's scarf had fallen back, and her braids hung windblown in her eyes. She tossed her head, a fierce smile on her face.

Cassia scanned the press of bodies, looking for Knight. *"Ckuundat! Oona kaetlii?"*

His shaggy head lifted from among the pack. His jaws gleamed with blood.

Cassia shook her head. "How can a specter have blood?"

"How does the moon have blood?" Kella replied. "Ayur only gives her blood when she is pleased."

"What are the consequences if Knight partakes of it?"

"Only the goddess knows."

Cassia set Monsoon's fortune blade aside and scrambled forward. Monsoon reached to stop her, but before he could catch hold of her, she shimmied down the dune on her heels and backside.

She landed at the rim of the boneyard on her hands and knees and met Knight's gaze.

He looked at her over the heads of the wild pack. A dog beside him was licking at his shoulder.

She commanded him to her. When he did not respond, she crooned and cajoled. When the old liegehound training tongue got her no response, she switched to Divine, calling him in the language of Hesperines.

He lifted his head and bayed at the Blood Moon.

"Cassia," Monsoon warned, "be careful. He's not himself. He's—"

"Let her," Kella said. "She needs to know."

Cassia lifted her gaze to the crimson light. What had her hound become, living out here for days on the sustenance of spirit?

She reached into her inner pocket for Nodora's flute. Taking a deep breath, she gave it a sharp blow.

Knight froze, his ears perking.

Now she positioned her fingers over the holes and played gently, trying for the notes that usually calmed him.

He padded nearer, his ghostly brothers and sisters milling around him. He halted at the edge of the boneyard. Almost within reach.

She repeated the strain. He made a little whine in his throat, cocking his head.

Not daring to move, she kept playing, luring, reassuring. He took one more step forward.

She held the flute and the note with one hand, while she eased her other hand out slowly. Nearer, nearer. At last her fingers were close enough for him to sniff—or bite.

His nostrils flared. He leaned forward. She felt the damp, cool touch of his very natural nose.

"Remember me?" she said softly. "I'm Cassia."

He broke out into barks that split across the desert. She had never heard him make such sounds, except for one occasion when he had been locked in the kennels and separated from her all day.

He leapt over the border of the boneyard and came to her.

They tumbled back onto the sand together, and he licked her tears off her face. There was no sign of the blood that had stained his mouth. He looked like himself. He smelled like himself. He shed and slobbered all over her, as always.

She touched his shoulder, where the other dog had licked him. There had been a wound there. Was that where one of the lithic edges had struck him? Now it was another scar running under his fur.

She clung tightly to the flute, her eyes on the Blood Moon, sending silent gratitude to Nodora for Hespera's music.

There came the sound footsteps, and Monsoon's tall form came between her and the moonlight. "Are you both all right?"

"Oh, yes." She smiled into Knight's fur.

Kella halted Tilili a few paces away. The cat twitched her tail and put her ears back, but didn't hiss.

Knight, sprawled halfway across Cassia on his belly, looked at the cat. Cassia could not begin to interpret the look that passed between the two predators.

"Kella," she asked, "did you say Ayur is the goddess of all nocturnal hunters? Does that include Tilili and Knight tonight?"

Kella's brows rose. "I suppose it does."

"Huh," said Monsoon. "You can always trust an Azarqi to negotiate a truce."

"The goddess of the moons does favor diplomats," Kella said.

Cassia looked once more toward the goddess's pack, only to find the hounds gone. The boneyard was as silent as if no living thing had trod there in centuries. But Knight was safe and alive in her arms.

Cassia looked up at Monsoon, then Kella. "You have my gratitude."

Kella sheathed her dagger. "Tonight was an adventure I look forward to recounting around my mother's campfire."

Monsoon put away his blades as well. "The night Ayur and Mweya hunted together. Who'd have thought?"

Her indigo lips curved in a smile again. "You kept up pretty well, for a city boy."

It seemed Ayur had fostered more than one miraculous truce tonight.

"Now we can get back on course toward Ipika." Cassia shut her eyes and cleared her mind, focusing on her inner sense of direction. She raised her good arm and pointed in the direction the jinn's boon was leading her. "That way."

"That's northwest," Kella said. "We'll head that way after a rest."

"There's still time before dawn," Cassia protested. "We don't have to stop yet."

"We need to keep our compass in good condition," Monsoon replied.

"I can keep going." Using Knight to steady herself, Cassia made to stand up.

Her knees buckled. Monsoon caught her and eased her back to the ground. All the way down. Oh, it felt good to lie down.

He pressed a hand to her brow. He was a rather comforting person, when he wanted to be.

But the curse he uttered was not comforting. "Your fever is even worse."

"I have a fever?" Her eyes slid shut. Nice to close her eyes.

He clicked his tongue. "Didn't you notice? You've had it all night."

"Sorry. Carry me some more? Don't mean to make you feel like a pack bird."

"...place to camp?" Monsoon's voice again, angled away from her.

"Not here." Kella's voice. Closer. "...need to get away from the boneyard..."

"...water?"

"...northwest..."

Their words faded from her awareness. She could still feel the sureness of Knight's weight against her and the comfort of his fur. She forgot everything else and slipped into oblivion.

Time passed in a chilly haze. Now and then she woke, reached out. One time she felt Knight. Another time, Monsoon's iron grip and the rush of wind.

Then it was Lio who held her midair, dancing with her across the starstrewn sky over the Maaqul like it was a festival night.

She laughed. "I knew you'd find me."

He kissed her neck, so gentle. "I will kill the one who did this to you."

No, that couldn't be Lio. He didn't make death threats. A dream.

Finally she woke on her back. The same stars overhead. "Northwest?" she thought she asked. Was that faint voice hers?

"Rest," Monsoon commanded.

She shook her head. "Ipika. Northwest."

Kella's hand stilled her. "We're going, Cassia. Just rest."

61

days until

NOTIAN WINTER SOLSTICE

44 Annassa, 1597 IS

OASIS

"SHE'S CLOSE." LIO'S VOICE rumbled out of his throat like sand and drifted off on the wind.

He peered at the reflection ahead. Was it a Craving mirage? It looked like water, winking at them in the moonlight from between two stony ridges.

"Tonight's the night," Hoyefe rasped jauntily, pausing to rest with his hands on his knees. "I'm sure we'll find her, and you'll finally get that well-deserved drink. I won't begrudge you in the least. At least one of us won't die of thirst."

"We'll find water again soon." The confidence in Tuura's voice didn't reach her aura.

Too quietly for mortal ears, Karege asked Lio, "Can you see that?"

"I thought it was a trick of my eyes," Lio admitted.

"It looks like water"—Karege's nostrils flared—"but I can't smell if it's water."

"That's the direction Cassia is in," said Lio.

"Then we'll go," Karege replied.

They dragged themselves onward. Karege assisted both mortals with levitation so Lio could focus his Craving-scattered thoughts on the mind ward. His chest felt hot, his skin cold in the desert air. The wind shifted, sending a shiver over his skin.

The scent came to him on that dry breath of wind. The promise of survival, the fragrance of Sanctuary. He gasped, as if he could drink the smell to soothe his parched veins.

"I smell water," Karege announced.

Tuura sighed a prayer. Hoyefe let out a laugh.

Lio hadn't even smelled the water. All he could smell was… "Cassia. She's here."

The Ashes cheered.

"Go!" Karege gave him a push. "We'll catch up."

Lio found a burst of strength he hadn't known he possessed. He ran. The desert blurred past him. Russet ridges bathed in the Blood Moon's light parted to admit him into a ravine where the Eye of Light shone on a long pool of water.

Cassia's scent grew stronger. The mind ward drew nearer. At last, a flutter in his ears. Her heartbeat.

He let out a cry of frustration that he couldn't step. Pain tore at his wound as he moved faster.

He heard voices. Monsoon's, anguished, yelling in Sandira. A woman's calm, worried tones, answering in Azarqi. Lio wanted them to be quiet so he could listen to Cassia's heart.

They came into view in the shadow of a palm. Monsoon knelt on the ground, his wings flared. The woman stood beside him, her hand on his shoulder. Knight was stretched out there, pressed against…

That small, limp form was Cassia.

Monsoon leapt up, rounding Lio. Fury twisted the man's face. He grabbed Lio by the remains of his collar and lifted them both off the ground with a beat of his wings. "How could you do this to her? After everything her sister did to protect her! Look how ill she is—because of you!"

"Get out of my way!" Lio let out a blast of raw magic.

The impact tore Monsoon's grip from him and sent the man hurtling a few paces, but he caught himself midair with disconcerting ease. The woman, riding a cat as a mount, leapt between them.

Lio had no time to waste on the mercenary. He went down on his knees next to Cassia. Knight licked Lio's hand as he gathered Cassia into his arms. She was out cold.

The woman spoke. "We've done everything we can to care for her. She's not suffering thirst or hunger."

No, no, no. The Craving shouldn't be able to do this to a human. "How long has she been in a faint?"

"She's drifted in and out of consciousness for two days."

He felt for the mind ward, praying he could reach her mind and rouse her. The moment he connected with his spell, her spirit cried out for him.

He didn't even Will his magic into her. Raw power surged out of him and charged through her. Her body bowed in his hold.

Hespera's Mercy, what was happening? Was he hurting her?

His magic flowed, as if a vein ran from his essence to hers. Exhilarating energy throbbed through his weary body.

She gasped for a breath, and her eyes shot open, dilated and unfocused. Her hand clutched at his chest, catching the tatters of his robe. He held her hand there, cradling her against him. There was no pain in his chest now, only the warm flow of his massive magic distilling into the small woman in his arms.

The color returned to her skin, and her heart pounded, fast and strong. At last her gaze focused on his face, and she spoke, her voice as hoarse as if she'd been screaming. "Lio."

"I'm here." He rocked her. "I'm here."

"I knew you'd find me."

"You're safe," Lio said into her hair.

"What did you just do?" Monsoon demanded.

"I'm feeding her my magic," Lio realized. The pull hadn't stopped. It threaded him to her, siphoning his power into her body.

"You can do that?" the woman asked.

Monsoon's shoulders sagged, and he rubbed his face. "Thank all our gods."

Cassia needed more magic. And Lio needed blood. He rose to his feet, lifting her. She rested her face against his chest, breathing deeply.

"I will tend her," Lio said. "You two should wait here for Karege, Tuura, and Hoyefe."

"Mweya's Wings." Monsoon shook his head. "You found half the Ashes?"

"Karege found me. He can tell you everything." Lio lifted his gaze from his Grace and looked at the woman, who wore a fortune blade of her own. "You must be Second Blade Kella."

She nodded, eying him with wariness.

"Thank you for protecting Cassia." Lio turned away.

"Thank Monsoon, too," said Cassia.

Lio paused, not looking at the man. "Thank you."

Monsoon said nothing as Lio carried Cassia away through the grand ruins surrounding the oasis.

The ridges sheltering the ravine proved to be the remnants of walls. The pool stretched on for some distance, bordered by crumbling pillars and palm groves. Broken tiles shimmered beneath the water, hinting at the ancient civilization's beauty, now lost to the same desert that had tried to take Lio's Grace from him.

Lio took Cassia around the curve of the wall until they were out of sight of the others. Knight followed so closely that his fur brushed Lio's calves. Finding a soft bed of reeds under a tree, Lio lay Cassia down. He added veil spells to the natural shelter of the palms. Knight had posted himself nearby, facing the bend in the wall.

"Good dog," Lio said.

Knight's tail wagged.

Lio stretched out over Cassia's trembling form. The sight of the bandage on her arm filled him with helpless rage. He smoothed her sweaty hair back from her face. She was crying.

He kissed her eyelids and damp cheeks. "Shh. No need for tears now, my rose. I'm here."

Her gaze was fixed on his bandages. "What did they do to you?"

"Added insult to injury. Nothing you can't fix. Tell me about your arm."

"A flesh wound."

"The Ashes' diviner-herbalist is on her way. She can make a poultice that will help."

She didn't even ask him about the other Ashes. "I don't need a poultice."

"I know, my Grace, but I want to be very careful as I give you what you need." He worked a cleaning spell on their wounds and the rest of them.

"Oh," she sighed, "being clean. That's a good start."

He laughed, even as his heart ached. "My soap-loving Grace, thinking of cleanliness at a time like this."

"No scrubbing for days. You know it drives me mad."

He stroked her hair again, thinking of all the times she had tried to wash away her bad memories. "I know."

"Lio." She released a shaky breath, stroking his face with her good hand. "We really must break this habit of getting separated."

"This won't happen again." He couldn't stop to wonder if he had the power to keep that promise. He needed to give her every possible reassurance. And let himself believe it, too.

He pressed the gentlest of kisses to her brow. Her skin was feverishly hot now. "Do you feel cold?"

"No. Now I feel like I'm on fire." Her hot hand on his cold cheek felt good. "But you're freezing."

"Don't worry about me."

"You know that's not how this works."

"My Craving has been much worse. But yours, Cassia—I'm so sorry. I never thought you would get symptoms like this. Everything will be all right now." He kissed her temple, her cheek. Rivulets of his magic eddied between them, reassuring him her strength was growing.

"Lio." The love and gratitude that swept out of her as she said his name was like an embrace. Her fingers hovered at his chest, as if she wasn't sure where to touch him. "I don't want to hurt you."

"You're worried about hurting me?"

The pain in his chest had become a distant noise compared to his roaring Craving. His fangs were at full length, ready to sink into the inviting softness of her throat. His own instincts demanded that he feast on her without ceremony.

But he would handle her with the care she needed. *Goddess, help me be gentle.*

He cushioned her in his mind magic, searching for all the pain in her body. Their thoughts blended, and his chest wound seemed to disappear, replaced by the numbing ache in her arm, the sting of blisters on her feet, and various other discomforts in between. Reaching into the parts of her mind that experienced the sensation of pain, he banished her every hurt.

"Even better than being clean?" he asked.

"Mmm. A tie, perhaps."

Knowing it wouldn't hurt her now, he began to unwind her bandage.

"Lio, I don't need a poultice," she said again.

"No. You need me."

When he uncovered her wound, what he saw confirmed his fears. The reddish poison of the desert discolored her veins, radiating from a deep puncture wound, down her arm and up her shoulder.

"Let me see your chest," she demanded.

He shook his head. "There's no need to put you through that."

"Your pain is my pain. Your wounds are my wounds." She reached for his bandage.

He caught her hand. "No."

"Lio, I am your Grace!"

"And there's no reason for that image to linger in your mind for all of time."

Her aura hummed with protest, but she let her hand fall. "As you Will."

She wouldn't like what he was about to suggest, either. For the first time, he didn't want to ask for her permission to drink from her. But he must.

"Cassia, I need to get the poison out of your wound."

"What? You mean—drink from my arm?"

"You will feel no pain. I'm no healer, and a bite won't be enough to repair a wound like this, but it will help."

"If they hit you with one of their weapons, then you already have poison in you. You don't need more!"

"My body can tolerate it. Your blood will cleanse mine."

"Those stone blades *can* harm Hesperines, otherwise you wouldn't be wearing a bandage. There's no telling what harm it will cause you to drink from my wound." She tried to slide away from him, but she was too weak to get far.

He eased her back into his arms. "Let me take care of you."

Tears swelled in her eyes again. "Oh, it's not fair to ask me like that."

He smiled. "I know."

"Show me your wound," she said. "Then you can drink from mine. If I watch your injury while you drink, I can stop you at any sign that my blood is doing you harm."

"Cassia—"

"Those are my terms, my love. And if I ask you to stop drinking at any point, you must heed me."

He sighed. "Always."

He sat back on his heels and eased out of his torn robe. He hated for her to see how stiff his movements were. He couldn't hide a wince.

"Let me."

Her plea drew him back down to her. This time, when she reached for his bandage, he didn't stop her. She unwound it, her aura trembling with more anger with each layer she pulled away.

The color drained from her face again. "Hespera's Mercy."

Goddess, he regretted this. He slipped a hand behind her head, fearing she might faint again.

"What could do this to you?" She traced one of his discolored veins across his pectoral.

"It doesn't matter what it is. It's not stronger than Grace, than us."

"Do you really believe taking blood from my wound will heal us both?"

"Yes."

"Then drink from me, my Grace."

He lowered his head to her arm. Her hand lingered on his chest, just beyond the edge of his wound, light as a bird's wing.

Her injury had reopened, and blood welled sluggishly from the jagged incision. He covered the dagger wound with gentle lips and probed it with his tongue.

His fury at those who had harmed her made his fangs strain to their full length. He framed her wound with his canines and bit down.

She tasted like Cassia. Not like jinn magic or Hypnos's door. She tasted pure and alive.

He drank deeply, pulling the marked blood out of her and swallowing it down. Whatever strange magic it was, his Hesperine senses couldn't detect it. All he could feel was her hand caressing him and her filling with his magic as quickly as he filled himself with her blood.

His Craving eased by minute measures. Then the sensations of healing began in his chest cavity. His teeth tightened on her, and he regretted it. But her hand stroked through his hair, holding him to her.

He dug his fingers into the moist sand on either side of her while his flesh knit together and his skin closed. At last, all that remained was the intense heat where his magic rushed from him to her.

He made himself seal his bite and lifted his head to check on her. Her wound had stopped bleeding, and the swelling had faded. Her veins were all delicate blue beneath her skin, clean and natural. He looked into her eyes and took her hand, pressing her fingers to the smooth, unmarked skin on his chest.

"You were right," she said with relief. "Our bond is stronger than our wounds."

It felt so good to hear her confirm it. He could give her what she needed. *He* was what she needed.

Not his medallion or his diplomacy. His power. Everything she required was inside of him, and he would give it all to her.

"I love you," he vowed.

"I love you too." She sounded hoarse still, but content.

He felt her brow. "Your Craving fever has broken. I don't want you to catch a chill."

"You'll keep me warm." She smiled, one of her lips cracking.

He kissed a tiny speck of blood from her mouth.

She cuddled against his chest, which her blood had made whole. "I never want to move again."

He held her close. "Good. Because you need to stay right here."

"I suppose I will let the rest of the world wait for a moment." She stroked the site of his healed wound. "There's a gap in your chest hair now. That's simply unfair."

"Oh, thorns. That will take an embarrassing amount of time to grow back."

She pressed her mouth to the raw, new skin where the sword had pierced him. He shivered as her kiss banished all memory of his pain.

"Now tell me how you got this," she said.

They recounted their ordeals for each other, with embraces and kisses to remind each other it was over.

"Now sleep," he murmured. "Everything can wait until after you rest."

"Then we can decide what to do next…" She sighed.

"Together."

A TASTE FOR DANGER

MAK STOOD BEFORE THE crucible, which hovered over the forge, suspended in place by levitation enchantments. Within the stone vessel swirled the molten, blood-red metal that would become—he hoped—his second perfect batch of adamas.

He pulled his senses out of the complex layers of geomagic in the depths of the forge. "The spells feel right to me. They should hold the perfect temperature for the next few months."

Nike nodded in approval. Still Mak hesitated to take his eyes off the crucible, or even breathe on it wrong.

"Come along, mother hen," Nike said. "Don't stand here clucking over it until the midnight sun comes for you."

Here in the northern hemisphere, where Nike's forge lay hidden in Orthros Boreou, the days grew longer and longer this time of year. The short hours of this night were already nearly over and with them, Mak's last chance for a smithing lesson until after the midnight sun set for another year.

He sighed. "Why couldn't you have two forges, so we'd have one in the south to use while we're all in residence at Orthros Notou?"

"Brilliant idea. We should break the Queen's laws not once, but twice."

"Your forge is not illegal."

"Hmm, no, only the weapons you intend to craft here."

"If I promise to only craft adamas garden hoes, could we have a second forge in the south where I can practice?"

She pursed her lips. "Well, the greatest obstacle to having a second forge has always been replicating the forge itself. The spells are so precise and require so much power."

Mak nodded. "The forge is an even rarer creation than the weapons you crafted at it."

She crossed her arms. "I suppose it would be easier to perform such a feat twice if I had an assistant. One who has skill and experience regulating geomagical smithies."

Mak's heart leapt. "You can have every last drop of blood in my veins— well, as long as we leave enough for Lyros. When do we start?"

"I'll consider it," she said darkly, but a smile tugged at the corners of her mouth.

He laughed and stood back from the forge, stretching his overworked muscles while the Gift restored them. "I'm ready to go back to Orthros Notou, then."

"Actually, before we step back to the southern hemisphere, I have an errand here in Orthros Boreou. And you're coming with me."

Mak stood at attention. "You do? I am?"

"I know I would only waste my breath if I told you to step back to the southern hemisphere without me while I stay behind here in the north and take care of something." She beckoned to him and headed for the door.

Mak trotted after her. "You're right, First Master Steward. I would be derelict in my duty as a warrior in the Stand if I let you go alone."

"You would be derelict in your duty as a younger brother if you did not follow me around and pester me for my secrets."

He grinned. The truth was, he was relieved. If she had told him to go home without her, while she stayed here in the northern hemisphere… here on the same side of the world as Tenebra…

He would have feared she planned to go errant again and disappear for another century, leaving their family to grieve once more.

And him to miss her.

Not having her in his life had been much easier before he knew what he was missing.

He followed her across the workshop, past adjoining storage rooms, to the antechamber. She halted at the entrance to the underground forge. "Have you ever explored out here?"

"No," he admitted. "I always step in and out. Your wards are so tricky, I wasn't sure what would happen to me if I tried to use the door."

"Wise." She bit her palm and held out her bleeding hand to him. "I'd best attune the lock to you as well."

"I'm honored." Before she could change her mind, he pierced his own palm with his fangs and took her offered hand.

When their blood met, magic charged through his veins, lifting him off the floor. He sensed a silent auric rumble in the walls around him, then a grinding inside the door. He landed on his feet a little too hard.

"Bleeding thorns," he said. "It's a good thing I never tried the door."

"But the wards like you now. They know Blood Argyros when it flows into them." Smiling, Nike stepped back and motioned for him to go ahead.

He took hold of the adamas bar across the door, bracing himself to heave it. But it lifted, light as a feather under his touch.

The door opened up and outward. A heap of snow cascaded away from them. Mak levitated out into the polar night and found himself on a mountainside.

He took in the stunning twilight landscape. Pale fog spread below them, obscuring the ravine below. Craggy, snow-clad peaks surrounded them. A plethora of brilliant stars shone down, undiminished by city spell lights.

Not even Hesperine cartographers had charted these high, forbidding reaches of the Umbral Mountains. There was not a soul out here but him and Nike. Just the two of them and the Goddess's night sky and eternal ice.

Nike took a deep breath, then let out a sigh. He could understand why she had chosen this place to inspire her craft and forge a Sanctuary.

"This way." She levitated away, a little spring in her spell.

Now that she had broken the silence, he drew breath to speak. The air was thin and frigid in his lungs. "Where are we going?"

She didn't answer, only shot upward toward the stars.

He hurried after her with a surge of levitation, his work robes whipping around him in the icy wind.

They levitated higher, higher. His limbs felt heavier, and pressure built behind his eyes. The fog far below seemed to gather in his mind.

Like every young Hesperine, he knew the dangers of levitating too far. At great heights, blood magic became unstable. If you were lucky, you would sink back to a safe level. If you weren't, you would pass out and fall like a stone to whatever painful landing awaited you below. Lio or Kia probably understood the arcane and astronomical reasons why, but what Mak had learned were Stand safety practices.

"Nike?" he called up. "Just how high do you intend to go?"

Her only answer was a defiant laugh that echoed across the mountains.

Mak found the sound even more heroic than her tears. The Victory Star had not lost her taste for danger.

Mak laughed too and pushed himself higher. Another chance to prove he could keep up with his mentor.

Even as the Goddess's heavens seemed to wrestle with him, warning him to return to the ground, the massive magic above them drew nearer. Like a sky within the sky, the Queens' ward sparkled on his auric senses, a comforting darkness.

Nike kept going.

They flew through the ward, light magic scattering around them like countless sharp diamonds, and left the shadowy caress of the ward.

Mak gasped in the meager air. At last he spotted it—a shape soaring above them, a patch of darkness between them and stars. He recognized the shape of its wings. A vulture.

It ceased its circling and flew into Nike's arms. She caught it close, and they spun back down under the protection of the ward.

Now that she had secured her goal, she wasted no time returning to the ledge in front of her Sanctuary. Mak followed her into the warmth of the forge.

The familiar chamber filled with the foreign scent of myrrh that emanated from the bird. The silence reminded Mak the creature had no heartbeat, the sign that it was bloodless—undead.

The bizarre messenger bird gave him a sanguine look over Nike's shoulder, resting its ugly head against her neck. Mak suppressed a shudder. He didn't know how she tolerated touching a reanimated corpse. The minion of a necromancer, Hesperines' sworn enemies.

But Nike had assured Mak she knew the necromancer to whom the buzzard belonged, and that he was a valuable source of information inside the Magelands.

"Now I understand your errand," Mak said. "Treacherous as this place is, it's closer to Cordium than southern Orthros is."

"In my last letter, I asked his master to send him this way instead. To see if he could withstand the mountains for a shorter flight."

"And faster delivery?"

"I admit to some impatience." She set the bird down on her worktable, but it did not seem eager to leave her arms. It snuggled against her while she removed the metal cylinder from its leg.

"I know you have a long, long list of hopeless admirers," Mak muttered, "but a bloodless vulture among them?"

"Well, a liegehound adores Rudhira now. That makes us even."

Mak couldn't help laughing at the thought of Knight begging for the First Prince's attention. Come to think of it, the bird's beady eyes were about as pathetic as a begging dog.

Mak muttered a curse and reached out to scratch the bird's chin. The vulture shut his eyes and ruffled his feathers. His emotions might feel like a void in the Blood Union due to his bloodless nature, but his happiness was obvious.

Nike must have been impatient indeed, for she unrolled the necromancer's letter in front of Mak, although she turned so he couldn't read it over her shoulder. Her gaze scoured the scroll.

"Any new information on Methu's possible whereabouts?" he asked.

"My ally has a lead."

"Nike, that's…marvelous news."

But Mak's heart sank. He had let his hopes levitate too high.

His smithing lessons were over for the season. Now she had information that could revive her quest. She had no reason to stay, and every reason to leave again.

He tried to push away his disappointment. His feelings were so much less important than the hope of finding Methu after all these years.

Mak knew what he would do if anything threatened his Trial brother. The last letter from Lio and Cassia had made Mak want to drop everything and go find them. Lio had reported nothing more dangerous on their travels than heavy rains and muddy roads delaying their progress. And yet something about all their recent letters set off Mak's sense of danger. He couldn't shake his worry for them, even though it didn't seem justified.

He could not imagine how Nike lived with Methu's loss night after night. Wondering what had befallen him. If he was suffering in the war mages' custody even now. Or if, after a century of holding out hope he could be rescued, she would discover that she was wrong, and he had truly passed on to Sanctuary to be with Hespera.

But he also knew what his parents had lived with every night that Nike had been missing.

He tried to find the right words to say, but he was much better at taking action. He stood there debating with himself while she wrote a hasty reply on a veiled length of paper.

She rolled the answer and a bundle of other scrolls into the cylinder. The papers that might break their parents' hearts once more.

Nike picked up the vulture again. It chortled and nibbled on her braid. Mak was uncertain whether it was too stupid to understand what was happening, or simply very good-natured about toiling across frozen mountains and an entire continent to go back to Cordium. Either way, it let her carry it to the door, kiss it on the head, and send it off into the cold night.

They stood outside the forge and watched it go.

"Nike—" he began.

"My ally must investigate further. He will write to me about what he finds in his next letter."

Mak let out a breath he hadn't known he'd been holding. "I'm sorry. I know how much you want real answers."

"I have inured myself to disappointments."

"There must have been so many."

"Yes. But there have been blessings, too. I must admit…the most distracting interruptions to my quest have proved to be…very dear." She gave a huff, her eyes fixed on the bird.

"What do you mean?" Mak asked.

She tore her gaze away and grinned at him. "Alkaios. Nephalea. Cassia." She reached out and ruffled his hair as if he were Bosko's age. "My meddlesome little brother."

"Ha." He used a classic Steward dodge to evade her, and she let him. She carried so many regrets. But he was not one of them.

"Does this mean you'll go dancing with us on the docks tomorrow night?" he asked.

"Absolutely not. The answer is still no."

He crossed his arms. "I followed you to a rendezvous with a bloodless vulture without question or complaint."

"Don't pretend you weren't delighted to indulge your curiosity."

"Aren't you curious to learn the new dances? Even a very little bit?"

"No."

"I'm the Steward who is refraining from reporting you for consorting with an illicit avian. You should try harder to stay on my good side."

She snorted. "I cannot go dancing with you tomorrow night. I promised Mother we would go for a horseback ride."

Mak resisted the urge to crow in triumph. He'd best not rub it in.

His and Father's efforts to mend the rift between Nike and Mother was succeeding. Now Orthros's two greatest and most stubborn warriors had progressed from sparring together in the arena to taking up their old pastime of riding.

"Well," Mak said, "I don't dare steal you from the Guardian of Orthros. She might make me regret it during our next training exercise. Will you go dancing the night after that?"

"No!" Nike said with a laugh. "Thorns, you refuse to give up, don't you?"

Mak crossed his arms. "It is my duty to distract and interrupt you."

And to keep reminding her of all the reasons to stay here in Orthros, to enjoy the surprising blessings that had come out of the curse of her quest.

60

days until

NOTIAN WINTER SOLSTICE

45 Annassa, 1597 IS

SHADOW AND SUNSHINE

S

HE AWOKE IN THE shelter of Lio's embrace. His veils stood between her and the rest of the world. Everything would be all right.

She turned in his arms to look at him in the dusky light. Or was it nearing dawn? Regardless, he appeared wide awake. His hair fell tousled about his face, and his beard was scruffy. Her silken sorcerer had gone wild in the desert.

She reached up and tucked a wave of his hair behind his ear. "Watching me sleep again, my love?"

His exquisite mouth curved in a smile, and his long lashes lowered over his eyes as his gaze slid down her body. "I never take that simple miracle for granted."

She touched the healed place on his chest, reassuring herself that he, too, was safe now. He was right that she would have the image of his wound in her mind forever. But also the certainty that her blood had healed him.

It felt so good to lie against his warm body in the cool air. "How long was I asleep?"

"You spent the Dawn Slumber with me."

Her heart gave a jolt. So it was twilight. Another day had passed, a new night had fallen. "Every hour could cost Ipika."

Lio put a finger to her lips. "I don't want you to set foot outside my veils until we've made certain you're well."

"I suppose you're right. It won't help us find Ipika if I collapse." Cassia sighed, nestling closer to him. Just a few more minutes.

Her stomach chose that moment to let out a noisy rumble.

Lio smiled and slid down beside her to kiss her belly. "All right, I will allow you out of my veils for food. You need to eat something besides my magic."

"But you're my favorite food," she protested.

"I know." His dark blue eyes gleamed with masculine satisfaction. "I won't be jealous of the gourds if you eat them, too."

They donned their clothes, such as they were, and left their Sanctuary. Knight trotted eagerly at their sides toward the smells of cooking, clearly feeling more like himself. Hand in hand, she and Lio followed the scents around the curve of the wall to the other side of the ruins.

There was no one there. No mercenaries, no fire, no smoke. But the scent of roasting bitterblade filled the air. Cassia looked around the seemingly deserted ruins, her skin crawling.

The colonnades all led to one place. A great doorway, half sunk in the ground, flanked by time-worn slabs of desert stone. The whole temple where Cassia had taken shelter would fit inside that structure. But the yawning, dark gate didn't look like a refuge.

"What is it?" Lio rubbed her back.

Something about the door pulled on her senses. She tried to concentrate on it. Her arm wound gave a throb, and she put a hand to it. "Nothing."

Lio frowned in concern. "You need a poultice. Let's find the others."

"Where is everyone?" she wondered.

"Right here," announced a man's gallant voice.

Colors burst in the air before her eyes, manifesting into a rain of flower petals. Suddenly she could see the mercenaries gathered around a campfire. They sat on fallen columns and ruined stones, cooking gourds and palm nuts.

She took in the sight. Here were four of the legendary Ashes.

And one lone eagle. Monsoon sat on his own on one side of the campfire, Kella and her comrades on the other.

As Cassia and Lio approached, Monsoon rose to his feet. "Cassia, you're…" He swallowed. "…walking."

That didn't sound like half of what he had meant to say. She put a hand on his arm. "How's your foot? No danger of it turning to silk, I hope?"

He snorted, and she knew he was back to his normal self.

Lio's hand tightened in hers. He said nothing to the man who had carried her across the desert for days and fought for her survival. Monsoon didn't look at him.

One of the Ashes broke the tension. His hair was as impressive as his gold roster status, but that wasn't the first thing Cassia noticed about him. The way she felt safe near him told her he was a Hesperine, even before he beamed at her and showed his fangs.

"Well, if it isn't Cassia and Knight!" he said. "I'd know you anywhere. Those freckles and the dog."

Cassia gave the elder a Hesperine wrist clasp. "Karege. You will always have my gratitude for everything you've done for Lio."

He patted her hand. "It was great fun. He kept me entertained with your tales of war mage assassination plots. You youngbloods are certainly shaking up Orthros."

Cassia smiled. "We try."

Another mercenary stood and gave Cassia a flourishing bow, offering her a bouquet.

She blinked, then reached out to take it. Just before her fingers touched it, it transformed into a bird and flew away.

"Hoyefe, master fencer and illusionist?" she guessed.

"You know my reputation. How delightful."

Cassia arched a brow at him. "You are not at all what I expected for an alumnus of Imperial University. You must take that as a compliment, as we're a Capital family."

He gave her a charming laugh. "Don't listen to the rumors, my dear. We know how to have fun at Imperial, too."

The gentleman appeared to be quite the rogue, with his fashionable tunic hanging open over a perfectly sculpted bronze chest. He had the physique of a fencer and the taste of an artist, to be sure.

He lifted her hand and kissed her knuckles. "My apologies for startling you a moment ago. I'm maintaining the most thorough and confounding illusions over our party, since the Accord Breakers have a nasty habit of dancing right through our Hesperine friends' veils. Did you and Lio enjoy the benefits of the sun-deflecting spells I employed throughout the day?"

"Ah. That's why I woke so early." Lio clasped Hoyefe's wrist. "That is much appreciated. Thank you."

"My pleasure. And yours, I hope." Hoyefe winked at Lio.

Lio smiled innocently. "My apologies for being so irritable for the past several days. The Craving tends to ruin a Hesperine's good manners."

"No hard feelings. My illusions wouldn't have done her justice." Hoyefe leaned closer. "You have excellent taste in Hesperines, my dear."

She was blushing, but she laughed. "I'm very happy Lio and I have an eternal taste for each other."

Lio seated Cassia beside a woman with a bright head wrap and a staff. This must be Tuura the diviner. She sat halfway between her comrades and Monsoon like a peacemaker.

She had the kind of smile that made a person feel instantly reassured. "Hello, Cassia. It's such a joy to meet you at last."

Cassia smiled back. "I feel the same way."

Kella looked Cassia up and down, her eyes full of things she clearly wanted to say, but could not. "In one piece, then?"

"Thank you, Kella. I am well."

"I can't let anything happen to you."

Cassia smiled. "I wouldn't dare break when you all need me for a compass."

"I won't let anybody break. The rest of us are all bandaged and covered in herbs. Let me see about your arm now."

Cassia sat still while Tuura examined her wound. There was no pain, only Lio's presence in her mind. Knight posted himself beside them, with Kella between him and Tilili. The cat dozed, as if she had better things to do than notice a dog.

"Good, good," said Tuura. "Lio has already worked on this, I see."

Lio bent near. "Did it help?"

"Oh, yes," Tuura answered. "For Cassia, let's mix some of your saliva in the poultice."

Cassia was glad Tuura kept Lio busy. She could tell her Grace needed something to do, preferably for her. Even after he had drunk the taint in her wound from her body with his own fangs. Even though he was managing her pain with his thelemancy even now.

He would be on high alert for some time after their separation. So would she, and gods help the Accord breaker who had put a sword in her Grace, if it came to a rematch.

Karege was looking their way with concern. "Mind your shoulder, Peanut."

Cassia bit her lip. "If I may ask, how does a gold roster mercenary acquire a fortune name like 'Peanut'?"

Tuura chuckled. "Peanuts are a staple in the little village where I grew up. Every season, every meal, every dish. There are always peanuts in there somewhere. When I left to see the world, I vowed never to eat a single peanut ever again."

"Has your fortune name helped you succeed?" Cassia asked.

"Yes! I had a close call once, though." Tuura cast a chiding glance at Hoyefe.

The illusionist grinned, stretching out by the fire. "The peanut butter mustache looked fetching on you."

Tuura shuddered. "It's a good thing Kella woke me before I licked it off in my sleep."

"Spoilsport," Hoyefe said to their second blade.

"Who, me?" Kella shrugged. "Tilili loves peanut butter. I couldn't keep her from licking Tuura's face."

Cassia's stomach rumbled again.

While Tuura and Lio worked on her arm, Kella handed Cassia a roasted gourd on a stick. "Eat."

Cassia took it in her good hand and dug into the food.

Monsoon laughed. "Made friends with the bitterblade, did you?"

"You were right about Kella's cooking," Cassia answered with her mouth full.

Monsoon tossed Knight a bite of something, and her hound eagerly accepted the handout. "Knight appears to enjoy snake as much as Tilili does."

Tilili batted the other half of the snake between her paws.

Karege watched sadly. "Waste of a good snake."

"*I* never waste a good snake," said Hoyefe, to his friends' laughter.

Tuura smeared the finished poultice on Cassia's arm. "Remember the time Ukocha found that viper in her bed?"

Karege groaned. "Oh, the smell."

Kella wrinkled her nose. "I admit, burnt snake doesn't smell all that lovely to humans, either. There was nothing left of that one for me to cook."

"And yet, she didn't even singe the bedclothes." Hoyefe sighed. "Now there's a woman with finesse."

Cassia glanced at Monsoon to see his reaction to Hoyefe mentioning heat, bedclothes, and Ukocha.

The lone mercenary had donned his mask of ill temper again. "How many more Ashes are we looking for out here, besides Ukocha?"

"This is all of us," Kella answered.

Monsoon startled. "There are always seven Ashes. What happened to the other two?"

Kella skewered a gourd with her fortune blade. "After we lost two of our best, we never found decent replacements. There are five Ashes now."

"You came out here with only five?" Monsoon demanded.

"That makes us five times smarter than mercenaries who always fight alone."

So they had found all of Ukocha's comrades. Why not the first blade herself?

Was she still alive to find?

And what had become of Ipika, without any protection?

"Cassia," Kella said, "I don't want to push you when you've just recovered, but as soon as you're able to guide us onward, we need to get moving."

"Of course." Cassia checked her inner sense of direction. Her arm spasmed, and she knotted her hands.

"Relax your arm," Tuura requested.

She tried. Lio's mind magic trickled through her, carrying away her tension, while his gentle hands held her arm for Tuura. Cassia gave up trying to sense Ipika until they were finished.

Once they had re-bandaged her wound, Lio sat down next to her and put his arm around her waist. Leaning into him, she closed her eyes, concentrating on the tug of the jinn's magic.

She had to grip his hand to keep herself from clawing at her wound.

His body tensed against hers. "What's wrong?"

Cassia looked into the dark mouth of the doorway that led down beneath the sands. "Chuma's mother is inside the ruins."

As soon as the words left her mouth, she felt disoriented. A wave of vertigo overtook her, and she sagged against Lio.

He caught her close. "Are you ill again? Do you—"

"No," she groaned. "Oh, no. My inner compass is…gone."

Silence reigned around the fire. Cassia was glad Lio was holding her up, because she thought she might sink into the sands from the sheer weight of her despair.

"I'm so sorry," she said. "It seems the jinn's boon has…worn off, now that we've reached our destination. I know Ipika is in the ruins. But I cannot guide us to her down there."

A strong hand took hold of hers. She looked down at Kella's blue fingers.

"Blaming yourself achieves nothing," Kella told her.

"I promised Chuma," Cassia said.

Tuura patted her other hand. "And you've risked your life to keep that promise."

"Who needs a jinn boon, anyway?" Karege scoffed. "You lot have two Hesperines."

Lio lifted Cassia's chin. "Together, we can find her."

She looked into his eyes, feeling him in her thoughts, and his conviction seemed to run into her veins. Now that she was with him again, she truly could believe anything was possible.

"We're going in," Kella announced. "Tonight."

The mercenaries fell quiet and heeded their second blade. It was clear that in Ukocha's absence, Kella led the Ashes.

"We should be prepared for anything," she said. "There's no telling what dangers we'll encounter."

"I don't know," Hoyefe mused, "the ruins seem like a sensible enough place for Chuma's mother to take shelter."

"If you like cave-ins, booby traps, and surprise jinn," Kella snapped.

Hoyefe lounged on his elbow, holding a gourd as if it were the finest wine. "I might like surprise jinn."

Kella gave him a quelling look.

"It's hardly unheard of," Hoyefe went on. "Your Azarqi legends are full of scintillating human-jinn pairings."

"Which always ends badly for the human," Kella said.

"It's the Accord breakers we should watch out for." Karege scowled at the gate. "Those ruins look like a perfect place for them to ambush us again."

"I want all of us to understand our roles before we enter," Kella instructed. "Everyone will follow me. Tilili's ears can pick up the tiniest sounds far underground, so she can warn us of potential cave-ins."

Then she looked at Hoyefe again. "You'll maintain the invisibility spells to protect us against ambushes."

He grinned at her. "Are you certain you don't want me to disguise us? You'd look fetching as a water jinn."

Kella did not appear amused. "Invisibility, Hoyefe."

"They'll still be able to hear us," Monsoon pointed out.

Hoyefe smirked. "But good luck landing an arrow or dagger in a target you can't see."

"No use bothering with veils," Kella went on. "Karege, we need you to watch our backs."

Karege made a fist. "Tackle anything that moves. My favorite duty."

"What matters most is that we don't get separated again." Kella turned to Tuura. "Is there anything at all you can do about the spirit tears?"

Tuura cleared her throat. "I thought you'd never ask. I've been studying the spirit tear residue as we searched for everyone. I've concluded that I cannot close spirit passages in the Maaqul."

Kella cursed and started to speak.

Tuura interrupted her with a smile. "But I can still cast spirit shackles."

Karege beamed. "Of course you can."

Cassia tried not to sound apprehensive. "If I may ask, are those anything like Hesperine blood shackles?" The restraint spell Hesperine warders used was not pleasant. She knew that from Lio's experience, when Mak and Lyros had cast it to stop him from giving into his Craving for Cassia in front of the Tenebran embassy.

Lio's smile suggested he was remembering the same night, particularly the part where her kiss had broken the spell. "Yes and no. Spirit shackles can prevent someone from spirit walking or going through a spirit gate, just as blood shackles can keep a Hesperine from stepping. But Tuura's spell uses ancestral power, rather than blood magic, so the underlying methodology is different."

Cassia was glad to hear Lio lapsing into his usual scholarly tone. He was feeling more like himself. "That sounds powerful."

Lio bowed in Tuura's direction. "Only very powerful diviners can cast them."

Tuura patted Cassia's hand again. "Don't worry in the least. I know it sounds dreadful, but I'm a very friendly shackle caster. I'll make the spell as comfortable for everyone as possible."

Hoyefe's mouth curved into a smile. "Are you suggesting you'll lock us up in padded shackles, Tuura? All of us at once? With surprise jinn? This might turn out to be our most enjoyable adventure of all time."

That got a chuckle out of everyone, even Monsoon and Kella. Cassia paused to marvel that she was in the middle of a desert in the Empire, laughing at naughty jests with mercenaries. If someone told the courtiers back in Tenebra what Lady Cassia's life looked like now, no one would believe her.

"I still advise everyone to avoid the weapons." Tuura's cautious tone dampened everyone's humor.

"Yes," Cassia agreed. "The jinn I met called them 'lithic edges' and said they give humans and Hesperines the power to move as the jinn do."

Tuura frowned. "Curious. These weapons clearly have power—and poison—we don't properly understand. And remember, if they hit me, I'll be unable to use my magic."

"Nobody will even scratch you, Peanut," Karege promised.

"Don't you get yourself scratched up either, Noon Watch. I'm bringing a batch of poultice, but I know you'll never let me use it on you."

"Lio," Kella said, "with your mind magic, you have the farthest range for locating auras. I want you to concentrate on sensing Ipika."

"Of course," Lio agreed.

"If we do get ambushed, can you also try to disable the Accord breakers with thelemancy? The more of them you can stop before they use the lithic edges, the fewer spirit shackles Tuura will have to maintain."

Cassia wound her fingers in Lio's. "Truth be told, when Lio is near, battles are often superfluous."

He ran his thumb over the back of her hand. "If they make the mistake of attacking us while I am awake, they will not be a threat."

"How fast can you master their minds?" Kella asked.

"Faster than they can form the thought of throwing a dagger."

She appeared impressed. "Cassia—" she began.

"I will not stay behind," Cassia preempted her. "I will not let Lio out of my sight, and I will follow Ipika's trail to the end, no matter how far down that is."

"Of course I won't leave your sight." Lio wrapped both arms around her.

She looked at him. "I thought you were going to tell me to stay somewhere safe."

"None of the dangers of the Maaqul have deterred you so far. I know better than to try. For the record, that does not mean I'm happy about it."

She gave him a quick kiss.

"Good," said Kella, "then I won't have to argue with you. Hesperine rhetoric is infuriating in scholarly debates. Cassia, you and Knight are with Karege."

"Excellent," Cassia replied. "Tackle anything that moves. I'll direct Knight to do the tackling."

Karege grinned. "The Stewards won't be the only Hesperines in history to fight alongside a liegehound."

Smiling, Cassia turned to Monsoon. "Will you help us tackle enemies?"

"No." He didn't smile back. "I will make sure no Accord breakers target you."

Lio's magic hummed dangerously. "Nothing will happen to Cassia while my heart beats."

Hoyefe frowned. "Why would the Accord breakers want to target Lio's dumpling in particular?"

"You didn't see their tattoos?" Monsoon looked around at the Ashes.

"We were too busy getting tossed across the desert," Kella said. "What tattoos?" Then her face froze, as if she had just had a terrible realization. "A circle of stone fragments on the palm?"

Monsoon nodded.

"What does it mean?" Lio demanded.

Monsoon looked away. "They're a group of vigilantes who hunt down any shadowlanders in the Empire. We don't know their identities, but we've all met them in battle in the past. We call them the Broken Hands because of their tattoo."

"Well." Cassia kept her voice calm. "That explains a great deal."

If Ipika was in the business of helping people like Cassia, no wonder the Broken Hands were after her.

That also meant Cassia was walking into the ruins with a target on her back.

Lio touched her hair, holding her close to his chest. "I won't let them hurt you."

She looked up at him. "I know. Remember when we faced the Collector. We promised each other we wouldn't lose. And we didn't."

But her reminder of their victory against the Old Master didn't seem to reassure him. He just looked haunted.

Cassia swallowed. "Tell me truly. Am I a danger or an asset to Ipika in the coming battle?"

"Asset," Kella answered. "You've braved the Maaqul to rescue her. I look forward to seeing that determination in battle."

For the first time in weeks, Cassia didn't feel like a weak human. "Thank you."

Kella smiled. "Not to mention, if they're focused on targeting you, the rest of us can take advantage of that distraction."

"Cassia is not bait," Lio objected.

She squeezed his hand. "No, just a diversion with a very mean dog."

That roused a laugh from everyone, and she thought Mak would have been proud of her for thinking of a jest in the moments before battle.

"I want you all to know," Cassia said to the mercenaries, "I don't take for granted what you've done for me. I know I'm a fugitive."

"Falsely accused," Karege said.

She put her hand in Knight's ruff. "Well, except for the part about mauling a Sandira guard."

Monsoon huffed. "I've done worse to him in the Court of Claws, to be honest."

"The Ashes don't tolerate injustice." Anger simmered in Kella's voice. "We judge a person by one thing only. Not where they came from. Not what language they speak. By their deeds." Her jaw clenched. "You've shown us who you are, Cassia. You came out here to rescue all of us, and you turned down the power and riches of the jinn to help find Chuma's mother. If only—" Kella stopped, making a frustrated noise. She sounded as ready as Cassia for the secrecy to end. "What I'm trying to say is that… an old friend of mine would have been impressed with you."

Cassia blinked back tears. "Thank you, Kella."

"I won't let anything happen to you. If we meet the Broken Hands, I want prisoners. But I'll accept corpses."

"I can make sure we take prisoners," said Lio. "As many as you prefer."

"How many do you want for questioning, Hoyefe?" asked Kella.

"I like to have at least three to tattle on each other, although I could make do with two."

"Two or three then, Lio," Kella requested, "depending on how many minds you're comfortable controlling at the same time."

Cassia didn't like to remind him of the battle in Martyrs' Pass, but she felt the need to mention it now. "Lio once held hundreds of minds for the duration of a battle."

There was a moment of silence around the campfire.

"Well," said Kella, "that's gold roster-worthy. Lio, Cassia, consider yourselves honorary Ashes. That means you wield your power to the fullest—but also that you follow my orders."

"Understood, Second Blade." Lio bowed.

"It's an honor to fight with you," said Cassia.

The corner of Monsoon's mouth lifted. "If they're going to be honorary Ashes, they need honorary fortune names."

Karege crossed his arms and sat back, considering Lio. "Sunshine."

They all laughed, and Lio groaned.

Kella tilted her head at Cassia. "And for our defector from Tenebra, Shadow."

The mercenaries applauded.

Lio smiled at her. "Perfect."

"And for you, my light," Cassia replied.

"Make ready," Kella said. "We're heading in."

While the Ashes broke camp, Lio drew Cassia aside. His veil spells swept around them.

She stroked his chest. "I know you're afraid for me."

Without another word, he kissed her until she was liquid glass in his hold.

Then he pulled back and looked into her eyes, his own fraught with emotion. "Be careful."

"By our Oath, my Grace, I will. Knight and I have your back."

"And I have you." His voice echoed along the walls of the mind ward.

INTO THE RUINS

E VEN LIO'S HESPERINE EYES couldn't see far into the grand,
ruined doorway. The Light Moon had set. The Blood Moon's glow
splashed into the entrance, illuminating a flight of broad, shallow
steps that led down out of sight.

"Spell lights, please," Kella requested.

Lio half expected Hoyefe to conjure a lightworks display and naked
dancing girls, but the man only cast a simple, glowing orb like Lio did.
Their lights revealed the stairs to be pitted and worn, but not crumbling.
Knight leaned toward the gloom, sniffing the air.

"Should we levitate down, in case the floor can't be trusted?"
Karege asked.

Kella shook her head. "The steps look sound enough. We need to stay
on the ground where we can fight. Even the instant of reaction time to set
us back down could cost us in an ambush."

Karege nodded. "Understood."

"You're welcome to levitate us to safety if we crash through the floor,
though." With that unpleasant prediction, Kella urged Tilili forward. The
Ashes followed her down, choosing their footing with care.

But Monsoon balked on the threshold. "Of course this whole disaster
would end with us going underground."

"Do you have a fear of caves?" Cassia's aura colored with both concern
and amusement.

She had actually come to *like* the vulture, as impossible as that
seemed to Lio.

"No," Monsoon groused. "I hate any place too confined for me to fly."

"Will your foot be all right?" she asked.

"Thanks to Tuura, I'll manage. But I won't be able to use any of my best aerial attacks down there."

"You didn't rely on those when we saw you fighting in the Court of Claws, and those rhino guards still had a very bad night."

The corner of Monsoon's mouth turned up in a crooked grin. "Told you I was the best."

"And so humble, too." Cassia gave Monsoon's arm a poke.

Lio captured her hand that had made the teasing gesture.

Monsoon started down the stairs, limping along with his bandaged foot. "It's no boast when it's the truth, *nyakimbi.*"

The endearment stunned Lio. That was the same word Monsoon called Chuma.

A turmoil of emotion overtook him, feelings he couldn't explain to himself. He wanted to hurl Monsoon away from Cassia as he had the night before, this time with a blast of magic that would make sure the mercenary could not fly back to her.

Lio held her close as they followed Monsoon down, wishing he could pull her back up into the moonlight. Knight came at Cassia's heels, his toes clicking on the stone.

The moment they passed through the doorway, pain darted through Lio's chest. Cassia yelped and clutched a hand to her arm. He wanted to ask her if she was all right, but he couldn't get air into his lungs.

Hoyefe staggered, putting a hand to the wall. "Well, that's unpleasant."

Kella hunched her shoulders. "Tuura, thoughts?"

Tuura's hand tightened on her staff. "The magical disruption is stronger in here. Our lithic wounds seem to be responding to it."

Karege shook his arm. "'Responding' is a nice way to describe the feeling of someone digging around in your insides. Bleeding thorns."

Lio checked Cassia's bandage. No blood. "I got the poison out. This shouldn't be happening."

"Does yours hurt?" She eyed his chest.

"Yes," he admitted.

Kella started forward again. "We've all fought through pain before. A little sting like this isn't about to stop us from finding Chuma's mother."

Their footfalls echoed down toward their unseen destination.

"Do you sense anything, Lio?" Kella asked.

He resisted the urge to liken the atmosphere to a tomb. "No."

When they reached the bottom, Cassia let out a sound of wonder. "What is this place?"

The inside walls of the sizeable chamber were sculpted with majestic skill into doorways and pillars, stairways, and arches that rose up to the high ceiling.

"It's the same architecture as the temple." Monsoon touched a hand to the engravings on a nearby wall of striated, red stone.

"The jinn told me it was built by humans," Cassia said. "So this must have been, too."

"If the jinn was telling the truth," Karege said.

"They never tell lies." Kella tilted her head back. "You just can't trust a thing they say."

"Does anyone recognize the carvings?" Lio asked.

Hoyefe studied one of the pillars. "This is not the work of any civilization known in Imperial art history. Marvelous. We are the first people to appreciate its beauty in who knows how long."

"No clues about whose magic we're dealing with, then." Kella shook her head. "Let's keep going."

"But which way?" Karege levitated to peer through a second-story window. "Ipika could be anywhere in this maze."

Lio let his thelemancy fill the many doorways surrounding them and sweep through whatever mysterious passages lay beyond. "I still can't sense anyone."

Karege landed next to him. "If she's still outside your reach, this place is enormous. We could wander in here for days."

"We need to mark which way we've already been," said Kella.

"Blood works," Karege suggested.

Cassia shook her head. "Then the Broken Hands would follow us. I'll remember our route."

"How can you keep track of this labyrinth?" Kella asked.

"I spent months sneaking around in secret passages in Tenebra," Cassia said. "I learned to memorize my route without marking my way."

"Well," Hoyefe said with appreciation, "aren't you accomplished in subterfuge."

"There's a reason I call her Lady Circumspect." Lio smiled.

"Well, I would have to be, to keep up with a sneaky Hesperine sorcerer."

Lio's smile faded. His Hesperine sorcery was not doing them any good at the moment. "Let me try sensing for Ipika once more."

She took his hand. "Let's do it together, with blood to amplify your spell."

He squeezed her hand. "Good idea."

Gently, he bit the soft flesh at the base of her thumb, feeling her shiver at his touch. He swallowed a sip of her blood before scoring his own palm with his fang and holding their bleeding hands together.

"Fair warning," Lio said, "you all might feel this."

Sped by his and his Grace's libation, his power leapt from him. He sent targeted bolts of thelemancy down each corridor in search of auras.

Cassia's aura thrilled to his spell, the mind ward humming. But the Ashes had a mighty vocabulary of profanity from around the Empire.

"Don't cause a cave-in!" Kella snapped.

"Don't worry," he reassured her. "Stone is my father's craft. I know just when to stop before I wreck his workshop."

Karege laughed. "Newblood accidents."

"According to Lio's father," Cassia said, "the statue he made from the pieces turned out better than what he originally had in mind." With his eyes shut, Lio felt her brush the hair back from his face. "Anything?"

In the quiet after his spell, he sensed it. "There's a spark of something—not an aura. Magic of some kind. But it doesn't belong here... and it's fresh."

He opened his eyes and drifted toward the glimmer. He found it tucked away on the back of a pillar—a small scorch mark. The others gathered around him to look. He touched the burnt spot and felt the same sting in his fingers as he had at the ambush site.

Kella said it before Lio did. "Ukocha was here!"

Cassia gave a sigh of relief. "Ipika has her protection down here."

Karege laughed. "Our first blade didn't seem too worried about the Broken Hands following her if she marked her path."

"Knowing her," said Kella, "she wanted to lure them after her and into an ambush of her own."

Hoyefe put his hands on his hips. "With no respect for the artistic value of the architecture at all!"

"Can you follow her trail through the ruins, Lio?" Tuura asked.

"Certainly. In this case, Hesperine sensitivity to fire magic is a strength, rather than a weakness."

Karege nodded. "Especially enhanced by the range of your mind magic and Cassia's blood."

Cassia gave him a playful smile that promised she was happy to enhance him again.

He kissed her hand before sending a spell light ahead of them through a doorway. "I sense the next spark this way."

With Kella in the lead, they passed under an arch onto what appeared to be an underground road. Tilili's reflexes alerted her to no traps along the way.

Ukocha's marks led them through the wonders of the subterranean city. Plants Lio had never seen hung from stone window boxes, their filmy, luminescent fronds thriving without the touch of the sun. Cave-ins blocked doorways into mysterious chambers. In the basins of once-lively fountains, deep pools remained, unstirred for time out of mind.

At every turn, Ukocha had written her signature in fire magic. They found her signs tucked in the rubble, half hidden under the fall of a plant, or reflecting on the water.

A narrow lane forced them to walk single file. While Knight went ahead of Cassia, Lio stayed close behind her, a hand at her waist. He knew he shouldn't mind having any ally at his back, not even Monsoon. But the rustle of the man's feathers made Lio grit his teeth, his fangs spoiling for a fight.

The narrow lane opened up into a large chamber, and they all gasped. A broad plaza stretched out before them, bordered in beautiful dwellings built into the cavern walls. Dust had dulled the tiles of the floor, but Lio could make out faded patterns of black and gold.

Who had lived here? Who had built the temple that had saved his Grace's life an epoch later? What had become of these people, with whom he had a bond of gratitude beyond their time?

With great care, Hoyefe brushed some of the glowing plants away from a statue with a missing head. "Time has hidden her face. But her body still speaks. One could imagine she is an early precursor to the goddesses from Old Delta Imperial temples, and yet even more sophisticated."

"That would make this ruin several millennia old." Lio let that sink in. He was standing in a place far older than the most ancient Hesperines.

"Well, that explains why even centuries-old Azarqi scholarship has no record of this place." Kella turned Tilili in a circle. "Which way? So many roads lead from here."

Monsoon flew up to one of the balconies and perched on a wide stone railing. "If we stay in the passages wide enough for my wings, I can keep watch from these upper levels and have a better vantage point in case of an ambush."

Kella halted Tilili next to Lio. "What's the broadest corridor that looks like it will take us in the right direction?"

Lio sighed and pointed. "Let's try that one."

Kella led the way again, and Cassia kept her hand in Lio's, their blood drying between their palms. The swoop of wings alerted them to Monsoon's glide through the gloom overhead.

When the grand boulevard turned away from the direction Lio felt they should go, they entered one of the stone dwellings in search of a route through it to a parallel road. They picked their way past the fragments of pots and a ruined stone bench.

When they stumbled over a dice game scattered across the floor, they halted.

Hoyefe tossed one of the dice in his hand. "This is what we art history experts call the rat-licking lowlife style. It dates from the present-day New Delta Imperial jinn's breath dens."

"The Broken Hands were definitely here." Kella sounded grim.

Then Tilili batted one of the dice across the floor with a paw. A laugh escaped the second blade. Suddenly they were all laughing together. The weight of the stone around them felt lighter for that instant.

"Well," Karege said, "the enemy isn't here now. They may have left the dice, but they took their winnings."

"They left in a hurry." Tuura tapped her staff on the floor. "Through a spirit tear."

Tilili padded to the back of the room to sniff a gap in the wall, then began to purr. Lio followed her nose and his senses to a swath of scorch marks on the rubble. "Here's why. It looks like Ukocha blasted in through here."

Kella gave another laugh, menacing this time. "She ambushed them this time."

Hoyefe cradled a soot-covered stone in his hands and moaned. "Why did it have to be the wall with a mural?"

Lio grimaced. "This ruin needs a restoration expedition after this, to be sure."

Tuura clicked her tongue in sympathy.

They took the passage Ukocha had opened for them, on course toward the next glimmer of her fire magic in the distance.

The closer they came to the spark Lio sensed, the more he was able to follow his sense of smell. The reek of alchemy led them out into another plaza. He stopped breathing, and Cassia coughed.

"Sorry I don't have a handkerchief," he said with a wince.

She shook her head, smiling. "You mean you don't keep a stack of silk hankies from Orthros when you're lost in the Maaqul?"

"Shameful, I know. What sort of Hesperine champion am I?"

"Mine," she answered.

A wide, shallow pool occupied the center of the plaza, and beside it were a couple of worktables scattered with alchemy supplies. Chopped herbs and broken bottles had fallen to the floor, their stains marring the beautiful tile of the ruined city.

"*Definitely* not historical." Hoyefe wrinkled his nose.

Cassia stopped by one of the tables, going still.

Lio touched her back again, standing close. "What is it?"

She pointed at a stone vessel. "I think that was lithic poison."

Dried reddish stains clung to the sides of the bowl and had boiled over onto the surrounding table. They were barely visible under more scorch marks.

"What kind of experiments were they doing here?" Lio couldn't stop himself from pulling Cassia back, as if that bowl could reach out and harm her.

"I would have taken a sample," Tuura said, "but it looks like dear Ukocha was not interested in the pursuit of knowledge at that particular moment."

They found their direction again and left the plaza on a broad road. Here they found pickaxes, shovels, and crates filled with samples of stone.

"An excavation." Hoyefe sounded personally insulted. "Those vandals!"

Ukocha's signs were no longer hidden. She had blatantly melted many of the tools into misshapen lumps.

Kella lifted the lid of a crate, then put it back. "This would be the place for a jinn surprise. These Broken Hands have a death wish."

Hoyefe sniffed. "If any jinn appear, I will personally assure them that *we* at least appreciate this place's historical and artistic importance."

"The jinn I met didn't seem much swayed by personal assurances," Cassia said. "It told me the temple had returned to the desert. It does seem the jinn have taken ownership of all this now, even if it used to belong to humans."

Lio didn't say it, but the worry hanging in the air told him they were all thinking it.

Perhaps they couldn't sense Ipika because she had already met a jinn.

Again Lio sent out a flash of mind magic, checking for auras. Nothing but more embers of Ukocha's spells. His magic rebounded to him, fueling his frustration.

His power had led him back to Cassia. His magic would help her finish her quest, too.

They followed his senses onward.

At the next intersection of their path with another road, Lio's chest began to throb.

He slipped a bit of thelemantic pain relief into Cassia's mind.

"Thank you," she murmured.

Kella winced, gingerly rubbing her shoulder. "We're getting closer to the disturbance, aren't we, Tuura?"

"The heart of it seems to be just ahead," the diviner confirmed.

"Huzzah." Now Hoyefe conjured a small lightworks display over Tuura's head.

The road ended in an archway taller than any they had yet seen.

Beyond it, they found the grandest plaza of all. Lio and Hoyefe expanded their spell lights to shine across the broad floor and up into the highest levels.

There was a black and silver sky of beautiful, broken tiles at their feet, and the stone of the depths soared over their heads. Story after story of masterfully hewn buildings rose all around. The oppressive beauty weighed down upon Lio, even as the power in the air seemed to make his senses float. Nothing could make him feel like this but magic, and yet he sensed no magic here at all.

Obelisks ringed the room in pairs. Where they stood in darkness, they appeared to be a deep black-red. But everywhere his spell light touched them, he recognized the faded reddish-colored stone of the desert. Each obelisk was carved of the same material as the lithic weapons.

Kella halted them in the middle of the chamber. "This is where the anomaly is coming from, isn't it? The obelisks."

Tuura had her eyes closed. "The magic is so old. Older than anything I've encountered before. I'm trying to understand it."

"We can't stay here," Kella said. "Lio, check for auras, quickly."

Lio's heart was pounding in his aching chest. "I can't sense anyone. Not even all of you."

Cassia gripped his hand. "Not even me?"

The silence in his blood was terrible. "I…I can't even feel your mind ward."

She wrapped her arms around him.

He reached deeper, past his thelemancy to his Gift. There. His Grace, flowing in his blood. Thank the Goddess. "I can still feel our Union."

She sighed with evident relief. "Nothing can break that."

"Just stay close to me."

"I will, my love. And we've still learned something from your power. We know Ipika and Ukocha are in the ruins, but you can't sense either of them. That means they're here, near the obelisks."

"Search fast." Kella pointed to the higher stories. "Karege, Monsoon, start at the top level and work down. The rest of us will begin at the bottom and work our way up. If you find anyone, give us a shout—but not too loudly."

In the quiet that chased her words, there came the softest rush, like a hearth fire springing to life. He and Karege opened their mouths to speak a warning. But their words went unheard in the roar of fire that rolled down over them all.

Lio pulled Cassia into his arms and spun to put his body between her and the flames.

THE HIDDEN BLADE

HEAT BATHED CASSIA'S SKIN, and light glared in her eyes. But then she was floating in the shelter of Lio's arms.

As he levitated her out of harm's way, Knight bounded past below them, fleeing to safety with liegehound speed.

But the fire never reached where they had been standing. Cool wind yanked at their clothes. All the air in the chamber seemed to rush toward Monsoon. Deprived of breath, the flames extinguished.

Cassia stared toward the source of the fire, a balcony across from her and Lio. A woman emerged from her hiding place there. Flames licked at her battered leather armor and blood-smeared skin, their orange and blue tendrils kissing her burnt sienna cheeks. On eye level, she and Cassia met each other's startled gazes.

"Ukocha," Cassia breathed.

"Ukocha!" Kella shouted from the ground.

Monsoon stood in front of the Ashes, panting, his feathers still ruffling in an eddy of his wind magic that swirled around him. He called something up to Ukocha in Tradewinds, and she answered in the same language. Monsoon snapped his wings, his mouth twisting, as if he wanted to say more.

Cassia touched Lio's sleeve and murmured, "Did he just tell her he deserved that fire spell, but she should save it for when no one else is present?"

Lio's lips twitched. "And she informed him she was saving it for the Accord breakers, not planning to waste it on him. But then she complimented his reaction time and said he hasn't lost his touch taming fireballs."

"They're being such warriors about it, aren't they?"

"Not what I would say to my lost love after a long separation, to be sure."

"How well I remember, Glasstongue."

The Ashes gathered under the balcony and saluted their first blade. Lio swept Cassia closer to Ukocha's vantage point.

Here she was. Solia's protector. The dusty scarf over Ukocha's hair, her chapped, bleeding lips, and the makeshift sling around her arm did nothing to diminish her presence. There was beauty in her muscular frame and harsh expression that defied any artist's gentler notions.

Looking into her face, Cassia felt a deep sense of recognition. How could this woman she had never met seem so familiar?

Ukocha looked down at Knight, then back up to Cassia.

"Now you see why I'm here," Monsoon said, and this time Cassia understood him. Of all the tongues a Sandira shifter might have chosen to speak with a fellow Imperial mercenary, he made a point to use Divine.

"Well," Ukocha answered in kind, "not much surprises me anymore. But this is a surprise."

"I need to look at that arm," Tuura interrupted. "Shall I come up to you, or are you coming down?"

"I don't need a poultice." Ukocha scowled. "What we all need is answers from each other. But not here. Noon Watch, how fast can you step us out of this desert?"

Karege rubbed his face. "We can't step. That's why it was so much trouble to find everyone."

"This magical disruption is at fault," Tuura explained. "You can sense it, can you not?"

Ukocha nodded and muttered a string of filthy curses Cassia had only heard in privateer taverns. "Any idea what time of day it is, Karege?"

"We have a couple of hours before dawn, I'd say," he answered.

"No point in trying to reach the surface tonight, then," said Ukocha. "We'll spend the day underground, then find our way out at nightfall."

At the thought of staying down here through Lio's Slumber, Cassia's skin crawled. But she knew Ukocha was right.

"You all come up," the First Blade ordered. "I have a campsite nearby, at a strategic location. We can regroup there."

286 of Vela Roth

Lio set Cassia down on the balcony, keeping an arm around her. She leaned over the railing and called Knight. With a leap bred into him for hunting levitating Hesperines, he jumped from the ground to the balcony. Cassia was gratified to see him sniff Lio as much as her. Her hound must reassure himself both his people were in one piece.

But her heart ached with a lifetime of questions as she turned to Ukocha. "I'm Cassia."

"I can tell." Ukocha held out her good hand to Knight.

He sniffed her fingers and wagged his tail.

Cassia touched her Grace's arm. "This is Lio, my intended."

Ukocha's brows rose.

Lio bowed. "It's an honor to meet you at last, First Blade Ukocha."

She looked him over. "Karege warned me most Hesperines are more polite than he is."

Lio's mouth twitched. "I'm happy to be impolite to the enemy alongside you and your Ashes, should the opportunity arise."

A smile broke through her grim expression. "I hope it does."

They had to save one more person. Chuma's mother was still in danger. And that meant Solia's secrets still could not pass Ukocha's lips.

Cassia dreaded asking Ukocha what had become of Ipika.

Monsoon flew up to the balcony and crouched on the thick stone railing. His face was fixed in an expression Cassia knew well, the hard armor one needed to contain a roil of conflicting emotions. But the regret in his eyes escaped his defenses.

His gaze went to her bandage. "That's your sword arm."

Ukocha tilted her head back to look up at him. "I'm still alive. And so are you. You even found Cassia."

"She found me. But the enemy also knows she's here. They're no mere Accord breakers hunting for treasure. They have the tattoo."

"What in the ancestors' names are *they* doing digging for rocks in the Maaqul?"

"I wish I knew," Monsoon said. "If I'd had any idea the Broken Hands were here, I would never have brought Cassia to them on a platter."

"Old friends and old enemies in one day," Ukocha muttered.

"Which category do I fall into?" Monsoon asked.

"I'm surprised you have to ask. Did Chuma send you?"

After a hesitation, "Yes."

"Did you take her flying when you saw her?"

"She'd never let me leave without doing that." He smiled.

"Ask her which category you're in, then," Ukocha told him.

The rest of the Ashes joined them on the balcony with the assistance of Karege's levitation. Ukocha stroked a purring Tilili under the chin. "Shame you missed most of the battle down here. Sending the rats running with their tails on fire was very entertaining."

Kella gave Ukocha a stiff half-embrace around their wounds and Tilili's affectionate head bumps. "We saw evidence of the fighting, but it took us forever to find you in this jinn-cursed complex."

Somehow Hoyefe managed to give Ukocha a salute with the air of blowing a kiss. "Your battles were magnificent, as always."

"What?" Ukocha scoffed. "No vapors over the scorched artwork?"

"I'll save my laments for when I'm not in range of your fire spells, First Blade."

"Good plan. You can apologize to the Imperial Museum for me as soon as no one is trying to kill us."

"I feel the need to point out that someone is always trying to kill us. It's the nature of our profession."

"This way." Ukocha led them through a door to the interior of the ruin.

Karege held out a hand. "Might an old friend assist—"

"I don't need my arm for walking," Ukocha cut him off.

"You lost a lot of blood," Tuura said.

"This isn't the holy goat race." Ukocha kept walking.

"Of course not," Karege said. "No one carries First Blade Ukocha."

"That would never happen," Hoyefe agreed. "Except for that time when—"

Karege smacked Hoyefe's arm.

The illusionist cleared his throat. "Nevermind. It's lost to memory, just like all the places we've buried our enemies over the years."

Their battered party trudged through a labyrinth of audience halls and bedchambers and other rooms of mysterious purpose, where only stone furniture, pottery, and cave plants survived.

They were ascending a narrow stair when Lio's nostrils flared. Before she could ask him what was wrong, he glanced ahead of them at Hoyefe.

The illusionist paused on the steps, as if composing himself.

"Tuura—" Karege warned.

Hoyefe took one more step, only for his knees to buckle.

The two Hesperines caught him before he tumbled down the staircase.

Cassia stood right behind Lio in the close space, her hand on his back. "What's wrong?"

"He's bleeding. Heavily."

At the top of the steps, Ukocha beckoned. "Bring him up. Hurry."

They followed her into a spacious stone chamber. Knight darted ahead, investigating every corner and sniffing for danger. Cassia stayed close to Lio while he and Karege laid Hoyefe down beside a banked campfire. The flames revived at Ukocha's nearness.

Tuura knelt beside the illusionist. "I knew he was hiding something!"

But his spells were gone now. On one side of his tunic, an ugly patch of dried gore was now visible, newly dampened by a fresh rush of blood. Cassia had lived in a war-torn kingdom long enough to know she was looking at a possible death sentence.

"A belly wound." Monsoon bowed his head over the fallen mercenary.

Kella brought Tilili close and urged her cat to lie down beside Hoyefe. "What was he thinking, not letting Tuura tend a belly wound?"

Ukocha sank down by the fire. "How bad is it?"

Karege and Lio exchanged a glance, and Cassia knew what they were thinking. If only the Gift could save Hoyefe now, this might be the hour when the Ashes gained another Hesperine among their ranks.

"Would he consider it?" Lio asked Karege.

"It's not his style," Karege said with a sad smile, his voice thick.

Tuura pulled up Hoyefe's tunic. They waited in grim silence for her verdict.

"He'll live," she pronounced.

Everyone breathed.

"The blade missed his organs," Tuura continued, "but he needs stitches. Now."

Lio handed Tuura items she asked for, and Cassia tore new bandages for Hoyefe from the scraps of clothing everyone was able to spare. When Tuura's poultice touched his skin, his eyes fluttered open.

He lifted his head to glance at himself, then grimaced and lay flat again. "Ugh. Now you've all seen me in a state of nature. I do hate it when an illusion fails."

"Why didn't you tell us you were injured?" Kella demanded. "What if you'd passed out during a battle, and we'd lost your invisibility and your sword?"

"I didn't pass out," he replied.

Kella gritted her teeth.

Hoyefe gave her perhaps the most genuine smile that had yet appeared on his face. "Thank you for your concern, my dear. And yours, Peanut."

The diviner held up her needle and thread.

"I revoke my thanks," Hoyefe said. "That's not the kind of concern I want."

"It's the kind you're about to get."

"Marvelous. Back among the living, just in time for stitches. I'd prefer the old sword wound to new needle punctures, please."

"Not a chance." The look Tuura gave him was surprisingly fearsome. "Don't do that again. Everyone's lives are my responsibility as our healer."

Hoyefe winced. "Yes, and you had more pressing matters to attend to than the fool who was on watch when everyone was ambushed. Like the shoulder wound our first blade sustained because of my lack of vigilance."

Cassia realized something for the first time. Hoyefe wasn't wearing a fortune blade. That had been an illusion, too.

He reached into his bag of "tricks" and pulled out his knife, offering it hilt first to Ukocha. "I intended to do this with a bit more finesse than sprawling flat on my back in a hostile location, but there's no time like the present. First Blade, I hereby tender my resignation from the Ashes, in acknowledgment of my failure to protect you and our comrades."

Ukocha looked at him with steel in her gaze for a long moment.

"Did I ask you to resign?" she said at last.

"No, First Blade," Hoyefe answered.

"Do you think that battle would have gone any differently if someone else had been on watch instead of you?"

"We'll never know, because I was the one on watch."

She pushed his hand and the knife back toward him. "I do not accept your resignation. Use that blade to help us fight our way out of this pile of ruins, as soon as we get you back on your feet."

A smile tugged at Hoyefe's mouth. "As you say, First Blade."

Kella snatched the blade from Hoyefe's hand and helped him buckle it back on. "We just need to get our fencer back into fighting condition before the Broken Hands come back for another round."

"I'm always up for another round," Hoyefe said, "but perhaps a bath first."

"Stitches first," Tuura declared.

Hoyefe glanced from Lio to Karege with a pouting expression. "Awake for stitches, but unconscious while two good-looking Hesperines carried me. The world is unfair."

Karege rolled his eyes, while Lio and Cassia exchanged an amused glance.

Cassia gave Hoyefe's shoulder a gentle pat. "Truly an injustice. No one should miss being carried by Hesperines."

Hoyefe gave a dramatic sigh. "Very gracious of you to spare your gentleman for a moment on my behalf."

"You won't feel the stitches," Lio promised. "It seems my mind magic is functioning."

Tuura nodded with a sigh of relief. "This chamber is far enough from the obelisks."

"We can sense auras again," Karege confirmed.

Cassia felt Lio's magic touching the mind ward the same way he held her hand, a simple, sweet assurance that they could reach each other.

While Tuura saw to Hoyefe's wound, Kella and Tilili made their own patrol of the room. Knight gave the cat a polite berth and settled next to Cassia.

Kella peered out the open windows and single doorway. "Third story, only one narrow stair leading up here, but four escapes to adjacent rooftops. Nice find."

Ukocha nodded. "Even if the Broken Hands decide to pop in, I've placed so many fire traps that they won't be able to take two steps in here without losing their feet."

Cassia's arm tightened around Lio on instinct.

He went very still, glancing around them. "At the risk of sounding like a silkfoot, is there anywhere I shouldn't walk?"

Karege laughed. "Don't worry, Sunshine. Only enemy toes make Ukocha's fire traps explode. You'll come to appreciate walking on prickles around her."

Lio smiled at Cassia. "Excellent. I have the greatest appreciation for prickly women."

"I am not prickly," she protested, laughing.

"On the contrary, my rose, your thorns are one of my favorite things about you."

"Very well. If you're so determined to be prickled." She gave him a poke in the ribs.

He chuckled and caught her hand. "See there. I knew your thorns would come out."

Cassia had lost that debate at record speed, but surrender was well worth seeing him smile.

"Get a veil," Monsoon muttered from his watchful post by one of the windows.

"Come now." Hoyefe's voice was cheerful, if strained, as Tuura tied off his bandage. "Let the two lovebirds enjoy the giddy heights of their recent reunion. And don't interrupt all this inspiration for my next play. It appears I shall live to write it, and I've decided it must be a romance."

Lio kissed her hand without remorse, although Cassia did feel rather abashed. She hadn't meant for their flirting to rub salt in Monsoon's wounds.

But she needed her Grace's teasing. She could withstand Broken Hands and ruins and not knowing where Ipika or Solia were. Lio was here. He was the one thing that was right in her world when everything else went wrong.

"What happened to Ipika?" she asked at last.

"Ah," was Ukocha's only reply.

"First Blade," said Kella, "Cassia is under the impression that you were leading your Ashes on a mission through the desert to bring Chuma's mother home safely. After we got separated, she and Lio helped us all find each other. They've joined our contract as honorary Ashes."

Tuura smiled and patted Cassia's arm. "Our Shadow got a boon from a jinn and asked it where Chuma's mother was."

Karege clapped Lio on the shoulder. "And Sunshine here traced your fire magic through the ruins."

Ukocha gave Lio and Cassia a nod. "It sounds like thanks are in order, to both of you."

"Don't thank us yet." Cassia had come all this way, only to stand before Ukocha and tell her that they had failed. "We have to keep looking for Chuma's mother."

"You found her," Ukocha said.

Understanding dawned on Cassia. She saw past the muscles, scars, and crows' feet and realized she was looking at Chuma's future. "How did I not see it?"

"I've made many enemies," Ukocha replied. "I've gone to great lengths to ensure they never find my family. Few people alive know that Matriarch Ipika and First Blade Ukocha are the same person. But each of the Ashes places one secret in the Ancestors' Keeping."

Cassia thought of Chuma with that dagger in her hand, facing the Golden Shield. "Mumba and Chuma and the village are your secret."

"Thank you for entrusting the truth to us," Lio said.

"Should we take an oath?" Cassia asked.

Ukocha shook her head. "I'll accept fighting your way across the Maaqul to rescue me as a sign of your good intentions."

Reaching into the sleeve of her robe, Cassia pulled off Chuma's bracelet and held it out to Ukocha. "She gave this to us to help us find you. You should have it back now."

Ukocha held her daughter's bracelet on her lap. She ran dry, calloused fingers over the smooth beads. It was the only motion she made as Tuura began to examine her wound.

"I don't need herbs," Ukocha said again.

Tuura ignored that and pulled another gourd shell of poultice from her medicine bag. But when she peeled back the sling, her hands stilled.

Cassia couldn't see much of the injury over the diviner's shoulder, but Lio must have gotten a good glimpse. He didn't stare, and his face was composed, but Cassia could feel his anguish.

She gripped his hand, sick at heart, but Willed him to remember they had done all they could.

"You cauterized it," Tuura said.

Ukocha slid the beads between her fingers, again and again, as if it were a meditation. "I was bleeding to death."

Lio's voice was too calm. "I thought this enemy didn't aim to kill."

Ukocha's fingers tightened on the beads. "They had a hard time aiming at all through a wall of fire. I would have made plenty of kills, if not for that arrow."

"Is that the reason you came here?" Cassia asked. "Not to protect someone, as we believed, but to stop the Accord breakers?"

Kella nodded. "My people gave us the contract after it came to their attention that someone was interfering with the ruins out here. They sent us to apprehend them before they angered the jinn. Of course, at the time, we merely thought they were Accord breakers, and had yet to realize they're the Broken Hands."

"What happened to you after we got separated?" Hoyefe asked Ukocha.

"I took care of the bleeding and went looking for water. I made it to this ruin. When I saw signs of an excavation, I knew they would be coming back."

Tuura rubbed her brow. "So you laid a trap for them. Alone."

"We're on a contract"—Ukocha gritted her teeth—"and I had a score to settle."

"We'll have to ask my people to modify the terms of this contract," Kella said. "These are enemies we cannot apprehend."

When Tuura finished bandaging the wound, Ukocha's hand stilled on the bracelet. She met Cassia's gaze. "Looks like we'll have time to talk. You have questions, I know, and you've waited years for answers. I won't make you wait an hour longer."

Cassia felt Lio touch the mind ward, reminding her that she did not face the past alone.

After a drink from her water flask to wet her parched tongue, she spoke. "Please tell me everything you know about my sister."

SEVEN SECRETS

UKOCHA DREW HER KNIFE and laid it across her knees. With a ritualistic cadence, she spoke words that stirred both reverence and familiarity in Cassia, although she couldn't understand. She heard them at home whenever Annassa Soteira spoke her ancient language.

Kella closed her fingers around the filigreed silver hilt of her knife and unsheathed it. She chanted in Azarqi.

Hoyefe was next to draw his slim, elegant fortune blade and recite something in Dynastic. Then Tuura, in a tongue Cassia couldn't name.

When Karege spoke in Divine, she understood. "My Ashes, bound by fortune, seven truths our ancestors keep. Draw your blades, thus to show that Solia's secret we shall speak."

There came a silence. What broke it was the brush of Monsoon's fortune blade from his scabbard. He laid the long knife across his knees and invoked the Ancestors' Keeping in the Sandira language.

The whispers began, their voices strangely comforting. They swept around the chamber like an ethereal wind. The room felt full, as if the past and present were too much to fit within it. A murmur caressed Cassia's ears.

Seven ivy vines in my bright spring garden
To tear down every wall
Seven ivy vines that built my fortress
Each as strong as my own

She gasped. Then the whispers departed through the windows and echoed away into the ruins.

Cassia stared at Monsoon. "You're one of the Ashes?"

"Was," Kella cut in. "He is a *former* member of the Ashes."

"But still a bearer of our secrets," said Ukocha. "The Ancestors' Keeping is binding until death."

"You knew her," Cassia said to Monsoon. "You knew my sister and couldn't say anything, all those times we talked about her."

There was none of Lio's usual forgiveness in his gaze. "You could have told us we were on the trail of your former comrades."

Monsoon's face was impassive. "Then you would have asked me even more questions I couldn't answer."

Cassia shook her head. "You asked me so many questions about her, when you already knew the answers to them. Why?"

"Being a good listener is a free service, remember?"

She smiled at him. "Now you can tell me everything."

Ukocha began. "Thirteen years ago, when Ziara came inland to find us, I knew whatever favor she wanted must be a big one. Perhaps she needed me to find out where one of her enemies had retired. Or roast a beached kraken. But no. She wanted something more dramatic than that. She asked me to help a shadowlander."

"I know the Ashes have a strict code of honor," Cassia said. "I'll always be grateful to you for not turning Solia into the authorities."

"What inspired you to grant her such clemency?" Lio asked.

"Potential," Ukocha answered. "The same thing that made Ziara bring Solia here in the first place. That girl had a fire in her that would drive her to achieve great things—if it didn't kill her first. It was very much a question whether she would control her anger, or it would come to control her." Ukocha gave Cassia a considering look. "I think you know what happens when anger controls you."

"It destroys you," Cassia said.

Ukocha nodded. "She was a survivor. She wouldn't have made it that far otherwise. But she was in danger of not surviving herself."

Cassia leaned forward. "What did Ziara ask you to do for her? What was Solia's plan?"

"Training," Ukocha replied.

Cassia's eyes widened. "Training for...what?"

"Battle. I agreed to teach her to defeat her enemies, but with different weapons than gowns and whispered secrets."

Cassia sat back, her thoughts suddenly spinning into parts unknown. "You taught her the battle arts? How can that be? Ziara said she couldn't even look at a sword."

"By the time I was done with her, you couldn't keep a sword out of her hand."

The image came to Cassia of her sister, with her soft hands and sweet smiles and shining presence. That goddess, transformed into one with a sword, her eyes blazing with her inner fire.

"Scion Angara," Cassia breathed.

Why had she never considered it before? She had risked death to remake herself into a woman who would not be bound by Tenebra's mold. Why had she let her sister remain frozen in her mind, exactly the same as the last time she had seen her? Why hadn't she allowed her image of Solia to grow beyond the role Tenebra had forced on her?

"But Ziara was right," Ukocha continued. "At first, Solia was a hazard. So I partnered her with my other new blade, who was already a skilled warrior when he joined us. He had a way with her." She nodded to Monsoon.

He laughed softly, gazing into the fire. "I was the only person who could spar with her without losing half my skin. Most fun I've ever had."

Something plucked at Cassia's thoughts, but didn't quite sing.

"When we were sure she wouldn't die in the first five minutes," Ukocha went on, "we took her with us on a contract. After that, if the Imperial authorities had come for her, a legion of ice mages couldn't have pried her from my side. We needed her." Ukocha gave a wicked smile. "Besides, I liked her."

"Cup and thorns." Karege put a hand to his ear. "You might have to say that again. The mortals will think they misheard."

"I've made my point," Ukocha returned.

"She became my dearest friend, Cassia," said Kella. "It was so hard not to say anything to you all the way through the desert."

Cassia's sister had somehow won the loyalty of these incredible people.

"You're saying," Cassia realized, "that she *joined* you?"

"I sponsored her myself," Ukocha said. "When I vouch for someone, the administration issues them a fortune blade without asking questions."

"Her secret was her origins," Monsoon murmured, "and you, Cassia."

"But this is not the land of her ancestors," Tuura explained. "We could not give our secrets to her foremothers. But even so, she placed the truth of her past in the keeping to our ancestors."

Kella nodded. "She put herself at the mercy of our ancestors' power, without being able to wield it in return."

"She trusted you." Finally, Cassia could imagine what Solia's life in the Empire had been like. The Ashes had been her confidants, her comrades. Her family. "She loved you. And found happiness with you."

"She rose from the Ashes of the shadowlands." There were no dramatics in Hoyefe's sincere tone. "And burned so very brightly."

"She thrived in the mercenary life," Tuura confirmed. "She became whole."

Lio smiled, rubbing Cassia's back in reassurance. "Clearly, Solia found her Solace and Sanctuary here in the Empire, as surely as you did with us in Orthros."

Tears of relief pricked Cassia's eyes. "I'm so glad I crossed the Maaqul with all of you."

The Ashes met her declaration with laughter.

"That settles it," Ukocha said. "We're recruiting this one. Anyone glad to cross the Maaqul has the makings of a great mercenary."

Kella gestured at Lio and Cassia. "Care to make your honorary status permanent?"

Cassia sniffed, laughing through her tears. "What do you think? Shall we hit the road for a life of adventure?"

"You, in battle on a regular basis, where you might get hurt?" His fangs lengthened in her defense. "Please, no."

"Perhaps after I'm a Hesperine and can scare thick-headed outlaws with my fangs."

"Not even then. I'll never be glad you had to set foot in the Maaqul. But yes, I thank the Goddess we've had the honor of traveling with the Ashes."

Cassia dried her eyes. "Did my sister have a fortune name?"

Monsoon met her gaze. "That wasn't part of the secret."

At last, the pieces fit.

Do you want to talk about what happened?

I can't.

"Oh, Goddess," Cassia said. "Sunburn."

There it was, Monsoon's smile for the woman he had loved and lost. That woman had been Solia. "We had nearly eight years together."

Instinctively, Cassia held fast to her Grace's hand. Eight years. More time than she'd even been with Lio yet. Far less time than she could look forward to.

"What happened?" Cassia reached out and touched Monsoon's shoulder. "Can you talk about it now?"

He rubbed a hand over his face.

"Why didn't she stay with you? With the Ashes?" Cassia held onto the handkerchief, the delicate silk crushing in her tightening fingers. "Where is she now?"

A sudden gleam of light caught Cassia's eye. Ukocha, turning her knife so it caught the light. For the first time, she noticed what was engraved on the hilt. The symbol of an acacia branch. Just like Ziara's flag.

"Cassia," Ukocha said, "you've heard of the Battle of Souls?"

"Your reputation as a victor is well known."

Ukocha nodded. "Once you win, everyone who can hold a butter knife begs you to train them to compete. Even those who have no hope of making it past the first round."

The firelight swayed across Monsoon's face. "The temptation of the prize makes people do mad things."

"What is the prize?" Cassia asked.

"A boon from the Empress," said Lio, "according to my father."

"Well. I've seen men kill for lesser ends. I can easily imagine the frenzy to grasp such a favor from the most powerful monarch in the mortal world."

"And that's just the top prize for the winning champion," Monsoon went on. "If you make it far enough in the rounds, you can also get an officer's commission in the army...a reference to Imperial university...a mercenary job so lucrative, you can retire wealthy as a king. The longer you last, the more renown and connections you gain that can make any future you imagine for yourself a reality."

With her good hand, Ukocha tossed her knife and caught it. "But only one person can walk away with the victor's acacia branch and the Empress's boon. Ziara asked Her Imperial Majesty for the *Wanted*, the ship of her dreams, to replace the one lost at the bottom of the sea."

"May we ask what boon you requested?" Cassia said.

Ukocha's smile was as sharp as her dagger. "I haven't collected mine yet."

Lio whistled. "An outstanding boon with the Empress."

"Irks her to no end." Ukocha laughed. "But what can she do?"

"Have you not decided what you want?" Cassia asked.

"It was never about the boon for me. I just wanted to win. After I did, I attracted all sorts of fools who thought I'd spend the next eight years training them. I only met one aspirant who was worth my time." She pointed her knife at Monsoon. "The Sandira warrior who pledged himself to the Ashes to prove his mettle. But before I knew it, my shadowlander recruit had the acacia in her sights, too."

Cassia gaped. "My sister wanted to compete in the Battle of Souls."

Monsoon's chest rose and fell on a heavy, silent sigh. "We were always at our best when we challenged each other. So we agreed we would enter together. We were so sure. We could taste it. If we battled each other, we would make it through every round. It wouldn't matter which of us won. We would celebrate together."

Cassia could see it now. "Which one of you became the victor?"

Monsoon raised a brow. "Convinced one of us succeeded?"

"Yes." She looked at the fire in his eyes. "I'm sure, too."

"Your sister took the acacia, Cassia," Monsoon told her.

Lio let out a breath. "She is a legend."

"No." Monsoon's voice grew hoarse. "She should have been."

Cassia felt her pulse pounding down to her fingertips. "What happened to her?"

Ukocha opened her mouth to speak.

Monsoon held up a hand. "I will tell her."

He turned to Cassia and took both her hands. She felt Lio's hands on her shoulders, bracing her.

Hespera's Mercy. She had come all this way and hoped so hard. For bad news.

Monsoon spoke like the friend and leader who had guided them across the desert. "I thought she was going to request citizenship. The Empress would be honor-bound to grant it, even if she was a shadowlander. We thought this was her chance to live without fear."

Goddess, he was so calm, even though she knew speaking of it must tear open all his wounds. Cassia pushed words through her tight throat. "That would have given her the right to marry you, wouldn't it?"

He looked down at his hands. "Her citizenship is the boon I would have claimed, had I won."

"Why wouldn't she ask for that?" Cassia wanted that to be the truth.

"The night before our final duel," Monsoon continued, "the battle that would decide which of us took the acacia, she told me the truth. She planned to ask the Empress to give her the resources she needed to return to Tenebra and challenge the king."

"No." Cassia squeezed her eyes shut.

Solia had found her Sanctuary. Why would she give that up for Tenebra? Why hadn't she chosen her happiness, her future, as Cassia had?

"She couldn't abandon you," Monsoon said gently. "She was determined to return and save you. Even if she had to overthrow Lucis to do it."

Cassia's thoughts spun. "But she never came back. What happened, Monsoon?"

He bowed his head. "The Empress refused her boon and had her arrested. Solia has spent the last five years in prison."

Cassia's stomach rebelled. She focused on not being sick and was glad that took all of her focus. She didn't want to think about where her sister was at this very moment.

Lio's cool fingers caressed the back of her neck. His magic touched her mind, and her belly calmed.

Kella was there, touching Cassia's face as she had when they first met. "I'm so sorry, Pup. She tried so hard for you."

Cassia leaned her face on Kella's shoulder. "Why wouldn't they just deport her and let her go free?"

"She took the fall for us," Kella explained. "She confessed to crimes she didn't commit, which got her a prison sentence instead of deportation. All to make the Empress believe we were innocent of harboring her."

"That's why you weren't arrested?" Cassia asked.

"Sunburn had a plan in place," Ukocha answered. "On one of our contracts, we happened to acquire a less-than-legal artifact from a rogue mind mage we defeated."

"A mind hook?" Lio asked. "Those are very illegal, and with good reason."

"Naturally we couldn't let it fall into the wrong hands," Ukocha went on. "Instead of destroying it, Solia wanted to keep it. Not to use, you understand. She made us all agree that if she ever got caught, she would turn over the mind hook to the authorities to convince them she had used it to deceive us about her origins." Ukocha's mouth tightened. "We believed she would never have to do that."

"But she did." Kella's voice was harsh with anger, despite the years that had passed. "She was loyal to the last. She made everyone believe she had exploited the Empire's heroes. She went to prison, and we got sympathy. We have tried not to squander her sacrifice. At least, some of us have." Kella shot Monsoon a look. "Now Monsoon has more to say."

His lip twisted. "Going to let me tell her this part alone, are you?"

"Striking out alone was your choice," she returned.

Ukocha pointed at the doorway, but her voice held none of Kella's rancor. "There are fire traps protecting the courtyard, too, if you three would like somewhere private to talk."

Monsoon rose to his feet, snapping his wings. "Cassia, Lio, if you'll join me outside? There are...family matters we need to discuss."

How true that was. He had almost become Cassia's brother-in-law, Lio's Grace-brother.

"Of course." Cassia got to her feet, her knees like jelly.

Lio held her steady as they followed Monsoon out to the remains of a once-beautiful courtyard. Knight sniffed at the luminescent plants that overgrew the ancient stones. It was deceptively peaceful.

There would be no peace for Cassia, not until Solia was free.

WARPATH

L IO HELD CASSIA, AS he had every step of the way on this journey, which had begun the first night he had ever held her in his arms.

Goddess, I don't want this for her. Why grief upon grief for my Grace?

He offered her no words of comfort. He said exactly what he knew she needed to hear. "We will rescue Solia."

Cassia leaned against him, her hand in Knight's ruff. The dog pressed close to his distraught lady with a soft whine.

Then she drew herself up, straightening her spine. Lio knew the look of his Grace rallying and donning her armor to tame the beast of her emotions.

"Yes," Cassia gritted. "We'll get her out."

"I tried." Monsoon's calm was gone. There was a warpath written in his aura. "There wasn't anything we could do at first. The arrest was very public. The Golden Shield made an example out of her in front of all the spectators at the Battle. A shadowlander had taken the acacia."

A heavy sigh escaped Lio. "The Empress would have felt she needed to save face."

"Yes." Monsoon's lips twisted. "There was nothing to be gained by starting a melee with the Golden Shield in the middle of the arena. Considering the magic at their disposal, Karege didn't dare veil himself and step away with her."

Cassia shook her head. "She wouldn't have wanted you to do anything to make yourselves look guilty."

"That's what everyone agreed," Monsoon ground out. "I respected that. No one wanted Ukocha to get arrested and taken from her family. So I went alone."

"That's why you left the Ashes, isn't it?" asked Lio. "To keep searching for Solia."

"Kella never forgave me. She took Solia's loss hard and wanted me to stay loyal to the Ashes. I know it hurt everyone for me to leave when that wound was still raw. But I had to."

"That way, if you got arrested, you wouldn't bring the others down with you." Lio would have done exactly as Monsoon had.

"I spent years prying information out of the Empress's clutches, and I wasn't particular about how I did it. I've been in the underbellies of her most secure prisons. If I had found Solia, nothing could have stopped me from breaking her out. But I've never been able to find out where they're holding her. When I told you I could find and rescue anyone, it was a lie. She's the one person I couldn't save. The person who mattered most. I'm so sorry, Cassia."

She took his hands this time, and Lio couldn't begrudge him that comfort.

"What makes you think you have anything to be sorry for?" she asked.

Monsoon blinked hard and looked away. "Thank you. I...came a long way to hear that."

Lio had been separated from Cassia in the desert for days, in agony over her fate, blaming himself. He had been trapped on the wrong side of the Orthros-Tenebra border from her for half a year, living in fear for her.

The man Solia loved had existed like that for five years.

"Monsoon," Lio said, "you did everything you could."

"But it wasn't enough. Whatever prison the Empress reserves for shadowlanders remains a secret."

"Are you sure—" Cassia began. "Is she—"

She couldn't finish that sentence. Lio hated that she even had to think it.

"She's alive," Monsoon said. "Justice here is not like Tenebra."

"And Imperial prisons are better than Tenebran ones?" Cassia asked.

"Much better," Monsoon answered.

That did little to lift Cassia's aura. "She could have had her freedom and happiness with you if only she'd asked for a different boon."

"She wouldn't have had you, *nyakimbi*. She could never reconcile herself to abandoning you in Tenebra. Sometimes the guilt was quieter, sometimes it ate her up inside. I tried to reassure her that she had done her best."

"She did," Lio said. "The situation in Tenebra would never have allowed her to return safely."

"But she blamed herself. You don't understand what she was like when she arrived here. She needed…" Monsoon sighed. "She had to fix herself before she could do anything to help others. And even after she came into her own, what then?"

Cassia shuddered. "I meant it when I said I'm not angry, and that the best thing she could have done is survive."

Monsoon nodded. "If she had gone back, she could never have stood against the king and his allies. There was no chance she could even find and take you away in secret."

Cassia shook her head. "The king holds his possessions tightly. Even the ones of meager value, like a bastard girl."

Monsoon took a step closer. "You are so much more than that."

For once, Monsoon and Lio were in complete agreement.

"I know that now," Cassia said, "but it took a Hesperine to help me see—and to pry me from Lucis's grasp."

Lio touched his Grace's hair. "Little did he know that he lost the jewel of his kingdom."

Monsoon crossed his arms and came no closer to Lio, but his aura was sincere. "Thank you for keeping her safe."

Lio was unsure the man wanted his sympathy, which he might mistake for pity. "I will always wish Solia and Cassia could have escaped Tenebra and come to the Empire together so that both of them could have been spared all of this."

And so the males who loved them might have been spared it, too.

"No one wishes that more than I do," Monsoon said.

Cassia rested her hand on Lio's chest, her arm around him. "I couldn't have given up the one I loved, the life I wanted. I wish she hadn't."

Not for the first time, Lio contemplated the strength in her small hand. She could have taken hold of her sister's legacy. She had reached for him instead. No matter what happened, he would always know that she had chosen him above everything else in the world.

Monsoon would never have that.

The man glanced at them, then away. "Thank you for your vote of confidence. But no one could talk her out of the plot she'd been working toward since before you were born. She and many others devoted their lives to that cause—or lost them."

"She told you how she was planning to overthrow the king?" Cassia asked.

"I know everything. When she awoke from nightmares of your father, I was there. When she wept at the thought of what he might be doing to you, I held her. And when her scars healed, and she learned to live for herself instead of existing for revenge, I kept hating him for her."

"He is everything you imagine him to be," Lio said.

"Have you met him?" Monsoon asked suddenly.

"Yes," Lio answered.

"Then why is he still alive?" Monsoon demanded.

Because Lio had been wrapped up in diplomatic cords that night. Not now.

"Lio and I aren't assassins," Cassia said. "We're diplomats. We persuaded the free lords to make a treaty with Orthros. They're meeting right now to remove Lucis peacefully and put one of our allies on the throne."

"Mweya's Wings. That's what you meant when you said you'd made arrangements."

"Lucis will be deposed, and a just king will take the throne. I have a life in Orthros. Solia doesn't have to save anyone. There's no reason for her to ever return to Tenebra. She can have the life she wants—the life you two wanted together."

Monsoon's pain filled the Blood Union. "It's too late."

"She sacrificed everything for me." Cassia's aura steeled. "That ends now. If Lio and I can drag the free lords into an alliance with Orthros, we can certainly extricate one woman from the Empress' prison. We will find her, and we will set her free."

"It can't be done, Cassia." Monsoon sounded so kind as he tried to destroy the last of her hopes. "If it were possible, I would have found a way."

"Don't give up. The three of us together—"

Monsoon flared his wings. "It took me years to finally admit defeat. I can't save her. But I can do one thing for her. Keep you from sharing her fate."

Cassia faced him, her hands closing into fists. "I will not let my sister sit in prison for the rest of our lives."

"I know it will take time to accept. Until then, at least I can trust your silkfoot to keep you from doing anything dangerous."

With that, Monsoon quit the courtyard. Lio heard the swoop of wings echoing through the subterranean halls. Knight trotted after him, growling, then stalked back to Cassia's side.

Cassia turned to Lio. "We need a plan."

He had one. The time had come to tell her what it was.

"What we must do is clear," she said.

Yes, it had been clear to him before tonight. He had just needed time to find a way to explain it to her. To himself.

She began to pace, Knight trotting faithfully back and forth at her heels. Lio watched the sight before him. When Cassia paced, lords lost their seats on the council. Heretics escaped the mages' pyre. Kings toppled from their thrones.

But this time, her brilliant schemes would only put her in more danger.

"We cannot avoid it any longer," she said. "We must reckon with the elders and the Imperial authorities to clear my name. If I can secure diplomatic immunity, we'll be in a position to negotiate for Solia's release."

Lio turned the fulgurite in his hands. The glowing plants lit eerie sparks inside the glass. "I'm afraid that won't work, my rose."

"I know it will be a nightmare of waiting and bureaucracy. But it's clear the only course of action is for Orthros to officially intercede with the Empress for Solia's sake."

For once, Lio was struggling to find the words he needed to say. It was more difficult than he had predicted to tell her this. Especially right now, when her eyes were alight with the dream of her ambassador's medallion.

Her shoes brushed back and forth on the stone. "Surely we can persuade the Empress to consider extradition to Orthros, at least. Perhaps she would even commute Solia's sentence in exchange for certain guarantees.

Although I shudder to imagine what those demands might be." She looked in the direction Monsoon had flown. "Exile from the Empire is not what I want for her. But she would be with us, and everyone who loves her would be welcome in Orthros."

"Cassia," Lio said evenly, "I have reached the conclusion that diplomacy will not work any longer."

She frowned at him. "Basir himself said the Empress might be willing to foist a troublesome shadowlander off on the Hesperines."

"That was before she sent the Golden Shield to arrest my Grace. Over a millennium and a half of alliance with Orthros—your citizenship papers—none of it was enough to stop her from persecuting you. I will place no more faith in her."

Cassia halted. "You can't really be suggesting the alternative."

"It is the only alternative."

"Breaking a notorious criminal out of the Empress's secret prison?" She gave a tight laugh. "Lio...if our concern is avoiding an international incident, that is not the way to go about it."

"That does not concern me."

"For all his skill, Monsoon couldn't find and rescue her."

"I am not Monsoon."

"We already know you cannot step to her."

"Stepping is hardly the only magic at my disposal."

"I know. You have Hespera's power." She swallowed.

"The Golden Shield tested my spells and could not take you from me. They will not stop me from rescuing your sister."

"When I allow myself to imagine what we could do, I confess, I'm tempted, Lio. I'm still close enough to the person I was in Tenebra to spin that out in my mind. Your magic would make many things possible." Cassia's voice broke.

"Cassia." He sat down on a stone bench and held out his arms.

She came to stand before him and slid into his embrace. "But that's not how we use our power, is it? You've always told me that with Hespera's great Gift comes great responsibility. We must be gentle and just. And risking Orthros's alliance with the Empire is not what diplomats do."

How long ago those nights seemed, when as an initiate ambassador, he had so passionately explained his creed to the bitter Lady Cassia. Now here she was, the voice of Hespera.

What did that make him?

Her gaze dropped and landed on the fulgurite. She covered his hand with hers where he held the disfigured glass. "What is this?"

"A reminder." He sucked in a breath, as if there was something that could suffocate him. "Eudias's magic forged it during the battle. I took it from the ruins at Rose House."

She caressed his face. "Oh, Lio."

He lifted his gaze to hers. "The truth is, I lost my medallion of office in the battle against the Collector and haven't seen it since."

She trailed her fingers through his hair. "I know."

"You knew?"

"Of course. I've been looking for it everywhere, but even Knight couldn't sniff it out."

The hound rested his head on Lio's knee, looking up at him with soulful eyes. Lio sighed and rubbed Knight's ears.

"Was I wrong not to say anything?" Cassia asked. "You are always so patient with me when I'm not yet able to speak of something that's troubling me. I was trying to wait until you felt ready to talk about your medallion. About Rose House."

"No, now is the right time. There's something I need to tell you."

Her aura swelled with concern and a sharpness he knew well. Her determination to fight. For him. No matter what. "What's wrong, my Grace? You can tell me anything. You know that."

She needed to know he would fight for her, at any cost. Any cost at all. "I've decided to resign from the diplomatic service."

Now that he spoke it at last, the horrible confession slipped out of him easily. He didn't feel different after he'd said it. In fact, he was pleasantly numb.

Her aura seemed rather numb, too. "What?"

"I'm not a diplomat anymore. The paperwork will simply make it official."

Her hands fell to his shoulders. "I don't understand. I know you once tried to leave diplomacy and go errant, but that was temporary, when ambassadors weren't allowed in Tenebra. You were only trying to get to me. But you found a diplomatic solution to our separation. You called the Solstice Summit."

And invited an Old Master into Orthros.

She sat down beside him. "Why would you give up being an ambassador? You've worked for it your entire life. You're brilliant at it."

"Not brilliant enough."

"What do you mean? Just think of everything we achieved during the Summit. We succeeded, Lio."

"Yes, we succeeded. But diplomacy isn't why we won. We won because I poured magic into the Old Master's maw. We made it across the Maaqul because my magic links our minds. In the end, power was all that mattered."

She searched his gaze, her aura pulsing with alarm. "I thought the outcome of the Summit had restored your faith."

"Everything we've been through has finally taught me to have faith in my magic. Not my words. Not anymore."

Realization crept through her aura. "You've already made up your mind. And you wouldn't have done that without thinking through everything carefully. It's been eating at you for…how long? And you said nothing. You decided—alone."

"I was too busy trying and failing to keep you safe to stop and discuss matters over coffee."

"You've listened to all my woes about my sister, and you said nothing about struggling with the decision to give up your life's work."

"I had to think it through."

Hurt welled up in her. "You clearly haven't. Orthros needs Ambassador Deukalion. That hasn't changed."

She didn't understand his decision.

He had never expected that. And Goddess, how it hurt. He had thought his Grace would understand.

"Ambassador Deukalion isn't who you need," he tried to explain. "You need one of the most powerful thelemancers in Hesperine history."

"Ambassador Cassia needs her partner. What about your reassignment to Imperial affairs? Our future as diplomats together in a cozy home office, showing the Empress's dignitaries around the city?"

For her to think he was the one dashing their dreams cut even deeper. "I don't give a bleeding thorn about Imperial affairs, and all I'd like to do with the Empress's dignitaries is shred their minds the same way I did your arrest warrant. We were quite done with Tenebran diplomacy, and now we are done with the Empire, too."

"No. I will not let the charges against me ruin the lives we want to build together. To rescue Solia—to make sure Tenebran politics never interfere in our lives again—we can face all of that as Orthros's ambassadors. That is who we are."

He cupped her face in his hand, the fulgurite digging into his other palm. "I will do whatever I must to keep you safe. And while I do it, I cannot be concerned about how my actions reflect on Orthros. I cannot tread with the caution of diplomacy. I must be free to protect you with all my power."

She clutched his arms. "No. You can't give up your life's work because I lost control with the guards. I won't let my transgression against the Empress destroy your career."

He tilted her face up, holding her gaze. "None of this is your fault, my Grace. To Hypnos with my medallion. Our family is more important. You are more important. All I want is for everyone we love to be safe, together. So you and I can live our life together in peace."

"You know that's all I want, too. But even if we can find Solia, if we break into the Empress's prison, it will destroy peace, not protect it."

"We are not going to search for her and break into the Empress's prison."

A relieved sigh escaped Cassia.

He gathered her into his arms, the most treasured person in his eternity. "I will find her, and I will infiltrate the prison. After I've taken you home."

Anger turned her aura to ice. "Deukalion Komnenos, that is the wrong kind of heresy. If you think I'll sit safely at home while my Grace goes errant, you need to have Uncle Argyros examine your mind."

"My uncle broke an army with his mind. My father walked the path of war for centuries. When one of our bloodline is in danger, I will not stand down. And by the Goddess, when someone threatens my Grace, I will remind them that Hesperines have fangs."

Cassia sprang to her feet, her fury sweeping through their Union, beautiful fuel for his determination. "I will not let this happen. When one of our bloodline is in danger, I should be at your side. When someone threatens my Grace, I should be there to fight with you, for you."

"Now that we know what has happened to Solia, it is clear you're in too much danger here. It won't help her if I must break both of you out of an Imperial prison."

All the light in her aura went out. The fight. The anger. And the feeling left him bereft.

"If I had gone through with my Gifting," she said, "you wouldn't be considering any of this."

"Cassia," he tried to reassure her, "we all know why you couldn't. It would have been too difficult, even dangerous, to endure your transformation with Solia's fate hanging in the balance."

"You shouldn't have to make these sacrifices just because I'm not—" She cut herself off.

Intense shame cut through her.

It pierced his heart. "Cassia. You have nothing to apologize for. Once Solia is safe, you will feel ready, and you can have the Gift Night you deserve."

"I should have gone through with it," she said in a small voice, "but I didn't. Because I'm not...I'm not..." A sense of fragility trembled in her aura.

He got to his feet, and she didn't resist when he pulled her into his arms. "What are you trying to say?"

She hung her head. "I'm not ready," she whispered, "for my Gifting. Even before we found out about Solia, I...was never ready."

His arms tightened around her. "But you said you were."

"I was trying so hard to be. I should have been. I told myself I was. But I was lying to everyone and to myself. That's why I was so relieved when we delayed it."

"You could have died." The words wrenched out of him. "Think what could have happened when the visions of your past overtook you, and you had to reckon with your choices. You tried to put yourself through that before you were ready? You were about to risk your life—to let me endanger your life! Why? Because you thought we expected it?"

"Because I wanted it!" she cried. "I want it so much. I want my Hesperine future. But I can't have it, because I'm not ready for my Gifting. And I don't know why. All the conversations with the mind healers. Learning how to be Hesperine. All the time becoming part of your life, your family. I don't know what it's going to take, Lio. But I do know you cannot give up everything that's precious to you because I am holding you back."

He rose to his feet. "You are what is precious to me."

"You waited so long to tell me I'm your Grace, because you wanted me to choose my own future in Orthros. Your life was at stake, but you wanted me to have my freedom. What of your future? Your freedom? There must be more to your life than me."

"There will be nothing left of my life if something happens to you."

For some reason, that was what made her tears spill over again. Her hurt and shame only deepened.

"Cassia, I—"

She shook her head. "I promised you that you would never have to do without me again. That I would be a Hesperine."

His power pulsed out of him, and he felt her heart beating against his chest in tandem. "You will be. If waiting for you to be ready is what I must do—Cassia, I have forever. And if rescuing your sister is what I must do—I have power."

"Don't think your power is our only resort," she pleaded. "Don't give up on your medallion. If you'll only wait to make any decisions until after we talk to the elders about my arrest warrant—"

"You were right when you said I've already made my decision."

Her anger and misery and denial crashed through their Union, even as Lio sensed the sunrise nearing. Far, far above, out of sight beyond the weight of stone, dawn drugged his power, mocking his strength. He didn't want to leave her like this, with so much unresolved hurt throbbing between them.

She made the decision for him by turning her back on him and fleeing through the door, toward the sounds of the other humans.

Lio leaned his back against the cracked wall of the courtyard and slid down to sit among the glowing fronds. He rested his head on his knees, gathering his veils around himself out of pure instinct as Slumber crept up on him.

He would sleep alone, without his Grace in his arms, when he had only just gotten her back.

...that's not how we use our power, is it?

Lio had accepted what he must do. Unleashing his power upon the threats to Cassia, to her sister, to their future did not seem difficult.

What was much harder was the knowledge that his Grace was ashamed of his decision.

59

days until

NOTIAN WINTER SOLSTICE

46 Annassa, 1597 IS

THE ONLY CORD

LIO WOKE TO THE sensation of her teeth on his skin.

Strange smells around him. Soft plants under his head. In the back of his mind, hurt lingered. Something had been wrong.

He didn't care what. She was nibbling her way down his chest.

"My Grace," she whispered. Her warm breath soughed across his stomach.

Too much effort to lift his head. He lay back and let her roaming hands push his robes out of her way. Her incisors scraped below his navel, teasing a path downward, tightening his groin.

The next thing he knew, she slid up to lie beside him. His eyes came open, meeting her hazel ones.

The hurt was there too. What had happened?

"Casssiaa?" he slurred.

"You said I'm welcome to bite you in your sleep…" She licked her lips. "What is your position on sleep kissing?"

His Craving honed in on his Grace, offering herself to him. His nostrils flared, and his fangs unsheathed. "I'm not asleep."

Her mouth came down on his. She bit his lips, deepening the kiss each time. When she bit his tongue, his hands came to life and fastened around her hips.

Need awoke his preternatural strength, and he lifted her onto him. She straddled him and rocked her clothed krana against his bare rhabdos. His body roused fast and hard.

Her aura nipped at him, hungry. No need to think. He gave her his magic. She bucked on him, crying out.

But then she tore her mouth away from his. "No. I'm here to give you what you need."

There was something wrong about that assertion. But his thoughts were soft and slow, save the sharp imperative to get her blood inside him and his body inside hers.

She clawed her hair away from her neck. Taking his face in her hands, she lay her throat against his mouth. Her tears splashed onto his brow.

She was hurting. He poured more magic into her, a tide to erase her pain. She wept, but not with sadness now.

He fastened his fangs onto her throat. Her blood flooded into him, heavy with sweet flavor. He dragged at her vein, relishing every rush of sensation through his sleepy limbs, down his back, to the tips of his fingers and his curling toes.

Her robes were in the way. He shoved them up over her waist, his fingers digging into the soft flesh of her thighs. He felt a quiver of anticipation go through her. Panting, she nuzzled his neck, dampening his skin with her tears. He parted her legs wider, about to lift her onto his rhabdos.

"No." She pushed away, yanking her delicate throat where his fangs held her.

Alarm and blood focused his awareness. She would hurt herself like this. Heeding her refusal, he let go of her hips. He wrapped his arms around her gently, tightly, just long enough to seal the wound at her neck, before he let her go.

She crawled off of him, looking wild and wanton and exquisite with her robes hiked up and blood smeared across her throat. "I thought I could give you what you needed. But I can't even do this for you. My own wants are too much."

Lio pushed himself to a sitting position, heaving a breath.

Her anger and pain the night before came crashing back to him. It only made him want to pull her near again, part her thighs, and make her climax until they both forgot what had been wrong in the first place.

His fangs ached, and his body burned. But he wouldn't impose on her, not after the things they had said. The things they had left unsaid. "You don't owe me anything tonight, Cassia."

"I knew you would say that." She scrubbed at her tears. "You feel guilty, and you'll refuse to drink from me, even though you need your magic to be at full strength. That's why I..."

"Bit me in my sleep."

"Before your mind could start to overthink things. It would have worked, if I didn't want to..." She put a hand over her mouth, shutting her eyes.

"Bite me harder?"

She scrambled to her feet to leave him.

Oh, no. He would not let their near feast end like this.

Denying his own needs was one matter. But he would never leave his Grace hungry.

She had spent her advantage of surprise; his Hesperine power was awake now. She would give into the Craving long before he did. He would see to that.

He stepped in front of her before her next heartbeat, and she ran into him. He caught her and held her against him, chest to chest. "You need to feast."

"So do you," she protested.

He opened his magic to her. Intense warmth grew in his breast as a current came to life between them, pulling his magic into her.

"I mustn't..." she whispered.

"Why not?" He traced a finger down her spine.

She shivered against him, but she shook her head. "Not until you do."

He bent his head and spoke low in her ear. "But I could give you so much, long before I bite you."

Her hands fisted in the front of his robes, her aura tugging at his magic. "I have more self control than this...I must..."

"When have you ever needed self control with me, my Grace?" He fed a flood of power into her demand.

Her knees buckled.

He caught her close. "Do you want to stop?"

"No," she gasped, "I want too much."

"There's no such thing."

He backed her into the courtyard, deeper into the veils that sealed them off from the rest of the world. He carried her down onto a bed of gleaming fronds.

"It's not safe," she said. "What if I—"

"I won't let you. Trust me." He caught her hands in his and pinned them above her head.

He paused over her, looking into her eyes for any sign of distress, running his mind magic gently over the surface of her thoughts.

He knew all the things that pleased her…and everything that frightened her. He would never forget or forgive the necromancer who had poisoned her, leaving her delirious and haunted by nightmares of being strapped to a bed.

Cassia wove their fingers together. "Your hands holding me…your mind descending upon mine…this is nothing like my illness…"

He let his thelemancy blanket her.

Her eyes slid shut. "I need you," she moaned.

That was surrender. He pulled her robes out of the way with his teeth.

Along the smooth curve of her breast, he gave her a taste of pleasure. Her aura drank it down, and each wave echoed in his own body. He licked the pebbled texture of her nipple, then sucked. Her Craving drew him in, and more of his magic surged out of his heart and under her skin.

His fangs throbbed. Her throat was so near, her vein beckoning. Her pulse raced for him, promising a rich and rapid feast.

But he devoured only the taste of her skin, the sound of her sighs. The scent of her lust.

He lifted his gaze to see her teeth bared. She tossed her head, but there was no way she could reach him with her mouth.

"I've got you, Cassia." He positioned himself between her thighs. "Relax and let me give you what you need."

"Yes," she gasped.

He drove hard and deep into her krana, sinking into heat as intense as the current of magic flowing between them.

"My Grace," she cried. She arched beneath him, pressing against his hands.

He drove down again, holding her steady against the ground. "That's right. Your Grace. Not a diplomat. Not a Hesperine errant. Just your Grace."

He held her gaze, filling the mind ward with his power the way he filled her body. Her climax rolled through her, shuddering in their Union and pulling a growl from him.

He watched her undulate on the waves of his magic crashing through her. He fed her his body, pounding into her demands until she lay still beneath him, soft and warm and wet.

He held her there, hard and hungry inside her. "I want you to understand, Cassia. If it will buy your safety...I'll hand my medallion to Hypnos."

"Lio—"

He lifted one of her hands to his throat, tangling their fingers in her braid around his neck. "This is the only cord I need. This tie to you. You are all I need. Do you understand?"

She tugged on the braid, bringing his face closer to hers. "I won't let you give up. I won't give up. Do you understand?"

Her gaze lingered on his fangs. His Craving mocked his self-discipline.

Cassia yanked his mouth to hers and scraped her tongue across his fang. The life inside her raced into his mouth, and his instincts raged. As he buried his fangs in her throat, her shout of triumph echoed around them. The surge of power between their bodies broke his control and wrenched pleasure out of him in one wave of blood and magic after another.

Their hunger turned to satisfaction. They lay still together. He felt her soft breaths on his neck.

His neck. Within easy reach of her bite.

He startled and pulled back. Her hands closed around his buttocks, holding him to her. He saw the defiance in her eyes and realized the only blood on her mouth was her own.

He licked a smear of blood from her lower lip. "Your Will is a force to be reckoned with, my Grace."

"I'm not done," she told him.

How he wished they could linger here until she was done with him. But he knew she meant she was not done arguing her case against the decision he had already made.

"We have to leave." Still he didn't move. "Now isn't the time to discuss it further."

She raised a brow at him. "Is your magic at full strength now?"

He gave her a salute to the victor. "But I am not done, either."

OBELISKS

THE MOMENT THEY ENTERED the plaza and Lio lost his sense of Cassia's aura, he felt lost.

He held her hand tighter, although their rift the night before made her seem even farther away.

"I don't like going past the obelisks again," Karege rumbled.

"The only other route will take too long," Ukocha said. "Do you want to spend another Dawn Slumber down here?"

"On second thought," Karege agreed, "let's tiptoe through the heart of the disruption one more time."

As their weary party trudged across the grand chamber, Kella frowned at Hoyefe. "If you need help, Lonesome, you'd better speak up."

Hoyefe put a hand to his side. "I am in *terrible* pain. I may fall to pieces at any moment. I need handsome Hesperines to carry me the rest of the way."

Tuura tutted. "Not after my poultice and stitches, you don't."

"Precisely. I had to have *stitches*. Clearly I deserve to be comforted by a couple of strapping immortals."

"Nice try," Karege said.

Monsoon didn't say a word, much less join in their banter. Cassia kept glancing at him, as if there were a great many things she wanted to say, but she was silent.

They were nearing the center of the chamber when Cassia clutched a hand to her shoulder with a grimace.

Their quarrel fled from his mind. The pain in his chest didn't matter. He reached out to catch her as she stumbled.

All around them, the other mortals cursed or grunted in pain. Their wounds were their only warning before robed figures sprang out of thin air from between each pair of obelisks.

The Broken Hands outnumbered them five to one, and Lio couldn't feel their auras. The Blood Union was like elusive whispers he couldn't understand.

With blades and bows drawn, their enemies advanced across the plaza from all sides. Shrouded faces turned back and forth, searching.

Hoyefe's invisibility spells were all that stood between them and the ambush they had feared. Lio and Karege stood in Hesperine silence while the mortals measured their breaths. Cassia leaned into Lio, as if she could absorb his stillness into her.

He couldn't feel the minds of their enemies. But his thelemancy was still there inside him, at his fingertips.

Lio sent his magic out in a wide blast that would catch every enemy in its path.

The Broken Hands staggered. Lio laughed. A few dozen were much easier than hundreds. He made a controlled strike upon their Wills that would render them unconscious.

His power crashed upon a bastion of mental defenses. The Broken Hands shook themselves and stalked closer.

These were not weak-minded brigands.

An archer let an arrow fly. Lio dodged aside, pulling Cassia with him. The missile's flight ruffled his sleeve.

Lio fired back with a concentrated spell. His magic struck the archer's thoughts, only to speed into a dizzying mental labyrinth. Not mind wards. Twisting defenses expertly constructed to foil the most qualified intruder.

Invisibility wouldn't stop this ambush.

"They're theramancers," Lio warned. "Every one of them."

"For shame," Tuura cried. "They've weaponized our affinity."

A volley of arrows cut across the plaza.

Lio carried Cassia down to the ground. Levitation cushioned their fall as he covered her with his body. But none of the arrows reached them or their allies. He heard wingbeats, then the howl of wind and the clatter of arrows scattering.

Lio lifted his head. "They're tracking our minds to detect our positions."

"Stay in motion," Ukocha ordered. "Don't stand in one place. Hoyefe, keep us invisible. We won't make it easy for them!"

By the time she finished speaking, she had already dodged to a different position, where her voice would not give her away.

With Monsoon blowing the arrows off course, the rest of them scrambled to their feet again.

"The obelisks have all become active spirit gates," Tuura said. "They're trying to pull us through. I must focus on anchoring us. Can you battle their minds?"

Lio bared his fangs. "Yes."

THE CAUSE

MIND HEALERS HAD HELPED Cassia talk about her past and cured her inner wounds.

They had never brandished weapons at her.

She spotted a figure on a high balcony overlooking the fray. Brilliant emerald eyes gleamed at her through the shadows and seemed to look right into her. She saw through them to an ageless garden.

The jinn had led her to Chuma's mother, but also into an ambush.

Something resembling a smile crossed its strange face, and it disappeared.

Well, she and Lio had faced worse than jinn and the Broken Hands.

She stood in front of him and pulled his arms around her. He held her, just as he had when they had faced the Collector.

Kella's daggers flew, landing in two chests. Her targets went down on their knees. Two other Broken Hands dragged their wounded comrades toward a pair of obelisks. They disappeared through a spirit gate, abandoning the battle.

Karege let out a cheer. "Four in one go! That's our Second Blade."

Their triumph faded when four more Broken Hands raced out of a different spirit gate.

"Stand your ground," said Ukocha. "Guard each other's backs!"

Lio's arms tightened around Cassia's shoulder. The new attackers' steps slowed.

"*Ckabaar!*" Cassia cried.

Knight lunged at the oncoming warriors. His jaws locked on one man's arm.

"*Ckastaa!*" she commanded.

Knight hurled the attacker away from him. The man flew between two obelisks and disappeared.

The rest of the reinforcements pushed forward, but slowly, as if every step cost them. Lio's whole body was tense, his magic ebbing and flowing like a sparkling shadow around her.

Six Broken Hands collapsed on the ground. The rest kept coming.

Cassia reached up and pressed her wrist to Lio's mouth. She felt the bite of his fangs. Eight of the Broken Hands cried out and went flying. Their backs hit the face of the ruins. When they slid to the ground, they did not rise again.

She glanced back to see Lio lick her blood from his lips. "I won't let them near you."

With another howl of wind magic, Monsoon dove down from a high balcony. Claws sprang from his hands, and he sank them into one attacker's shoulders. Her scream echoed across the plaza. He carried her into the air and tossed her through the obelisks.

Together, they all picked off Broken Hands from the oncoming force. Not fast enough.

"It's no use," Cassia cried. "Every time we get rid of one, another comes in their place."

The robed warriors closed in around them, a circle of swords and daggers.

Ukocha smiled.

The world seemed to fall silent as half a dozen of the oncoming Broken Hands ignited. They stumbled back toward the obelisks with fire eating at their robes. Like living torches, they hurtled through the spirit gates and were extinguished.

"Ukocha!" The Ashes turned their first blade's name into their war cry.

Karege roared and barreled into the nearest Broken Hands at Hesperine speed. Cassia's mortal vision lost sight of him, but she could track him by the fallen enemies he left in his wake. Some hit the ground, while others ran into their burning comrades and caught fire. Spirit tears opened to swallow them and the flames.

Hoyefe's jokes and tricks were gone now, his face still and grim with focus. He lashed out with his sword, disarming a Broken Hand before the enemy could react to an invisible opponent. The next attacker was even less lucky. He fell, clutching his side as blood bloomed on his robes.

Another assailant drew a sword on Hoyefe, only to spring back from him, fleeing a billow of flame that spread outward from the mercenary's blade. The Broken Hand backed right into a blast of fire raining down from Ukocha's direction. Hoyefe laughed, and the flames around his sword turned into a shower of acacia leaves, an illusion.

Kella and her cat danced between two warriors, fighting both at once. Tilili pranced amid Ukocha's flames like a kitten playing with fire. Kella's dagger hamstrung one enemy. Tilili pounced on the other, sinking in her claws with all four paws. The Broken Hand tumbled backward with a scream.

When an attacker thrust a long sword at Kella's back, her cat leapt over a burning line on the ground, carrying them to safety. She landed on the shoulders of an enemy on the other side and dug in with a snarl.

Tuura stood in the center of the storm, as calm and still as its eye. Magic emanated from her, deep and steady, like comforting arms holding Cassia in the world.

Monsoon glided back and forth over the battle. Everywhere he stirred the air, the wind from his wings blew life into Ukocha's spells, turning her gusts of flame into storms.

For the first time, Cassia saw the Ashes fight together.

"Ckabaar!" Cassia called again, her chant in their battle.

Knight was a battering ram with jaws, one the enemy couldn't see. No sword arm was safe from his bite. No warrior could withstand the impact of his weight. Cassia sent him left, right, and center. His fangs and fur were all that stood between the attackers and her Grace.

Cassia saw Lio's hand everywhere in the fight. An archer aiming at Monsoon's wings fell to the ground, unconscious. A warrior lunging in Kella's blind spot dropped his sword and stood in place, his goal forgotten. Lio cut a path through the onslaught, marking his passage in a trail of powerful mages with broken minds.

The Broken Hands shimmered in and out of sight, using spirit tears to reposition themselves in battle. Shouts and snarls echoed across the plaza, and steel crashed against stone in a contest between teleportation and invisibility, theramancy and thelemancy.

Cassia was no warrior, but she had trained with the Stand. She could tell the Broken Hands used magic like experts and fought like warriors with a cause.

The cause of killing her?

How many had pledged themselves to eradicate shadowlanders? They seemed endless. Again and again, a shimmer in the air carried a mortally wounded Broken Hand away and delivered a fresh assailant.

"So much for corpses," Kella snarled, as the man impaled on her long knife disappeared.

Ukocha cursed. "The cowards won't stay here long enough to die."

Tilili let out a hiss, her ear bleeding, and raked her claws at the enemy who was trying to yank Kella out of the saddle. Hoyefe was surrounded, harried by three swordsmen. Karege came into sight, trapped under half a dozen Broken Hands. Tuura swayed on her feet.

A Broken Hand appeared out of thin air on a balcony and leapt off, landing on Monsoon's back as he swooped by. The two men grappled midair, plunging toward the ground.

The wind ceased, and a volley of stone arrows streaked across the plaza.

Lio turned, sweeping Cassia off her feet. She felt his body jerk against her and knew he had just taken a bolt meant for her. She screamed with wordless fury and clung to him, although her bare hands were of no use against the lithic edges.

"I've got him!" Tuura called, her voice strained.

"*Ckabaar!*" Cassia snarled, the only magic incantation she had. Her one weapon leapt into action again. Knight's barks and snapping jaws drove back two Broken Hands trying to press their advantage against Lio.

"I need your wrist," Lio ground out.

She pressed her wrist to his mouth again. His jaw clenched, his fangs digging deep. Then the arrow tore itself out of his shoulder, swiveled, and shot into the nearest Broken Hand.

With Lio holding her like this, Cassia couldn't see what damage the arrowhead had done. "How bad is it?"

He took one more long draught of her blood before sealing her vein. But he had no time to answer.

The archers fired again. Their stone arrows flew toward Ukocha's bastion of flames. Then halted midair and launched themselves back at the Broken Hands on an unmistakable current of Hesperine levitation.

While Lio was concentrating on the arrows, Cassia sent Knight after an enemy with two daggers, an instant before the attacker came within arm's reach of her Grace.

One of their daggers caught Knight's shoulder, a glancing gash through his thick fur and hide. An angry command tore from Cassia, and Knight mangled the attacker, but not before he took another slice on his back.

Amid Knight's fallen opponents, another Broken Hand shimmered into sight. Cassia sicced Knight on him, too. But the air wavered. He appeared to her left. On her right, Knight leapt through empty air.

The Broken Hand's shroud faced her, as if his unseen gaze met hers. Her wound throbbed.

That was when she saw his ripped, bloodstained sleeve and the bite marks on his arm. Right where Knight had bitten him under the overhang. Here was the man who had put the knife in her flesh and banished her through a spirit tear.

This was the enemy who had run a sword through her Grace.

"Ckabaar bentaa!"

Knight streaked toward the man for a rematch.

The air shimmered at the man's hand, and a spear appeared in his grip. He aimed at the level of Knight's chest.

"Loma!" she shouted. *"Loma hoor!"*

Knight retreated. The man spun on his heel and aimed for Cassia.

She blinked, and Lio stepped. His hand closed around the attacker's spear shaft. The mind ward sang in Cassia's head, and the pain in her arm dulled. The Broken Hand's knees buckled, and he sank to the ground, holding his head.

Lio's fangs flashed in the spell light. The spear snapped in his grip and fell to the ground.

He blurred in a pattern she had seen him use in Hippolyta's Arena.

The man crumpled, now covering his face with his hands. Blood rushed out from between his fingers.

The Broken Hand closed his other hand around the spearhead. His tattooed hand, some part of Cassia's mind recalled.

With a sudden burst of strength, he surged to his feet. Then he was gone.

When his hand closed over her mouth, it was already too late to scream.

His other hand clamped on her wound. Pain seared her, as if fusing his grip to her limb.

Everything around her blurred. Waves like desert heat rippled through the air. A force dragged at her body, at her spirit, as the whispers of the ancestors chorused in her ears.

Another power pulled her the other way. Tuura?

Cassia thought she would tear in two.

I've got you. Lio's voice, whispering within the ward. *Hold on to me.*

She reached for him with all her senses, pouring all her Will into their connection.

His power rang through the layers of the ward. She saw into his spell. Together they sent a thousand fragments of mind magic shattering into her captor and felt his thoughts bleed.

But her captor did not let her go.

"No!" she screamed.

Only the ancestors answered her.

MIRAGE

L IO STOOD MOTIONLESS WHERE his Grace had been, baring his fangs at an enemy who was no longer there.

There were no more attackers. There weren't even any bodies.

The Broken Hands were gone, and they had taken Cassia with them.

Despite all his promises to protect her, the enemy had snatched her from his very arms.

Lio found his voice. "I have to get out of the disruption. To track the mind ward."

He levitated away from the others at Hesperine speed. When his senses burst into full awareness again, he landed hard, bracing a hand on the wall of the ruins.

His surroundings were a blur as he withdrew deep into his mind's eyes to seek the ward. He called out with his thelemancy to the farthest ends of his range in search of his Grace, his beacon.

He felt only the emptiness of the world without her.

In the numbing quiet, he heard Knight's paws approaching. He truly could track a levitating Hesperine at unnatural speed.

He raced over to Lio and pressed against him with a pitiful whine. Lio held the dog's head close, as Cassia was wont to do, and rubbed his drooping ears. If only Hesperine mind magic worked on liegehounds so he could offer Cassia's faithful friend some comfort.

But there was no comfort to be had.

He raced back to the plaza, Knight keeping pace with him. The Ashes stood waiting for his verdict. Their kind, angry questions seemed to deal him a dozen cuts.

Monsoon was the only one who said nothing. He just stood there beside Lio in silent support, and Lio found that he felt deeply grateful for that.

"I cannot sense the ward," he said. "Wherever they've taken her, it's within the disruption."

Ukocha gestured with her good arm to the ruins around the plaza. "We'll search the entire area affected by the obelisks. I've gotten to know every bolthole while I've been down here cleaning the place out. Wherever the rats are hiding, we'll find them."

Lio shut out the voice of doubt in his mind that argued the enemy would never remain so near. He focused on Ukocha's plan, on the one action he could take that might help Cassia.

Lio had to remember the liegehound command for tracking. *"Seckkaa!"*

Knight took off across the plaza, sniffing and digging by turns. As the hound retraced Cassia's steps in the battle, Lio followed him, and so did Monsoon. The man still said nothing, but he stayed with them, even when Knight's hunt left him trotting in circles around the place where Cassia had disappeared.

They took him into the chambers surrounding the plaza. Down the secret tunnels Ukocha had found. Up the crumbling stairs to higher levels. All while the Ashes fanned out to search every other nook and cranny. With every passing minute, every accruing hour, the chill of Lio's despair became a freezing numbness.

When they all regrouped in the plaza at last, he stumbled on a crack in the lavish floor tiles. The luminescent plants seemed too bright in his eyes. The ancient statues around them gazed back with peaceful, blank eyes while his world crumbled.

"She isn't here," he admitted aloud.

"But she's still alive," Karege told him, his encouragement bracing in the Blood Union. "You would know if she weren't."

"Yes." He sank once again into the depths of his Gift, where Hespera's power bound him to his Grace. Cassia's life force in his blood was his only reassurance that her heart still beat.

Tuura put a comforting hand on Lio's arm. Her voice was so calm, her conclusion undeniable. "There must be more obelisks in another location.

They must have taken her elsewhere in the Maaqul, where the disruption is also powerful enough to prevent you from sensing her."

Cassia could be anywhere. It would take them weeks, months, lifetimes to scour every ruin in this vast, unmapped inferno of the Maaqul.

Cassia didn't have time for that.

The enemy had taken her alive. But there was another enemy that would soon threaten her life: the Craving.

He had seen what had happened to her during their separation in the desert. How long did she have before her illness became even more dangerous?

Grace. Hespera's greatest blessing. Her people's greatest weakness.

"No." His voice echoed back at him from the surrounding ruins. "There is another way."

Hoyefe frowned at him. "By the look on your face, I'm not sure we'll like it."

Lio bared his fangs, which had yet to sheathe since the battle. "The jinn will tell me where she is."

"See here, youngblood." Karege planted a staying hand on Lio's chest.

"They led us into that ambush," Lio hissed. "They must make it right."

Kella positioned Tilili beside Karege, as if they could block Lio's path. "That's not how the Desert Accord works. They'll consider the scales balanced because the jinn did fulfill Cassia's request to lead her to Chuma's mother."

"Cassia and I are citizens of Orthros. We are not bound by any treaties with the jinn."

"What are you," Karege asked, "a moonflower from the diplomatic service, thinking you can negotiate with jinn?"

"I have no interest in negotiating," Lio replied.

Ukocha considered him with a hard gaze. "I strongly advise against it, Sunshine."

At this moment, he was still under her command. And yet, she did not phrase it as an order. "I respect your position, First Blade."

"The Ashes must uphold the Accord," she replied. "We cannot antagonize the jinn. But we can stand with you."

At Lio's shoulder, Monsoon drew his sword. "Nothing I do will reflect on the Ashes any longer. If the jinn give you any trouble, we'll see how they like Mweya's way of 'negotiating.'"

Lio felt no ray of hope, but he had this—the loyalty of these courageous, honorable people from every corner of the Empire. The support of Solia's family. Of all the treasures hidden in the fabled Maaqul, he and Cassia had found the greatest one of all. "I won't ask you to do this…but you have my eternal gratitude for offering."

"We have your back," Monsoon promised.

Lio stood in the center of the plaza with Knight and the Ashes around him. "Hidden ones," he called out to the jinn, "I have cast aside my veils. Face me in the open."

The ruins remained void.

"Nothing that happens in the desert escapes your notice. I know you hear my words. Will you not answer?"

Only the silent stones replied.

Lio raised his voice. "You have taken she who is mine. You will give her back."

"Insolent child," came the alien voice, rippling like the heat of the day Lio would never see. "You imagine we come on command? You presume we owe you anything?"

"Do you deny one of your kind is allied with her captor?" he demanded.

At last the jinn made their soundless, sudden appearance.

They lurked in doorways. They held court on the balconies above, too many to count. Some seemed made of smoke, others formed of parts from beasts that existed only in tales. There was unmistakable menace in the way they surrounded him and his allies.

Blocking the exit was the jinn who had first allowed Cassia, Lio, and Monsoon into the desert.

"Who are you," it sneered, "to extract a penalty from us?"

He was her Grace. "Her protector for eternity. Our bond defies your desert. Your magic. Time itself."

"What affair is it of ours if another mortal is lost in the desert due to the foolishness of humankind?"

"It is your affair when she belongs to Hespera." Lio turned in a circle, letting them see his fangs. "I am no mortal for you to play with. I am no

Imperial citizen to tread carefully before you. I am as immortal as you, and you have taken the one I love. Tell me where she is!"

A wind, unseen and unheard, seemed to ripple through the jinn.

"You do not have the power to ask anything of us," said the jackal-headed immortal.

Lio had reached into the well of his magic before and had yet to find where it ended. A goddess's power ran through his veins. He would gladly become the first Hesperine to find out how his power matched the jinn.

"I am not asking," Lio replied. "If you would like to find out if I have the power to get what I require from you, then let us put the matter to the test."

Lio looked into the hollow eyes of the jinn before him and reached into the vast expanse of stars inside his own blood.

Self control was a lifelong, careful effort. Releasing his power was the instinctive act of an instant.

Fury, endless as immortality, rolled out of him. With it came a blast of power. He readied himself for the impact against whatever strange minds he would discover within the jinn.

No collision came. His power echoed into the empty halls.

The jinn had disappeared.

"No!" he shouted. "How dare you flee! Do not hide yourselves from me."

But there was no answer. They had dealt the cruelest blow they could. Retreat.

It was over.

Until the whole surrounding world disappeared, so quietly and with such stillness that Lio didn't feel as if he had moved.

He found himself in a garden, surrounded by greenery taller than his head. The fragments of four broken moons shone overhead, showing him the riotous colors of all the flowers around him. The air was sweet with their perfume and cool with moisture.

Like a paradisaical twin to the accursed landscape where the Collector had once trapped him in a waking dream.

Where in the Goddess's name was he? Was this...some realm belonging to the jinn? Did it somehow exist, but not, in the same space as the desert?

"What have you done?" he shouted at the jinn.

There came no reply.

He shot up on a burst of levitation to get an overhead view of the garden, to spot a way out. But no matter how high he rose, the greenery rose with him, blossoming and proliferating, inviting him into an endless maze of life.

While Cassia's life was in danger.

When he had offered her his love, he had known what it could cost her. But in the future they had imagined together, he had never foreseen this.

He would be the death of her.

SHATTERED HOPE

WHEN CASSIA EMERGED ON the other side of the tear, the whispers didn't cease. The ancestors only grew louder.

She lashed against her captor's hold. He let her go so fast that she stumbled. Finding her feet, she fled.

The voices followed her across a vast terrace, as if this were a busy meeting place full of people she couldn't see. Massive pillars carved from desert rock ringed the area to either side of her. No doorways there to offer escape.

Pushing her ragged body, she raced to the railing ahead of her, only to catch herself on it and careen to a halt. She sucked in a breath of hot desert air.

The sky above was dark and swirling with stars. Beneath it lay a city bathed in sunlight. Far below the high balcony where she stood, the metropolis spread out as far as she could see. Larger than the Sandira city. Grander than Haima or Orthros's northern capital, Selas. She could not begin to imagine how people had ever built such towers and mansions, courts and boulevards.

This architecture was the same style as the temple and the underground city. But the temples here made that one look like a mere shrine, and the dwellings in the caves like a little village. The wonders before her were the most magical things she ever beheld, although they were still and silent.

Except for the voices. *"Hear. See. Hope."*

There was no hope here. Nothing moved but the wind. Nothing grew. She beheld the beautiful carcass of a city long dead.

The sand piled in dunes under the galleries. The impossible, unseen sun bleached the skeletons of broken towers. Everywhere Cassia looked, she could see through the jagged teeth of collapsed roofs into the private spaces of the people who had once lived here, where the remnants of their lives lay in fragments.

In the very center of the city stood an array of megaliths. Some were blunt stumps, others tall and pockmarked with damage. But the massive stones had once been arranged in a careful pattern. She had seen it before—on the palms of the Broken Hands.

The monument appeared dark red in shadow, pale red in sunlight. The same kind of stone as the lithic weapons, as the obelisks.

Her gaze fell to her arms. Her hairs stood so on end, she might have walked across a carpet in Orthros at midwinter. The magic here was deep as the sand and behaved even more strangely.

Could the megaliths be the source of the disruption Tuura had described? Were they some kind of spirit gate, like the obelisks?

Did that mean Lio couldn't sense her mind ward here?

The most sickening panic she had ever known made her slide to her knees. Worse than facing the king. Harder than watching war mages destroy the shrine of Hespera. More terrifying than the Collector.

Lio couldn't find her.

She couldn't get back to Lio.

"Find. Try. Hope."

Curled on the floor, shaking, Cassia found a thought that anchored her. This was the Craving.

"Lose. Fear. Survive."

This fear was the Craving. A survival instinct.

That's what fear was, wasn't it? Survival. A warning of danger from inside her so she could protect herself.

Anger she controlled was power. Fear that helped her...was power too.

"Rage. Stand. Endure."

Thank you, fear, she thought. *You have served your purpose.*

It was time to stand and use her power.

She dragged herself to her feet and turned back to the inside of the room.

In the center was a long stone table, spread with scrolls, tomes, and all manner of lithic weapons. Her captor stood at it, his hands spread on its surface.

There was the bandage on his arm where Knight had bitten him. Those were the robes of the Broken Hands. But he had removed the shroud from his head. Despite the mess Lio's fists had made of his face, she recognized him.

"Welcome, Cassia," said Dakk.

What a fool she had been to trust him. She should have listened to her instincts. They hadn't been unfounded fears leftover from Tenebra. She had known, deep down, he would betray her.

Dakk gestured to the chair across the table from him. "If you're ready to join me, please make yourself comfortable."

There was nowhere to go but forward. She approached him, the table between them. Her gaze fell to his hand. There was the emblem she had first seen when Monsoon had stepped on his wrist. The one he had hidden under gloves in Marijani. "May I compliment you on your tattoo? It goes so well with your broken nose."

His expression was the too-calm one of a very angry man. Her enemy had a temper, she noted.

He tossed aside the stained rag in his hand. His nose had stopped bleeding. "Our healers are rather busy at the moment, thanks to you and your allies. I won't trouble them to spare my vanity."

Gone was the dapper young student. She looked around at the grand chamber, the documents on the table, his air of authority. "Who are you?"

"Always your friend, I assure you."

"You certainly have a strange way of showing it."

"You are a prisoner, to be sure, but I am not your jailer. I only want to help you, Cassia. I can set you free."

"Then send me back through a spirit tear to Lio. Best do it quickly, before he gets angry."

"The Hesperines won't be able to find you here. This is the safest place in the world for you. Won't you sit down?"

Gaining trust was a highly effective interrogation technique. He had employed it once before to great effect. She thought back to everything they had talked about while he had laughed with her in the Sun Market. Cup and thorns. She had made an easy mark.

He was interrogating her again now. That meant the mind ward stood against him, and he couldn't use his magic to get the information he wanted from her.

Cassia was very good at resisting interrogation and finding out what she needed to know in return. She must turn the tables on him and learn information that could help her escape.

With a show of hesitation, she took the chair he had offered her. He sat down on his side of the table, picking up a nearby clay pitcher. He poured water into a cup and slid it across to her.

"Certainly not," she refused.

"You will need to eat and drink something during our time together. This isn't the most hospitable place, but I will do my best to provide everything you need."

"You hardly seemed concerned about that when you banished me across the Maaqul with your dagger."

"I didn't have many options with your dog and your carrier pigeon looming over me."

Had he wanted to capture her instead, even then? That could have been the aim of the ambushes at their camp and later in the underground city, but she had been too well defended.

The Broken Hands wanted her alive. What did they have in store for her?

She straightened her posture and put on a cool expression. "You didn't want to snatch me out of Marijani for a private chat?"

His smile didn't reach his eyes. "Stabbing you in the Sun Market might have drawn unwanted attention."

She thought of the discoloration in her veins and how her arm had throbbed when he had touched her. How much could she get him to reveal about how the lithic edges worked? "Oh, I see. Your stone dagger cast some kind of magic on me that allows you to bring me through spirit tears."

"Yes. Now that you've had lithic material in your blood, I can bring you here from anywhere I please." He lifted his palm, showing her the tattoo. "I carry my lithic mark with me everywhere. Now, so do you."

Cassia's skin crawled, and she resisted the urge to claw at her arm. Lio had drunk the poison from her veins himself. She would have denied Dakk's assertion that he had some hold on her, except that she had experienced the truth of it for herself. He had managed to break Tuura's anchor and take her from her Grace.

Who was this man, who wielded all these strange secrets just to apprehend the few shadowlanders who made it to the Empire? There must be something more complex at work here than dedication to the Empress's policy of isolation.

"I understand you are opposed to the presence of shadowlanders in the Empire. Perhaps we can settle our differences, because my allegiance is to Orthros, not the shadowlands."

"I have no quarrel with you, Cassia. Only the one who sent you."

She frowned. "You have a quarrel with someone in Orthros?"

"Come now. You don't have to play the citizen of Orthros game with me. I knew you were a shadowlander all along. When my friend who works for the port authorities let me know about a Tenebran arriving in the Empire in possession of magical artifacts, it was my duty to investigate."

Cassia suddenly recalled the kind young woman who had gone through her gardening satchel. Cassia hadn't even noticed the design on her palm, because it had blended in with the many tattoos that covered her hands and arms.

Dakk watched her face. "Yes, Cassia. I have friends everywhere. Marijani. The Sandira Kingdom."

"The arrest warrant."

"I tried to handle things with delicacy. A quiet arrest would have been better for everyone."

Here was the enemy who had destroyed her reputation and pursued her through the Empire. He was more than just a desert outlaw. This conspiracy ran far and wide.

Dakk shook his head. "But you do love creating a scene, don't you? You made such a dramatic one during the Summit."

"If you're aware of the negotiations between Tenebra and Orthros, you know I defected to Orthros. I assure you, whatever your interest is in Tenebra, I cannot help you."

"That so-called battle with the necromancers was very convincing. Even my source believed it. But you and I know the truth, the secrets we keep from everyone, to protect them from the danger that is always near. I admit, I myself have never stood so close to that danger as I do now. You must understand, I cannot allow you to spread it throughout the Empire."

Cassia could think of no clever response this time. He was deluded. "What are you talking about?"

"I told you, there's no need to feign innocence with me. I know about the ancient necromancers who hold Tenebra and Cordium in their thrall. They are the shadow cast over those pitiable lands. I have devoted my life to ensuring they never breach the Empire. No one has made so bold an attempt to bring their power here as you have. I cannot allow you to unleash the Master of Dreams upon the Empire."

"How dare you," Cassia spat. "I have looked the Collector in the eye. I have fought him for all I hold dear. Do not imply I'm working for him."

He lifted his hands in a defensive gesture. "I am not one to judge you. I know how he controls people. You didn't have a choice, did you?" He lowered his hands slowly to the table, holding her gaze, his eyes full of pity. "Somewhere, deep down, no matter what he has done to you, there is still a spark. Your desire to be free of him."

Cassia braced her hands on the table and leaned forward. "I was never his. Lio and I taught him the price of trying to add me to his 'collection.' And I will teach you the cost of mistaking me for any servant of his."

"You don't have to lie to me. You don't have to persist in the act he sent you here to perform. I meant it when I said this is the one place you're safe from him."

"I am safe behind the Queens' ward. I was safe in Orthros."

"So the Hesperines believe, of course. My compliments on your expert manipulation of them. Few mortals have ever succeeded at besting them. They have been a bane of my people's existence all along."

"I've never met an Imperial who had a grudge against Hesperines."

"Oh, I know. All the Empress's citizens are eating out of Orthros's hand. They give into the temptations of magic, pleasure, wealth. They don't realize that Orthros is a gaping doorway for evil to enter our lands.

But they'll see the light when they realize the Hesperines endangered us by allowing you to come here. I will be the one who finally breaks the Empire's alliance with Orthros."

This reached farther than Cassia had imagined. Dakk didn't only fight to keep shadowlanders out of the Empire. He wanted to cut off ties with Orthros as well?

Destroying that alliance of nearly sixteen centuries was unthinkable. The Empire would lose the life-saving magic of Hesperines.

And human guests were the lifeblood of Orthros, in every sense. The Hesperines could never survive without them.

"Orthros has always been a boon to the Empire, not a danger," Cassia protested.

"Hesperines cannot be possessed, it is true. The Old Masters cannot spread their magic here through an immortal. But it was only a matter of time before they found a way to send a possessed human through Orthros to the Empire."

"You think I'm like Eudias," she realized. "You think I'm the Collector's way of sneaking into the Empire."

"My people have always known that one day, a wolf would enter among the lambs. I admit, the wolf chose a very unexpected sheep's clothing to wear." He gestured from Cassia's head to her toes.

"Lio freed Eudias from the Collector's possession. If the Old Master had ever attempted such a thing with me, Lio would have stopped him."

The question remained. The one that had always troubled her about the battle. Why hadn't the Collector tried to possess her or abuse her mind?

It didn't matter. He hadn't.

"I'm sure Lio thinks that," Dakk said. "Let me guess. He was eager to cast the mind ward for you. It's a brilliant disguise. The Hesperine thelemancy all over your mind is so dramatic, it makes it even more difficult for someone to detect the way the Master of Dreams had tampered with your thoughts."

"How dare you," she repeated. "You had no right to examine my mind without my permission."

"I'm sorry the Master of Dreams has subjected you to this. First his intrusion, then enduring a Hesperine's mind ward. My magic is very gentle by comparison. No one should have to suffer what you have. That is my life's work. Protecting people from your ordeals. Let me help you."

"I don't need your help." What Dakk implied couldn't be. Lio's protections weren't disguising something so horrible from their own people.

"Did you wish that Lio had the power to save you? One thing I don't think is a lie is your emotional attachment to him. It must have been hard for you, knowing his closeness to you makes him vulnerable to the necromancer. If you tell me what you know about how the Old Master is using the Hesperine, I can help Lio, too."

"You have this all wrong." She would maintain the truth at any cost. "Queen Soteira herself has used her mind healing on me. If I were possessed by an Old Master, she would have detected him and driven him out."

"Eudias slipped by her."

"Because the Old Master possessed both Eudias and the Gift Collector, Skleros. Whenever Queen Soteira scrutinized one of them, the Old Master retreated into the other. But with both Eudias and the necromancer gone from Orthros, the Gift Collector has no one else to hide in when Queen Soteira looks at me. She would have detected his presence in a heartbeat."

"Even if there were a Hesperine mind ward on you?"

"She examined my mind before that."

"Were Eudias and the Gift Collector still in Orthros at that time?"

Cassia swallowed down a wave of nausea. But she wouldn't admit aloud that Skleros had been the one who made her ill that night, and Eudias had been outside her sickroom door through the entire ordeal.

Dakk shook his head. "What the Master of Dreams has done to you is clearly of a different and more threatening nature than his possession of Eudias or even the Gift Collector."

There is the scar of necromancy here, Annassa Soteira had told her.

That had been because the Gift Collector had just poisoned her. Surely that was all she had sensed.

"Lio would have found the Collector in me."

"The Master of Dreams is an ancient mage with skills a young thelemancer like Lio can't even fathom."

"He defeated him. He saved Eudias."

"It does seem the Collector cut his losses that night. But he could afford to. Because he left you behind."

"Lies. All of it."

"Hesperines don't have access to my people's research. We have been the sole guardians of this knowledge for time out of mind." Dakk swept a gracious hand to indicate the length of the table. "See for yourself what knowledge I possess. Hesperines can't even dream of the ancient secrets passed down to me. I am the only person alive with the expertise to help you."

Cassia concluded that everything on the table had been arranged to manipulate her thoughts as well. Not surprising. As long as she kept that in mind, it was still worth looking to see what she might learn.

She spotted a familiar seal of matched speires, already broken in two. An outraged sound escaped her. "Those are letters from home."

Dakk didn't stop her from snatching them up. She opened the first one, finding a letter from Mak and Lyros that she had never seen. She rifled through the stack. Letters from Zoe, from Apollon and Komnena, from Uncle Argyros.

…a blessing that your search progresses…

…wish you could stay in one place long enough to meet…

…keep us informed of everything you're learning about Solia…

…I miss you…

…where are you?

"You've been intercepting our mail," she accused. "You must have been writing to them, making them believe all was well."

"My forgers are the best in the Empire. And our conversations gave me plenty of material for impersonating your writing style. I'm a mind healer, Cassia. I can make anyone believe me. Trust me. Even you, when we were strangers in the Sun Market. Even your friends at home, who only feel my influence through lines of ink."

They have weaponized our affinity, Tuura had said.

Cassia knew how easy it was to trust mind healers, even for someone so reticent as she. It was the nature of their magic. One's defenses felt unnecessary with them.

The same power that Komnena, Rudhira, and Queen Soteira used to help Cassia open her heart had become a tool for manipulation in Dakk's hands.

"Does Uncle Argyros even know we wrote to him for help?" she asked.

"I couldn't allow Orthros's diplomats to become involved. The Hesperines would have taken you back to Orthros before I had a chance to apprehend you."

"How could you do this to Zoe?"

Under the blood on his face, a guilty expression emerged. "She believes you're safe. There is no cause to let a child become frightened."

Cassia hugged the letters from home to her chest, as if she could absorb Orthros's magic through the paper. She didn't know what to make of her strange enemy. Had he given her these to flaunt his control over her…or to reassure her?

He gestured to the rest of the documents on the table. "These are records of my people's traditions. Everything we inherited from our ancestors."

There was a map of the city. A diagram of the megaliths as they must have appeared before they were broken. Beautiful ancient manuscripts with paintings that reminded her of the one on the wall of her cell. A book of poetry.

"Much of our wisdom has been lost," Dakk said. "Some have lost faith in our calling. They forget the danger and with it, the teachings that protect us from it. So much has slipped through our fingers like sand. That is why I will never uncurl my fists."

"Who are your people? What is this place?"

"Come see." He stood and strolled to the railing.

She joined him there, glancing up and down at the structure in which they stood. The terrace appeared to be part of a palace complex.

"Daughter. Daughter. Behold."

Something about the drop made Cassia especially dizzy. Her arm throbbed.

"Open. Open. Hear."

"Can you hear them?" Dakk asked quietly.

She said nothing. His words threatened to distort her thoughts enough. She didn't need the whispering ancestors muddling her mind, too.

"Has the Master of Dreams deafened you to their voices?" Dakk pressed.

"Reach. Reach. Take hold."

"The ancestors speak the clearest here." He sounded reverent. "The natural phase and the spirit phase weave together."

"Where are we?"

"It has borne many names in myth and history. But my people know it by its true name: Btana Ayal. In a tongue you recognize, it means Shattered Hope. The Diviner Queen who built it had to destroy it with her own hands. That was the price of protecting us from the Old Masters. This is the sacrifice she made to keep our lands safe from them."

He turned to Cassia. "My people are her adherents, who stand vigil in the ruins, like the megaliths. Any one of us would make the ultimate sacrifice to ensure hers was not in vain. We are Hope's Fragments—the Rezayal."

He spoke with such conviction, such grief, Cassia found it hard to believe he was spinning a tale to manipulate her. She looked at his tattoo, a mirror of the stones below. Whatever the real history of this city, he believed his version of it.

Cassia ran a hand along the time-worn stone of the railing. "You were never Accord breakers. You have always tended the ruins."

"They are ours, and the jinn know it."

Cassia cursed inwardly. "Was that jinn who led me into your ambush a friend of yours, then?"

"I would not be fool enough to imagine any jinn is a friend. But a number of them have proper respect for the Rezayal's role in the desert. You are not the only one with immortal allies."

"The Azarqi sent the Ashes after you. That's how much they think of your 'role' in their desert."

"They have the gall to brand us as brigands! We, who have been stewards of the ruins for generations. They call our excavations vandalism." He withdrew a lithic dagger from his sleeve. With an act of Will, Cassia didn't flinch away.

"Your sister's appearance in the Empire was a call to action. I have been readying the Rezayal for imminent attack ever since. Thanks to my research, we have learned to craft weapons with extraordinary power from the megaliths. Naturally we had to excavate ruins for additional material."

"Why are you telling me all of your secrets, Dakk?"

He rested the blade across his palm. "I want it to be no secret that we are well prepared. Let the Old Master in your mind hear my threats."

"You don't understand. The Master of Dreams is our common enemy. I have fought his influence over Tenebra. I know what he has done to the people there. I would never work for him."

"I believe you. How did he make you do it?"

"He didn't!"

He paused, quiet for a moment. Then let out a sigh. "It's entirely possible you aren't aware you're working for him."

His kind tone twisted through her, pricking little wounds in everything she believed about herself and Lio, about Orthros, about the rules of the world.

"We have the same enemy," she insisted. "I would gladly help you protect the Empire from the Master of Dreams. I love this land, the homeland of so many of my friends and family. We should work together. Make me your ally, not your prisoner. Let me give you all the knowledge I have— and help me to return to Orthros so I can continue guarding it against him, too."

His expression was sad. "I wish I could, Cassia. I truly do. But anything that comes out of your mouth could be the lies he wants me to believe. The only way I can be sure of the truth is to take it from your mind."

She laughed in his face. "You think you can take anything from behind a mind ward crafted by one of the three most powerful thelemancers in Hesperine history?

He held up his hands. "To eradicate the Old Master's influence from your mind, I *must* get past the mind ward. I must seek a way in to heal you. I will use what I learn to protect the world from the Old Masters. And I will set you free."

That was when she realized there would be no negotiating with him. He was too devoted to his cause, too deluded by his convictions. How could she possibly rely on diplomacy when she faced an enemy who wouldn't see reason?

"You could have had me for an ally," she said, "but you have made me your worst enemy."

"I am very sorry to hear that."

She braced herself for a mental attack. But it was his hands that grabbed for her. She fled, only to collide with him when he emerged from a spirit tear in front of her.

His hand shackled her arm. Pain drove from the site of her wound into her skull.

Terror rose inside her as she fell. Whatever he was about to do to her mind, she would be unconscious, unable to fight back.

58

days until

NOTIAN WINTER SOLSTICE

47 Annassa, 1597 IS

THE BEST INTUITION

MAK COULDN'T REMEMBER WHEN his father's library had felt like this.

At one of the bookshelves carved into the walls, Lyros was luring Bosko to read with the promise of military strategy books. Kadi and Javed sat on the thick Imperial carpet, playing with Thenie together.

Mak's father had left his study alcove, right in the middle of moon hours. More dispatches joined the pile on his desk every night, but for the moment, he had abandoned his toil to sit on a couch with Mother. He balanced his coffee on his knee, one arm around her. Her long auburn hair was unbound from her speires.

At the coffee table nearby sat Nike. Her emotions weren't entirely unveiled, and she had her stack of papers in front of her as a shield. But she was here, not closeted in her residence.

For the moment, their father's sanctum was not the headquarters of Orthros's diplomatic service. It was just the family library.

After weeks of Mak and his father's combined efforts, they had gotten every member of Blood Argyros to relax together. And they had gotten Mother and Nike talking.

"I can't decide," Mak's mother was saying. "Alkaios and Nephalea could benefit from more sparring in the snow, but I don't want to neglect their underwater training, either."

"Perhaps a swimming competition for all the Stewards?" Nike suggested. "We could swim a relay through the Veins. Haima's natural canals have always made an excellent training environment. The sucklings could watch from the cliffs above."

Mother smiled at her. "We haven't done that in years. An excellent idea."

Mak sat with Zoe on his lap and tried to enjoy the results of his effort. But he couldn't.

Lio and Cassia were not here.

"Can I see that letter again, Zoe?" Mak asked.

"Of course!" She held up Lio and Cassia's latest letter, which she had been re-reading. She pointed to a sentence. "I still don't understand that part."

Yes, that was the part that bothered Mak, too. "Try sounding it out again."

Her brow furrowed, her little lips moved, and finally she said, "Perfumery."

"Well done, Zoe."

"But Cassia hates scent oils. Why did she go there?"

Wisdom from the mouth of a suckling. Cassia abhorred perfume because it conjured painful memories of her sister's kidnapping.

"She has started to feel better about some things that used to make her sad." Even as Mak said it, he didn't believe his own reassurances.

This letter had given him a sense of wrongness ever since it arrived, and it only kept getting worse the longer he thought about it.

Lyros was at his side before he had finished his thought. "Zoe, Bosko found a book on goats."

She was off of Mak's lap and over at the bookcase in the blink of an eye.

Lyros sat down next to Mak. He brushed a piece of Mak's hair back from his brow, taking the letter in his other hand. "Still worried, my Grace?"

"Is it just me?"

Lyros hesitated. "No, but I understand why they can't stop for a family visit. They've explained why at every stage of their journey. Their leads could go cold in the time it takes for us all to have a cup of coffee together. Not to mention that some of the places they've been traveling aren't fit for sucklings."

"You and I could keep up."

"If we weren't helping our Trial sisters with the vote." *And if you weren't making such progress at the forge.*

Were arms to protect their people in the future really more important than Lio and Cassia's immediate safety? Was being here for his family in moments like this more important than going to look for his Trial brother and sister?

Mak sighed. "When did I start overthinking things? That's your line of duty."

Lyros's finger trailed across his temple again. "I think this just reminds you too much of Nike. But Lio and Cassia aren't hiding from us."

"They're errant without us, and they might need our help. Just like Nike did all those years."

"I also think politics make you itchy, and you'd rather be out there than sitting in the Firstblood Circle for that vote tomorrow night."

A few nights. That was all the time they had left to make sure the Eighth Circle had enough votes to defeat Elder Firstblood Hypatia's measure.

"All of that is true." Mak shook his head. "But there's something else… something worse."

He looked around at the comforts of home, at the miracle of their entire bloodline sitting here together, alive and well. "I can't shake the feeling."

He pulled Lyros deeper into their Grace Union, letting him sense the dread lurking in the currents of Blood Union that tied them to Lio and Cassia.

Lyros winced. "I can't deny I feel it, too, but…it doesn't make sense."

"None of it does. That's why I know something is wrong. Why are we sitting here doing nothing about it?"

"What do you think we should do?" Lyros asked.

"The vote and the forge and all of it can wait for an hour or two. We should step to wherever in the sunbound Empire they are and see with our own eyes that they're not in trouble. I know it's emotional and not strategic. I know I'm acting impulsively and not thinking through any of the questions plaguing my mind. But what I cannot do is sit here worrying about them a moment longer." Mak drew breath to make his case to his Grace.

Lyros stopped him with a sweet kiss on his mouth. "When do we leave?"

Mak blinked. "That's all? You don't need me to lay out my plan of action and explain the reasoning behind each step?"

"No. I need my Grace to have peace of mind, and I'll do anything to accomplish that. Let's go."

Mak pulled him closer for another kiss, resting his forehead on Lyros's with a sigh of relief. "Thank you."

"I do have a couple of strategic suggestions, though. We should go now, while it's night in many areas of the Empire. And we should make a quiet exit, just the two of us, and assess the situation."

"Agreed. Everyone else will want to come, but…"

"Lio and Cassia might be wading through a swamp or bargaining with a shady informant. No place for hovering parents or impressionable sucklings."

Mak surveyed the room. Zoe and Bosko had settled onto the rug with Thenie, Javed, and Kadi to browse through some illustrated bestiaries. Time for the hard part. "We will have to disappoint everyone."

"They'll be all right."

"I still hate ruining this night." He sighed. "We have to make sure there's one thing that won't be ruined."

"Yes."

Mak truly didn't have to explain. Lyros understood. They were headed into this fray together.

Lyros was his Grace, and he understood. The feeling filled Mak's chest, and no matter how often it came over him, cup and thorns, it felt grand.

Taking Lyros's hand, Mak got to his feet and strolled over to the coffee table. It wasn't until they drew near that Mak noticed the sparkle of amusement escaping his sister's veils.

Nike looked up from her papers, clearing her throat. Was she stifling a chuckle? "No new information in the latest letter."

Mak sensed Lyros raising a subtle veil over their conversation and squeezed his Grace's hand. "You won't be sneaking off to check for vultures while Alkaios and Nephalea are on patrol tonight?"

"No. I don't expect another delivery until tomorrow night."

Mak's instincts, so keenly on edge, told him his sister was forlorn about that. "So why do you keep re-reading that, if there's no information in it?"

"Perhaps there's a clue I missed."

Mak prided himself on his ability to make his sister laugh. Few people could anymore, and none so often as he.

So how could it be so easy for a death mage in Cordium to get a chuckle out of her? The thought of someone with a bloodless vulture attempting a jest gave a whole new meaning to gallows humor.

"So you're not going anywhere for a few more nights at least?" Mak asked.

She glanced into her empty coffee cup. "It will take me at least that long to get enough of this new coffee. Father is threatening to call it Reunion Roast. Please help me persuade him such a fine welcome home gift deserves a name devoid of alliteration, puns, or implications about roasting me for my absence."

Mak laughed in surprise. "Father is jesting about coffee names? Don't discourage this marvelous progress."

Lyros smiled. *Nike's quest won't take her out of Orthros for the moment. Good timing. We can be back before her next missive from Cordium.* "Grace-Father has found his sense of humor. Clearly all is well on the home front. It's safe to carry out our plan."

Nike's smile faded. "I don't get the sense this is the usual mischief of little brothers."

Mak took a deep breath. "We're going to look for Lio and Cassia."

Would she tell him to leave the Hesperines errant to their quest? Or encourage him to go after his Trial brother and sister?

She set aside her papers. "Their letters have failed to reassure you?"

Mak glanced at Lyros. "I know they should."

"We'll simply go say hello and make sure all is well," Lyros said.

Nike looked at him. Her gaze was so much like their father's at times, as if she were peering into his soul. "What does your Union tell you, Mak?"

"That something is wrong."

"Go. Don't wait a moment longer. A mere moment can change eternity."

"Thank you, Nike." He would go, no matter who tried to stop him. But going with her blessing mattered.

She sat back in her chair and looked across at their parents. "Shall we

Vela Roth

start planning the swimming competition? And perhaps drink another pot of this marvelous coffee while we're at it?"

Their mother and father joined them, wearing pleasant smiles. But only for the sucklings' benefit. Their parents' powerful veils wove in the fabric of spells around the table.

"What's wrong?" Mother asked.

Lyros squeezed Mak's hand. *Do you want me to give them the well-reasoned version of our plan, to ward off parental doubts?*

Not this time, my Grace. I'm not the naughty son anymore.

"We're going to find Lio and Cassia," Mak announced. "We'll return before the vote. The Union is warning me that something is wrong, and I won't rest until I know they're safe."

His father let out a sigh and put a hand on his shoulder. "I'm so glad to hear it. I've been fighting the urge to ignore their assurances and send someone after them. I keep reminding myself that they are not sucklings, and it doesn't do for mentors to become meddlers. But your interference will be welcome, I suspect."

His mother nodded her approval. "Go and make sure they aren't in need of wards or fists."

Mak looked around at the most powerful elders of his bloodline. His parents, who had always loved him. The sister he had always looked up to.

He had finally proved that they could trust his judgment.

It's high time they caught on, said Lyros. *I've always trusted your judgment.*

Thank you, my Grace, but I know you didn't avow me for my decision making.

Nonsense. The first time you kissed me—in spite of all my doubts and overthinking—I realized two things. There are times when you know better than I do, and you're as good a kisser as you are a warrior.

Mak couldn't stop himself from smiling.

Mak's mother stepped out of sight, then returned with two scrolls in hand. Black paper, tied with black ribbon and sealed with black wax that gleamed with little white stars in the shape of the constellation Aegis. "Here are official Steward papers, only to be used if the Stand must enter the lands of our allies to assist with a crisis. These passes allow you to step into the Empire and travel anywhere within its borders, bypassing the gate authorities—as long as it is for the protection of someone in danger."

Mak gaped. "I didn't know there was such a thing."

She laid one each in Mak and Lyros's hands. "They are usually reserved for Master Stewards. But I know I can trust you with them."

Mak's heart swelled. "You have our gratitude, Mother."

"What will you tell your Trial sisters?" his father asked. "I know how concerned you must be to leave now, on the final night before the vote."

Mak's smile faded. His help hadn't done them much good. But they did need Lyros, and now Mak was dragging him off.

As if they had sent a summons via courier, Xandra, Kia, and Nodora stepped into the library at that precise moment. Mak blinked at them in surprise.

"Sorry to intrude, Ritual Father," Kia said without any real remorse. She gave Mak's father a peck on the cheek.

That was Kia for you. Always irreverent, never intimidated.

Father's mouth twitched with amusement, his aura warming with affection. "You know intrusions by the Eighth Circle are always welcome in my library."

Nike chuckled. Now a point to Father for making her laugh. "Goddess knows the First Circle has intruded here a number of times."

"Hm." Father considered. "I might sooner call that a stampede."

"Do you hear that?" Kia hooked her arm in Mak's. "We must aspire to be more disruptive. I shall not be content until we qualify as a stampede in the tradition of Nike, Rudhira, and Methu."

But under her usual brazenness, Mak sensed her worry. "What brings you by? Lyros and I were about to come find you."

Xandra offered Mak a scroll secured with a veiled blood seal. The Imperial purple wax, pulsing with magic, was stamped with the constellation of House Kassandra. "She asked us to give this to you. She said you'd know who to deliver it to."

Kassandra had foreseen this, too. Mak hoped this was her favorite version of his possible decisions. "I think it's for Lio and Cassia."

"Then you feel it too." The air around Xandra was unusually warm. "It's as if I can smell smoke, but I don't know where the fire is."

The same fear flowed in Nodora's aura. She put a hand on Lyros's arm. "Do you know what's wrong?"

"No." Lyros looked at Mak. "But Mak does."

"It's definitely Lio and Cassia," Mak said. "You all sense it in our Trial circle's Union, too."

"You're going to check on them." Kia didn't even phrase it as a question.

Xandra pressed her hands palm-to-palm the way she did when she was trying to calm herself. The heat surrounding her began to abate, but not much.

Mak would hate it if he ruined her first political triumph and handed a victory to the isolationists. He was a Steward. It was his sacred duty to support the royal family in all things, on and off the battlefield. And Xandra was *his* royal, his Trial sister.

"Yes, we're going," Mak said, "but I hope we can go with your blessing, Eighth Princess."

The heat around her flared. "Oh, thorns, Mak, don't get all formal and honorable with me, or I might cry. I'm so angry I can't go with you."

Mak's grimace turned into a grin. "Oh. You aren't upset about us leaving."

"Of course not." She must have won her battle with her temper, for the heat around her snuffed out. "Go rescue the Eighth Circle's diplomats."

"Thank you for trusting my instincts," Mak said.

Kia opened her arms for a hug. "We knew you'd have a clearer sense of what's wrong."

"You did?" He gave her an extra big squeeze.

"You have the best intuition of anyone in our Trial circle," she informed him, as if reciting a statistical fact. "I'm too intellectual, Lyros is too analytical, Nodora is too sensitive, and Xandra is…" Kia paused to search for words.

"Oh, just say it." Xandra blew her hair out of her eyes. "I'm volatile, and it clouds my judgment."

"But you, Mak," Kia went on, "your heart is so big that you feel everything, and you're so steady and strong you can make sense of it."

There was a reason Kia and Mak had always been close, and it wasn't just because their parents were each other's Ritual parents. She might be a scrollworm of the highest order, and Mak might be a warrior through and through. But they both always spoke their minds.

"Well, thorns, Kia," he said. "Those words mean a lot, coming from you."

The righteous anger that had clouded her aura lately now broke, and she gave him a sincere, affectionate smile that he hadn't seen in far too long. "Now then, what's your plan?"

Lyros pulled Mak close. "She's right, my Grace. We'll do things your way this time."

It took Mak and Lyros mere minutes to step back to their residence, change into their Stand regalia, and pack their field kits. Just as they had always trained for. But this time, it was no exercise.

We're actually doing this, Mak said in their intertwined thoughts. *Going to the Empire with official papers.*

Thank the Goddess our Steward passes let us step past the entry authorities.

Thorns, yes. I couldn't bear to deal with administration at time like this. But even so…

I know. These papers are for times of crisis. They make our worries for Lio and Cassia feel all the more real, doesn't it?

Mak gritted his teeth. *I can't help feeling like we could be stepping into…anything.*

Lyros put one muscular arm around Mak's waist and pulled him close, covering Mak's mouth with his. His hand tangled in Mak's hair, tugging on his Grace braid and sending tingles along Mak's scalp.

Mak's thoughts skidded to a halt, his worries retreated, and for a moment, he let himself forget everything except his Grace. The strength in Lyros's body, the sureness of him in the Union. The slide of his tongue across Mak's own and the need to tighten his hold on Lyros in return.

When Lyros pulled back, Mak blinked at him.

I love that stupid grin on your face, Lyros reminded him.

I don't remember that being part of the packing routine we trained for.

It is now. I'm not charging into danger without kissing you properly first. And look, we still beat our speed record for field readiness.

Wish we had time for a proper feast before we go.

We'll celebrate when we've made sure everything is all right.

We certainly will. Mak held Lyros to him an instant longer, then sighed and slung his small, black canvas pack over his shoulder.

When they stepped back to the library, the rest of the family and their Trial sisters were waiting, now joined by Alkaios and Nephalea. They all gathered round as he and Lyros prepared to step.

Nephalea straightened the shoulder of Mak's robe, and he thought he was making progress turning her into his honorary elder sister. "Alkaios and I will take your patrols if you're gone very long."

Alkaios gripped Lyros's forearm. "We didn't save Cassia all those years ago for her to run into trouble in the Empire, of all places. Go bring her and Lio back."

Mak and Lyros joined hands. In unspoken agreement, they raised wards around themselves and focused on their Trial brother's aura. The link with Lio was always so easy, after all the years of closeness, not to mention Ritual drinks among their Trial circle.

But not this time.

A chill crawled up Mak's spine. *I can't find him. Tell me you sense him.*

Lyros's hand tightened in his. *I'm sorry, Mak, but I...I can't tell where he is.*

"What's wrong?" Nike was the first to ask.

"We can't step to Lio," Mak explained.

"That may not be a bad sign," Nike replied. "The first night he and Cassia tried to find Solia, no one could step to her. Perhaps they've reached her and are now under the same concealing magic that has been protecting her."

"I hope so." But the dread in the pit of Mak's stomach made him doubt it.

"We can try focusing on Cassia next," Lyros suggested.

"And amplifying the spell with blood," Mak said.

They pierced their palms and tried again, this time with their blood mingling. But Cassia was nowhere to be found in the Union.

Mak's dread had turned to pounding alarm. *Where in the Goddess's name are they?*

Let's be thorough, Lyros said. *We should try Knight as a focus.*

Never thought we'd need our lessons in sensing liegehounds to go to one instead of away from them.

Time to innovate.

Mak shut his eyes, winding deeper into the intimate, shared space where his and Lyros's magic, thoughts, and emotions lived together. With the combined force of their Wills, they sought the elusive, resistant presence of Cassia's liegehound.

"I can scarcely believe it," Mak exclaimed. "We've got a focus on Knight."

"We're going," Lyros announced.

They stepped. Dryness seemed to suck the air from Mak's lungs. He smelled roasting goat and heard the wail of an imzad.

Hypnos's nails, he swore silently, *this is no muddy road in the rainy season. Are we in the sunbound Maaqul Desert?* Lyros replied

They opened their eyes to find themselves in the middle of an Azarqi tent.

They were surrounded by six warriors who were armed to the teeth, their drawn blades gleaming in the light of a campfire. The amount of magic bristling in the tent was even more threatening.

One of them was a Hesperine. And one of them was a fire mage with an aura big enough to burn down a city. This could get ugly.

Mak heard a familiar whine. Knight lifted his head from his paws. He lay in a dejected heap nearby, in the clutches of...a cat. Yes, that was a very large cat with huge teeth and long claws.

Mak was already running through fighting moves with Lyros in their Grace Union, faster than thought. But before they sprang into action, Knight leapt to his feet.

Mak tensed to tackle the cat, but she let Knight go with a soft bat of her paw.

The dog all but threw himself at Mak and Lyros. Mak wrapped a protective arm around Knight's shoulders.

"You must be Mak and Lyros," the Hesperine boomed.

A dapper man with an elegant sword and light magic in his aura gave a dramatic sigh. "Why are all the best-looking Hesperines taken? You two could have had so much fun with me."

"I wouldn't advise flirting at this time, Hoyefe." A woman with a heavy aura of mind healing tutted at him. "That's a good way to get your sword removed."

"No need for a scuffle." The Hesperine sheathed a knife on his arm.

Mak's gaze followed the blade. A Hesperine with a dagger. A fortune blade.

The musclebound elder, whose hair must surely have a legend of its own, gave Mak and Lyros wrist clasps that could have crushed mortal bones. "I'm Karege."

"I know that name," Lyros said. "It's on a plaque in the arena in Haima. You trained with the Stand for a time, didn't you?"

"Why, yes, too long before your time for us to have met. But I feel as if we have. Lio has told me so much about you two."

Mak's heart leapt. "You've seen Lio! Where?"

"That will take some explanation, I'm afraid," said the muscular woman sitting closest to the campfire with her arm in a sling.

She was the source of the fire aura. Suddenly the fortune blades and her affinity fit together in Mak's mind. He looked around at the famous mercenaries, who had felt like a threat a moment before. He liked them already.

"First Blade Ukocha, Victor of Souls." Mak gave her a slight bow.

Lyros did the same at his side. "You're the Ashes. Lio and Cassia did find you."

"But where are they now?" Mak asked.

"You'd better sit down," said a petite Azarqi woman who was curled up next to the cat.

"I will break the news."

The ominous words came from the man who alerted Mak's sense of danger the most. A shifter. His wings were remarkable enough, but it was his magic that set Mak's fangs on edge. This man was more powerful than any mortal in this tent. Any mortal Mak had ever met, in truth.

He rose to his feet with predatory grace, and Mak tensed on instinct.

He's trouble, Lyros agreed.

Hopefully to our enemies, and not us, said Mak.

"I'm Monsoon." He extended a hand. "Cassia is like a little sister to me. That's all you need to know. If we have a hope of saving her, we have to get Lio back from the jinn."

There was a roar in Mak's ears. "What in the Goddess's name have the jinn done to Lio?"

Monsoon snorted. "The question you should be asking is, what did he do to them?"

LOST AND FOUND

L
IO DID NOT GIVE up searching for an escape until his thirst warned him how much strength he had wasted.

He needed to act. Needed to *fight*. Bleeding thorns, he could not bear to stand still.

But he didn't know how long a battle with the Craving he might have ahead of him.

He must try to stay strong, to be of some use to Cassia.

He sank down onto the verdant floor of the garden next to a pool, its tranquil waters a mockery of him. He sat there in the shreds of his travel robes, still covered in the dust of the Maaqul that he had not bothered to banish with a cleaning spell. All he had with him in this strange prison was, of course, the accursed lump of fulgurite he could not seem to let go of.

This was what the eighth bloodborn, one of the three most powerful thelemancers in history, had come to. He had let them take his Grace. And now he had gotten himself trapped where he could do nothing to save her.

He put his head in his hands. *Goddess, what have I done?*

"We have graciously decided to allow you visitors." The voice of a jinn broke the quiet of the garden, its ethereal tones rustling with the leaves and perfuming the air with the flowers. "Do not test our generosity."

His captors were coming to pay him a visit? Lio tensed, but did not move. He didn't even know what to prepare himself for anymore.

He was out of brilliant plans.

The jinn with the green eyes and feathered head appeared. It was the immortal who had looked down on the ambush as if greatly entertained, the creature who had tricked Cassia into getting captured.

So this was Lio's jailer.

The jinn advised, "It would be unwise to pollute the garden with more of your magical outbursts."

When two deep shadows appeared beside the jinn, Lio thought it was just another figment of this bizarre realm. When two familiar auras joined him in his prison, he thought his senses deceived him.

It wasn't until his Trial brothers fully manifested that he realized they were really there, Stand regalia and all.

This was no jinn illusion. He felt them in the Blood Union.

"Mak," he rasped. "Lyros. How?"

They stood at attention, the image of Orthros's finest warriors. Mak wore an expression Lio barely recognized. Confident. Powerful. Stern.

But his aura felt like one of his hugs, telling Lio everything would be all right. And warning him that if he didn't play along, he was an idiot.

"Firstgift Komnenos," his cousin said, "we are here to request your release into the Stand's custody. It has come to our attention that while traveling in the Maaqul as a private citizen of Orthros, you have performed magical acts to which the jinn take offense."

The jinn's feathered crest rose. "We could not allow him to continue wreaking havoc on the scales of balance. His magic is very powerful. The direct confrontation he craved would be undesirable. We merely placed him in a comfortable place where he could cause no further damage. It was a great inconvenience to evacuate our people from this garden so they would not be endangered while he is our guest."

So the jinn did deem him powerful enough to be a threat. Lio found it hard to appreciate the confirmation in his current state.

Mak's expression was like stone. "Let it be noted that on behalf of the Queens, the Stand protests the jinn's response, given Hesperines' long history of goodwill to all peoples."

"As your citizen so forcefully argued," the jinn replied, "no treaties dictate Hesperine behavior toward us, nor ours toward you. Without precedent to guide us, we evaluated the situation and acted accordingly."

"We assure you," said Lyros, "our elders will hear and consider your grievances against our citizen, and our diplomats will determine an appropriate response."

The situation felt like another feature of the dreamlike landscape. Lio was no longer a diplomat. Not only had he lost his medallion in the rubble of Rose House and broken Cassia's heart with his resignation, he had just made a mess of his people's relations with the jinn.

The feathered immortal paused, as if considering. Or perhaps consulting silently with its hidden comrades. "Based on Hesperines' past deeds—despite this individual's misconduct—we have reason to believe your elders will keep their word. We are willing to release Firstgift Komnenos into the Stand's custody, on the condition that you place him in blood shackles and remove him from the Maaqul. He will not be permitted to trespass here again."

Goddess, no. "Cassia is still in the desert. I—"

"Firstgift Komnenos," Mak interrupted, "the jinn have not extended you the opportunity to speak in your own defense."

Again that rush of reassurance in the Blood Union.

Lio was out of plans. But Mak, clearly, was just getting started.

Lio gritted his teeth and let his trust fill his Union with his Trial brothers.

"We accept your terms," Mak told the jinn.

"Very well." The creature cast a dismissive gesture at Lio with one clawed hand.

The pool between him and his Trial brothers evaporated, replaced by a tiled courtyard. Lio wanted to run to them, but he stayed where he was and kept his mouth shut.

His Trail brothers flanked him and drew a circle around him in their blood. When they closed it and clasped their bleeding hands, he felt their wards shackle him. Their other hands closed around each of his arms.

Then the blessed sensation of a Hesperine step spirited him out of the jinn's prison. The inside of an Azarqi tent took shape around them. Knight leapt up to greet Lio with frantic barks and shedding.

Now Mak did pull him into a crushing hug that squeezed the breath and despair out of him.

Lio had not felt this glad to see his Trial brothers since the night they had broken down a door at the gymnasium to discover he had the Craving.

Lyros slung an arm around his shoulders, yanking him close for an embrace, too. "Monsoon told us everything. About Cassia. And Solia."

Lio said it so no one else would have to. "It's my fault."

Mak's outrage buffeted Lio. "Don't you dare shoulder the blame. None of this would have happened if we had been with you. You and Cassia went into battle without us! When I think of how our wards or just our fists would have changed the outcome—" He rubbed a hand over his eyes. "I'm so sorry, Lio. You needed us, and we didn't know."

"You're here now," Lio said, "when we need you the most. But I'm sorry you had to waste precious time picking up the pieces I broke."

Mak's mouth tilted. "That was admittedly a very big mess."

"You're so perfect all the time," Lyros mused, "I suppose we'll let you live this one down."

"Speak for yourself," Mak said. "I'll relish telling the Blood Errant all about how we had to arrest our own Trial brother to bail his rowdy fangs out of a magical jinn prison. This was even worse than when Uncle Apollon came to prevent our expedition, and this time, it wasn't my idea."

Mak spoke as if there would be a future when all of this became a grand tale of their adventures, instead of…the end.

"Cup and thorns," Lio said, "I am grateful for you."

"You should be." Mak smiled and held out a scroll.

Mak didn't just have a plan. He had a letter from the Oracle.

"Thank the Goddess. She must have seen where Cassia is." Lio handed Mak the fulgurite so he could open the scroll with both hands.

Dearest Lio,

    Time is of the essence, so I want to spare you a visit to ask me where she is. They have taken her to the place my sight cannot reach.

    But Grace Union reaches everywhere. Trust Cassia and yourself.

               —Your Ritual Mother

"What is her prophecy?" Lyros asked.

Lio stared at the brief lines. What had he hoped? That she would hand him the Akron's Torch so he could carry it to victory?

His plan had failed that night, too. His diplomatic play had only made matters worse.

"Not even Hespera's oracle knows where Cassia could be," Lio said.

It was already too late.

His power was useless against her enemy, against the distance between them, against the time now slipping through his fingers, draining her life away.

There was no magic in the world that would reveal his Grace to him. Not the oracle's. Not the jinn's. Not his own.

He could feel Zoe's little hands in his. He could see the look on her face. He heard himself trying to tell her that Cassia wasn't coming back, and he would soon follow her to Sanctuary.

He couldn't even imagine what his sister's aura would feel like in that moment. His mind stopped him there, putting a horrible blank where Zoe's emotions would be.

He had missed his chance. He could have saved Cassia's life on her Gift Night, and he hadn't.

"But you have a plan, clearly." Mak turned the fulgurite in his hand, peering at it in the spell lights.

"No." The word slipped out of Lio, his final denial. His surrender.

"Then why are you carrying it around like this?" Mak asked.

"It...reminds me of Rose House." Of his limits. His failures.

Mak peered at him. "You mean you don't know what's in here?"

"Glass," Lio said. "Eudias's glass."

"Yes. Protecting what's inside." Mak took the fulgurite in his broad hands and cracked it like an egg.

Black and luminous, the broken pieces reflected light onto the metal that had been fused inside, both lost and safe. A silver disk engraved with the sun and moons, the opposing forces of the heavens in harmonious alignment.

Lio's medallion of office had been right here all along.

He finally saw that there was more beauty in the fulgurite than in the finely crafted panes of his stained glass window at Rose House. The Collector had failed to shatter the most valuable work of art in that building. Lio and Eudias had crafted it together.

It hadn't been force that had freed Eudias from the Master of Dreams. It had been words of compassion.

Lio had thought he had protected the young mage. He should have realized his friend had also protected him.

"I'm sorry I wasn't there for that battle," Mak said.

"You saved me from it tonight," Lio told him.

His cousin slapped the medallion in his hand. "Looks like this is what you need, then."

Lio lifted his head. "Cassia was right. Diplomacy was always the answer. The only way to get her back is to negotiate for her."

He was her weakness. He was her blessing. He was her Grace, and he would save her.

57

days until

NOTIAN WINTER SOLSTICE

48 Annassa, 1597 IS

MIND GAMES

ASSIA TRIED OPENING HER eyes. Light speared her skull. She squeezed her eyelids shut again. She felt like someone had used her brain for clay on a potter's wheel.

Lio had said that creating the mind ward would make her feel ill for a little while afterward. This was normal.

"Remember," came a whisper. *"Wake. Rise."*

No. Not normal. Lio. No, no, no...

She felt for the mind ward. Still there, woven into her every thought. Her Will was safe.

She lay there, tears of fury and gratitude escaping her closed eyelids. Whatever Dakk had tried while she was unconscious, it hadn't worked. Lio's power had held.

After a moment, she forced her eyes open, throwing an arm up to shield them, and heaved herself into a sitting position. Vertigo turned her belly inside out. She leaned over the side of—it was a cot. And there was a pot next to it perfectly positioned for her to be sick in.

When she was done, she tried to gather her thoughts. They felt sore, like abused muscles. Curse Dakk and his vile magic. She couldn't tell how much of her illness was due to his spells or to the Craving. There was no way to guess how long she'd been away from Lio.

Now that her eyes had adjusted, she saw that she was in a square stone room. Sun shone in a window on the other side of the chamber, beaming in a blinding golden rectangle on the floor. Here, out of the direct sunlight, the room was cool.

There was also a doorway. Edge to edge and top to bottom, it was covered in the wavering air of a spirit tear. Cassia could only see more stone walls through it.

She eased to her feet, steadying herself on the wall. She shuffled over to the patch of sunlight and looked out the window.

The wall of this tower was a long, sheer drop. The masons who had built it had been far too skilled. All this time later, the stones fit together so flawlessly she could not see a finger or toehold anywhere.

She turned to the door. Was the spirit tear a trap? Or could it lead her to a different room where she could devise a way to escape?

There was only one way to find out. Knowing Dakk wanted her alive, she had little to lose by testing the boundaries of her prison.

She walked through the spirit tear.

And found herself right back inside her cell.

She resisted the urge to kick over the cot. She should conserve her strength.

She studied the room, looking for anything in the bare space that might be useful. For the first time, she noticed the painting on the wall opposite the cot.

She drifted over to the faded design. It depicted two rows of people, each moving toward each other. Faces of charcoal and ochre and amber smiled at her from another time. Everyone carried something—a scroll, a basket, stone, wood—all working together on a great endeavor.

What it was, she could not see, for the center of the painting, that thing all the celebrating people looked toward, had worn away, leaving behind nothing but a rough patch of stone.

Compelled to touch something so ancient, to feel a physical connection with these long-lost people, Cassia brushed a finger with the utmost gentleness over a seedling carried in the hands of an olive-skinned woman.

They bore no resemblance to the fanatic who now occupied their halls. What would they think of what Dakk did in their memory?

Her fury gave her strength. She would stay awake for as long as she could. Whenever the next round of interrogation began, she didn't want him to catch her vulnerable.

She paced to keep herself alert. The sunlight faded, replaced by the eerie lights of night. She couldn't see the moons or the stars, only a day-time sky over the darkened city.

How long had she been here?

How much time did she have before her Craving made her helpless?

She turned around again to walk back the way she had come. A flask of water and a small basket of flatbread were waiting for her on the floor. She hadn't seen how they'd arrived.

She stared at them. Were they drugged? Would they loosen her tongue? She had no fear of that. All she would tell Dakk was the truth.

She needed all the strength she could muster to resist the Craving. Food was no substitute for Lio, but it would help her body hold out longer.

She sat down to eat the bread and drink the water. More time went by, and she didn't feel any different.

Dakk's voice startled her. "How unfortunate for you, Cassia. The drug doesn't work on you."

She looked around. There was no one with her in the cell. But she could hear him, as if he stood right next to her.

"His mind ward is tied to your blood," Dakk said. "Your very veins resist, and my alchemy cannot give you an easy path to speaking the truth."

"That's a fancy trick," she said, "but it doesn't scare me."

"An Old Master rules your world. There must be very little that can frighten you. But I will prove to you that the Rezayal are more powerful than he is."

She laughed. "It took a sixteen-hundred-year-old artifact of Hesperite Sanctuary magic and one of the most powerful thelemancers in Orthros's history just to wrest an apprentice from his grasp. You think I'm impressed by the power of one mortal man puttering about in a heap of rubble?"

"I am not one man. I am just one fragment. Break me, and you will only cut yourself on more pieces. We are everywhere."

"You sound remarkably like the Old Master himself. He likes to brag about how he has eyes and ears everywhere."

"How dare you!"

"I dare just as you dare." She stood up, lifting her chin, whether or not he could see her. "You should have kept on with the friendly tactics. You'll find I don't respond well to intimidation. I've been bullied all my life by

376 & Vela Roth

a monster much scarier than you, and I don't mean the Old Master. My father tried every trick in the book, and he couldn't cow me, although he has a throne and a sword to use against me."

"Is that why you accepted the Old Master's help? Did he make you feel strong against your father?"

"All my strength against my father is my own." She put a fist to her chest. "I know their secrets, Dakk. I can describe in detail the Old Master's relationship with the King of Tenebra. But you said you don't trust my information, so I'll keep it to myself. All those conversations I overheard in the king's solar. The necromantic ritual I witnessed. The things Lio told me about the impact of the Collector on Eudias's mind. It's a shame you won't accept me as an ally, because I'm a fountain of information about our enemy."

"You'll find I don't respond well to temptation."

If that wasn't his weakness, she would find it yet. She would keep him talking.

"Have you considered what you'll do when Orthros takes action against you?" Cassia asked. "Lio's bloodline won't take kindly to you endangering our lives by separating us."

"You have managed to make them all believe he needs you."

"You truly underestimate Hesperines. Especially Lio. He's Firstgift Komnenos, you know. His father and uncle are elder firstbloods, and he was tutored by the Queens. I'm not so unimportant myself. Princess Konstantina is my mentor."

"Reciting names you learned in Orthros won't help you."

"Do you truly wish to risk angering the Second Princess of Orthros? Even you must respect how powerful a mind healer she is. Say all you like about how Hesperines don't understand the Old Masters. But you must know she's an isolationist. She wouldn't tolerate me if she thought I put her people at risk."

"Orthros's welfare is not my concern. My duty is to the Empire. So is the Empress's. We are of one mind in that, although she sometimes must be guided by us when her methods differ from ours. We were once one of the great powers holding up her throne, and yet now she thinks to rule without us. When we must choose between her will and the safety of her people, we are above obeying her commands. Our mission is more ancient than her rule. And her rule is more ancient than Hesperines."

"Kassandra," Cassia said. "She was an Imperial princess. Almost the Empress. Surely you know she is an oracle. She is Lio's Ritual mother and a friend to me. Just imagine when she uses her sight to find me."

He laughed. "Her power cannot penetrate here. You are quite out of any Hesperine's reach."

"But your people aren't," she said. "And neither is the Empress."

Let the games continue.

A LESSON IN DIPLOMACY

I T WAS JUST AFTER sundown when Lio and his fellow Hesperines stepped the Ashes to the center of Ukocha's village. Doors swung open, filling the night with light, happy relatives, and the scents of cooking.

Chuma burst out of Ukocha's home and ran to her. *"Bamaayo!"*

Ukocha's whole face lit up with a smile, and she held out one arm. Chuma came to a halt in front of her mother, looking from Ukocha's face to the sling.

Ukocha reached out and wrapped her good arm around Chuma, pulling her close. Mumba caught up to them and enfolded both his wife and daughter in his embrace.

The sight of them holding fast to each other blurred before Lio. "Cassia fought so hard for this moment. She should get to see it."

"She will," Lyros said. "You can show it to her with your thelemancy—and later, in your Grace Union."

Ukocha shooed away the village healers and declined a celebration of her return. She went straight to her home with Chuma and Mumba, motioning for her Ashes, Lio, and his Trial brothers to follow.

She sank down onto a bench by the ancestral hearth, Mumba and Chuma sitting on either side of her. At her beckoning motion, the flames rose. Chuma imitated her, and her own fire flowed from her hand to join the power of her foremothers.

Mercenaries and Hesperines squeezed in around her ancestral fire for a council. Not a council of war, this time. Lio weighed his medallion in his hand.

He was grateful that Ukocha explained everything to Chuma. By the time she finished, the girl's aura was sparking with anger, and Lio wondered at the magic and secrecy that had kept him from realizing she was a fire mage like her mother.

"Well, you'll find Cassia," Chuma said with absolute confidence. "You'll rescue her. And now that more Hesperines are here to help, you'll finally be able to help Monsoon rescue Sunburn, too."

"That's right," Lyros reassured her. "The Stewards of Orthros don't rest until everyone is safe."

Mak smiled at her. "Cassia helped me get my sister back. We'll rescue her and Solia, too."

Monsoon said nothing. Lio knew he couldn't bear to make promises to Chuma that he did not believe they could keep.

But they needed him if they were to rescue Cassia and then Solia. And Monsoon needed to be part of that rescue.

Lio would have to convince him it could be done. Which meant he had to keep believing it himself.

"We are Hesperines," Lio said. "Attempting the impossible is how we became immortal. The same can be said for the Ashes' legend. We will not be defeated by the Broken Hands."

"What information do we have about Cassia's captors?" Lyros asked. "Every detail. We need to know our enemy."

"They are vicious," Monsoon answered. "They never surrender, and they don't see reason. We learned that the hard way. They would have hounded Solia and us to our graves if not for her arrest."

"Kella, what do the Azarqi know about them?" Lio stroked Knight's fur. While he and Cassia fought their Craving, Knight suffered from his liege bond to Cassia. Lio would do everything he could to help Knight endure, too.

The hound's newfound friendship with Tilili was proving a great help. The cat lay against him, purring with a vengeance.

Kella took the opportunity to dig a burr out of Tilili's fur. "The Accord breakers came to my people's attention only recently. Now that we know they're the Broken Hands, I suspect they've been out there for much longer than we realized. But without our knowledge. I have no idea where their strongholds might be."

Hoyefe stroked his freshly groomed goatee. "I once questioned one of their operatives personally. I gave him a very enjoyable opportunity to tell me all about himself. As much as I appreciate the physical secrets he shared with me, alas, that was all he revealed."

"You probably understand the most about them," Lio said to Tuura.

"More than you imagine." She pressed her lips together.

"Tuura is too modest to say it," Karege boasted, "but she has connections with all the important mind healers in the Empire."

"Hmph," was Tuura's reply. "Only because they want something from the Ashes' gold roster diviner. When I was a peanut grower's daughter, they were not so interested in friendship."

Lio leaned forward. "What more can you tell us about the Broken Hands?"

Tuura's frown deepened. "There is a certain unspoken expectation among mind healers in the Empire. If you get wind of illicit necromancy, you inform those who wish to know. If you discover a shadowlander, you whisper in the right ears. Since the Broken Hands revealed their affinity for theramancy, I am convinced they are the diviners who have been behind this ancient conspiracy all along."

The fire cast Monsoon's scars in sharp relief. "A secret society holds the mind healers of the Empire in their sway, and you have never mentioned this to us before?"

"The less you know about them," Tuura answered, "the safer you are. Their history, motives, members…all are closely guarded secrets. But I have found myself deep enough in mind healer circles to hear their name: the Rezayal."

A chill went through Lio's blood. Their enemy was greater than he had known.

But Mak snickered. "Secret society? Tattoos? A fancy name? Do they expect anyone to take them seriously as a threat when they resort to such theatrics?"

A smile tugged at Lio's mouth. "Well, they also have magic weapons that can banish you to die in the desert."

Mak gave an even darker laugh. "I'd like to see how their 'lithic edges' hold up against adamas."

"Pathetic strategy, really." Lyros waved a hand. "They have three secret identities—Accord breakers, Broken Hands, Rezayal—and none of them are a secret to us any longer."

Trust the Stewards to cut a seemingly enormous enemy down to size.

"Finally, all that unpleasant politicking has come in handy," Tuura mused. "I have no contacts in their web that we could use against them, however. I've made a point to avoid them."

Karege scowled. "They don't sound like the types to take no for an answer. If they've threatened you—"

Tuura smiled and patted his hand. "It's true that at one time, there were dreadful consequences for not bowing to their will. But it has become easier to stay out of their way in recent years."

Lyros exchanged a glance with Lio and Mak. "That sounds like a possible weakness. So their power has been waning?"

Tuura nodded. "But they still have many allies in high places. Even in the High Court."

Mak raised a hand. "Sorry, but memorizing the structure of the Imperial government was not a part of Stand training. Remind us warriors what the High Court is."

"Happily," Lio said, "as long as you'll help me get my Bones of Adamas move right next time we're practicing in the arena."

"Deal," said Lyros.

"The High Court," Lio explained, "is a council of diviners, all renowned experts in Imperial mind healing arts. At least one of them attends the Empress during each of her audiences. They ensure that no one uses illicit spells when petitioning or advising her, so evil magic does not affect the outcome of her decisions."

Mak grimaced. "So their purpose is to protect the fairness of government...but we think they're being influenced by the Rezayal's corruption."

Tuura replied, "The High Court is deeply divided between those who, like me, resist the Rezayal's influence, and those who wish to bend the Empress to their will. The Rezayal prey upon candidates for the High Court early in their careers to attempt to place their allies on the council."

"Such as mind healing students," Lio realized, "the ones at Imperial University from noble families, who are High Court hopefuls."

Tuura rested her staff against her knees. "Oh, especially them. The oldest aristocratic lines are most deeply entwined in the conspiracies. Their young heirs often cooperate in order to advance."

"Harkhuf!" Mak's fair skin flushed with fury. "That bloodless scavenger. I'll pry him off our Trial sister's arm and throw him out of Orthros myself. After all the times I tried to be pleasant to him, even though he made my hackles rise…"

"Goddess." Lyros grimaced. "Your intuition was right—again. To think, I encouraged you to give him the benefit of the doubt, when he might have been working with the enemy from within Orthros."

Tuura frowned in thought. "That name sounds familiar."

"Harkhuf Addaya Khemkare," Lio said. "He's studying in Orthros right now. When he returns to the Empire, he intends to take a position in the court of the Empress—his cousin."

"Oh dear," said Tuura. "That's where I've heard him mentioned. The current Chief Diviner of the High Court is interested in taking him under her wing. Someone like him will already be tangled up in the Rezayal's plots, whether he likes it or not."

Lio discovered he still had the strength to be angry. "It was he who wrote to the Empress, praising Cassia's and my deeds during the Solstice Summit. He advocated for us…or so we thought."

Lyros shook his head. "Who knows what information he could have been giving them all along?"

Lio cursed. "Now I regret skipping his symposium on the political intrigues of the Court. I might have picked up some clues."

Mak crossed his arms. "Surely not everyone is happy to lick this invisible faction's boots on their way to the top. There must be mind healers made of stronger stuff than that weasel Harkhuf, honorable theramancers who are tired of answering to the Rezayal."

"Many," Tuura said. "The Rezayal are seen as something of a relic. However, they still have enough members in positions of power to make it impossible to throw off their yoke."

Lio turned his medallion in his hand. "So, they are an enemy with one cause, many faces, and no fear. A seemingly unbeatable opponent."

"You have no hope of negotiating with them," said Monsoon.

"That doesn't matter," Lio replied, "because we will negotiate with everyone around them until we have them surrounded, and there is nowhere safe for them to hide."

"'We,'" Monsoon said with approval. "Good. You're not entertaining any foolish ideas about attempting this without us."

Lio looked around him at the Empire's heroes. "You have all done more than Cassia and I could ever ask. You owe us nothing. If anything I'm about to suggest compromises your honor or puts your people too much at risk, I will not question your decision to not involve yourselves."

Kella flicked another burr into the fire. "We're talking about an unbeatable enemy. That's an opponent worthy of the Ashes."

"The trouble is," said Lio, "we cannot use blades to defeat them this time."

Kella raised a brow. "Do you think steel is all we know how to fight with?"

"No," Lio answered, "I don't think that for a moment."

"My Ashes are with you," the First Blade promised.

Lio let out a breath. "I am profoundly grateful for that. Because I recently forgot a basic lesson in diplomacy, to my great detriment. An ambassador cannot accomplish anything alone."

Mak shot him a look. "Who knew you needed some warriors to teach you a lesson in diplomacy?"

One side of Monsoon's mouth lifted. "Fancy that. I think that was one of my first lessons as a mercenary. I might have forgotten it for a while, as well."

"It's about time you remembered," Ukocha grunted.

Mak was grinning from ear to ear. "The Stand and the Ashes on a quest together, with a Victor of Souls in the lead. I don't care if we're fighting with words or pea shooters, this will be magnificent."

"These two young warriors need fortune names," Karege declared, "if I might suggest we make them honorary Ashes like our Shadow and Sunshine."

Lio threw one arm around each of his Trial brothers. "Hear, hear."

Ukocha looked Mak and Lyros up and down. "I find myself wealthy in qualified recruits lately. If you ever want to put away your speires for a while and come errant like Karege, you have but to ask."

Mak and Lyros's auras fairly glowed with pride, and then both gave her a bow.

"The Stand needs us for the time being," Mak said with great courtesy, "but we are deeply honored by the offer."

"And will gladly accept honorary membership," Lyros agreed.

Ukocha nodded at them in satisfaction. "What misfortunes shall your names spare you from, then?"

A mischievous smile spread across Mak's face as he gave his Grace a long look. "Art Class."

Lyros covered his face in both his hands and groaned.

"Perfect," Lio agreed, grateful Mak could make him laugh, even now. He pondered his cousin. "But what for you, Mak?"

Mak crossed his arms. "Not 'Library.' I'll have you know, I've spent plenty of pleasant hours in my father's sanctum lately."

"Not 'Politics' either," Lio said with a smile. "You aren't avoiding them anymore."

Lyros tilted his head at Mak. "Wisdom."

Mak put his hand to his chest, as if stabbed in the heart. "Oh, you would have to remind me of Wisdom's Precipice."

"Of course." Lyros gave him an innocent look. "But it seems desirable to avoid 'wisdom' for other reasons...such as when it tries to overrule your intuition."

Mak's expression softened. "Hadn't thought of it that way. I'll take it."

"All right, recruits," Monsoon said, "what's our plan?"

"We battle the enemy head-on in the light," Lio said, "before the Empress and her court, with the most impressive delegations she has ever seen. We'll expose them for the threat they are so that the greatest power in the land will turn against them."

"Spoken like Ambassador Deukalion," Mak approved.

If Lio and Cassia had come here with diplomatic papers in the first place...if Lio had not resisted a diplomatic approach at every turn...it might never have come to this. He should have been willing to negotiate then.

But he had no time to waste agonizing over his mistakes. For Cassia's sake, he could only move forward and act.

"Lyros," he asked, "do you think this is a sound strategy against a force like the Rezayal?"

Lyros nodded. "I believe it to be the only viable strategy. With armed fanatics such as these, they will never change their minds or lay down their arms. They cannot be defeated with weapons—only by hearts turning against them. But it will not be an easy strategy, by any means."

"But it will be worth it," Ukocha said with a wicked laugh, "to watch the Empress destroy them."

Monsoon's eagle eyes glittered. "Even I could enjoy that—and I *hate* court."

Lio wetted his dry lips. "The challenge is, we have to act faster than Cassia's Craving."

Karege gave a fanged smile. "Good thing we're moving at Hesperine speed, then."

"Then we strike at their hearts first," Lio said, "the Empire's mind healers. Tuura, do you know other theramancers who are not aiding the enemy? Do you think they would be willing to join our efforts?"

She patted her staff. "They will leap at a rare opportunity to challenge the Rezayal. Hesperine involvement will strengthen their confidence in our plan, for the theramancers of your royal family are widely admired among us. Leave it to me. I can gather a delegation of mind healers from all parts of the Empire in no time."

"Thank you, diviner." Lio gave her a bow before turning to Kella. "To flush out the Rezayal in the Maaqul, we need to ensure we act with respect for the Azarqi. I recognize that I am in no position to negotiate with your people after offending the jinn. Do you think there is still hope they will ally with us?"

"I will secure my mother's support," Kella said, "and other clans will follow her example. As her daughter and the Second Blade of the Ashes, I have my own influence, as well."

"Your mother sounded very proud of your deeds," Lio remarked. "May I ask if it's unusual for an Azarqi princess to become a mercenary?"

"Our royal women don't confine themselves to thrones. My mother has always appreciated how I've chosen to define my role. Other sister states in the Empire are not so flexible."

"Your people prize your independence, clearly."

"Yes, and we don't bow to manipulation, and we don't like sharing our desert with anyone but the jinn. These enemies have put the Accord at far greater risk than you ever did, and if this is what it takes to stop them, we will send a delegation."

"You have my gratitude, Kella," said Lio. "If I can ever make amends…"

"Helping us apprehend the Rezayal is a good start," she assured him.

Hoyefe rubbed his hands together. "Now then, let us discuss how you can benefit from my talents."

Lio nodded to his fellow light mage. "You are an alumnus of Imperial University, are you not? You must have many friends in aristocratic circles in the Capital. Perhaps even some in the Empress's court?"

"Precisely." Hoyefe's gaze glittered with anticipation. "I would fancy calling in a favor or two. Or granting a few. There are conscionable friends and former lovers to rally…conniving nobles to tempt with the promise of undermining rivals and increasing their influence…and perhaps a few opportunities for blackmail."

"We'll leave the court in your capable hands," Lio said.

"My hands aren't even my greatest asset." He wiggled his fingers. "These are the moments I live for. Secrets and lies…beautiful, worldly aristocrats…games of persuasion… Mmm. That settles it. My new romantic play must be a tale of court intrigue."

Now Lio looked to Ukocha. "First Blade—"

"No need to ask." She rubbed her injured arm. "The Cifwani Matriarchs will want the Rezayal's heads after everything they've done. And I excel at delivering heads."

"Is that so, Victor of Souls?" Mak asked with interest. "How do you include deca—" With a glance at Chuma, Mak shut his mouth.

"Decapitations?" Chuma finished for him. "Yes, you can perform them, even when using spellsword attacks."

Lio swallowed a surprised noise. He couldn't imagine Zoe talking about beheadings, even in a few years. But then, Chuma was Ukocha's daughter.

"Really?" Mak asked. "I would think there wouldn't be enough of the enemy's head left after your fire spells."

Lio could definitely imagine Bosko saying that, though.

"Well," Chuma continued, "with savanna chimeras, you have to behead them first, *then* set the pieces on fire. Otherwise they don't die properly."

Ukocha smiled at her daughter. "Chuma killed her first chimera last year."

Chuma touched the pendant at her throat. "See? Here's the tooth."

"We're so proud of our first bladelet," Kella said. "She will make a mighty mercenary soon."

"We'll give you a demonstration," Ukocha promised, "if diplomacy fails and we need to behead someone. Preferably not during our audience with the Empress, though."

Lio swallowed. If diplomacy failed…he could not allow himself to imagine the consequences. "Might I impose on you for one more favor, First Blade? Actually, a favor from your friend Captain Ziara. I assume she is on good terms with the officials who issue arrest warrants in Marijani."

Ukocha laughed again. "I can certainly get word to her. Who do you want arrested—or quietly ignored?"

"I'd like to know who issued Cassia's arrest warrant, and I want it canceled. I also want the merchant governors to know that offending Orthros is highly unwise."

Ukocha's mouth tilted in a grin. "Ziara will love this. The privateers have a long history with the Rezayal. There's a mind healer aboard every privateer ship, per the Empress's mandate, to ensure they don't bring any foreign necromancy back with them. The Rezayal have their hooks in many of those theramancers."

Monsoon snapped his wings. "You also knew about the Rezayal?"

"To an extent. Like Tuura, I was not aware they and the Broken Hands are the same enemy. But I've been friends with Ziara and Tuura for a long time, and they have ears on the ground." She gave Monsoon a pointed look. "Unlike eagles in high nests."

"Yes," Tuura confirmed, "Ziara's first mate is even less friendly with the Rezayal than I am."

"Now, if you want blade demonstrations," Ukocha said to Lio's Trial brothers, "watch Huru when she's playing games with that knife of hers. Heads aren't usually what she cuts off, though."

Lyros's aura brimmed with amusement. "Likes to teach mortal men a lesson, does she?"

Lio thought of Huru casually tossing her lethal blade. "I can imagine she and Ziara would not take kindly to the Rezayal's interference. But of course the Rezayal would keep a close eye on the privateers, since they are the Empire's only point of contact with the shadowlands." He looked from his Trial brothers to Karege. "Besides us."

"I thought Orthros's alliance with the Empire was unchallenged." Lyros shook his head. "The idea that there could be a faction within the Empire that is hostile to us..."

"That would endanger everyone's way of life," Mak said.

"I dare say they have no influence in Orthros, though," said Karege. "Ha. I'd like to see them try anything under the Second Princess's nose."

The thought of Konstantina sent a jolt through Lio, and he looked at his Trial brothers. "Oh Goddess. The vote. It must be taking place any night now..."

Mak scowled. "It's tonight. The Firstblood Circle is probably convening as we speak. But if you think we're going to let you out of our sight for a moment, then I may well cast the blood shackles on you again."

"Mak is right," Lyros said. "We belong here."

Lio took a deep breath. "I'd rather not let you two out of my sight, either. But I think you need to go back to Orthros, with Karege, if all of you are willing."

"See here—" Mak began.

"We need Uncle Argyros's help," Lio admitted.

"Argyros is your uncle?" Karege interjected. "And your father, Mak? You don't say. Well, aren't you all cozy with the Blood Errant? The Lion of Orthros's son, the Victory Star's brother and Grace-brother."

"Rudhira the Blood-Red Prince is my Ritual father." Lio might as well play all his cards now.

"And you're bloodborn like the Midnight Champion." Karege laughed. "Last I heard, Apollon's little bloodborn was an infant. But here you are, all grown up and already paired, at that. I suppose it has been a long time since I went back to Orthros to catch up on things."

Lio braced himself for a ferocious argument from his cousin. Mak glared. Then he crossed his muscular arms over his barrel chest.

Then, "You're right. We need to tell my father what's happened to

Cassia. And Lyros and I need to be at the vote to tell the entire Firstblood Circle about this new threat to Orthros's alliance with the Empire."

Admiration swelled in Lio's chest. It seemed Mak had decided that politics were his fight, now. "In that case, the Firstblood Circle had best be prepared for what you have in store."

"I don't think they are at all," Lyros said.

Mak's face set in a stubborn frown, and his aura closed, as implacable as a fist. Lio knew that look. His cousin had gotten an idea and had just as quickly come to a decision.

"Mak?" Lio queried. "What are you planning?"

"Do you trust my instincts?"

"Of course. Your intuition has always been better than any of ours."

Mak let out a breath. "Thank you, Lio. It means…more than I can say, really, to know you think so, too."

"Did I ever give you cause to doubt it?" Lio asked in dismay.

Mak shook his head. "No. I think I did. But not anymore."

"What do you say, Karege?" asked Lyros. "Would you like to come with us and watch Mak handle some diplomacy the Steward way?"

"I wouldn't miss it."

Lio grimaced. "You may find you have some difficult elders to deal with once they discover what Cassia and I have been doing."

Karege laughed. "I don't concern myself too much with what the elders think."

"That's why we need you as a liaison to the Circle. We need an Imperial Hesperine to address what's at stake for the Empire and Orthros, in no uncertain terms."

He patted his fortune blade. "I'll go home and handle some diplomacy the Ashes way."

"You can't come with us, can you?" Mak asked, his aura twinging with understanding.

"No," Lio said. "I…simply can't."

"I couldn't leave either," said Lyros, "if it were Mak in danger."

Lio swallowed and nodded. "There is one more ally we need—the one who will be the most difficult of all to win to our side. I must attempt to negotiate with him myself."

Monsoon eyed Lio. "It doesn't escape me that you've left me for last. I'm not going to like what you have to say, am I?"

Lio put this hands behind his back. "I'm going to apologize."

"I knew it. Sentimental silkfoot."

"I never thanked you for protecting Cassia, all those times when I could not."

"Of course you didn't thank me. You wished it had been you."

Monsoon understood. In fact, Lio had come to realize that he and Monsoon understood each other better than most anyone. "I should have given you my gratitude long before now. You were protecting her all along, for Solia's sake. I'm sorry I was so wrong about you."

"I wouldn't let anything happen to Pup. Especially when I couldn't save Solia."

"You still can. If what we're about to do works to rescue Cassia, it will work to get Solia out of prison. Cassia already had a plan to negotiate for her extradition before she was taken." Lio offered Monsoon his hand. "We won't rest until Solia is free. You have my word."

Monsoon clasped his forearm with a warrior's strong grip. Hope stirred in the man's aura. "We'll do it. The official way, this time. Which means we need the support of my people."

"Most of all. The Sandira Kingdom's power is second to none. If they join our cause, it will truly shake the Empress. Considering the king's reputation, I know how difficult it will be to win him to our side. But I have negotiated with the King of Tenebra and lived to tell the tale. Do you have any connections at the Sandira Court that can get us onto the King's Hill?"

"Really, Monsoon?" Kella shook her head. "You've told them about being one of the Ashes and just how well you knew Sunburn, but not your family?"

Monsoon shifted on his feet. "You know I'd prefer to be oblivious about them myself."

"Who are they?" Lio asked.

Monsoon sighed. "Just come with me. But first, you might want to change into something that will make a good impression."

COURT OF KINGS

THE HOUSE BEHIND UKOCHA'S was smaller, but no less welcoming. Lio felt at home as soon as he set foot inside with Monsoon. The hearth was cold, but an aura lingered here, and not just the powerful emotions rolling off of the mercenary. The residual energy felt familiar to Lio somehow…her presence reminded him of someone… of Cassia.

"Solia," he realized.

Monsoon rubbed the back of his neck, his wings folded tightly. "Whenever we were in Ukocha's village, this was where we stayed. I'm surprised no one else has moved in by now."

"It sounds as if Ukocha wanted you to feel welcome, if you returned."

"I haven't entered this house in five years."

"I wouldn't have, either."

Monsoon stalked away from Lio and disappeared behind a room divider. "We can wash up and change here."

Behind another divider, Lio glimpsed a bed with a bright geometric blanket and carved wooden headrests. He paused at a bookcase laden with volumes Tuura had described and ran a hand along a sword rack that now held no blades. His gaze arrested on a small painting, a masterpiece in contemporary Imperial style, signed by Hoyefe. The subject was a skinny girl with an upturned nose and freckles, holding a puppy and smiling. Cassia, as she must have looked in Solia's memory.

"Don't touch anything," Monsoon added from behind the divider.

With Hesperine speed, Lio opened his pack and set about transforming himself from a desert vagabond back into a proper diplomat. Then he posted himself by the door to wait, arms crossed to show he respected Monsoon's request.

When Monsoon stepped out from behind the room divider, Lio almost didn't recognize the man. Like Lio, he had washed up and trimmed his beard, but his transformation was something more than that.

Monsoon carried himself differently. He had exchanged his mercenary gear for a ceremonial sword and Sandira waist-wrap. He also wore a sash that draped behind his neck and criss-crossed his chest to tie behind his back, leaving his wings free. Feathers, bones, and charms adorned the fabric.

Lio didn't understand the full meaning of all these symbols of status, but he knew regalia when he saw it. This was not a man who had washed out of the royal guard.

He inspected Lio, then nodded. "I had a feeling you'd dragged formal robes across the Empire, silkfoot. How about wearing that medallion?"

"I don't have cords, but I can present it to whomever we're going to meet, if necessary."

"That will do. Ready to step us to the Sandira Court?"

"Now that we are making an attempt at acting officially, perhaps it would be better not to step over state borders and past guard posts?"

"Stepping at my request *is* official."

This grew more and more interesting. "Where shall I aim?"

Monsoon rubbed his well-groomed stubble. "Jinn bollocks. If we're going to do this, might as well go the distance. Set us down on the Royal Way."

"The boulevard that runs through the city to the King's Hill?"

Monsoon nodded. "Unfortunately, yes."

"Whatever you say."

Monsoon clasped Lio's arm as he had earlier. Lio applied his Will to the challenging task of stepping a shapeshifter.

But it was effortless compared to his last attempt. Monsoon's magic wanted to return to the kingdom of his ancestors. They landed easily on the stone pavers of the Royal Way at the heart of the Sandira metropolis. One of the city's enclosed courts rose above them, the fitted stones of its round walls a testament to the great masons of the Sandira. The guards at the entry bowed deeply, then snapped to attention.

Monsoon gave them the barest nod, saying to Lio, "Levitate just behind my right shoulder, please."

Monsoon took wing, and Lio did as he had requested. As they followed the course of the Royal Way in midair, the guards at each court they passed bowed, and joyous shouts rang out.

From within the mightiest enclosures and the humblest, thatched-roofed huts, people hurried out. The broad boulevard filled with the countless residents of the city. Torchlight gleamed in brilliant orange trails below, and music rose up to them.

Monsoon spun in the air to a cheer from below.

"I think they like you," Lio said.

"Nah. The Sandira are just friendly."

Lio's keen ears made out the name that the people below were singing. Tendeso. "You're the famed Prince Tendeso of the Sandira. The king's brother."

"Don't rub it in."

"Wouldn't dream of it. I gather it *is* unusual for a Sandira prince to become a mercenary?"

"This is one of the not so flexible sister states Kella meant. The king's advisers appreciate my role about as much as a black eye."

"What do they expect younger sons to do?"

He gave his wings a heave, climbing higher over the crowd. "I'm not the younger son. They expected me to become king. Until the anointing ceremony, when the ancestors, for reasons only they understand, chose my brother instead. No one knows what they should expect of an elder son without a throne, so I make a point to stay out of the way."

Lio kept pace with him in silence for a moment, wary of probing wounds. "It sounds like something a queen without a throne would understand."

"Yes." His voice softened, almost snatched away by the wind. "She did. More than you know."

They flew over the procession to the King's hill. By the time they reached the stony rise, a welcoming party waited on the broad terrace before the king's complex. Lio found the sight breathtaking.

Under luxurious fabric awnings waited a glittering array of courtiers flanked by royal guards. The Sandira nobility wore wraps, gowns, and shoulder capes artfully draped to display the power granted by their ancestors. Their wings, tails, and skins were proud evidence of their lineages. They were some of the most powerful and beautiful people Lio had ever beheld.

Word of the incoming Hesperine must have already reached the hill. A small delegation of people Lio knew from the diplomatic service were already present as well, shining in Orthros silks and ambassadors' medallions. One wore the tablion of a master ambassador.

Monsoon landed before the illustrious gathering, and everyone bowed low. Lio made sure to stand just behind his right shoulder.

Then Monsoon bowed deeply to the young man in the center of the glorious company.

The king was dressed in the most elaborate regalia of all. His wings had the same markings as Monsoon's. His face was narrower and less rugged, his body not so honed, but there was no mistaking the family resemblance.

Every single person on the hill radiated varying degrees of disapproval, except for the king, who was as delighted as an initiate who'd been smiled at by his favorite athlete.

A herald with the wings of a kestrel spoke out in Dynastic, as was customary at many official gatherings. "Welcome to His Royal Highness, Prince Tendeso of the Sandira Court, Blessed by Mweya, the Divine Ancestor of Kings…" The titles went on.

When the herald stopped, the king gave him a look.

With a nervous glance at the nobles, the herald cleared his throat and added, "Runner up in the Battle of Souls, Gold Roster Blade."

The king nodded.

"Welcome to Ambassador Deukalion," the herald continued, "Firstgift Komnenos, of the Diplomatic Service of the Queens of Orthros, friend of our prince."

Lio bowed deeply to the king.

The young man barely noticed him. He was looking at his brother, his face alight. "You came." He turned to the dour minister beside him. "Did I not tell you my brother would come if I held a feast for him?"

The white-haired minister, with the privilege of elders, did not mince words. "Your king invited you to a feast weeks ago."

"I paid him a visit." Monsoon's statement was toneless.

"For a few hours, before you departed again on another...*contract*." The elder pronounced the word like something you'd find in the privy, not on the gold roster.

"I am here now," Monsoon stated.

"In the middle of the night, rousing the court from our beds."

Monsoon didn't snort, but Lio felt it in his aura.

The elder gestured to Monsoon's arm. "You come before your king with that blade on display?"

The king kept the smile on, although his aura was distressed. "My brother's famous deeds have brought honor to us, and his earnings on the gold roster help feed our people."

"I have indeed worn my blade to this sacred hill," Monsoon announced, "for one purpose. A new danger threatens our people, one that cannot be fought with a knife. This enemy deceives us from within, thinking to bend us to their will. Only with the might and wisdom of royal leadership can we defeat this foe." He unbuckled his fortune blade and knelt before the king, offering him the knife. "To face this challenge with you, My King, My Brother, I surrender my fortune blade to you and with it, my life as a mercenary."

"Monsoon," Lio said, perhaps for the last time.

His eyes wide, the king put a tentative hand on the blade. "You're coming home?"

"Yes, Anesu."

Slowly, the young king wrapped his lean hand around the dagger. He held it to him for an instant. Then he offered Tendeso his hand.

Tendeso's strong, scarred fingers wrapped around his brother's soft ones. Anesu pulled him to his feet and embraced him. Their auras choked with years of unspoken emotion, although they showed nothing on their faces before the court.

"Make ready for the feast," the king ordered. "My brother is home. We will celebrate, then we will confront this threat together with all the power of our ancestral kings."

A BLESSED MATCH

THE DOMED HALL WHERE Orthros's government met in Haima
stood proudly on a high outcropping at the center of the city.
From every direction, bridges crossed the Veins to carry Hesperine elders and Imperial dignitaries over the canals below. Or, at the
moment, to admit two Hesperine youngbloods and an Imperial mercenary
who were late to the vote.

As Mak, Lyros, and Karege crossed to the main entrance of the Firstblood Circle, not a soul was to be seen on any of the bridges. Mak could
sense the many auras gathered inside the Circle.

Karege shook snow off his sandals and laughed. "Well, we're a long way
from the Scorched Verge, aren't we? Time to charge into a very different fray."

The doors were closed upon the proceedings. Few Hesperines had the
authority to open them once the voting had begun.

Mak held out his hand to Lyros. *Time to use more of our Steward privileges.*

I love our service. Lyros took his hand, and together they Willed the
doors open with a satisfying bang.

The three of them strode inside before the eyes of countless Hesperines. Silk-clad elders and youngbloods alike looked down from the seats
that ascended in rows toward the domes overhead.

Mak cast a glance up at the mosaics on the ceilings far above. A glorious rendition of the Firstblood Rose representing Orthros's founders
adorned the center dome. But his gaze went to the constellations of every
bloodline that marked the smaller domes over their respective sections. He
sent a mental salute to his father's Gifter. Eidon had been a scrollworm, too.
Mak supposed this could be the most Eidon-like thing he might ever do.

Hypatia stood at one of the podiums on the floor of the Circle. Kia's mother emanated her usual dignified disapproval.

At the opposite podium stood Xandra in her royal robes of black and white. She lifted a hand to Mak and Lyros, her face lighting up. Karege joined them in giving her the heart bow.

Xandra's seat in the royal section was empty at the moment. Usually the rows behind her, reserved for her future descendants, were empty too. But tonight, they were packed with all the partisans their Trial circle had worked so hard to win to their side. Young Hesperines from many bloodlines had abandoned their seats behind their elders to occupy Xandra's section. Kia, Nodora, Alkaios, and Nephalea sat in the front row and cheered, disrupting the dignified quiet of the amphitheater. Everyone sitting behind them joined in.

On the other side of the royal section sat Rudhira, the rows behind him lined with members of the Prince's Charge. The force of Hesperines errant who fought at his side in Tenebra had come to defend their cause, and they took up the cry.

Mak grinned. *This feels more like a match in the arena already.*

We should do this more often, Lyros agreed.

Hypatia spoke over the noise. "The time for displays of partisanship has already drawn to a close. The vote is about to begin, and the debates have made it clear you still lack a majority."

Mak's heart sank. All this effort, and Hypatia still had more votes? Was Orthros really still so set in their ways?

"You cannot bring forth more supporters at this stage," Hypatia continued, "especially when they do not show the Circle the courtesy of arriving punctually."

Mak doubted anyone outside their Trial circle could feel it, but he sensed the stir of Xandra's anxiety in the Union. Even so, she spoke with composure and confidence. "The Stewards of Orthros are never absent without dire cause. Let us discover what tidings they and their companion bring us."

Standing in her customary place with the Queens, the Second Princess spoke. Clearly she was still fulfilling her role as the Royal Master Magistrate, although she would not vote tonight. "Let the proceedings pause to admit another voting member. Dear Firstblood Karege, how lovely to welcome you into the Circle. A rare occasion."

Mak looked from the princess to Karege and raised his eyebrows.

Karege put his hand to his heart and gave Konstantina a gallant bow. "My Princess, you grow more magnificent with each passing decade. If I receive such a welcome from you every time, I may be tempted to take part in politics more often."

"You've known you will always receive a warm welcome from me, since the night I bestowed a white rose upon you, when you were yet mortal. I take heart that you are involved in the matter at hand, whatever it may be."

Hypatia made the circle petition and a protest. "If there is a crisis, the Stand is to report to the Guardian of Orthros before disrupting the government."

Mak's mother held out her hand in the circle petition next. His father held her other hand, sending Mak and Lyros encouragement through the Union.

For the first time in nearly a century, Nike occupied the seat of Firstgift behind them.

Konstantina nodded to their mother. "Elder Grace Hippolyta, advise the Firstblood Circle on the matter at hand."

"My Stewards were on a sanctioned foray to assess the safety of two citizens of Orthros traveling in the Empire. They would not interrupt this vote unless they bring us troubling news."

A hush fell over the Circle.

"The Empire is safe for our people," Hypatia huffed. "How could any of us possibly meet with danger there?"

Mak glanced at Blood Komnena's section. Lio's parents were in the front row, but they had not brought Zoe with them.

Mak spoke up, projecting his voice as if he were addressing a gymnasium full of spectators. Politics wasn't so different from a fighting match, after all. "Cassia has been taken captive, and she doesn't have much time."

Mak thought the stones would rattle with Uncle Apollon's fury. Aunt Komnena's fangs flashed.

Konstantina pressed her fingers to the railing in front of her. "Join Xandra on the podium and tell us what has happened."

They stepped to Xandra's side, and she clutched their arms, her palms hot. "What happened to Cassia? How long have she and Lio been apart?"

"It's bad," Mak said honestly.

"But do not fear," Karege said. "They have the Ashes' aid, and reuniting two lovers is much easier than beheading a giant snake, in my professional opinion."

Trust Karege to find an encouraging word at the moment. Mak intended to be like that when he was hundreds of years old.

Karege gave Xandra the heart bow, which made her blush. "Princess Alexandra, it is an honor to stand with you. Your Trial brothers have sung your praises and told me all about how you're unstuffing the stuffy elders. How marvelous to have a fire mage in the royal family. How can I help?"

Xandra laughed. "Are you certain it was my traditionalist sister who invited you to become a Hesperine?"

Karege winked. "Everyone knows she has excellent taste."

"She certainly does. Thank you for being our reinforcements tonight. The margin is so close—your vote could be the deciding one."

"That will make an excellent tale on long journeys. But first, Mak had best tell everyone what has happened."

Mak looked at Lyros, who shook his head. "The Firstblood Circle doesn't need a speech on strategy. They need a speech from your heart."

Goddess, Mak was about to make a political speech in front of Orthros's government. When had he become a diplomat?

No, he still wasn't a diplomat. He was a Steward of the Stand.

He was sick of arriving too late to use his fists. But battle moves and wards weren't all he had to fight with. He was here to do his duty, as he had since he had first donned his speires as a suckling, as he had during all his training as a newblood. As he had when, as a youngblood, he had first fought and killed enemies in defense of Orthros in Martyrs' Pass.

He glanced up at the constellation Aegis, arrayed with Eidon over his bloodline's seats. Then he gave his heart bow to the Queens, whose aching hearts filled the Union. "Annassa, Firstbloods, and heirs of the blood, thank you for hearing me under the stars of our foregivers. By Alatheia's light, I speak the truth according to my duty as a Steward."

Mak discovered it was easy to speak from his heart when he knew he spoke the truth. Conviction gave him the words he needed to describe what had befallen Lio and Cassia and what was now at stake. He knew it was not an eloquent speech like they might make. It was the speech only he could make.

"As we speak," Mak concluded, "Cassia is a prisoner of the Rezayal, who wish to cut off the Empire from the rest of the world—even from Orthros. They are willing to endanger innocent lives for the cause of isolationism. A cause like that has no place in our hearts. And voting in favor of it while our diplomats' lives are in danger is no way to honor the risks they've taken to save innocent lives."

Mak met Lyros's gaze one more time. *We are agreed, my Grace?*

I'm with you. This is the right course for us, and we will take it as partners.

Mak held his Grace's hand. "Throughout our history, when the Hesperine Embassy entered the hostile territory of Tenebra, members of the Stand always accompanied them. Steward Lysandros and I hereby request official reassignment. Annassa, if it is your Will, we would join our Trial brother in representing you in the court of the Empress—and wherever he and Cassia travel thereafter. Should the Guardian of Orthros and the Queens' Master Ambassador approve, we request to be appointed the bodyguards of the Eighth Circle's diplomats."

To Mak's surprise, it was not his mother or father who replied. Nike made the circle petition.

"Firstgift Argyra," Konstantina addressed her, "let your voice be heard again in this Circle at last."

"I would join my brother and Grace-brother at the podium."

"A powerful display of partisanship. You have the floor."

Nike walked down. Her march from her seat to the floor turned every head in the hall.

She joined Mak behind the podium and faced him. Her veils gathered around them for a moment. "Are you sure?"

He swallowed. "It's time for me to go errant."

She clasped his wrist. "It's time for me to stay home."

"What?" He pulled her closer. "Did the vulture arrive tonight? Did you get bad news from Cordium?"

"Yes and no. My ally sent a great deal of information—more clues, more portents. As always, I am left to interpret mysteries. To weigh possibilities. The decision is not easy, but it is mine."

"You can't give up on finding your Trial brother."

"Never," Nike swore, "but I can be here for you, my blood brother, right now. And if we happen to be home at the same time, another lesson at the forge?"

"About that…" A smile came to Mak's face. "I've realized no one needs my swords. They just need…me."

Nike returned his smile. "I'm glad you finally realized that."

"Could our next lesson focus on other uses for adamas?"

"An excellent plan. I've always known you would devise applications for it that I never imagined. Until then…"

She turned to the podium, dropping her veils. She opened her hand. She was holding her speires.

But she didn't place them on the podium. She gathered her long, hundred-year-bound red braid and bound it up in her speires.

"If the Stand is to spare these two decorated Stewards," she declared, "someone will need to patrol the border in their place. Guardian of Orthros, your First Master Steward is reporting for duty."

Mak could feel their mother's tears in her aura, although her voice was full of joy as she replied. "Welcome home."

Nike blinked hard. "Now, I believe there is a vote to be decided. Orthros, I ask you, why do you fear opening our gates to Tenebra? As the Guardian of Orthros's heir, I have protected our borders. As one of the Blood Errant, I have survived the most dangerous enemy territory Abroad. If men trouble us with their swords, they will meet with my wards. If this mage of dreams seeks to threaten our people again, he will meet with my thelemancy. There is not a single threat that can surprise me. Do you imagine for a moment that any harm can come to our Sanctuary, with my mother and me together at our gates?"

An even mightier cheer rose from their partisans and the Charge, with Alkaios and Nephalea letting out a battle cry, and Rudhira's aura fierce in support of his Trial sister.

Konstantina's voice chased their cheers. "Let the firstbloods speak for those they have given power and life, and cast their votes on behalf of their bloodlines."

Hypatia marked her vote in favor of isolation on the podium before her. Xandra and Karege folded their hands, their podium marked only by the tokens of their partisans.

Kadi need not stand in for their eldest sister this time. Nike announced the count from their section aloud, not hiding her satisfaction. "Zero votes from Blood Argyros and their tributaries."

"Zero votes from Blood Komnena and their tributaries," Lio's father announced himself.

"Insufficient votes from the royal bloodlines and tributaries," Rudhira declared.

"Insufficient votes from Blood Kassandra and my tributaries," spoke the Oracle.

Before the rest of the firstbloods finished announcing their tallies, Mak knew that they had carried the day.

Konstantina, with folded hands, cast a gentle gaze upon her friend. "Elder Firstblood Hypatia, I'm afraid your proposal has insufficient support. No limits will be placed on Orthros's future involvement in Tenebran affairs."

Mak turned to his sister. "That's how to be both our parents' heirs at the same time, wouldn't you say?"

She stood at the podium with the poise of someone who had done so before. "Let it never be said that the battle arts and diplomacy are not a blessed match. There is a reason our parents are Graced, after all."

In the flurry of activity as the official session ended, it grew crowded around the podium. Rudhira came to Nike's side and gave her the salute to the victor, then a hug. Konstantina herself descended to congratulate Xandra and speak with Karege. Aunt Komnena and Uncle Apollon pressed Lyros with questions, and he reassured them as only he could.

Mak found himself facing his father.

"Goddess bless, I'm proud of you," he said.

Mak didn't need veils. He felt no more dread. "You can rely on me, Father. Tonight and always."

"Together, we will employ diplomacy with the speed and impact of warriors."

54

days until

NOTIAN WINTER SOLSTICE

3 Ourania, 1597 IS

THE FACE OF DEATH

ASSIA COULDN'T PACE ANYMORE. The cot gave her body no ease, but it was still, at least.

Dakk's voice again. It was harder to concentrate on his words every time his voice rang out to interrogate her.

She tried to focus on the mind ward. Still there. The spells he kept trying wore her to the bone. But her Will was unbroken.

She couldn't say the same for her stomach after all his alchemy experiments. No use trying to eat anymore.

"Is the Old Master trying to secure his hold over you?"

Dakk spoke with three voices. Was that some new trick, or were her ears failing her?

She blinked. There were two paintings on the wall now. Twice as many lost smiles from the ancient past. She rubbed her eyes.

"Are you fighting him?" Dakk asked. "I see how he tortures your body with illness, Cassia. But I can do nothing to stop your suffering until I get through the mind ward."

"You're such a fool." She had three voices, too. Definitely her ears. "Don't you know what happens when a Hesperine and the one they love are apart?"

"Why do you persist in these lies? You and the Old Master both know I've already seen through the act he has dictated to you."

He was the one who persisted in his delusion. She wouldn't waste what remained of her strength to argue with him about his beliefs.

"Let me help you." Dakk's plea sounded so desperate that she could almost believe it.

A chill skittered through Cassia. She wrapped her arms around herself and closed her eyes.

The sluggishness of her own heartbeat told her the truth. The Craving could kill a human.

She was afraid to close her eyes, in case she did not wake.

But she must have drifted off, because she woke when a warm, soft blanket wrapped around her. A gentle hand smoothed her hair back from her sweaty brow.

"I'm so sorry, Cassia."

Dakk. She flinched away from his touch and forced her eyes open.

His face wavered in front of her like a two-headed monster. She tried to make her eyes focus, tried to muster her Will to fight.

He held a cup to her lips. She turned her head away.

"No alchemy," he said, in the voice of her friend from Marijani. "Just water, I swear. Try to drink."

"Ha. I'm not that gullible, Dakk."

"You need water."

"As satisfying as it would be…" She coughed, trying not to gag. "…to be sick on you, I'd rather not."

He stroked her hair again.

"Don't touch me." She found the strength to push his hand away.

"I hate that Hesperine for doing this to you. If not for him, I would have saved you from the Master of Dreams already."

"Saved me," she spat. "In a prison cell in the desert. Dashing rescue, that."

"You don't deserve any of this. I wish I didn't have to treat you like this to contain the Old Master's influence."

"I wish I wasn't going to die because of you. I wanted a better death."

"I'm so sorry." Could the anguish in his voice be real? "I wanted to save you, Cassia. I've tried so hard. I should have been able to."

She stared her death in the face. If this man was going to succeed where the king and heart hunters and the Old Master himself had failed, she would look him in the eye.

She managed to focus. The sight of him came clear before her.

Two lines of tears tracked down Dakk's face.

WORK OF ART

LIO HAD VISITED THE Imperial Capital before, but he had never entered the Empress's city through the spirit gate reserved for Orthros's dignitaries. He had never thought he would exit the portal in such a company as this.

Tonight, Orthros's official representatives to the Empress's court were a Hesperine mercenary and three rebellious youngbloods from the Eighth Circle. But Karege had a letter of recommendation from the Second Princess, and Lio came armed with proper diplomatic papers to match Mak and Lyros's Steward passes. Lio could not imagine a finer delegation.

Uncle Argyros, in his capacity as the Queens' Master Ambassador, had secured them an audience before the Empress with all the officialness, pomp, and circumstance the Firstblood Circle's hearts desired.

"This is even more fun than jumping off Wisdom's Precipice." Mak looked around them at the spacious gate courtyard lined with fig trees.

"Let's pray for a softer landing," said Lyros.

"From your lips to the Goddess's Eyes." Lio looked up at the Light Moon. Hespera's gaze shone down on the brilliant white clay walls of the Owia Dynasty's traditional architecture, which distinguished the oldest and most prestigious sections of the palace complex.

Lio found a smile for his Trial brothers, despite the Craving clawing through his veins. "There's no one I'd rather jump to my near death with than you two. It's a good thing you applied for reassignment, because I have no intention of ever going errant without you again."

"Don't worry," Karege advised, "I'm here to catch you all before you break yourselves on the rocks of Imperial politics. The Ashes have been at court before, you know."

All around the courtyard, through other portals, came their allies. Tendeso led the Sandira representatives himself, a procession of winged and horned nobles who emanated sophistication. Kella rode through with her Azarqi nobles. She was dressed in the silver jewelry and indigo finery of a princess, with Tilili wearing a tasseled saddle decorated with delicate chains and bangles.

Tuura led a council of diviners, their varying attire and accents representing peoples from all over the Empire. From the Cifwani gate, Ukocha brought the matriarchs with Chuma at her side. Captain Ziara and her privateers arrived with a stir, and Ziara and Ukocha greeted each other as old friends.

Hoyefe waved at Lio and winked from a nearby group of courtiers who had been waiting to formally welcome them all.

Your plan worked, my Grace, thought Lio. *I hope you'll be proud of how I have seen it through.*

Lio fingered the scrolls he carried, which Mak and Lyros had brought from his uncle, along with advice and plans.

If the damage makes the elders bleed, Uncle Argyros had written, I will help them see that the shattered glass is your latest work of art.

Lio's medallion now hung from his new set of cords. He was prouder of them than the ones his uncle had bestowed upon him at initiation.

He felt Cassia's absence as a constant agony in his body and spirit, but her words echoed in his blood. *You've always told me that with Hespera's great power comes great responsibility. We must be gentle and just.*

A diplomat could not accomplish anything alone. He was the one who stepped back and gave everyone room to speak. He was only as heroic as the people he brought together.

In the crowded courtyard, he beheld the work of many hours and many minds. Speaking and listening, debating and promising, together they had all found a way to the Empress's door, where they would unite against the conspirators exploiting them all. He was very proud to stand quietly here and know he was just one part of something greater than himself.

When one was a diplomat, this was what storming the hill looked like. Cassia's cavalry was coming.

The official greetings with the Empress's officials dragged on while Lio said the right things and quietly warred with his symptoms. He had managed a petition in front of the Firstblood Circle with the Craving. He could achieve his first audience with the Empress, too. It helped that at one point during the proceedings, Tendeso caught his eye and snorted.

Then it was over, and they were all walking along a wide avenue between palace buildings. More fig trees. More moon-kissed white walls with vivid geometric designs along the bottom, painted scarlet and soaking up the Blood Moon's light.

It was much easier, and much harder, to get an audience with the Empress than with the King of Tenebra. One didn't have to overcome centuries of hostilities, accusations of heresy, or war mage assassins. But it was a challenge to distinguish oneself enough to receive her attention.

Lio had known his first audience with her would come after a long effort. But he had thought he would need to establish connections with Imperial diplomats and cultivate cooperative efforts between Orthros and the Empire. Such as his forgotten proposal on contributing Hesperine light magic and glassmaking to Imperial libraries.

Instead he had fled with his fugitive Grace, become an honorary mercenary, and made some jinn very angry. It had been a warrior who handed his medallion back to him. Lio had never intended to take such a path to the Empress, but here he was, staring at her throne room's wooden doors, which were tall enough to make even a bloodborn feel small.

Lio was ready. But he and Cassia should have been walking into the Imperial court as partners.

I will make it right, he silently promised his Grace.

Next to him, Tendeso watched the doors swing open.

"Well," Lio said, "this is nothing new for you, Your Highness."

"Not my first joust, silkfoot," he confirmed.

"Any final suggestions?"

"When you smashed that Rezayal's nose in the underground ruins, you let down your guard on your left. You should work on that."

"I'll keep that in mind next time we're sparring in the Court of Claws."

"You shouldn't say things like that. I might take it as a challenge."

"It *is* a challenge, Prince Vulture," Mak said amiably.

"Of course," Lyros agreed. "We were at a *vote* while you and Lio were surrounded by Sandira warriors. We demand a rematch."

"Count me in," Karege spoke up.

Lio was glad to be surrounded by warriors he trusted, seeing who flanked the entrance. The Golden Shield.

The women's helmets appeared completely sealed, their metal eyes forged open, ever watchful. Surely some magic enabled them to see and breathe. Lio heard their hearts beating in their smooth, round breastplates.

He could not look upon them without anger. But his temper would not help him convince the Empress that Cassia did not deserve to be her elite guard's target.

The delegations entered the Empress's throne room. Energy washed over Lio, enervating and intimidating.

This room felt like the center around which the world revolved. Lio could feel it in the auras of the courtiers present, the best and brightest from every corner of the Empire. Here was where everything of import happened. Here was where the worthy set foot. Here was where history moved and had done so for millennia.

The whole chamber glittered with gold. The jewelry of the occupants, the treasures and statues lining the chamber, the fixtures holding the spell lights from the ceiling. Ceremonial masks hung upon the white walls, judging the proceedings with the gazes of the ancestors.

As the delegations proceeded down the central aisle between the onlooking courtiers, murmured conversations in countless languages followed their passage. Shoulder-to-shoulder with the Ashes, Lio approached the Empress's feet.

Lio's first real glimpse of Her Imperial Majesty was her toe rings and gilded sandals. Jewels had looked like spoils of war on the brutish Tenebran king, but on the Empress's feet, they looked as natural as a kiss. He and the other Hesperines bowed low, while her subjects knelt before her.

A woman adviser to her right spoke out in Dynastic, the tongue of the Owia, which served as the language of power in this era. "Her Imperial Majesty greets her sisters and their friends from Orthros. Be welcome in the shining presence of our Eldest Sister, daughter of the Queen Mothers, she who is anointed by the ancestors and pleasing to Zalele, Goddess of the Sun."

It sent a chill of awe through Lio to hear her invoke the symbolic sisterhood between the Empress and the states under her rule. This matriclan bound the Empire together not by birth, but millennia of cooperation.

With his fellow Hesperines, he straightened, as the rest of the delegations rose to their feet, and they all stood together before the most powerful mortal in the world.

The Empress sat upon a throne of solid gold, robed in cloth of gold, bedecked in heavy gold jewelry. The crow's feet at her eyes and the lines around her mouth looked as majestic on her as the precious metal. Her maturity was another symbol of her power, a sacred sign that she had the experience to rule. The gray at her temples blended into the gold dust that adorned her hair, which rose in a complex structure of braids and locks, intertwined with the masterpiece that was Imperial crown.

She was draped in so many layers of enchantments, he doubted an army of mind mages could read her thoughts or all of Orthros could discern her emotions in the Blood Union.

For mundane threats, a dozen of the Golden Shield stood arrayed around her, ready to draw their swords at any hint of danger or disrespect. One warrior stood apart from the others, right at the Empress's shoulder. As if tethered in place, she stared straight ahead.

And then the Empress spoke. Her rich, beautiful voice carried through the room, the perfect balance of authority and care. "It always delights us to see Hesperines in our court. We are pleased to speak with your delegation, Ambassador Deukalion."

He was unprepared for the impact of hearing his name from her lips, although he had known to expect the Imperial hospitality custom of welcoming foreign guests in the court first. "Your Imperial Majesty, it is the greatest privilege of my career to stand before you."

"How do you find our court?" she asked.

"The praises of history do it justice, for it is truly the cradle and crown of civilization. But art and literature cannot do justice to you. Your wisdom and beauty are as impossible to capture in song as that of my own Queens.

I rejoice that I may behold their sister monarch with my own eyes and hear her voice."

"Orthros's diplomats have spoken highly of you as the student of the Queens' Master Ambassador. We are certain we can expect great things from you, Ambassador Deukalion."

It would echo across continents: the Empress had complimented Ambassador Deukalion by name before her court. Whole futures could be built on two such sentences.

"What tidings do you bring us from our sister monarchs, Queens Soteira and Alea?" the Empress asked.

In this moment, when it fell to Lio to declare the delegation's purpose before her, Cassia's life and the safety of the Empire hinged on his words. He was grateful for every boring scroll on policy he had read as a student, every foolish public speaking exercise when he had balanced a bust of Alatheia on his head, and all the times he had nearly died, which had been rather more terrifying than this.

He was not afraid, and he knew what to say.

He *was* a diplomat after all. And he would never doubt it again.

"You have our gratitude for lending us your ear, Your Imperial Majesty," Lio replied. "We come before you to apprise you of a grave threat to your Empire and to pledge Orthros's power in her defense against this enemy."

"Our dynasty's bond of gratitude with your Queens has always prevailed, but been blessed by peace these many centuries. What enemy could threaten our combined might?"

"Hidden enemies, cowards who prey upon your people from the shadows. They have their claws in every state of your Empire, trample on your rule of law, and dishonor the sacred traditions of diviners. They seek to destroy our alliance. On behalf of my Queens and their diplomats, I assure you, Hesperine faithfulness to the Empire is too strong to be shaken." Lio himself had wobbled in the Maaqul, but he was here now. "Tonight, Orthros stands with your sisters against our common enemy."

He felt the weight of the Empress's gaze. Her full attention was a powerful spell, humming in all his senses. Her gaze flicked to his hand, then his face. She allowed their eyes to meet.

Light magic winked at his senses. Hers, he realized. The glow all over this room was hers. Her magical power infused the court and her person, as surely as her political power did.

He knew that whatever he saw in her gaze was what she permitted him to see, as much a flawless political maneuver as her words.

Her eyes gleamed with recognition. She shone with the keen anticipation of an expert strategist ready to make a move.

But who would she move against? Lio and Cassia, or the Rezayal?

The faintest smile adorned her full, gold-dusted lips. "Can I trust you to unmask my enemy, Ambassador Deukalion?"

"Yes, Your Imperial Majesty."

"Present your evidence."

"If it pleases you, the Hesperine members of the delegation will cede the floor to Captain Ziara of Marijani, Victor of Souls."

Only the queen of privateers would approach the Empress with a swagger.

"Captain Ziara." The Empress smiled. "What spoils do you bring us from your latest voyage?"

"Three remarkable gifts, Your Imperial Majesty. Allow me to present the second one."

With a flourish, Ziara offered the Empress a small but luxurious inlaid box of Cordian make. The treasure-trove from the Magelands was tied with a ribbon, and from it dangled a coral and quartz ring.

Just like the ring Lio wore on his finger even now, one of a matched set Ziara had given him and Cassia. The privateer captain's words came back to him. *We bring Her Imperial Majesty all sorts of unusual treasures that we know she'll find useful.*

The Empress stroked the lid of the box, running one fingertip over the ring. "What a lovely second gift. We are greatly pleased with the first one, as well."

Oh, well played. Ziara believed Lio could be useful to the Empress. Her Imperial Majesty wanted him for a purpose.

"But what of your third gift?" the Empress asked Ziara.

"A surprise," the privateer replied. "You will know her when you see her."

She must mean Cassia.

What would the Empress, who upheld the policy of isolation, want with the King of Tenebra's turncoat daughter and a Hesperine diplomat who specialized in the shadowlands?

Can I trust you to unmask my enemy?

Perhaps she was not so committed to isolation as she appeared. Could this be one move in a long game she was playing against the Rezayal?

A diplomat, finding himself neatly delivered into her hands under such circumstances, could make much of his opportunity to assist her.

"Have you also brought news from across the sea, Captain?" the Empress asked.

"My news from Marijani is more interesting," Ziara answered. "You remember my old friend Gomba, do you not?"

"He has not presented us with gifts in some time. We cannot imagine why he no longer sails."

Lio tried not to tense before the observant gazes of the court. Ziara had stolen Gomba's letter of marque, the Empress's permit to engage in piracy against her enemies. Lio knew that because he had helped her keep it out of Gomba's hands, which probably violated a dozen laws and international agreements.

"Your Imperial Majesty," Ziara said innocently, "has he not been by to explain himself to you?"

"No, we have not seen him since his last…highly unfortunate…visit." A knowing gleam came to the Empress's eyes, her expression satisfied.

Lio suppressed a sigh of relief. He gathered that the Empress sometimes found it advantageous for a privateer to mysteriously lose his letter of marque, rather than for her to officially withdraw it. How many such favors had Ziara enjoyed doing for Her Imperial Majesty over the years?

And would it help his cause that he had already played a part in their plots?

"Unfortunately," Ziara continued, "Gomba's activities in Marijani have been rather unfortunate as well. He recently lined the pockets of a merchant governor to have an arrest warrant put out on an innocent woman."

The Empress frowned. "Why would he bring such dishonor upon the name of my privateers?"

"At the suggestion of the mind healer on his crew. When I interviewed him about the matter, I noticed something curious. Gomba's diviner has an unusual tattoo on his palm. A circle of stone fragments in red-black ink."

Lio sensed around him for reactions. Many were amused, some bored. Then there were those whose emotions were shielded by theramancy.

The magic emanated from a group of officials who stood at the front of the courtiers in attendance. Their diviners' staves and the theramantic symbols woven into their robes marked them as the Diviners of the High Court.

The entirety of the High Court was here, both the Rezayal's allies and those who resisted. But which were which?

"Poor taste in tattoos is hardly a crime," the Empress remarked.

"But bribery is, and I cannot in good conscience allow filthy hands to pay off the merchant governors of my island."

The Empress lifted a brow at Huru, who stood a step behind Ziara. "Does Gomba's diviner still have the tattoo?"

The First Mate's smile was as sharp as her knife. "I can assure you, Your Imperial Majesty, the tattoo is still attached to his hand."

As to whether the hand was still attached, neither she nor Ziara commented. The Empress laughed, and the court took that as permission to join her.

She was masterful. Her every word and motion was a demonstration of the art of ruling. How blessed the Empire was, that millennia of tradition and effort were concentrated in a woman so capable of carrying it.

Whoever she decided was her enemy tonight—the Rezayal or the delegation—should fear.

"And this innocent woman," the Empress prompted. "I trust you rescued her from Gomba's ill intentions?"

"I saw her safely on her way," Captain Ziara said with a bow, "but I fear her tale does not end there."

When Tendeso stepped forward, the currents in the room changed. Power flowed toward the prince of the mighty Sandira and moved even the impassive Golden Shield at the Empress's shoulder to flex her fingers on the hilt of her sword.

The Empress gave him a regal nod. "Our brother, Prince Tendeso. It pleases us to welcome you before us again after all these years."

"It has been too long since I stood in your light, Eldest Sister."

"What word do you bring from our brother King Anesu?"

Tendeso spoke with such authority, there could be no doubt in anyone's mind that he had been born to rule. "When the woman Ziara spoke of arrived at the Sandira Court, an adviser long believed to be wise poisoned His Majesty's ear with deception, claiming the woman was a threat to our people. As a result, this innocent person faced false charges, and the royal guard faced dishonor."

The Empress lounged on her elbow. "With respect to our brother, King Anesu, on what grounds should the Eldest Sister involve herself in an internal matter?"

"We are pleased to assure you that we have apprehended the one who insulted and betrayed our king: a diviner from one of our noblest families." Tendeso raised his fist, then opened his fingers. "She too has the lithic tattoo on her palm. It is clear the traitor to the Sandira owes allegiance to the same cause as the corrupt privateers in Marijani. It is clear this threat spans the borders of your sister states."

His voice rang out to the whole court. "The unmasking of this traitor led to the discovery of many more at work within the Sandira Court. We continue to find them at almost every level, seeking to bend our might to their cause. Let it be known that the Sandira King will tolerate no such challenge to his rule, nor will he allow these conspirators to harm his people. He has broken the power of this secret society in his own land, and we the Sandira declare ourselves their enemy everywhere in the Empire."

That should strike terror in the hearts of the Rezayal. Although Lio felt no auras shaking in fear, he did sense complex theramantic concealments weaving tighter through the High Court. But there was too much magic at work among them for him to pinpoint whom.

"As for the innocent woman," Tendeso concluded, "I escorted her safely to the Cifwani Matriarchate myself."

Lio and Monsoon had agreed to tactfully omit that he had grabbed Cassia and flown off with her against her will. The Empress didn't need to know that Cassia had tried to break Monsoon's ribs, or that Lio had wished to finish the job.

Now Ukocha approached the Empress. Lio marveled at Chuma, who exhibited no sign of nerves. She felt excited, through and through.

"Matriarch Ukocha, Victor of Souls," the Empress greeted her, "have you come to claim your boon from me at last?"

"If only the reason for our audience were so pleasant, Your Imperial Majesty. I am here with my heir to bring further evidence of the threat to our people. Allow me to present my daughter, Chuma, the future matriarch of my clan."

The Empress gave Chuma a warm smile. "What a momentous day for your clan, for you to take your place at your mother's side before us."

"Thank you, Your Imperial Majesty," Chuma said with poise.

"Until now, I believe, you have remained the famed Ukocha's treasured secret."

"It's time for me to fight her battles at her side."

"You are welcome among your sisters," the Empress proclaimed, "and you have our ear."

"Eldest Sister," Chuma addressed her, "my clan gave hospitality to the traveler fleeing unjust arrest. Her actions toward us prove her innocence and goodwill toward the Empire. She gave us her labor in our fields, and when my mother was in danger, she leapt at the chance to help. She went with our allies to reinforce the Ashes—in the Maaqul desert."

That sent a stir of murmurs through the crowd, and Lio felt hope. Surely the pure bond of gratitude between Chuma and Cassia would sway hearts and minds.

"She fought bravely at my mother's side," Chuma went on, "against enemies with the same tattoo on their palms. They dealt my mother this wound. But they also hold positions among our very own Cifwani Matriarchs."

"This is a very serious accusation," the Empress cautioned gently.

"Yes, Eldest Sister." Chuma raised her chin. "Someone sent Cifwani soldiers to hunt for the innocent traveler as soon as she crossed the border, so my mother and I set out to discover who. Before you and your court, I name our enemy. The Diviner Matriarch, the Cifwani Queen Mother's closest adviser, has the tattoo on her palm."

"You are as bold and brave as your mother," said the Empress. "You have represented your people well tonight. We look forward to seeing all that Ukocha's daughter will achieve."

Chuma's aura shone, and Lio thought Ukocha's pride might erupt in a fire spell.

"I trust Princess Kella brings us further tidings from the Maaqul?" The Empress beckoned to her.

Tilili's paws were soundless as she came forward. "Queen Mother Hinan sends her greetings, Your Imperial Majesty."

"Our regards to your mother, and honor to you for your scars, earned in battle for the common good of our Empire. What troubles the Azarqi?"

"Eldest Sister, my people have tended the Desert Accord like a garden in the Maaqul for the safety of the entire Empire. Recently, warriors with shrouded faces have disturbed the ruins and riled the jinn. And yet, when I and my comrades battled them to stop their crimes, a jinn aided them against us."

The murmurs of surprise and concern grew louder.

The Empress frowned. "Matters are so far gone that jinn take sides in a mortal contest?"

"These Accord breakers are marked with the lithic tattoo." Kella raised her hand, showing her blue palm to the court. "They wield mind healing for harm and carry weapons with dangerous spiritual power. The Ashes have found their hiding places deep in the Maaqul, in a region where a mysterious disruption bends and breaks the very laws of magic."

From the corner of Lio's Hesperine eyes, he saw a clue. A minute betrayal of concern that mortal eyes would not even catch. A mere flex of a woman's fingers around her staff. She stood at the center of the High Court, an elder whose deeply lined face seemed etched in a solemn frown. An ornate gold sphere adorned the top of her staff. She was the Chief Diviner of the High Court, the most powerful mind healer in all the Empire.

Kella bowed from Tilili's back. "The Azarqi ask for your aid against these criminals, Eldest Sister."

"This conflict in the distant reaches of the Maaqul is of great concern to us," the Empress replied, "as are our relations with the jinn. We will respond accordingly."

"Thank you, Your Imperial Majesty. But I fear this threat already draws much closer than the desert."

Kella withdrew, and Hoyefe swept forward. He wore Owia finery, adorned with heavy gold jewelry and wrapped in a knee-length robe of brilliant yellow that draped from one shoulder. He gave the Empress an exquisite bow. "Your Imperial Majesty, what a joy to behold you again. Your light shines brighter every time I return to you."

For the first time that night, she extended her hand. She allowed Hoyefe the privilege of kissing her rings. "Lord Hoyefe, tell me these dire tidings have not banished your inspiration."

"Far from it, My Empress! Such adventures fill me with the divine spark of creativity. Once your wise leadership has allayed our troubles, I promise you an excellent play based on these events…with a few embellishments."

"The first performance must be a private showing here in my palace, as always, for myself and my companions."

"Of course, Your Imperial Majesty. But might I make a few suggestions regarding the guest list?"

She raised a brow in invitation.

Hoyefe placed a hand on his breast. "Any arbiter of Imperial fashion will have noticed that over the centuries, gloves have by turns taken the court by storm, then fallen out of favor. Like similiar trends such as tattooed sleeves and illusory hand paint. I believe these patterns of fashion betray rising and falling allegiance to these enemies who sport palm tattoos."

Lio was not prepared for the amusing sight of various courtiers adjusting gloves or tucking their hands behind their backs in an attempt to go unnoticed.

"Let a new fashion indicate true loyalty to you." Hoyefe extended a hand, as one might invite a lady to dance. On his bare palm shone the sacred Owia symbol of the sun, which was known to shine through illusions. "We, your true devotees, are prepared to divulge every detail regarding the conspiracy within the court. Every bribe, threat, and act of treason besmirching your esteemed house."

Hoyefe's supporters in attendance lifted their hands in a gesture of petition toward the Empress. All of their palms glowed gold with the sign of her sun.

"Who?" the Empress challenged. "Who is this enemy against whom you bring allegations? I must know their identity, that the evidence may be properly weighed and justice decided."

In the quiet, Tuura stepped forward, her staff tapping softly on the floor. "Your Imperial Majesty, allow me to name your enemy."

"Diviner Tuura," the Empress replied, "your service on the gold roster has brought much good to our people. Share your wisdom before our court."

"These conspirators are well known to the diviners of your Empire. In secret, this faction has curried favor, while punishing any who would not tolerate their schemes. I bring theramancers from many sisters states, witnesses who will attest that these enemies have endured in our lands for generations. We are the diviners who remain true to our calling to practice healing and uphold truth, from the highest courts to the humblest villages. Tonight, we speak their secrets for all to hear."

Now she struck the floor with her staff. The impact seemed to reverberate through every aura in the room. "They are the Rezayal."

At last, Lio could sense who recognized the name and who did not. The Empress and the Chief Diviner of the High Court both knew it well.

The Empress did not glance the Chief Diviner's way. But a spark of light on the woman's staff drew Lio's gaze to her. Could anyone else see the smile the Empress bestowed upon him? Or did her light magic reserve it for him?

He made his and Cassia's final move. "Your Imperial Majesty, the Rezayal have also threatened the people of Orthros within the borders of your Empire. The woman they sought to arrest may be known to you, for your cousin, His Highness Harkhuf Addaya Khemkare, has met her during his studies in our homeland. Her name is Cassia, Newgift Komnena."

The Golden Shield's hand tightened on her sword once more, but the Empress offered neither confirmation nor denial. It seemed they would dance around the secret that Lio had just named the shadowlander her elite guard hunted. "This is of grave concern to us, as it must be to our sister monarchs."

Lio went on to describe Cassia's connections in Orthros in the most ostentatious, diplomatic terms, dropping the name of every ancient Hesperine who favored her. He concluded, "She is to be my partner for eternity and take her place in our founding bloodline. Her highest ambition is to serve our people as a diplomat, a champion of peace. We traveled here to celebrate our forthcoming promises and enjoy the wonders of your Empire. Yet the Rezayal have pursued us at every turn. Even now, Cassia is their captive in the Maaqul."

The Empress wielded even her expression of anger with skill and majesty. "It is a severe offense to threaten the lasting friendship between Orthros and the Empire."

Mak touched the black scroll at his belt. "Your Imperial Majesty, as Stewards of Orthros, it is our duty to protect the Queens' people. We are ready to fight alongside your authorities to ensure Newgift Cassia's safe return."

Lyros spoke with equal self-assurance. "The Queens fear for both Ambassador Deukalion and Newgift Cassia, for as long as she is the prisoner of the Rezayal, both suffer mortal danger from their separation."

"We know the malady of which you speak," said the Empress. "Ambassador Deukalion, how long can you endure?"

"As long as I must. Past experience has given me fortitude. My fear is for Cassia. A few nights without me are enough to make her gravely ill. I believe the Craving could be fatal to her if we are apart for much longer."

The Empress's expression of sympathy made one feel as if there were nothing in the world she could not mend, not even the Craving. "What reason could anyone in my Empire have to make an enemy of Newgift Cassia?"

"She was born in Tenebra," Lio answered.

"So were many Hesperines who traverse my lands."

Lio kept his veils tight over his apprehension. Now for the moment of truth before her court, when he would say what they both knew aloud. "She is yet mortal, Your Imperial Majesty."

The Chief Diviner of the High Court struck the floor with her staff.

At last, the Rezayal made their move. They must think this was a round they could win.

But Lio and Tendeso had made certain they were prepared.

"By the Empress's command," came the Chief Diviner's voice, "no Tenebran may set foot in the lands under her protection. So it has been for generations. How boldly you make accusations before her court, while confessing to this shadowlander's crime."

"Cassia is no longer Tenebran," Lio replied. "She has forsaken that land, and the Queens have formally granted her Sanctuary."

"She remains a shadowlander as long as she remains mortal," the Chief Diviner protested. "You try to exonerate her by spinning tales of conspiracy, but clearly, the truth is simple. A shadowlander came here illegally, and various sisters states tried to apprehend her, according to the law. Any diviner from Marijani to the Cifwani Matriarchate who advised their ruler to arrest her was speaking the wisdom of the ancestors."

"Eldest Sister," Tendeso said, "Esteemed Chief Diviner, this very debate was also of great concern in my king's court. We found it necessary to review the letter of the law. Allow me to quote from the decrees of the ancient Empresses who first codified our protections against shadowlanders. 'No persons from the continent comprising Tenebra and Cordium may enter the Empire, but the people of Orthros shall be welcome.'"

"Prince Tendeso," said Lio, "help those of us who are guests in your lands to understand the esteemed laws of the Empire. Am I correct that this decree does not specify whether the 'people of Orthros' must be immortal?"

"That is correct, Ambassador Deukalion."

The Chief Diviner appeared affronted. "The people of Orthros are understood to be Hesperines."

Lio kept his tone courteous. "What of citizens of Orthros who await their Giftings?"

"It is unprecedented for them to travel here before their transformations," she returned. "Fangs are clearly what distinguish a shadowlander from a citizen of Orthros."

"With respect, Chief Diviner, that is not the case under our laws." Lio offered two scrolls to the Empress. "Your Imperial Majesty, allow me to display Newgift Cassia's personal citizenship papers, granted to her by the

Second Princess's magistrates, as well as her diplomatic travel pass issued by the Queens' Master Ambassador."

The Empress lifted a hand. As if tugged on the end of a spell, the Golden Shield at her shoulder stepped forward. The soldier took hold of the scrolls with one hand. She fixed Lio with a stare over Cassia's papers. He looked back into her ever-still gaze without flinching before releasing the scrolls.

She unrolled them and stared at them in silence for a long moment before showing them to the Empress.

"Heed my counsel," the Chief Diviner warned. "My duty is to protect the Imperial Court from the influence of evil magic. Do not allow a few new papers to call the wisdom of our ancestors into question."

The Empress's gaze softened. "Your devotion to our safety is unquestioned. You have protected us since we were a tiny child learning to walk in the footsteps of our foremothers. Your counsel has been heard. But it is the purview of the Queens of Orthros to determine who their people are. These documents make it clear that they consider Newgift Cassia a full citizen of Orthros."

"That may be the letter of the law," said the Chief Diviner, "but not the spirit of it. Any human from that continent is dangerous, regardless of whether she arrives through Orthros."

Mak spoke up. "Esteemed Diviner, the Stewards are on constant guard against any enemies that might enter our Queens' lands, and we would never allow danger to pass by us into yours."

Lyros nodded. "We can attest that Newgift Cassia has aided in Orthros's defense many times, nearly sacrificing her life to protect us against threats from the shadowlands."

"She is Orthros's greatest defender against Tenebra and Cordium," Mak said, "and by extension, the Empire's. Her loss is a blow to all our safety."

"Some threats cannot be fought by warriors," was the Chief Diviner's ominous reply.

Karege cleared his throat and moved forward to flank Mak and Lyros. "Warriors are not the only line of defense Orthros offers."

"Karege," the Empress greeted him, "I wondered if our court would hear your wisdom tonight. What a loss it was for the Empire when you

424

left us for immortality, and yet what a gain, that generations of my dynasty may know you. What are your thoughts on these matters?"

"Your Imperial Majesty, you know how I love to roam your lands. But the threat of the Rezayal and Newgift Cassia's plight are of such concern to me that I returned to Orthros. I have been consulting with other Hesperines of Imperial heritage, including Second Princess Konstantina and Elder Firstblood Kassandra. What threat could get past their magic and foresight to enter the Empire from Orthros?"

"An eminent mind healer and the oracle, my own immortal relation," the Empress replied. "Their assurances carry weight indeed."

"They're both quite fond of Newgift Cassia," Karege added.

Lio laid out their final argument. "Your Imperial Majesty, we plead for your help in recovering her. Only your power is great enough to save her from enemies with such reach as the Rezayal's. We ask that you show her your mercy and your enemies your might, as we stand with you against these traitors to the Empire."

In the quiet that chased his words, the delegation and the court awaited the Empress's verdict.

"In the light of wisdom," she spoke, "which shines from Zalele, the truth is clear. The Rezayal have committed treason against us."

Victory, delivered on a few words from her lips. The swift death blow to the Rezayal's centuries of existence.

The Empress looked at the Chief Diviner. "Can any who place themselves above the law be allowed to continue?"

The silence between them stretched on. A bead of sweat touched the temple of the Chief Diviner. "Certainly not, Your Imperial Majesty."

"Esteemed Diviner," the Empress pressed, "what is your counsel? Are not these Rezayal wielders of evil magic and a terrible danger to the Imperial court?"

Lio stood and watched the Empress put the Chief Diviner's loyalty to the ultimate test, even as she extended her wizened adviser a length of rope with which she might save herself.

Would the mage bow to the Empress or stand with the Rezayal?

At last the diviner lowered her head. "Yes, Your Imperial Majesty. Clearly they must be reminded who rules this Empire and sets its future course."

She had chosen to remain at the Empress's right hand, rather than fall from grace with the Rezayal. They had lost their voice in the High Court.

Everyone here had just beheld, in that one tense exchange, the beginning of the Rezayal's downfall.

The Empress looked out across the court. "We will have an audience with each delegation that has brought charges. We will hear the enemy's misdeeds. The names of every conspirator shall be given to my Golden Shield. Nowhere in our Empire will be safe for the Rezayal."

She rested a gentle gaze on Lio. "Do not fear for Newgift Cassia. Let it be known that she is welcome in the Empire, as are all people of Orthros. She will be restored to you and our sister monarchs."

For the first time that night, he felt weak in the knees. "We believe they are keeping her prisoner in the Maaqul, where ancient monuments interfere with spells. It is not possible to step there, and only the Rezayal are capable of spirit walking in that region. Searching the area with mundane methods would take more time than Cassia has."

"The Rezayal cannot hide her from my sight. There is no corner of my lands I cannot reach." The Empress inclined her head to the Chief Diviner. "Your knowledge is great. I am certain you have an idea of where this place could be located. In your wisdom, surely you can devise a way to spirit walk there and take my Golden Shield with you."

That bead of sweat that had been trembling on the diviner's temple now rolled down her cheek. "Yes, Your Imperial Majesty."

The Empress beckoned once more for the Golden Shield. The soldier surrendered Cassia's papers to Lio and knelt before the Empress.

"You will lead the search," the Empress commanded. "I want Newgift Cassia returned and her captors brought to me."

The Golden Shield stood and backed away. She halted in front of the Chief Diviner and subjected her to a harsh golden gaze. The Empress's elite guard who had been the greatest threat to Cassia were now her defenders.

The Empress extended her hand to Lio.

He accepted the high honor of bestowing a kiss upon her rings. "Your Imperial Majesty, you have my gratitude."

53

days until

NOTIAN WINTER SOLSTICE

4 Ourania, 1597 IS

ANCESTORS

A T LAST, DAKK LEFT Cassia alone.

Time passed. She felt forgotten in a tiny eggshell under a mountain.

This was worse than being lost in the desert. Then, continuing to walk had given her hope.

"Hope. Hope. Ours."

Her only companions were the whispers. She wished they would leave her alone, too.

All those reassuring words she had heard in the spirit gates had been lies. Every step she had taken through them had only led her here. To the end.

The Craving kept dragging her toward unconsciousness. Each time, she went under in fear that she would not surface again.

When she came to, she clung to awareness, to her Will, to her thoughts. Her proof that there was life left in her yet.

Curse the Collector. She had escaped him, only to be blamed for his crimes. She had been so close to her Hesperine future, only for her human past to ruin everything.

Just as she had feared would happen during her Gifting. She had never made it that far, and it had happened anyway.

"Hope. Hope. Ask."

"Leave me be."

She had tried so hard to become her Hesperine self. The Cassia who had saved the Hesperine embassy from assassination, who had defected to Orthros and battled the Collector at Lio's side. The Cassia who put others ahead of herself, and in doing so, gained more and more joy of her own.

The Cassia who loved Lio.

She did not want to meet her end here, as her human self.

She pulled her knees to her chest and wrapped her arms around herself. "Hespera," she rasped with the remnants of her voice, "was I not worth saving?"

She drifted in and out of consciousness and her memories. She thought of all the people she had sold out to save her own skin. She had dealt countless tiny wounds over the years to people whose names she didn't even remember.

They would remember her, though. After she was gone, she would be a voice in their minds, making their lives worse, measure by measure, making their wounds ache more and more.

Cassia did not feel a bit of compassion for that self.

So why should Hespera?

Her head roared, and darkness claimed her again. She roused to a realization.

That was why she hadn't been ready. All along, she had not thought that human version of Cassia worth saving. She had seen no reason why the Goddess would, either.

How could she forgive herself for the pain she had caused others? How could she enjoy immortality while her cruelty poisoned their brief mortal lives? She knew the misery of carrying that voice of cruelty in your mind, the way it shredded you every day.

You are nothing.

The king's voice was still there. All her life, he had made sure to remind her how ashamed of her he was, how ashamed she should be of herself. She hadn't heard his voice as often lately. The bells of Orthros had drowned him out. But he was always there.

No bells here. But she heard a clarion from Orthros within her. There was another voice in her life now, too.

We could not ask the Goddess for a truer or braver heart...a blessing so immeasurable... We are so proud of you, Cassia.

Apollon...Papa.

Just like Cassia, he had felt unworthy. Yet he had not said that Hespera had destroyed his human self to make a new Hesperine of him.

She is the greatest sculptor there is…revealing the best of me.

Could Cassia find the best of herself?

She looked through the humiliation inside her. It was so hard. Was there anything left of her beneath it?

She didn't want to be this Cassia. She had never wanted to be.

Oh. *Oh.*

She was not the one who had made that layer of herself at all. It was the king's work. He had chipped away at her from the day she was born, chiseling her into his image of her.

This revile for her human self was not her own. The awakening of her conscience had made her ashamed of her past deeds. But the one who had made her ashamed of herself was the king.

She had thought finding her sister would help her lay her past to rest. She had thought if she once again had her sister's love, she could love herself.

Even Solia did not have that power. Only Cassia did.

Such deep wounds did not heal in days or weeks or even months. They might well require a lifetime of care. A Hesperine lifetime.

She wanted to have that chance. To undo her father's wounds. To forgive herself for the wounds she had dealt. She could not heal all the people she had hurt, but she could put kindness into the world to balance the pain she had once caused.

She didn't have to be a Hesperine to do that. Kindness was a human power, too.

What other human power did she have?

Courage. Human Cassia had placed herself between the Collector and a room full of mortals. Perseverance. Human Cassia had stared down a heart hunter's crossbow and refused to surrender. Selflessness. Human Cassia had risked her own life to save the Hesperine embassy.

Human Cassia had first felt an inkling of her worth in her sister's abandoned garden, lighting a vigil candle for her with Lio at her side. She had shared with him the tale of each woman Lucis had destroyed, a rare moment when she had spoken of her mother, Thalia. Cassia had declared herself the survivor, the last woman standing.

I am not nothing, she had said.

Human Cassia had all the women who had come before, her guiding lights.

"*Light. Light. Survive,*" said the whispers.

"I'm listening," she whispered back.

"*Yours. Yours. Ask.*"

"Are you my ancestors? May I ask you for help?"

The whispers increased, layer upon layer, and she couldn't make out their words.

Woe is she who does not understand the tongue of her ancestors, the jinn had said.

"I'm sorry I did not heed you. I understand better now. Please, teach me more in my hour of need."

The whispers clarified into a single voice that gained strength until Cassia felt as if the speaker were right in front of her. The woman's voice felt familiar, her words even more so.

"Know the voice of your ancestor," she said, and Cassia could understand.

"Who are you?"

"The first mage of your lineage. I was born in the land now known as Tenebra, long before it even had a name."

"So long ago," Cassia breathed. "Before the Mage King?"

"Long before him."

"During the Great Temple Epoch?"

"Longer ago than that."

"That was over six thousand years ago," Cassia exclaimed. "You must have lived in the Hulaic Epochs."

"Yes," said the first mage, "in the uncountable years lost to time. That was also when this city thrived."

"How is it that I can hear your voice here, where you never walked?"

"I did walk here. When I lived, the gate was open."

Cassia gasped. "There was a time when a spirit gate allowed travel across the world?"

"The Diviner Queen ushered in that golden age. She and her followers were rich in magic you cannot imagine. They built this City of Hope, a beacon to all. Their towns and temples spread across the land

and turned the desert into an oasis. Humanity prospered, and learning flourished.

"She opened a spirit gate here and led her people through it to explore a new continent and seek new knowledge. I was there the day she came to the land where you and I were born.

"She rewrote the laws of the world as we knew it. Until then, magic had been like the trees of the untamed forests or the wolves that roamed the wilds. A force of nature we feared and respected, but could not control.

"The Diviner Queen taught us to make magic into our garden, to befriend it like the dogs that guard the homestead. From the mountains of the north to the shores of the southern sea, the peoples of our continent joined in friendship with her followers from afar. We all had such ideals. We dreamed of building a great civilization.

"For a generation, we thrived together. My people went through the gate to behold the wonders the Diviner Queen had built here. Her followers came to our lands to nurture and to teach.

"But for some, dreams turned to ambition, and ideals turned to greed. They abused the power she had taught them. They rose, horrifying in their might, evil in their hearts. You know them."

"The Old Masters," Cassia whispered.

"They began life the same way I did. We were mere mortals, born to the plains or the forests or the rivers. They too stood empty-handed before the Diviner Queen when she arrived. When she filled them with her gifts, they repaid her with destruction.

"She had to collapse the spirit gate to protect the cradle of humanity from humanity's worst extreme. Here in the ruins of her city, where magic still echoes with that cataclysm, spirit and flesh meet."

"The megaliths were the gate, weren't they? That's where she made her sacrifice."

"I was among the faithful who fought for her that day. We stayed behind in the shadowlands, knowing we would never see the City of Hope again. We used all the magic she had taught us to hold off the Old Masters, so she could seal the portal for all time."

"Is that…how you became an ancestor?"

"I gave my life in battle against the Master of Dreams. My only regret is that my spirit cannot guide you in your fight against him.

"For the Diviner Queen did more than isolate one half of the world from the other. She closed off our lands from the spirit phase, so the evil ones could never open a gate to the motherland."

"There are spirit gates in Orthros," Cassia said, even as she realized, "but only in Orthros Notou. Never in Orthros Boreou, where we border Tenebra."

"There, no mage can reach into the spirit phase. But the consequence is that the ancestors cannot influence the natural phase. You were born under the Old Masters' shadow, in the lands where I must be silent. You are as an abandoned child, without the guidance of those who came before."

Tears slipped down Cassia's face for a loss she had never known she'd suffered. Death had taken her mother from her. But the Old Masters had taken the chance to speak to her, to know her, to live by her guidance.

"It had to be." Her ancestor's voice held the grief of the ages. "Imagine if the necromancers could abuse the spirit phase. All the world would fall to them, and then they would march upon the afterlife to conquer the ancestors."

Cassia had seen many evils in her life, but the vision of that future was more horrifying than anything she had ever imagined.

"Yet you and I meet here," said the first mage, "at the touch point of spirit and flesh, of old and new. By the grace of the Diviner Queen, I walked both lands. And so my descendants, your foremothers, may walk here at my behest."

Another woman's voice joined hers. She spoke in a tongue Cassia had heard snatches of from gray-haired grandmothers in village gardens. Words carved on Solia's ivy pendant, which had belonged to the Changing Queen. A language Cassia had never fully understood until now.

"Greetings, bearer of my secrets."

Goosebumps pebbled Cassia's skin. She spoke the old garden tongue of Tenebra, the language of Lustra magic, the power of the ancient wilds. "You're a Silvicultrix, wise in nature magic."

"I am the hawk."

"What does that mean?"

"Of nature's magics, there are three. The wisdom of plants. The wisdom of beasts. And soothsaying, the wisdom of humans."

"Of the three," said the first mage, "we may each give you one. From my soothsaying, I have given you the gift of tongues."

"From my beast magic," said the Silvicultrix, "you shall have the gift of sight."

Feathers rustled before Cassia's eyes, and then she could see.

The Silvicultrix stood over her. Short in stature, she was great in presence. Hawk feathers adorned her brown curls, and furs wrapped her body. Her eyes were as green as the wild woods.

Her fair skin was heavily freckled. Cassia might have laughed at the familiar sight if her awe had not left her speechless.

"The power will come forth in you," the Silvicultrix said.

Cassia found the strength to lift her head. "Are you saying I do have magic? Can it be one of these three nature magics?"

The hawk smiled. "You will understand."

A fragrance filled the prison like a thousand flowers. The Silvicultrix turned as another woman appeared beside her.

If an artist had painted Cassia and transformed her into a beauty, she might have looked like this. Lustrous olive skin, gleaming dark hair, a more glamorous vision of her own short nose and round face.

She had an arch smile, the kind that could inspire people to do anything, just for a glimpse of it.

Cassia didn't have to ask who she was. Even though she had never seen her, she just knew.

The ancient word for *mother* sprang to her lips. "Alma."

"My Cassia." Thalia put a hand to her belly. "My little sprout, now this strong and beautiful rose."

What should Cassia say? How could she, in this one moment, do justice to a lifetime of lost years?

She struggled to sit up, overpowered by the instinct to reach for her mother. If she tried to touch her, would she disappear?

Thalia sat down next to Cassia and pulled her into her arms. "Feel my gift to you."

It was no spectral embrace. She could feel her mother, soft and breathing, strong and alive. Thalia held her for the first time in her living memory.

Sobs came from deep within Cassia, and she let them out on her mother's shoulder.

Thalia rocked her in her arms and began to sing.

Five hawthorns sharp in my winter garden
Red berries in the snow
Five hawthorns ripe with winter bounty
To guard my little ivy

Her voice filled the bare chamber, driving back all the dangers surrounding them.

Six betony in my bright spring garden
No trouble can trespass here
Six betony of royal purple
But none so fine as my little ivy

Cassia felt the deepest assurance that she was safe. Loved.

Seven ivy vines in my bright spring garden
To tear down every wall
Seven ivy vines that built my fortress
Each as strong as my own

"I missed you," Cassia said, when she could speak.

"How I missed you, my dearest one."

"Was there any joy in your life?" Cassia asked. "It was not all grief, was it?"

"No, no. I was happy before I came to Tenebra. And after I went there, there was you. You made me happiest of all."

"You wanted me?"

"You were the best thing that ever happened to me."

Cassia dragged in a breath, choking on all that could not be. "I wanted more for you."

"You will have more, and that is most important to me."

She wasn't sure she should ask. Perhaps her mother didn't wish to speak of it. Perhaps Cassia didn't want to know.

But this was her chance. Now when the magic of the ages had aligned to give them this meeting, it was not the time to hesitate.

"Was he very cruel to you? How did you endure being with him?"

Her mother drew back and stroked her face. "You and I both deserved better. But we are more than what he did to us."

Cassia nodded. "I will be victorious over his wrongs. For both of us."

"You already are. I am so proud of you."

A lifetime of pain opened and healed within Cassia by turns. "That is what I needed to know."

"There is more I must tell you. Things you need to understand about my life."

"I want to know everything," Cassia confessed.

"When I arrived in Tenebra as the king's companion, word spread that I had come from a temple in Cordium. Assumptions were made that I was his concubine, and that I had been a handmaiden of Hedon in a pleasure temple. But that was not my life, Cassia. I was a powerful mage of the Mother Goddess Kyria in Corona."

Cassia gasped. "Garden magic."

"I had a rare dual affinity for plants and beasts. I could grow anything in my garden, train nearly any creature. I was one of the Order of Kyria's foremost flora and fauna mages. Until I manifested a third affinity, the rarest of all. Soothsaying."

Cassia's mind reeled. Nothing she had believed was true. "All three of the old magics?"

"My mother had warned me. Sometimes the third affinity manifested in the women of our line. I prayed that would not be my fate."

"I can understand why you wouldn't want that magic. The ability to influence others with your voice is a great power…but soothsayers are feared in the same way mind mages are."

"When I realized it was happening, I tried to hide it. But it was too late."

"Aren't all woman soothsayers sent to the temple of the Mourning Goddess Chera to serve the Oracle?"

"Banished behind a veil, silenced, where the truth we speak cannot challenge Anthros's power. The life I loved in my Kyrian temple vanished before my eyes. The shroud of Chera was closing around me. So when the King of Tenebra offered me an escape, I took it."

"What offer did he make you? Why?"

"He needed my magic in his bloodline for his own ends. I consented to our congress for the hope of a child." Thalia cupped Cassia's face in her hand. "Because I wanted you, and I had plans for you, precious one. You were never his. You were always mine."

Cassia blinked back tears. She could not let weeping cloud her vision now, when she had the chance to see her mother clearly for the first time.

She saw her mother's sadness now. "I could not remain with you to protect you from his designs. But I left you with a capable protector."

"Solia?" Cassia asked.

"She devoted her life to carrying out my plans."

"The plot was yours all along!"

"Solia will explain the rest to you. Tell her she has become the woman I always knew she could be. I love you both so much, my girls who refuse to surrender. You will always be my pride and joy."

The first mage's voice echoed through the chamber again. "The time is now."

"You must go," said the hawk.

Cassia clung to Thalia. "I don't want to leave you. Why must I go back to the silent land, where I cannot hear you?"

"There are people there who love you." Thalia helped Cassia to her feet.

Her hearing and vision were clear, her legs steady. Her fever had broken, and strength suffused her mind and body.

"Listen to all voices," said the first mage. "Learn from our past."

"See with keen eyes," said the Silvicultrix. "Keep our power present."

Thalia took Cassia's hands. "Fight with my hands. Build our future."

"I will," Cassia promised.

"Now escape," her mother urged her. "Our gifts will stay with you as long as you are within range of the shattered gate."

Her ancestors faded from her sight, and the whispers were quiet.

But Cassia knew she was not alone. She felt their presences all around her.

Her gaze fell to her hands. They looked the same. But she felt…

Magic was no longer an unseen fullness in the air or a shiver upon her arms. For the first time, it wasn't something she felt but couldn't touch. It was inside her.

She knew she had the power to escape. She only had to figure out how to use it.

"Listen," Cassia said. "See. Fight."

She closed her eyes and listened.

The whispers were quiet now, but other voices echoed from somewhere in the complex. It was as if the stone had opened up to communicate with her.

She could hear that people now filled the ruins of the city. Not spirits, but living mortals. Tense voices discussed the logistics of a crisis. Food. Blankets. Getting everyone to safety.

One voice came to her most clearly through the others.

"Grandmother!" Dakk spoke a language Cassia couldn't name, but she had no trouble understanding him. "Grandmother, thank the ancestors you made it to safety."

"It seems it is necessary for me to seek refuge here like everyone else." The woman's voice wavered with age.

"Here, Grandmother, take my chair."

"Don't fuss," she said. "The desert air is good for my bones."

"I wish you could have stayed in the village, where you are more comfortable."

"I go where I must for the cause, Dakkoul."

It sounded as if his grandmother had just used his full name. Oh, he was in trouble now. Cassia almost laughed, hearing her fearsome captor groveling to his elder.

But if the woman could make a man like him grovel, how dangerous was she?

"The Empress will regret this," Dakk swore. "Our people have been pouring through the spirit tears from all over the Empire, but no one can tell me what prompted her sudden war upon us. Whatever has emboldened her, she will pay for thinking she can rule without us."

"This is all due to your prisoner."

"What? We have operated under the strictest secrecy. None of our own would betray us." His voice descended. "I have personally ensured that."

"Then how is it that a Hesperine diplomat has announced, before the Empress and her entire court, that the woman is in your custody?"

Relief made Cassia sag against the wall. Lio!

"Impossible," her captor hissed.

"The Chief Diviner of the High Court sent word along a trusted route. One Ambassador Deukalion has described your entire endeavor to capture this Cassia."

"No. He is a foreigner. They will not trust his accusations against citizens of the Empire."

"He has the support of Marijani, the Sandira, the Cifwani, and the Azarqi, not to mention a coterie of aristocrats inside the Empress's own court and a council of rebellious theramancers. They have described our mark and spoken our name."

Triumph breathed new life into Cassia.

Lio had not abandoned his calling. He had once more taken up the cause of diplomacy and come to her aid alongside all their allies.

That's all I need, my love, she thought. *You work from there. I'll work from here. We will each create the opportunities the other needs. We will make a way.*

"But she is a Tenebran," Dakk protested. "It is he and those mercenaries who have broken the law by tolerating her presence here."

"The Empress has pronounced her protected as a citizen of Orthros."

"Our allies on the High Court would never allow that!"

"The Empress has waited for this opportunity for a long time. She is putting each of us to a test of loyalty. The Chief Diviner has already chosen her side. We should not expect to hear from her again."

"Cowards!" he spat. "Indolent cowards, growing fat at the Empress's feet! They have forgotten what sacrifice it takes to build lands such as ours."

His grandmother sounded tired. "They are cowards who hold our fates in their hands, Dakk."

"We will rally—we will rebuild—"

"It is over."

The silence that fell was profound.

"Was this girl worth it?" asked the grandmother.

"She is the key to discovering the Old Masters' plan of attack upon the Empire."

"You have uncovered further evidence of an imminent attack?"

"Ever since her sister arrived, we've known it was only a matter of time. Now Cassia's appearance is a sign of the Old Masters' rising aggression. It is our fate that the invasion will come in our time. I will not falter. Even if we must operate in secret, as outlaws, we will safeguard our homeland at any cost."

"What have you learned from her?"

"The Hesperine's mind ward continues to be an obstacle. But I have made progress ever since the week I spent with her in Marijani, studying the ward for weaknesses."

"I will deal with her myself."

"Her inner battle with the Master of Dreams has weakened her." Dakk sounded regretful. Guilty, even. "She cannot endure much more."

"We are out of time, in any case. Bring her to me."

"Cassia?"

Dakk's voice was suddenly right behind her. She turned to find that he had appeared in her cell.

"You can stand," he said with surprise.

Too late for her to feign weakness.

He looked her up and down, relief and regret warring on his face. "Your suffering has abated. I am glad of that, but… I hate to imagine what you surrendered to the necromancer to gain this reprieve."

Let him think what he wanted, as long as he didn't suspect the ancestors had revived her with their magic.

"Can you walk?" he asked.

"Yes." She would keep her own two feet under her at any cost.

He approached her slowly, with his dagger drawn. He had a spell at the ready, too. She could sense it, clear as day, as a sort of hum inside him, a halo of potential around him.

Until she could devise a spell of her own, she didn't want to give him a reason to use his. When she made no move to resist, he wrapped his hand around her arm. Her wound didn't throb this time, although Dakk was able to pull her through a spirit tear.

Why thank you, Lio. The stir you've caused got me out of my cell.

Cassia blinked, disoriented to be out in the world after so many days in a nowhere land of stone. She couldn't tell what time it was. Wind sucked at a carpet fastened over a window frame.

This chamber had furniture and rugs. A fire burned in an old clay hearth. On the warm edge there sat a woman stooped with age, her white hair like a cloud around her age-marked face.

She might appear frail, but her presence crackled with magic, which Cassia could sense as never before. Her magic had a similar flavor to the aura around Dakk, and she held a staff like Tuura's. Another diviner, then.

Dakk didn't release his grip on Cassia's arm. "No disrespect toward my grandmother will be tolerated."

"Of course not," Cassia replied. "You made that very clear during our friendly chats in the Sun Market."

His aura felt stronger to her. She had managed to get under his skin.

Cassia gave the elder a curtsy. "He speaks highly of you, Grandmother. It is clear he appreciates what great shoes he has to fill."

The elder lifted an eyebrow at Dakk. In someone less powerful and dangerous, Cassia might have read it as amusement. But this was the mage about to put her mind back on the potter's wheel. It was hard to appreciate the woman's sense of humor.

"Sit," she said.

Cassia took the chair nearest the window. Dakk stood over her with his hand on her arm. If she tried anything, she knew he could pull her through a spirit tear to anywhere he pleased. She would have to choose wisely when to make her move.

His grandmother turned to him and spoke in their tongue. Many of the sounds reminded Cassia of the names Btana Ayal and Rezayal. Had they preserved the dead city's tongue as a living language? She put on a blank expression and pretended she couldn't understand.

"She is braver than I expected," his grandmother said.

It was really a shame she was about to interrogate Cassia. Under other circumstances, Cassia might have respected a woman like this.

"She has no shortage of courage, to be sure," Dakk replied. "But feel how dangerous the Master of Dreams has made her. You can sense it, can't you, grandmother?"

"I sense that the scars of necromancy run deep in her."

Cassia didn't have to feign it this time, when her fear reared its head.

His grandmother studied her. "I also sense that she is powerful, although she doesn't know quite what to do with it yet."

Anxiety clutched between Cassia's shoulder blades. Would the elder find out about the ancestors' gifts before Cassia even discovered how to use them?

"I have tried not to underestimate her skill," Dakk said. "She has shown herself to be a cunning schemer."

Oh, yes. Scheming was Cassia's specialty. A scheme with the ancestors might be the one she was proudest of.

Her mother was proud of her.

Dakk hung his head. "I made the mistake of underestimating her sister. I hope I have sufficiently atoned for that error over the last five years. I will not allow this one to cause the same damage."

A thrill traveled through Cassia. Solia had given him so much trouble, he had been paying for it ever since. Now it was Cassia's turn.

His grandmother shook her head at him. "The damage is already done, and none of it by her."

Dakk fell silent, his magic shaking.

His grandmother spoke to Cassia in Tradewinds. "What is your name, child?"

"Newgift Cassia, soon to be Cassia Komnena."

Dakk looked as if he wanted to protest her assertion, but he didn't interrupt his grandmother.

The elder looked into Cassia's eyes with a gaze she recognized. It reminded her of Annassa Soteira. A mind healer could look at you in a way that made you feel it would be shameful not to tell the truth, that you were safe, and there was no need to lie.

That was fine. Cassia had nothing to say but the truth.

"Why did you come here?" the elder asked.

"To find my sister."

"Why do you want to find her?"

"I love her."

"What are the two of you planning?"

"I haven't seen her in fifteen years. I don't know what she's planning. But I will give her the opportunity to choose her own destiny, just as I have."

"You believe you have a destiny?"

"Yes. To go home to Orthros and plant some flowers in my new greenhouses. I've already given up a throne, defeated an Old Master, and crossed the Maaqul for the privilege. Don't imagine you can stop me."

"You see what a compelling liar she is," Dakk said.

His grandmother's face was unreadable. "You have indeed underestimated how dangerous she is."

They had. Cassia could feel the force inside herself. The sense of rightness.

She had watched people use magic. Listened to them talk about it. Surely she would be able to discover it for herself. It should come to her naturally, especially because she was in danger.

She focused her Will.

It wasn't a push. It was a release. She let it up out of her.

Heat flared in her chest and forehead. Her lips tingled, and her ears rang. A current ran down her spine and through her fingertips.

The magic took hold of her, changed her, and set her free.

The world was so much bigger. Colors looked different. She dragged air through narrow passages into her vast chest. She stretched.

Feathers brushed the back of the chair, and she felt it all the way to her shoulders.

She flexed her feet. Claws bit into the seat. Her claws. So satisfying.

She let out a screech and beat her wings.

With ungainly flaps, she made it over to the window and clawed at the carpet covering it.

Dakk was shouting, racing after her. She heard a lithic dagger fly toward her through the air.

The carpet came open. The blade landed uselessly in the fabric. Cassia tumbled out of the window and into free fall over the city.

The sunny sky spun overhead. The moonlit city below hurtled toward her.

I am the hawk.

Cassia spread her wings.

It was like the magic. Instinct. Air caught beneath her pinions and carried her aloft. She let out an exultant cry, and the voice of her lineage was heard in Btana Ayal once again.

This was so much more than flying with Monsoon. She had never felt so free.

The world lay at her feet. She could go anywhere.

The arrow seemed to come out of nowhere. She realized how to dive just in time and dropped below it, but it ruffled the feathers of her tail.

She spotted her attackers below. Robed archers spilled out onto the tops of towers and ramparts.

She screamed again and flapped hard, hoping to climb out of their range. But it took her too long to find an updraft. The arrows were moving too fast.

She dove to one side and managed to narrowly evade the batch of arrows. She could hear the Rezayal below shouting orders at each other. Heeding the warnings of where they would fire next, she tried her best to maneuver on her new wings. Life and death were fast teachers.

The next bevy of arrows flew higher, and she felt magic crackling in the air. She tried angling herself to fly between the missiles.

She lost her grip on the air, wobbled. An arrow clipped her wing. She shrieked her vengeance at them and tried to climb again.

Magic throbbed in the wound and through her strange new body. There was more magic inside her.

She had used the first mage's and the Silvicultrix's gifts. What had her mother given her?

Suddenly a powerful gust of wind knocked her off course. She turned her keen sight below again. She couldn't spot the source of the wind at first. But then she got a glimpse. A Rezayal without a bow was standing in one of the abandoned courtyards. That must be a wind mage.

Cassia gave into the flow of magic inside her.

It reached down, down through the air that carried her. She felt suddenly as aware of the ground as she was the sky.

She felt every stem and root of the thorn bushes that waited in the ruins. She Willed her magic into them.

There came a human scream. The wind mage twisted away from the spiny branches trying to consume him.

Her mother had given her the plant magic she had always longed for.

Cassia poured her soul into the soil of Btana Ayal. Thorn bushes shot from the sand and climbed the ancient walls, twisting around the towers, yanking bows from the archers' hands.

She flew over Shattered Hope, leaving thickets of devastation in her wake.

The outer walls came into sight. Beyond them, the desert and the sky.

She flew over the boundary of Btana Ayal. She was free.

She gave her wings a hard push, and a powerful current of air drove her forward with astonishing speed. She soared over the desert, spinning and diving a few times for the sheer joy of it.

This power would not follow her out of the range of the shattered gate. A yearning filled her. Would she ever know this feeling again?

The Silvicultrix had promised. *The power will come forth in you.*

Cassia must leave this place. She had to do the one thing her mother had asked of her. Build the future.

She flew hard, and the city receded behind her.

She heard no pursuers behind. There was no one but her and the presences that filled the desert, the souls who had come before.

She soared for hours over the desert. From here, it was beautiful. The open sky seemed to heal her, and the dry earth seemed to sate her thirst.

But the currents of power inside her faded as she went farther and farther. If hawks could weep, she would have shed tears.

She paid careful attention to the change inside her. She would surely lose this shape when she went too far from the city. She began to fly lower and lower.

The boundary hit her like a wall. She careened in the sky, and suddenly she was a tangle of arms and legs, not wings. She shouted with a human voice.

She landed hard on the top of a dune and rolled. With the wind knocked out of her, she couldn't even move to catch herself. The sand was cold on her naked skin. Grit filled her mouth and burned her hand like fire.

At last the world was still. She lay there, dragging at the air. She scraped a hand over her eyes and looked around.

At the sandals of one of the Empress's Golden shield.

Cassia's human heart seized in her chest. She looked up, up the woman's gleaming armor into her metal face.

And then the woman reached down and wrapped her in a blanket, lifting her as gently as if she were a child. She stood there holding Cassia, her frozen gaze never looking away.

A long moment later, her comrades rode over a dune, speaking in a language Cassia couldn't understand. Their golden horses circled round. The woman lifted her onto a horse, then mounted behind her.

Where were they taking her? Cassia fought for awareness, but the magic had drained from her, leaving behind exhaustion, thirst and Craving. With her face against a golden breastplate and the motion of the horse under her, she lost consciousness.

FINAL TEST

LIO FELT THE MOMENT when Cassia came within his reach again.
The activities of the Empress's court seemed to halt. The whole world seemed to disappear, except for the light of Cassia waxing by the moment.

Every instinct within him strained to step to her.

Mak took a step toward the doors, before Lyros put a hand on his shoulder to stay him.

"Ambassador Deukalion."

The Empress's voice summoned his awareness to her. Her tone was gentle.

"You look as if you have seen a goddess," she said.

"I have felt her, Your Imperial Majesty. Cassia is no longer in the disruption."

"You wish to go to her."

"I need to, more than anything."

His Trial brothers watched the exchange in tense silence.

"Do you doubt those I have sent to retrieve her?" the Empress asked.

To doubt the Golden Shield was to doubt the throne's protection and the Empress herself.

If this was the final test she posed him, he would not fail it. Not now, when he had come so far.

Cassia needed this from him. When this was over, they would need the Empress's trust in order to secure Solia's release.

"No, Your Imperial Majesty," Lio said. "I gratefully await Cassia's rescue."

The Empress gave a gracious nod.

Lio did one of the hardest things he had ever done. He waited while someone else brought his Grace to him.

"Your Ritual separation won't be any trouble for you after this," Mak said.

Lyros shook his head. "Who knew diplomacy could be such good training for that?"

His Trial brothers' support was all that had kept Lio sane while he waited for the Empress's agents to bring Cassia home. The ceaseless court audiences over the past nights had been exhausting. Lio reminded himself that every interminable conversation and careful negotiation was one step closer to Cassia's return. Each one was a move in their battle to rescue Solia.

Because that was how he slew monsters for Cassia. With patience and wisdom, with words and promises.

He secured the Empress's favor for them by standing still beside the throne.

There came a blast of magic on the other side of the doors. A powerful mage's traversal.

And then Cassia's aura filled the palace. His Grace. So close. She was here. She was alive. How could her aura feel so faint when she was so close?

The doors flew open and thundered against the walls. The crowd parted for a single Golden Shield.

She strode toward the throne with Cassia in her arms.

His Grace was in a faint, her heartbeat erratic. He could smell her blood somewhere under the blanket that covered her.

Lio's hands coiled into fists behind his back, and his power crested with his fury.

Whatever they had done to her, he would get Cassia justice, if it took him the rest of eternity.

Justice enacted via excruciating, crafted diplomatic maneuvers could be satisfying. Slow, yes. But he had all the time in the world. He had found his patience and his purpose in the slight figure who was now borne to him in another's arms.

The Golden Shield did not speak. She did not need to. She held Cassia before the entire court and let them see for themselves the results of the Rezayal's conspiracy.

Tendeso broke the silence. "For this, they have poisoned our lands. For this senseless cruelty against one innocent woman."

"My own physician will attend her," the Empress promised.

The Golden Shield lowered her head to the Empress over Cassia's limp form.

"Thank you, Your Imperial Majesty." Lio bowed deeply.

"Now be restored to your intended."

Released by her words, he closed the distance between himself and the Golden Shield. He held out his arms.

Her head lifted. Her voice echoed out of her mask. "She suffers this because of you?"

"Not a moment longer." He touched a hand to Cassia's forehead.

Her skin was drawn and clammy. Her breath rattled in her chest. Goddess, she felt so empty inside, as if only an echo of her spirit still haunted her body. An echo that cried out for him.

He felt for the mind ward, pulsing with the faint imprint of her heartbeat.

Their Union unfurled, and this time he was ready for the pull on his magic. He let his power feed her carefully.

Her chest rose and fell, and her eyes fluttered open. "Lio."

"I'm here."

At last, the Golden Shield placed Cassia in his embrace.

Lio held her to him as gently as he could, burying his face in her dusty hair. A sob caught in his throat. "I'm here."

Whatever she had endured, whatever she needed now to recover from it, he would be with her every step of the way.

52

days until

NOTIAN WINTER SOLSTICE

5 Ourania, 1597 IS

ARCANE MYSTERY

CASSIA DRIFTED IN AND out of awareness. A jumble of voices greeted her each time.

"Alma?"

Her mother didn't answer. The voices were not the ancestors, but they were kind. No threats from the shadows.

"You're safe, Cassia."

There. Lio's voice. Like the bells of Orthros, telling her she was home.

But unfamiliar magic rose and fell around her, rippling through her. She shied from it, trying to push it away.

"Easy there, trainee. Don't bruise the healers." Was that Mak?

"They're here to help." Lyros was here too.

"It's all right." Lio again. His hands held hers.

She didn't want any more magic, except his.

"There's plenty more where that came from." So much affection in his voice.

Then his power slipped through her, sweet and soft. She slept.

She woke to the sureness of Lio's arms around her. Everything was quiet. She opened her eyes and gazed up at her Grace's face.

He caressed her forehead. "We really must break this habit of you getting carried off."

She sniffed, not caring if she wept. "Lio."

He kissed her eyelids, then her tear-stained cheeks. "Shhh, we're together now. All is well."

Her Grace. Everything within her rose and attuned to him, bringing them into rhythm again. But reaching for him with her senses, she realized.

She was so empty. The magic was gone.

She clung to him, unable to find words to explain her sense of loss. She wanted to feel him with her magic. To know him with that ephemeral awareness. She wanted to be fully alive, with him, as she had in those moments when magic had flowed through her and she had spread her wings.

He rocked her in his arms. "Everything will be all right, my rose."

Then his magic breathed into her, and she gasped, so full of her Grace that there was no room for grief.

A whine reminded her of the world around them. She reached toward the warm, furry body that lay on her other side. Knight snuggled closer to her.

"Is he all right?" Her throat was so sore.

"Keeping vigil at your side has left him much improved." Lio reached out of her vision.

Cassia realized she was wearing a silk night robe, and she lay in a soft bed with a gauzy canopy. When Lio leaned close again, he held a golden cup to her lips. The lemon water soothed her throat.

When she was finished drinking, he set it aside and held her again. He was stretched out next to her in full formal robes, a sapphire glittering at his earlobe, his beard trimmed but hair tousled. He must have stepped right out of a diplomatic event to keep vigil at her side.

His power was a steady hum connecting them. "I almost lost you. Again."

"I promised you eternity. I couldn't break my word and die in the desert." She put a hand to his chest and touched his medallion. "But I had help."

"Do you want to talk about what happened?"

She thought back to everything. Btana Ayal. Her mother. "I have so much to tell you."

"The healers assured me they have restored you physically." Lio's eyes were full of pain, his question gentle. "But did the Rezayal hurt your mind?"

"Our ward held."

"They tried to break it?" His voice was gravelly with anguish.

"He didn't succeed."

"He? The man who captured you?"

She looked away. "It was Dakk."

"The university student who befriended you on Marijani?" Lio sounded as shocked as she had been.

I'm such a fool, came a version of her voice in her mind. *I haven't humiliated myself like this in a long time. It was a child's mistake, to let someone win my trust so easily. To open myself to such betrayal. I should have known better. I learned that lesson long ago in the Tenebran court.*

She silenced that voice of shame. She was done blaming herself for the harm others had done to her. The king's cruelty to her was not her fault. Dakk's abuse of her mind was not her fault.

That was the only lesson she need remember from her life in Tenebra.

"That's right, Cassia," said her mind mage. "And if you ever need a reminder, I will be here to give it to you."

"I admit, I'm in need of some reassurance." Although her breath hitched, she pressed on. She had to know. "I'm still not entirely sure what he tried. I wasn't conscious for much of it. I need you to check for me. You'll be able to tell if he…"

His hand stroked her hair steadily. When he spoke again, his tone was so calm and strong for her. "Yes, Cassia, I can examine you and find out exactly what happened. Are you sure you feel comfortable with thelemancy right now?"

"Yes. Having your magic in my mind was all that kept me sane. Don't hold anything back."

His magic brushed into her mind and rested lightly upon the ward, reassuring her he was here.

The relief of it brought another rush of tears to her eyes. "Come closer."

His power blanketed her, and she felt the chaste caresses of his magic upon her every battered thought. He was there in every twist and turn of the ward, checking its integrity, strengthening it with careful flashes of power. Lio's anger at Dakk was like a storm rumbling in the distance, ready to strike someone far away, while all she felt was the gentle rain of his magic.

The brush of his finger at her temple brought her back to awareness. He was blinking away tears. "He didn't steal one precious thought from your mind or so much as bruise your Will. But I can tell how painful it was for you while he tried."

"There's no sign that…anyone else has tampered with me, either?"

"Who?" he demanded. "Who else threatened you?"

She didn't want to give those fears credence by saying them aloud, but she confessed them to Lio. "If the Old Master had ever done to me what he did to Eudias, you would know, wouldn't you?"

"What? Cassia, what would even make you think of such a thing?"

"Dakk thinks I'm possessed. And I didn't want to believe him, but… it was hard to know what to believe in that place."

Lio framed her face in his hands. His dark blue gaze held hers as his magic twined further into her thoughts. "There is no one in your mind but you and me, my Grace. Dakk may boast of the Rezayal's research and theory, but he has never fought the Collector in a battle for someone's soul. I have. I can say with absolute certainty that you are as free and perfect as the Goddess intends for you to be." His expression softened. "In all your life, the only person who has ever left a mark on your mind is me. A privilege I'll treasure for eternity."

She wrapped her arms around him and held him, wordless with relief. The specters of her fears fled, banished by Lio, as always.

He rested his forehead on hers. "I'm so sorry for what you faced. Alone."

"I wasn't alone." She swallowed, then drew a deep breath. "Lio, the place the Rezayal held me prisoner was an ancient city…the ruins of one. They called it Btana Ayal. Shattered Hope."

His brows knit together, and he repeated the words to himself. "That's not any language I recognize. I've never read anything in the history books about such a civilization in the Maaqul desert."

"It existed in the Hulaic Epochs."

"Goddess bless. No wonder none of us could identify the ruins."

"It's a spirit gate, Lio. A massive, shattered gate that once connected this continent and the shadowlands. The queen of the city was a diviner who collapsed the portal to stop the Old Masters."

His lips parted, his eyes wide. "That…there's no historical record of that. It's a completely unknown discovery. This…Cassia, it will change everything we have understood about the entire world's past."

She nodded. "The phases are torn…or connected there, somehow. Everyone's ancestors can speak. Even mine. I wasn't alone, because they saved me." It sounded so impossible, saying it aloud, but she knew Lio would understand, would cherish this arcane mystery with her. "I met my mother."

Awe hushed his tone. "You spoke to Thalia?"

"I held her. I held my mother for the first time in my life."

Lio wrapped his arms around her again, pressing her to him to still the emotions that shook through her.

"Sometime," he murmured, "when your mind is not so weary, I would like to meet her."

"I want you to. I'll show you everything that happened in my thoughts, and it will be as if we were there together."

"You will never face that place without me again. And we'll remember her together."

"Oh, Lio, she wasn't a handmaiden of Hedon at all. She was a powerful mage of Kyria."

He pulled back and stared at her. "Garden magic."

"And beast magic…" Her hand tangled in Knight's fur. "…and soothsaying."

His lips parted, his beautiful face frozen in utter wonder. "The triune affinity?"

She wanted to kiss him, simply because he was her magic-loving scroll-worm who actually knew what she was talking about. "They gave me their magic. I couldn't take it with me beyond the gate. But for a little while, I had it, Lio. I had *my* magic. I can scarcely find the words to explain what it feels like…"

He pressed a palm to her heart. "I understand."

He did. He knew better than anyone, this gentle soul who carried two world-shattering affinities inside of him.

"You're a Silvicultrix," he breathed. "Cassia, it makes perfect sense. That's your mystery magic. Hesperine affinity readings wouldn't be able to detect ancient Lustra magic." The most stunning smile spread across his face, and he laughed. "My Grace, my theory that you have two affinities has been soundly disproved. You are going to manifest three."

She did kiss him then. Her Lio, who had just found out how truly powerful she might become, and looked as if he had been given a marvelous present by the universe.

"My Hesperine," she murmured against his mouth, "I do believe you like this idea."

"I was raised in Orthros. I have a proper appreciation for powerful females." He ran a hand down her body, tracing her form as if she were the most exquisite wonder he had ever touched, and a thrill swept through her senses.

"I had no idea you find power so attractive."

He raised a brow. "Didn't you? From the first night we met, I was enticed by your power. Now you'll have magic to match the rest of it."

"And my magic will be even stronger when I'm a Hesperine, won't it?"

"Of course, but thank the Goddess we delayed your Gifting. I never thought I'd say that, but I must acknowledge it was for the best for more reasons than we realized. We were prepared for any usual affinity you might manifest during the transformation, but not a mystery like Lustra magic. We don't fully understand what it can do or how it interacts with blood magic."

"You think it would have made my Gifting more difficult?"

"Dangerous, even. But there's no need to worry now. We have time to do plenty of research and learn everything we need to understand about your magic. Hespera knew what she was up to, slowing down our plan. You'll have your meeting with her yet, and it will be all the sweeter because you'll bring your own power with you for the occasion."

The power will come forth in you.

The hawk had promised her. And Lio believed it. She would have her magic again. And this time, she would get to keep it. Forever.

"How did you escape from the Rezayal?" Lio traced a slow circle over her hip. "You had to master your power so quickly. But perhaps Lustra magic is more intuitive than formal spell casting. And you would have benefited from manifestation resonance—that's the particular pattern magic has when it first wakes up in a person, you see. It makes acts of Will easier."

"Oh. Yes, that does make sense. I didn't have to try. I simply...let it out."

"Yes," he said, "I understand that too."

"It changed me. I *became* the hawk. I flew away from the city on my ancestor's wings."

He went quiet, running his hand down her arm, which had been a wing. He turned over her palm, tracing the line there, where she had drawn blood for many Hesperine spells. Now she carried a scar where an arrow had clipped her over Btana Ayal.

He kissed the scar. "You flew back to me."

"I always will, my Grace."

"And I will always help you fly as high as you can."

"I know. I was trapped with no way to use their power until your audience with the Empress. Thanks to everything you set in motion, Dakk took me out of my cell, so I was able to get away."

"How did you use your soothsaying?"

"I was able to understand what he and his grandmother were saying. I have so much information for us. Then, when I was flying away, I…" A smile came to her face. "I got to use my plant magic to awaken the thorn bushes growing in the ruins. The Rezayal will be pulling prickles out of themselves for days."

"Even our peaceful Hespera would heartily approve of such a use of her sacred plants."

"I'm so glad her thorns were the first plants I ever used magic on. They held back the archers and wind mage while I escaped the city."

He kept hold of her hand. "Letting someone else bring you back was the hardest thing I've ever had to do. But it took the Empress's power to get you to safety."

Her apprehension returned at the thought of the soldiers who had found her. "How did the Golden Shield know where I was?"

"The Chief Diviner of the High Court was in possession of a lithic dagger and knew the location in the Maaqul where the Rezayal were holding you captive. She betrayed them to the Empress to save herself and opened a spirit tear for the Golden Shield."

"They found Btana Ayal?"

Lio's mouth tensed. "The Chief Diviner claims the location is all she knew. When the Golden Shield arrived, it was as if there was nothing there."

"The city must be hidden by magic."

Lio nodded. "The Golden Shield were patrolling what appeared to be empty desert, searching for you, when you appeared out of nowhere."

"They didn't find the Rezayal? Dakk is still in the wind?"

Lio's fangs lengthened. "For now. But I promise you, my Grace, you will have the opportunity to introduce me to your friend from the Sun Market."

"Are we safe from him here?"

"You are safe everywhere in the Empire. The Empress has made the Rezayal her enemy and you her friend."

"I'm not under house arrest?"

"Certainly not. The Empress herself has exonerated you."

A tremendous weight lifted from her. "What a triumph, Sir Diplomat."

"I would never have been able to do any of it if I hadn't followed your advice." He brought her hand to his lips again. "Cassia, I'm so sorry we quarreled over my ridiculous idea to resign. After you were taken, I agonized over every word I said to you."

"It wasn't ridiculous. It was an important struggle for you and shouldn't be dismissed."

"It was the wrong decision, though, just as you said. I hope what I've done has made you proud."

She frowned, shaking her head. "Make me proud? I could burst with pride every moment I get to breathe the air around you. How could you think otherwise?"

He caressed her fingers between his, not meeting her gaze. "Everything you said about Hesperine principles was true. I'm ashamed you had to remind me."

"Oh, Lio. No. You thought I disapproved of your decision?"

"With good reason."

"I could never be disappointed in you. There's no one in the world I admire more. Whatever emotions you sensed in me that night, that is not what they meant."

"You were shocked. Hurt. And so passionately in disagreement with the entire notion."

"Because you didn't *tell me*. You didn't let me support you while you tried to make such a difficult decision." She stroked his chest, smoothing his cords. "I admit, I'm still not sure I understand why you wouldn't confide in me about it."

He stilled her hand over his medallion, holding her there over his heart. "I am your protector. I didn't want you to feel for a moment that my ability to keep you safe was in question. I was trying to be strong for you."

"You are strong for me in countless ways every night. One of those ways is how you listen whenever I'm struggling. Let me be strong for you, too."

"My Grace." He sighed and rested his head on her shoulder. "I will confide in you from now on."

"I will be a better confidant. I will listen to how you feel, instead of allowing my feelings to influence my reaction. I'm sorry I questioned your decision, instead of listening and trying to understand."

"You understand now."

She twined her fingers in his. "Partners. No matter the distance between us. Always."

"Yes. But I will do everything in my power to make sure there is never such a distance between us again."

"You don't have to promise me we'll never be apart. Just promise we'll always make a way back to each other again."

"You have my Oath, Cassia. I will always come back to you, if you will always fly back to me."

Their words wound them closer, and she lay there with him in their Union. He was so bright next to her, his magic so deep and dark where he rested in her mind.

Her magic had left her…but perhaps it had left her changed.

"Lio," she whispered. "Cast a spell."

He lifted his head. "What do you sense?"

He already understood. "You feel different. I *can* feel you better than I could before. Your aura is more vivid somehow. There is more…detail… to your presence. You feel…oh…you feel so good…"

His magic brushed over her skin, making her gasp. And then it flowed into her chest, making her shudder at the power that trailed down through her body to pool between her legs.

His gaze slid down her body. His eyes were bloodshot, his fangs wild. She could feel his Craving fever on his skin, and she knew he had just stopped veiling his symptoms from her. The knowledge filled her with a deep satisfaction.

He hid nothing from her. He was already confiding in her and letting her bear his wounds, too.

"What shall we do for your Craving, my rose? I am at your command, but I do not wish to tire you."

"Just be gentle," she whispered.

"Are you certain you feel able to Feast?"

"I need you."

His fangs unsheathed further, and the sight made desire coil tighter inside her.

He lowered his mouth toward hers. "There's just one small—well, rather large problem."

She shook her head. "I promise I feel well enough." She needed those fangs inside her. Now.

"I'm not sure he approves." Lio pointed at Knight.

Cassia turned her head, and her nose bumped Knight's snout. He began licking her face. "Oh dear. I suppose it is difficult to reach me around this furry obstruction."

"I feel bad asking the poor fellow to lie on the floor."

"Hmm. Do you suppose the Empress could provide us with a dog bone?"

"There's an entire basket of gazelle tibia over there," he said with a grimace, "from Her Imperial Majesty's royal game."

Cassia rubbed Knight's ears with both hands while he draped his tail and one paw over her. "Thank you, darling. I'm so very glad we're together again, too. But wouldn't you like to go sample some of those fancy bones?"

He didn't budge.

"I don't think bones seem important to him at the moment," Lio observed.

Knight turned and began licking his face, too.

Cassia laughed. "You two are closer because of your time together, I see."

"We kept each other company while we missed you. It's a very important bond of gratitude. No wonder he likes Hesperines, though. You talked him into it—a precursor to your beast magic, I expect."

I could train any creature, her mother had said. "You think I can make use of that even now, although my own magic hasn't manifested yet?"

"Yes, sleeping affinities usually grant some level of innate ability, and your brief experience with the magic of the ancestors most likely strengthened that."

"You said it's intuitive. An act of Will." She envisioned in her mind what she wanted Knight to do, strengthening the thought with her Will. "Knight, darling," she tried, "I'm hungry, and only Lio can remedy that, so you must give him some room. Do you suppose you could guard us from the foot of the bed instead?"

With a disgruntled whine, he hesitated. But then he wallowed down to the foot of the bed.

"Your magic is going to be very useful, my rose. Especially in bed." The fragrance of Lio's cleaning spell puffed across Cassia's face and the suddenly fur-free sheets.

"Moving the dog out of the way is not all I'd like to use it for. That is, if you would like me to."

"I fantasize about you using magic on me in bed. Now I know which affinities to imagine."

The possibilities sent a flush of heat across her skin. Could soothsaying enhance words of seduction? "I love how your magic feels. I want to give you that in return."

"You will. But right now, let me give to you."

He sat back, and silk rustled as he began to disrobe. She watched the spectacle, too exhausted to move, too bewitched by the sight of his lithe, sensual body emerging from those layers of formality.

The shape of his strong shoulders and slender waist, hugged by black silk. His pale skin and the new contours of muscle he had built on their rugged journey. His long runner's legs and narrow hips. He stripped away his underlinens, and she was reminded just how blessed she was to be a bloodborn's Grace. His height was not the only extraordinary endowment the Goddess had given him.

"I don't want anything between us," he told her.

"Undress me," she invited.

She let him levitate her to pull off her night robe. She sank back down into the soft bed, and he settled over her wearing nothing but her Grace braid and his medallion.

She caught the silver disk in her hand as his mouth met hers. At last, he gave her the kiss she had been tasting, all smooth tongue and sharp fangs and the flavor of him.

His weight on her was so light that she knew he was levitating. He slid his hand along the inside of her thigh. Her Craving survival instincts roared to life, more powerful than any weariness. Her body knew what she needed. When he palmed her between her legs, she arched her hips, rubbing into his touch despite the tremble in her limbs.

But she turned her head away. "I'm not too weak to bite you."

"Just hearing you say that makes me hungrier."

"I don't want to move. I want you just like this." She raked her mouth over his again, her lips chapped against his soft ones. "But I suppose we must..."

She trailed off, forgetting her words as his finger swirled over her kalux. If he kept on like this, she would climax so fast that she would forget it was wrong to sink her teeth into him.

"This is what you want?" He pressed his thigh against hers, parting her, his weight reassuring.

"Yes." She canted her hips to enjoy the pressure of his finger stroking inside her. "But we shouldn't..."

His hand withdrew, and his warm, damp fingers pressed her other knee down to the bed. "I want this too. I want to look into your eyes while you take me as deep in your body as I am in your mind. Will you look at me, Cassia?"

She gave him what he wanted, what she needed, too. She didn't look away as the tip of his rhabdos nudged the wet lips of her krana.

He slid inside her oh, so gently, so slowly that she whimpered. He joined them by measures, parting her a little more with each stroke. She lay there and let him fill her up, sealing their Union over all the wounds of being apart.

Deeper, deeper, until she was stretched and so full of him she could hold no more. But he gave her more. He braced himself on his arms and shifted his weight. The pressure was divine, chasing straight through her and burrowing her deeper into the soft mattress.

His magic pulsed where their bodies joined, and she clutched her krana around his shaft, crying out. A soft climax rolled through her.

He watched her with hooded eyes, holding perfectly still while her body shivered under him. "My Grace," he said, his voice husky, "I do believe you were hungry."

The release left her limp and needy. She shifted in the soft bedclothes, her toes curling at the hardness of his length inside her. "I'm still so hungry."

He lowered himself closer.

"I'm going to bite you." She wasn't sure if it was a warning, a challenge, or a plea.

"I've been working on a solution to that problem."

"You have?" She gasped as he flexed his hips. Goddess, he was so deep.

"Do you like my new earring?" he asked.

She blinked up at him, trying to remember how to speak. The sapphire, in a setting of silver thorns, glittered at her while pleasure made her see stars. "It's unfairly handsome on you."

Her gorgeous Hesperine gave her a wolfish grin and flexed his hips again. "Lyros made it for us."

"What?" That was the darkness in its gleam, teasing her senses, somewhere beyond the rhythm that was shredding her thoughts into nothing. "It's...warded?"

Lio leaned down even closer to her, bringing the pale column of his neck nearer. His mouth brushed her ear, his voice low. "The ward is just strong enough to keep human teeth from breaking my skin. You can bite me anywhere you like."

"Can you"—she licked her lips—"feel my teeth through it?"

"Oh, yes."

Her heart thundered, her mouth watered, and she gave into the overpowering instinct to bite his throat. Bleeding thorns, it felt so good, so right.

She heard him swearing, heard the scrape of his nails in the sheets. His whole body was taught with restraint as he covered her, cradling her beneath him.

She fastened her teeth on him and sucked. She felt his rough groan. His hand tangled in her hair, tilting her head to bare her throat.

He warmed her skin with a kiss. *I'll be gentle.*

She clutched at his medallion, pulling him closer still.

His fangs pierced her with a tenderness that brought tears to her eyes. His bite gave her more pressure, drawing out a flood of pleasure. He took slow sips from her vein, swiveling his hips.

They rocked together, locked on each other's throats, tangled in each other's bodies and minds. Every motion seemed to coax more power out of him, down into her body, where her hunger waited.

Yes, she sighed. *Give me more.*

I'm not giving. He sounded exhilarated, almost drugged. *You're taking.*

She pulled her mouth off of him with a gasp. She was doing this? Pulling his magic from inside him? *Is that...all right with you?*

Feast on me, my Grace.

A sense of power came over her. Half on instinct, half with effort, she reached with her inner senses. More, she Willed. She wanted more.

His magic pounded into her in a rush, and they both cried out, arching together off the bed. Under her skin, warmth bloomed into heat between her eyes, over her heart, between her legs. The rhythm of his magic and their bodies pulsed there, a triple beat.

How gentle—do you need me—to be? he gritted in her thoughts.

Just love me. She feathered bites along his shoulder. *Just relax and give yourself to me.*

His hands closed around her knees, spreading her legs wider. He pulled back, then pounded home, riding the surge of magic she dragged into her.

It gives you pleasure, too, she realized. *To feel your magic leaving your body.*

I never imagined this. Can't explain it. It's glorious. Take more.

It was easier every time. Her inner senses knew what to do. With that hidden place inside her, where she had wielded magic, she took another long draught of him.

His power spread, an erotic heat pumping through her heart and pooling between her hipbones. Energy and pleasure in a single current, every crest making her body arch beneath him. He drove deep into her every move, riding the ebb and flow with her.

My magic does as you Will. He shuddered, his body rigid with effort.

She could sense him on the brink. She could pull him over the edge with a mere tug, bring him to completion, send him spilling magic and his pleasure into her.

But she wasn't ready for this to end. She eased off, taking only sips of his magic. He drew a ragged breath, his thrusts falling into the rhythm of her draughts. It was perfect, the matching pulses of his magic and his body.

He nuzzled her face, then lowered his mouth to her neck once again. His beard rasped over her skin. He nipped her throat, asking. She gave his medallion another pull and urged him on.

He sank his fangs into her again. She bit his shoulder, hard. Not enough. There, his throat. Yes. *Yes.*

She bit down, and the muscles in his back bunched. Her loins quivered, and her jaw clenched.

Yes, just like this, in perfect Union.

She tapped the current of his magic once more and released him.

His power shattered into her. She couldn't see past the nova of magic in her mind's eye, but she felt him break in her arms. Heard his primal sound of ecstasy in her ear. He glimmered in her every nerve, an abundant shadow feeding the insatiable hunger within her.

But at last, she was sated.

Nourished and split apart, she lay trembling under him and trailed a hand down his tranquil body. She had Willed his control into nothing. She had given him this ease.

He seemed to come to his senses, for he sealed his bite. Then he rested his head on her chest, his blood-painted lips leaving a trail across her collarbone. "You're still an arcane mystery, my rose."

"Do you suppose we can learn to understand me together?"

"Oh, yes. Because I'm your mind mage—and you're *my* arcane mystery."

51

days until

NOTIAN WINTER SOLSTICE

6 Ourania, 1597 IS

MEDALLION OF OFFICE

"I WANT YOU TO STAY beside me," Cassia grumbled.

"The healers will be by to check on you soon," Lio replied, "they will not be pleased to find a Hesperine obstacle between them and their patient."

"A tall, handsome Hesperine obstacle." Cassia sighed.

No one had disturbed them since she had come to last night. She could have done with another night of making each other forget their ordeals before having to face the world.

Lio smiled as he straightened the bedclothes. He had already worked a cleaning spell on them and dressed. The sorcerer who had felled an army of heart hunters, the ambassador who had changed Tenebra, Orthros, and the Empire, the immortal who had taken her from the human world, now tucked the covers around her and fluffed her pillows with undivided attention.

"I love you, Lio."

"I love you, too." He gave her a soft kiss before sitting down in the chair beside her bed.

"You're recovering from the Craving, too," she protested. "You shouldn't have to sit in the chair."

"I'm still within reach." He took her hand.

She rested her cheek on their joined hands. "You're too far away."

"Alas, we must be appropriate. You're about to receive as many visitors as can make it past the gauntlet of the Empress's physician and the guards at every door and window."

Cassia eyed his formal silks. "Just what sort of visitors are we expecting?"

"You'll see."

Cassia glanced down at her veil hours robe, which he had retrieved from their travel trunks for her. "I feel underdressed."

"You, my rose, are recovering and exactly as you ought to be. Besides, your first visitors are Mak and Lyros."

Cassia grinned. "Somehow I don't think even the Empress's physician is much of an obstacle for the Stand."

Lio cocked his head toward a pair of wooden doors framed by the latticed windows. "They're arguing with your guard on the terrace as we speak."

"I would imagine an argument with the Golden Shield is more like a staring contest."

Lio got up and opened the doors. A verdant, spicy scent drifted in. Even at this predawn hour, the air was balmy.

Their Trial brothers joined them, filling the room with their Hesperine presences. They came in wearing full Stand regalia.

Cassia held out her arms, and Mak stepped to her side to give her a hug well worth crossing a desert for.

"We can't let you go anywhere," Mak huffed, sounding suspiciously close to tears. "If it isn't war mages and Gift Collectors, it's jinn and secret societies."

Lyros rested a hand on her shoulder. "And we won't let you go anywhere without us from now on. Either of you."

Mak tugged on the new silver-and-white silk cords belting his and Lyros's fighting robes. "The four of us are officially the new Hesperine embassy, whether you like it or not."

"Lio told me about your reassignment. I can't imagine anything better. We never should have left without you in the first place."

"But you were right," Lio said. "They had important things to do at home."

"Mak made an address before the Firstblood Circle." Lyros's voice glowed with pride. "You should have seen Hypatia's face."

"Oh, Mak, tell me everything."

Their Trial brothers pulled up a couple of chairs beside Lio. With their broad shoulders no longer blocking her view, Cassia noticed one of the

Golden Shield had slipped in with them and posted herself across the room from the bed.

The figure that had once terrified Cassia now reassured her. No matter how many of the Rezayal's agents might remain in the Imperial Palace, the Empress's elite guard wouldn't let them hurt Cassia. She wondered if this was one of the warriors who had carried her to safety from the desert, but it was impossible to tell.

Lio, Mak, and Lyros pulled veil spells around them, and she forgot the soldier was there while they all exchanged tales of what they had experienced. By the end, Mak was actually blushing at Lyros's boasting and Lio's enthusiasm for all he had accomplished.

"But what about your secret project with Nike?" Cassia asked at last. "Can you tell us about it yet?"

"It can wait," he said with a smile.

"Well, you and Nike will have time to work on it." Cassia smiled at him. "Your sister is home for good. Thanks to you."

"Mark my words, yours will be too, by the time we're done. But for that endeavor, there's something you'll need."

Lio, Mak, and Lyros stood and lined up beside her bed with an air of ceremony. She looked from one of them to the other. "What's going on?"

Mak smiled. "Father has something for you, and we have the great pleasure of delivering it."

Lio caressed her hair, his gaze full of emotion. "You shall have your ceremony before the Queens yet, but tonight, we are authorized to officiate in the field."

"On behalf of Hippolyta's Stand…" began Lyros.

Mak smiled. "…with the blessing of Blood Argyros…"

"…at the invitation of the Annassa and the Queens' Master Diplomat," Lio continued, "we hereby welcome you into the Diplomatic Service of Orthros."

Cassia's throat tightened. "I haven't lost my chance?"

"Let it be known in the Goddess's Sanctuary," Lyros declared.

"Let it be known in the lands of Tenebra and Cordium Abroad," Mak announced.

"Let it be known in the Empire of our allies." Lio's eyes gleamed with pride, his voice full of joy. "Henceforth, you are an official representative of the Queens of the Hesperines, empowered to negotiate for the protection of our people and the good of humankind."

A scroll appeared in Lyros's hands. He presented it to her, and as she unrolled it, a soft glow shone out.

Her name, her true name, was emblazoned at the top of the official decree: Ambassador Cassia Komnena. At the bottom, silver-and-white ribbons dangled from two glowing magical glyphs. One was the silver moonflower of the diplomatic service, the other a Rose of Hespera in the Queens' intertwined magic of white light and black shadow.

"Your cords." Mak unveiled the braid of silver, black, and white silk.

With great ceremony, he handed them to Lio. Her Grace held out his palm, and she felt the delicate brush of his veil spell pulling away. There in his hand was a diplomat's medallion of office, a match for his own.

He threaded her medallion onto her cords. Pricking his thumb, he sealed the ends of the silk into an unending ring with his blood.

Although she was sitting in a bed in her veil hours robe, the moment could not have meant more to her. As Lio leaned near, she bowed her head so he could place the cords around her neck.

"Congratulations, Ambassador Cassia." He pressed a kiss to her brow. "I am so proud to serve beside you."

Her medallion settled upon her chest, a comfortable weight that seemed to lift many other heavy burdens from her. A sense of accomplishment filled her, unlike anything she had once dared imagine for herself.

She pressed a hand to her medallion, her heart too full to hold it all. But she felt Lio in the mind ward, as close as her own thoughts, experiencing it all with her, giving her more room to feel.

She was holding in her hands a guarantee of diplomatic immunity and future success. But so much more.

She had not become the person Tenebra had molded her to be. She had defied all the king's judgments and decrees. She had become the Cassia she had chosen to be.

Hespera had already made her into her best self.

She held Lio's hand, beaming at him and their Trial brothers. "I am ready."

THE WAY FORWARD

MAK AND LYROS HAD brought a stash of mince pies and a travel coffee service from Orthros. The ceremony turned into a celebration, and the four of them got crumbs all over Cassia's lavish guest room. She carefully avoided getting any sticky fingerprints on her new medallion.

"You'll run out of handkerchiefs," Lyros predicted. "She's going to be polishing that every hour of the night."

Mak covered his eyes with one hand. "It's so shiny that it's blinding me."

Lio wiggled his fingers, and a light spell glared off her medallion. She laughed and waved it in front of their Trial brothers without remorse.

"Speaking of shiny things," Lyros interjected, "what do you think of Lio's new earring?"

She blushed terribly. "You have our eternal gratitude."

"It's a good thing you like it," Lyros said, "because I warded it onto his earlobe. I don't think even magefire could pry it off. Or adamas tongs. Or vigorous biting."

Cassia covered her face in her hands. "I'll never live this down, will I?"

Lio gave the sapphire a flick with his finger and winked at her.

It was so good to laugh with their Trial brothers. But she did feel rather sorry for the Golden Shield standing alone in the corner. They had offered her a cup of coffee and a pie, but she had declined with a silent shake of her head. Mak and Lyros had said they should not disturb her further, out of respect for the fact that she was on duty.

She had scarcely moved for an hour, but now her head turned toward the doors to the terrace.

At the same time, Lio cocked his head. "Ah, another visitor."

"He wouldn't be arriving on wing, would he?" Cassia asked hopefully.

"That's the one." Lio smiled.

A fist tapped on the door, and a familiar voice called, "Are you two decent? Or at least, less indecent than usual?"

Mak leaned back in his chair. "We pulled the turtle doves out of the love nest."

Lyros yawned at Mak. "I'm about ready to drag you to that love nest the Empress has given us next door."

Lio got up and went to let in Monsoon—no, Prince Tendeso.

Somehow the sight of him dressed like a royal did not surprise Cassia, and not only because Lio had told her about his identity. He carried his authority and dignity so naturally that she could scarcely believe she had ever mistaken him for a scoundrel.

He clasped Lio's forearm and spoke in Vulgus. "Oh good. I wanted to get here before you three passed out."

"You're up this early for us?" Lio asked in the same language.

"Don't flatter yourself. I haven't slept yet. Too much work to do." Tendeso crossed to Cassia's bedside. "You look well for someone the Maaqul ate and spat back out again."

"Greetings, Your Highness," she said. "Will you send the royal guard after me if I don't get out of bed to bow?"

Lio winced as he took his seat again. "Too soon."

"'Your Highness'?" Tendeso protested. "Really, Freckles? I thought I could count on you to give me a rest from all the formalities. Can't I get at least one good vulture insult?"

"No," Cassia informed him. "I don't use vulture insults on family."

He laughed and pulled up a chair, turning it around so he could lean his arms on the back. "I'm glad you're safe, *nyakimbi.*"

Mak gave him a salute. "You were rather helpful with that, for a vulture with meat breath."

"That's more like it," Tendeso replied. "I feel less royal already."

"You'll feel even less royal after our next sparring rematch," Lyros promised.

"Bring your best levitation moves, or I'll be disappointed. I haven't had this much aerial combat practice since Karege and I used to practice together."

Cassia glanced at his arm. How strange not to see his fortune blade there. "Are you all right?"

"My arm feels too light," he muttered. "All my fighting and flight moves seem unbalanced now."

That was probably the closest he would come to admitting how off balance such a change must leave his entire life. "The regalia suits you, though."

The prince before her gave her his cockiest mercenary grin. "It does."

"The night we met," Cassia said, "I saw the dust on your sandals. You had been walking through the poor neighborhoods in disguise, hadn't you?"

"Of course. I check the conditions of every part of the city when I visit." He glanced away. "Not that it's been very often."

"But your payments arrive regularly." Lio steepled his fingers. "A very big and important bird told me that's where all Tendeso's gold roster earnings go."

"I'm a prince. I don't need money. But our people do. The city has grown too rapidly in recent generations, placing a strain on the land and our resources. My brother works tirelessly to improve everyone's lives, but that takes coin."

"I believe I owe you an exorbitant amount of gold by now," Cassia said.

He shook his head. "Family doesn't pay."

"House Komnena would send resources for your people, even so."

"Oh, I know. My brother is highly satisfied with the gifts and trade agreements flowing between our court and Orthros since I took Lio home for a visit."

"Good." Cassia nodded. "What will you do now? Do you need to return home right away?"

"Actually, Anesu has requested that I remain at court for the time being to redress a number of matters affecting our state. We intend to work closely with our allies from Orthros."

Cassia looked from him to Lio. "This means we truly are joining forces to secure Solia's release."

"It does, my rose."

Tendeso's eagle eyes gleamed. "You think I'd let you rescue her without me?"

He had not surrendered after all. He was behind their cause, they had Mak and Lyros at their sides, and she and Lio both wore medallions now. It gave Cassia faith, too.

"We have the support of the rest of the delegation as well," Tendeso said.

"Plenty of friends who can throw a punch if needed." Mak hastened to add, "Not that I hope we'll need that during negotiations."

Lyros took his hand. "Your speeches will throw plenty of verbal punch, I suspect."

"The Ashes are staying to help?" Cassia asked.

"They'll be along anytime now," Tendeso replied. "I doubt our first bladelet will let the healers stop her."

"'First bladelet'?" Cassia smiled. "Chuma is here?"

When they heard her next visitors arrive on the terrace, Cassia braced herself for another argument with the guard, but the Golden Shield opened the doors for the Ashes without reluctance.

Chuma danced in, her mother strolling in behind her. "Cassia, I'm so happy to see you!"

"First facing off with the Golden Shield, now the Empress?" Cassia laughed.

Chuma wrinkled her nose. "And those annoying healers who said we had to limit your visitors."

"I should have known you're Ukocha's daughter."

Chuma hopped up on the bed with Cassia, while Ukocha took a chair. Cassia was surprised to see her still wearing a sling. Shouldn't the healers have finished repairing her injury by now?

Kella rode in and sat next to the bed on Tilili's back. Knight wagged his tail. His new feline friend showed him a bored expression, but began to purr. When Karege, Tuura, and Hoyefe joined them, Mak and Lyros had to step next door to their guest room and come back with more chairs.

Cassia found herself surrounded by family. "I confess, I wasn't quite ready for you all to adventure off on your next contract."

"The Ashes are with you." Kella looked toward Ukocha. "Our First Blade's leadership will guide us at court, as effectively as on the battlefield."

Ukocha did not answer right away. "Actually, I intend to spend some time at home."

"Of course." Karege picked another mince pie from Mak and Lyros's stash. "Enough of our salty company. Time to be home with Chuma and Mumba for a spell while you get rid of that sling."

"It will be some time before I don't need the sling." She paused. "A long time. In fact…" All expression left her face. "This arm won't be quite the same."

Their merry gathering turned to stunned silence.

Tuura gave Ukocha a questioning look, and the first blade nodded. The diviner explained, "The arrow pierced major veins, but also nerves. Ukocha had to cauterize it to save her life, but while that stopped the bleeding, it caused further damage to the nerves. Her arm will be mostly paralyzed for some time. With diligence and repeated spells from the healers, she can hopefully regain some motion."

The Ashes had never looked so angry. Cassia could see on their faces that they all wanted to charge back into the Maaqul and hunt down every last Rezayal until they found the one who had fired that arrow.

"I'll live," Ukocha reminded them, reaching across with her good arm to hold Chuma's hand.

"It will get better." Kella held her gaze. "And the next contract will be ready when you are."

"Thank you. I needed to hear that from you." Ukocha took a breath. "But I won't be taking any more contracts."

Kella's expression turned to steel, her gaze afire. "No, Ukocha. You don't stop fighting because of this. Remember what you told me."

Ukocha gave a nod. "I know."

"When I thought my dreams of fighting with the Ashes had ended as soon as they'd begun, you came into the healers' tent. You set this knife beside my bed." Kella put a hand to her fortune blade. "And you said the next contract would be ready when I was. It took me years to learn to fight with Tilili, but the contract was there, just like you promised."

"I'm not retiring because of my arm, Kella. You have my word. But

I won't deny nearly dying in those ruins made me think hard about my life. It's time for me to go home, because I made a promise to Mumba." Ukocha stroked Chuma's cheek. "The first one turned out so well. She's the best promise I ever made. The second one will make me happy, too."

"What promise?" Kella asked.

"When Mumba and I married, I promised him two things. We would have a child after the Battle of Souls, whether I won or lost. And I would retire once I was satisfied with how high I had climbed."

"You, satisfied?" Kella scoffed. "You're never satisfied. That's who you are. Always climbing higher."

Ukocha shook her head. "I found the top."

"You're capable of anything. How does someone like you even know where the top is?"

"It's the place where you realize something is more important to you than climbing onward: watching another go higher than you've ever been." Ukocha unbuckled her fortune blade and set it on her lap. "Ashes, you are no longer mine. You follow First Blade Kella now, and I look forward to seeing how far up she takes you."

Kella's eyes gleamed with tears, although not a drop fell. She saluted her mentor for what must be the last time. "You honor me, Ukocha."

"You have honored all of us with your many years of strength." Ukocha touched her motionless arm. "I will become strong again."

"You'd better."

"I have to. There's a tree I want to climb." She smiled at her daughter. "The view from the top is the best in the Empire."

"Say, Ukocha…" Karege's tone was too innocent. "You'll have time to learn all sorts of new things as you enjoy retirement. Even cooking."

She narrowed her eyes at him, but her gaze sparked with amusement. "If you weren't my longest-serving comrade and just as terrible a cook as I am, I'd singe your hide for the suggestion."

He grinned. "I know you'd never really do that to your fire-sensitive Hesperine friend."

"I might do it by accident, if I tried to learn to make food. Hmph. I may be taking off my blade, but that doesn't mean I've lost my fortune name."

"If you say so, Cookfire."

Judging by everyone's obvious efforts not to laugh, Karege was the only one who could get away with calling the great Ukocha by her fortune name.

"I remember the first time one of the Ashes decided to retire." Karege nodded sagely. "What was it you said? 'His grandbaby cooed at him, and all of a sudden he was ready to turn in his blade and sit in his village getting wrinkly.'" Karege leaned nearer Ukocha. "I think I see at least one new wrinkle since your earlier announcement."

"Shall we set a chair in the middle of the village for you?" Tuura asked.

Chuma put on a harassed expression. "Give me a few years before I'm expected to supply a cooing grandbaby."

"Ancestors," Ukocha said, "I am not ready for cooing. Or sitting still. Let me get used to the wrinkles first."

Everyone laughed, and fondness softened Ukocha's scarred face.

Kella looked around at the other Ashes, a challenge in her eyes. "Any more retirements tonight? I'm already three short."

"I'm too young to retire," Karege said.

Tuura shook her head. "I am not ready to go home and eat peanuts."

"Retire?" Hoyefe huffed. "Like fine wine, I only get better with age."

Kella blew a kiss to her comrades from the hilt of her fortune blade. "Glad you're all staying on. I've got plans. It will be a wild ride."

"Mmm," Hoyefe purred. "My favorite kind."

Karege laughed. "With you, Kella, it would have to be."

"Oh dear," said Tuura. "It sounds as if I'll need more poultice."

Ukocha chuckled. "I'll enjoy watching this. What will your blades do first under your command?"

"For now, we'll let the offers stack up," Kella replied.

"And gloat over the massive pile?" Cassia asked.

"Oh, yes," Kella said. "But we won't decide which to accept until we complete our current diplomatic battle. I'm busy trying to free my best friend from prison."

"I'm trying to find the words to say thank you," Cassia said.

"Deeds speak better." Kella smiled. "And we have seen yours."

By the time the Empress's physician interrupted their gathering, the Hesperines were beginning to yawn. Her entourage of healers, assistants, and servants scarcely fit in the room with so many visitors.

No amount of threats from the physician could have persuaded everyone to leave, but her concern for Cassia's healing did. Ukocha and the Ashes bade her good day, promising to return. Chuma and Karege were the last to go, and the first bladelet asked him riddles all the way out the doors to test how sleepy he was. The Golden Shield's metal face followed their every move as they crossed to the terrace doors and departed.

Tendeso moved aside with Mak and Lyros, but Cassia was glad to see he intended to remain. Once the healers had finished their spells, Lio was almost too sleepy to last through their report of her good health.

"I'm not ready for you to fall asleep yet," Cassia lamented.

He sighed. "Neither am I."

"Don't plan anything without us." Lyros tugged Mak toward the doors.

"Never again," Cassia promised.

"Sorry." Mak yawned on their way out. "Time to say good veil."

Tendeso returned to his chair by Cassia's bed.

Lio's eyes were already drifting shut, but he kept hold of Cassia's hand. "Keep her company for me?"

"Gladly," Tendeso answered. "I'll even promise not to fly off with her."

"It's all right…as long as you ask her first…" Lio's words and his breath trailed off.

She knew he was right here, and they were both safe. But panic stirred in her at the prospect of the day ahead without him.

"I'm glad you're staying," she said to Tendeso.

He gave her a knowing smile. "Couldn't let you grow bored watching him sleep. Besides, I'm better company than the Empress's statue over there."

"May I compliment you on your choice of language?"

"You're not going to complain that I'm forcing you to speak your least favorite tongue?"

"I'd wager it's the only one we can be absolutely sure the Golden Shield doesn't know."

"Exactly. I can't have all my dirty mercenary jokes reach the Empress's ears. It would ruin my princely image."

Cassia laughed. "You'll tell them to me, won't you?"

"I can come up with a few you didn't already hear in the Maaqul."

Cassia sobered, looking at the man who had carried her across that desert. "Tendeso…"

He made a face. "It really is strange to hear you call me that."

"Would you prefer I keep calling you Monsoon?"

"I must learn to answer to Tendeso again." He hesitated. "But Soli used to call me Tendo sometimes."

"Would it be all right with you if I did, too?"

"Yes. I think I could grow accustomed to that."

"You'll also have to grow accustomed to sentimental silkfoots."

"Oh, no. Are you going to apologize? Lio did that, too."

"Of course he did. I'm going to do something worse. I'm going to tell you how grateful I am."

His expression softened. "Eh. I'll accept thanks."

"You'd better." Cassia cleared her throat against the sudden lump there. "I don't blame you for being so angry at me when we first met. There I was, the reason Solia couldn't stay with you, the reason she's in prison now."

"That's not—"

"It's all right. Of course my appearance rubbed salt in your wounds. But in spite of that, you protected me."

"You're not responsible for anything that happened between Solia and me. I always knew that." He looked away. "Even if I didn't always show it."

"You did. You tried to warn me of the danger. You prevented my arrest. And that was just the beginning. I'm glad we're going to work together for her now, so I can perhaps make up for some of the time you lost because of her responsibility to me."

"You don't have anything to make up for, *nyakimbi*. It's not your fault."

It's not your fault. It had taken a deadly expedition into the Maaqul to wring those words out of him—and to show her what a deeply good man he was. "I'm sorry I didn't understand who you were."

One side of his mouth lifted in a grin. "When you ripped that arrest warrant in half and told me to get out of your way, you reminded me so much of your sister."

"Thank you for everything you've done for her sake and mine. You really are the best at search and rescue, whether you use interrogation, your sword, your wings—or your royal connections."

"Ah. Does this mean I get thanks and an admission that I was right?"

Cassia looked at his wings. "You were right, Tendeso. Especially about the ancestors. I wish I had heeded them before. When I finally did...they...I..."

He shook his head, smiling. "It's hard to describe, isn't it?"

"I can't express it, but you already know." She touched her arm. "I flew."

He sat up straighter. "You what?"

Haltingly, the words came. She found it so difficult to talk about with anyone other than Lio, but Tendeso was the one person who might be able to explain it to her.

"Do you have any idea how I can awaken my magic?" she asked. "Where does it come from? How does it work when I can't hear my ancestors?"

Tendeso leaned on the back of the chair again, frowning in thought. "My people's power comes from Eagle's favor. My ancestors cultivated a bond with Eagle over many generations, through responsibility and devotion. Ultimately, Eagle gave us the blessing of shapeshifting."

Cassia listened, trying to understand.

"My ancestor Mweya was the first to receive Eagle's wings. When he died, he became divine, and now he passes his magic down to us. But his power is only for his descendants. Each lineage must earn their own blessing."

"In the shadowlands, it must work differently. The ancestors can't give us gifts there. Lustra changers must draw their beast magic from a different source than Sandira shifters. But what?"

"I don't believe you can cause it to happen. Magic arrives on its own schedule. From what Solia told me, the conditions under which the triune affinity manifests are particularly mysterious."

"My mother said Solia could explain the rest. What else did my sister tell you?"

"I would never ask her to reveal the secrets of your woman ancestors to a man outside your clan. She learned much from your mother and had intended to pass that knowledge onto you. When we find her, you'll have the chance to ask her. My advice in the meantime? Be patient. Wait. Blessings can't be rushed, and the ancestors know what they're doing." He ran a hand across his sash. "I'm starting to appreciate that."

"Do you…feel better about how your inheritance turned out?"

He sighed. "My brother and I have so much work ahead of us. But we're working. Together."

"That sounds promising."

"It occurs to me that if I were king, I would not be here leading the Sandira delegation."

"You would have responsibilities at home."

"You have to understand, I couldn't use my royal influence when Solia was arrested. She had gone to such lengths not to implicate us or our families. I had no qualms about risking myself to search for her, but I couldn't risk my king, my people."

"Of course."

"Now we have altered the state of affairs. While I am here on my brother's behalf, I am in a position to join Orthros in advocating for Solia. I can fight for her again. My loyalty to my family and to her are not opposed. That…has never happened."

"Love makes a way."

"You were right, too, *nyakimbi*."

THE CASSIA GROVE

"**W**ELL, FRECKLES, DUTY CALLS, and I don't mean the fun sort with knives and knuckles." Tendeso sighed. "I'd forgotten how much of princeship consists of showing up for ceremonious meals."

Cassia raised a brow at him. "Surely the menu is better than snake jerky?"

"A silkfoot like you would find it so." He shook his head. "Can you spare me for an hour or three while I go impress Princess Nyakou?"

"The Empress's heir?" Cassia raised a brow.

"Yes, yes. Her unmarried daughter, who will eventually require a suitably royal ass to occupy the Emperor Consort's seat. Every Queen Mother in the court loves to remind me."

"I wouldn't worry about the threat of an arranged marriage quite yet. I happen to know that Orthros's Master Ambassador Rakesh has particularly close, ah, diplomat relations with her, and isn't likely to give up their private negotiations anytime soon."

"Oh, I see how it is. Your money is on the Hesperine moonflower."

"My money is on my almost-brother-in-law being safe at the princess's table. I'll spare you for now, for the cause. We'll need all the favor we can win from the Empress's daughter."

Tendeso stood to his full height and stretched his wings. "Leave that to me. I have not forgotten how to be suitably royal."

Cassia looked up at him. "I never doubted that."

"I won't lose the battle a second time."

With that promise, he departed through the terrace doors. A moment later, she heard the beat of his wings.

Now Cassia had nothing better to do than join Lio in sleep for a while, then submit to the Imperial physician's next visit. After the healer finished another round of examining, medicating, feeding, and bespelling, she pronounced Cassia allowed to leave the bed, as long as she didn't overtax herself. She prescribed a brief walk before she and her entourage finally filed out again.

Only the Golden Shield remained. She strode to the terrace doors. There was a certain marching cadence to her step, even though she was not in formation with her sisters. She opened both doors wide, letting in the wonderful outdoor smells Cassia had noticed earlier.

Silently she returned to Cassia's bedside and offered a hand. Cassia slid her fingers into the Golden Shield's palm. The armor that clung to her was warm like skin, although it had the smoothness of metal.

She helped Cassia out of bed. Then she pointed at the table nearby with a questioning gesture. Cassia looked to see if she needed anything there. Beside the water, tonics, and other niceties, there sat her gardening satchel, safe and sound. She reached for it, but the soldier slung it over her own shoulder to carry it for Cassia.

The Golden Shield supported Cassia as she walked out onto the terrace. Knight danced after them, his tail wagging furiously. When Cassia saw what awaited her, delight made its way through her weariness.

She gasped in a deep breath of fragrance. "Cassia trees!"

At last, after studying her namesake in books, she was seeing them in person for the first time. These cassia trees stood twenty to thirty feet high, their oval leaves verdant green in the sunlight. Their light yellow flowers shone at her like thousands of tiny golden stars in the branches.

She tried reaching within and connecting with the soil, as she had over Btana Ayal.

Nothing happened. But it would, eventually. She knew that now. It was only a matter of time before her very own plant magic manifested. Every time she thought of it, she felt a swoop of joy.

The Golden Shield kept a strong arm under Cassia's, supporting her while she drifted close to the nearest tree. She put her nose to the aromatic bark and inhaled deeply of the spice-to-be.

The soldier helped her along a pathway between the trees. Cassia wondered which one Kassandra had planted with her sister. She was unsure the Golden Shield would know, but she couldn't resist asking. "Could we find the tree the princesses planted together?"

The soldier inclined her helmet. She led Cassia on a short walk, further into the grove. There stood a majestic cassia tree with a bench beneath its branches.

"This is where they spent time together," Cassia asked, "before one became the Empress and another an Elder Firstblood?"

The golden helmet nodded once more and seated Cassia on the bench. Someone had left a carved wooden box there. Cassia was careful not to disturb it. The warrior placed a blanket over her legs, setting her gardening satchel within reach. Knight stuck his head on her lap for pets. She smoothed a hand over his ears.

She lifted her face to let the dappled sunlight fall upon her cheeks through the branches of the tree. She felt connected to Kassandra across the miles and to her sister across time. Somehow, Cassia felt closer to Solia, too, wherever she might be.

When the Golden Shield turned her back to Cassia, the sunlight fell upon her. It glowed on her armor, an effect almost divine.

She raised her armored hands to her helmet. Cassia's thoughts slowed to a halt.

The warrior lifted off her mask, and a thatch of golden hair spilled out.

Her golden armor dispelled, leaving behind only the golden fabric that wrapped her from shoulders to knees. Her limbs were honed with muscle, her fair skin tanned from years in the sunny Empire.

She turned to face Cassia.

Life and battle had chiseled her features. Emotion blazed in her sky-blue eyes. Nowhere in her could Cassia see the gentle princess who had cherished her as a child. She saw the warrior Solia had become, who was in every way her sister.

The world tilted as Cassia leapt to her feet with a cry. Solia caught her before she toppled over.

For the first time in fifteen years, Cassia held her sister.

Solia wrapped her in a fierce hold, cherishing her close, enfolding her in warmth. She felt exactly the same. When she had held Cassia for the last time, her embrace had been just like this. It was as if they had never let go.

Solia had always been this warrior and that princess.

"M-my sister. Soli."

"Look at you, Pup," came her rusty voice. "All grown up into a lady."

So many years. So many words they needed to say. But in that moment, Cassia let herself hold Solia and let Solia hold her.

Her sister sat them back down on the bench and rocked her. She rested her tear-streaked face on her sister's shoulder.

"You're safe," was all Solia said.

Knight danced around them, yipping like a puppy. Solia held out her hand to him. He crawled halfway onto her lap in an attempt to lick her face.

Sitting in the warm, golden sunlight of the Empire, watching her sister move and breathe and do something so simple and dear as pet Knight, Cassia felt like she would float out of her own body. None of it seemed real. "You're here."

Solia stroked Cassia's hair. "Do you remember what I used to do every time I had to travel somewhere without you? What we would do together when I came home?"

"How could I forget? No matter where you had to go, you always found something there to bring back for our garden. As soon as you returned, we would sit together like this so you could show me the surprise."

Solia picked up the wooden box, placing it across their laps, and lifted the lid. Inside was a collection of small pouches in a myriad of fabrics. Cassia lifted the one on top, a tiny purse of colorful stripweave. With reverent fingers, she opened it and peered inside.

"Jasmine seeds," said Solia, "from the grounds of Imperial University. Their fragrance is divine."

As Cassia sorted through the seed pouches one by one, Solia named the contents of each and told her about its characteristics and care.

"Peanuts from a tiny village. You know the one. Acacia from the Cifwani Matriarchate." She paused. "Flame lily from the Sandira Kingdom."

They traveled together through Solia's gifts and all the many places she had been with the Ashes over the years. She commented only on the seeds, although Cassia could imagine how many memories must be attached to each one. Here was a record of Solia's feats and a testament that Cassia had never been far from her thoughts.

This moment must be as overwhelming for her magnificent sister as it was for her. Perhaps more so. As the eldest, Solia had such a sense of responsibility on her shoulders.

Cassia had spent all this time with Hesperines, learning not to fear emotion. Learning to speak. Solia's time with the Ashes had taught her to feel freely and speak through her deeds. This box of seeds was her way of telling Cassia what she needed to say.

When they had seen every treasure in the box, Cassia closed the lid on the precious trove and smoothed a hand over the carvings. "Thank you."

"I know it isn't enough," Solia began. "That day I left you—your pleas for me not to go—I've heard them over and over again in my memories. If I had imagined I would never see you again—"

"But you have. Today. I am not thanking you only for the seeds. I want to thank you for everything you did all these years. I'm so grateful that you took care of yourself so we could be here, now, both of us safe and sound."

Solia looked into Cassia's face. "Is that really how you see it?"

"You won. We won."

Trails of tears spilled from her long eyelashes, over the sunspots on her face. "Everything I have done, I did for you. I want you to know that. Even when I stayed away, it was for your sake. To protect you."

"I never doubted your reasons, Soli."

"How can it be that after all these years, I can still do no wrong in your eyes?"

"After everything you've done for my sake, how could I look upon you as anything but a hero? You have been my guiding light."

Solia's voice was thick with emotion. "I have waited fifteen years to ask for your forgiveness."

"You thought there was something to forgive?" Cassia shook her head.

"Pup," she said, "what a woman you've become."

"I've waited fifteen years to find out if you might be proud of me."

"You needed to ask?" Solia pulled her close again.

She leaned into her sister. "Now we can decide what to do together."

"You have questions."

"So do you."

"Yes."

Cassia had an idea and smiled. Perhaps it was silly, but resurrecting their old rituals seemed to bring them both comfort. "Do you remember the game we used to play when you would tutor me?"

A smile came to Solia's face. Her smile looked exactly the same and even more beautiful on a warrior's face than a princess's. "You were ferociously curious about everything except what you were supposed to be studying."

"So you said we would take turns. You would require me to answer one question about my lessons. In return, you would let me ask you a question about anything I wanted to know."

"And I was hard pressed to answer some of them."

"I was incorrigible, to be sure."

"Still are, I can see. Well done."

Cassia grinned. "All right. You first. Ask me a question. I'll answer to the best of my ability, and then I may ask you an impertinent one."

Solia paused to think. Cassia thought this must be the most her sister had spoken their first language in several years. "Have you been happy?"

"Sometimes," Cassia admitted. "Have you?"

"Sometimes," Solia agreed. Another pause. "You do still have a garden?"

"Oh, Soli, I have the most enormous garden. Do you still read naughty books?"

Solia chuckled. "I did. Don't have much time these days." She glanced down at the drool sliding from Knight's jaws onto her calloused hand. "How has Knight held up?"

"I've been glad of him every moment of every day." Cassia searched for another light-hearted question. They had to work up to her asking how, precisely, Solia had gotten out of prison and become the Empress's right hand. "Do you like your big golden horse?"

"Ha. Yes. She's a treat to ride." Solia cleared her throat. "Have you been looking for me?"

"I've followed in your footsteps all over the Empire. Have you been looking for me?"

Solia cupped Cassia's face in her hand. "I never meant to frighten you. We weren't coming to arrest you. I was trying to bring you to safety before the Rezayal found you."

"It was you in that armor all along, protecting me."

"One of the Empress's trusted administrators at the Marijani docks alerted us to your arrival. I wanted to run to you, Cassia." Solia's fingers tightened. "But we had to handle the situation with care. Her Imperial Majesty sent one of her best agents to look after you. She was supposed to follow you everywhere."

"The woman in the Sun Market was spying for you and the Empress?" How falsely Cassia had judged the woman and Dakk.

Solia nodded. "When she returned with no report and no memory of what had happened, it was clear someone powerful had interfered with her. We knew you were in danger. At last the Empress allowed me to ride out. Were you there when I searched Ukocha's village?"

"Up in the tree, watching."

"Gods." Solia rubbed her face. "I tried so hard not to scare Chuma. That was not how I wanted to see our bladelet for the first time in five years. But it had become clear you were following my path across the Empire. I had to look everywhere I had been."

"That was you in Kella's mother's tent?"

"You were there as well?"

"Right in front of you, under Lio's veil spells."

Solia looked away.

"If only we'd known." Cassia rested her head on Solia's shoulder again. "If we think of all the wasted chances and disasters, we'll go mad. What matters is that we're together now."

Solia held her tightly. "You almost died in the Maaqul."

"You rescued me outside Btana Ayal. Thank you, Soli."

"When we find Dakkoul, I will arrest him myself—unless he gives me an excuse to run him through."

If Cassia had not traversed the Maaqul with the Ashes, she would have been entirely unprepared to hear such threats of violence coming from her sister's lips. But now Cassia would expect no less, for Ukocha had mentored Solia.

"Your turn to ask a question," Solia said.

"How did you get out of prison?"

Solia sighed. She hesitated for a long moment, contemplating the helmet resting beside her on the bench. "I was never there."

Cassia straightened. "But everyone witnessed your arrest."

"The Empress staged my capture to appease the Rezayal and end their pursuit of me once and for all. Her Imperial Majesty granted my boon. She agreed to provide the resources I would need to return to you, starting with this." Solia laid a hand on the helmet. "She promised to transform me into an even greater warrior than I was when I took the acacia."

Cassia took her sister's hand. "But at what cost?"

"The Empress seeks to end isolation—on her terms. I had to prove myself to her beyond question so she would know I'll safeguard her Empire's interests if she intervenes in Tenebra. Serving her as one of the Golden Shield was the only way."

"The Ashes spent five years believing the worst. The things they thought you suffered…"

"I know." The lines of strain on Solia's face deepened. "I would never subject them to that without cause. Because I know how it feels, Cassia. I was left imagining what your life was like under the king's control."

"I suppose neither the Hesperines nor the privateers brought any rumors of the king's bastard to the Empire before I met Lio."

"I had no news of you for fifteen years."

"But surely, once I arrived in Orthros, word of my involvement in the negotiations reached you."

Solia's jaw clenched. "Your arrival in Marijani was the first I had heard of you since leaving Tenebra."

"But during the Solstice Summit, Harkhuf wrote to the Empress about Lio and me."

"The Rezayal used him to control what the Empress, and thus the Golden Shield, did and did not know about the Tenebrans' role in the peace treaty, including yours. Harkhuf is merely their latest pawn. They've been intercepting information from Orthros for years, attempting to manipulate Her Imperial Majesty."

"Dakk has so much answer for."

"You see why I had to protect the Ashes from him after the Battle of Souls. Everyone had to believe that I had deceived them, or they would have faced the Rezayal's retribution."

"Could you not have told the six of them the truth, though? They have kept your secrets before."

Solia shook her head. "Do you know what happens to the loved ones of the Golden Shield?"

"They have to live in seclusion so no one uses them against the Empress."

"I would never sentence the Ashes to such a fate. They have their freedom." Solia put a hand on the helmet. "This was my sacrifice to make."

Tendeso had been right there, moments ago, within arm's reach of Solia. She had heard his vows to save her, proof of his enduring love for her. How did she bear it? Cassia wanted to ask, but she was uncertain her sister was ready to speak of him yet.

She knew Solia had broken Tendeso's heart. What did that heartbreak sound like from Solia's perspective? Had there been anyone to listen to her pain and empathize with her decision to place duty over love?

When she was ready to speak of it, she would have Cassia's ear—and all of Cassia's most persuasive words, convincing her she needn't make any more sacrifices.

"They would be so happy to know you're all right," Cassia said for the time being.

"The Empress has only given me leave to reveal myself to you. Until she releases me from her service, no one else can know."

"When will she do that?"

"It's my turn to ask a question," Solia replied. "How is Iris?"

The change of subject left Cassia reeling.

Oh, Goddess. Solia didn't know. And Cassia had to tell her.

Her face must have betrayed that their game was over, for Solia's hands tightened in hers. But she said nothing. Waiting.

Cassia thought back to the night Solia's trusted handmaiden had lost her life. It was still raw for Cassia, after she had relived it through Iris's eyes, thanks to Hesperine thelemancy.

She didn't know how to say the unspeakable. There was no comfort to be had when the worst had come to pass. All she could do was try to do Iris justice. "She met a hero's end."

Solia was on her feet, then at the edge of the tree's shade, her back to Cassia, her head bowed. She covered her face with one hand.

The day seemed to have grown warmer quickly. Sweat broke out on Cassia's brow.

"When?" Solia asked.

"That night at Castra Roborra. The same night you had to leave."

The sun felt uncomfortably hot in the silence. Solia's hand closed into a fist.

"No." She spun, facing Cassia, her gaze afire. "You were alone."

Cassia held Knight to her. "You had no way of knowing. When you left, you had every reason to believe Iris and I were both safe together."

"I left you alone with *him*." Her eyes flashed, her voice deadly.

"The Hesperines saved me. Just like the Ashes saved you."

"But *I* wasn't there for you. And neither was Iris."

"I know." Cassia swallowed. "I wasn't there for you, either."

Solia sat down heavily beside her. "You don't know the truth. The secrets we protected you from as a child. Iris was not there to tell you when you grew old enough to understand."

"I've wondered. I've surmised. The only thing I've known for certain is that you were going to overthrow him. You don't have to do that anymore."

"I must explain everything to you."

Cassia also knew how important it was to speak of the past aloud. It was the first step toward laying it to rest. If there was something Solia needed Cassia to know, she would listen. Then she would help her sister banish it all so they could have a better future.

"Go ahead," Cassia encouraged.

"That night at Castra Roborra was supposed to be the beginning."

After years of being haunted by her questions and asking them of everyone who had known Solia, now Cassia listened to her sister describe her fate in her own words.

"I suppose you still believe I was kidnapped," Solia said.

"How could I think anything else? I was in the king's camp outside the fortress where the rebel lords held you captive. I listened to Lord Bellator's messenger demand your ransom from the king."

"Bellator was not always my enemy. At first, he was one of my strongest allies in my effort to overthrow our father."

Cassia recalled Iris's words to Bellator about his betrayal. "You trusted him."

"Most of my 'suitors' were my partisans. Under the guise of courtship, I curried favor with them and cultivated our plot."

"While the king thought he was using you to manipulate them, all along you were outmaneuvering him."

"Bellator arrived with Lord Evandrus to escort me to Castra Roborra for a secret meeting. If all had gone according to plan, I would later have arrived at Desidia with the king none the wiser."

And Cassia would have met her and Iris there, and all their lives would be so different now. "What went wrong?"

"When I announced…the next phase of my plan, Bellator changed his mind. That coward. He turned on Iris and me. Lord Reman and Lord Mareus followed his lead. Only Evandrus's honor did not waver."

"But he was outnumbered."

"Bellator found himself deeply committed to a plot he no longer wished to carry out, with me on his hands. He feared my retribution if he released me. I could have sold him out to the king and made myself look innocent. He tried to salvage the situation and turn it to his advantage."

"That must be when he sent word to the king of your kidnapping and demanded concessions in exchange for your release."

"If he had stayed the course of my rebellion, his rights as a free lord would have been guaranteed. He should have known Lucis would never cede a scrap of power to the lords, especially not for my sake."

"That fool." Clearly, Bellator had lacked Solia's grasp of politics. And they had all paid the price.

"Lord Evandrus helped us persuade Bellator to set Iris free and send her to you." Solia drew a breath. "Did she make it that far?"

Cassia shook her head.

Solia sounded numb. "When Evander and I escaped together, we thought we knew what we were leaving behind."

"You escaped with Lord Evandrus's son?" Cassia asked. "What about the war mage who took you from the fortress?"

"Ah. I'll…explain that too."

Cassia squeezed her hands. Her palms were sweating. "Take your time."

"Evander's father sent him with me in the hopes of saving his son and preserving their line. We understood the sacrifice he and my guardsmen were making. I still pray for each of them by name every night in honor of our life debt. But I never imagined it would cost Iris her life, too. How did it happen?"

Cassia wanted to soften the blow somehow, but she owed a warrior's brave question a truthful answer. "The king refused to ransom you."

"Of course he did. I handed him a perfect opportunity to get rid of me. Letting him believe he had succeeded made him think the threat was over. That left me free to work toward his downfall in secret. He knew I was a danger, but Iris and I were so careful never to implicate her. He was assured of her loyalty. How did he find out?"

"He didn't. Bellator had to make the king believe he had gone through with his threats to kill you. You looked enough alike that he could fool the king into believing Iris was you."

Solia was quiet for a moment. "You're saying she died in my place."

"You know that was a sacrifice she was proud to make. She wouldn't have wanted you to stay and die with her. And she never would have left with you and abandoned me. Everyone did the best they could."

Solia's silence was longer this time. Cassia respected it. She would need time.

"Did you know it was Iris?" Solia asked suddenly.

"No."

"*You* thought I was dead?"

"Until a few weeks ago, when the Hesperines helped me find out the truth."

Solia pulled her close again. Cassia leaned into her, learning her new scent of gold and steel and Imperial spices.

"Oh, Goddess, Cassia. Iris would have told you I was coming back. I never meant…I'm sorry for all the wasted grief."

Not wasted. Her grief for the lost time would always be real. "I will never regret that you left that night, because it's the only reason we can be together again."

"What else don't you know?" Solia asked.

"What about the fire mage who traversed you and Evander out of the fortress? We thought he captured you and took you to the Magelands."

"On our side."

"An apostate, then?" Cassia guessed. "Not part of the Order of Anthros?"

"Yes."

Cassia heaved a sigh. Her sister had never been in the Order's custody. "Why go to Cordium then?"

"Evander had connections there. They would have hidden us while we rallied others to our cause. Unfortunately, it proved too dangerous for Evander and his surviving family for me to be near them, so I fled on my own."

"Why go to the coast?"

"I thought I could evade the Orders at sea. I intended to book passage on a ship, or stow away if I had to. Unfortunately, there was a war circle on my trail."

"Ziara told us about how she and Huru and their crew rescued you."

"If not for them, I wouldn't be alive today." Solia studied her hands, fiddling with the quartz and coral ring on her finger. "Did she tell you what the ring means?"

Cassia looked from her own ring to her sister's. She should have known such a gift from a woman like Ziara was no mere memento. "No."

"She attaches one to every gift she presents to the Empress."

Oh, the Empress's palace is full of gifts I've brought her. That's a privateer's business: stealing anything that will weaken the mages and strengthen the Empire… What could we do about a runaway princess…?

"Solia, did they save you? Or did they steal you for the Empress?"

"That was the only way to save me, Cassia. I was a gift for the Empress, fifteen years in the making. When Ziara brought me here, she gave me the chance to become the woman she believed I could be. Thanks to Ukocha, I survived and succeeded. The night before the final match in the Battle of Souls, Ziara came to me and gave me this ring. 'I knew there was acacia in you,' she told me. I'll never understand how she saw that in the broken girl she saved on the docks of Cordium, but I'll always be grateful that she did."

"She understood your political value when they took you aboard. They knew the Mage Orders were hunting you for the king."

"I told the privateers I was the runaway princess of Tenebra," Solia said evenly, "but the mages didn't know. The Orders were after me for their own reasons."

Cassia shook her head. "What? Why?"

"Because of this." Solia held out her hands, palms up.

Cassia's first warning was a prickle of heat, washing over her from her sister's direction. Then came a golden glow, as if sunlight were gathering in Solia's hand.

Fire blossomed on Solia's palm.

Cassia's jaw dropped.

Solia lifted her hand. The flames split and unfurled, burning in the shape of a flower with petals of brilliant orange and hot white. Perfectly formed. Utterly controlled.

At last, Cassia understood the path Solia had burned across two continents.

"You're a fire mage." Cassia had to say it aloud to make it sink in.

Solia touched her palms together, snuffing out the fire, then took Cassia's hands again with cooling fingers. "You need never fear my magic. It gives me power to protect you. After a lifetime of effort, I can make you that promise."

Cassia pressed Solia's hands. "I would never have thought otherwise."

"I owe you the truth. There was a time when the fire was a danger to me—and to you."

"You were struggling with this even when I was a child? When did you realize you had magic?"

"My power began to manifest when I was seven. The Orders' retribution upon girls with the affinity for fire was the lesser of my fears. I hid my power from the king, terrified of how he would use me. But without training, I quickly became a danger to myself and others. It was only a matter of time before I exposed my secret or killed someone. Maybe myself. Maybe someone I hated, like the king. Worse, maybe someone I loved, like Iris."

"How did you survive?"

"Thalia saved me."

"My mother."

"I heard you talking about what you saw in Btana Ayal." Solia's voice was hushed. "I am in awe of the ancestors' grace. It is one of the greatest griefs of my life, that you didn't get to know her as I did. But now you have met her."

"She told me she left me with a capable protector, and that you would explain everything to me."

Solia blinked hard, looking up through the branches of the tree. "From the time I could remember, my mother, the queen, was a walking specter. Marriage to Lucis killed her in spirit long before miscarriages and still-births destroyed her body. While she drowned her horrors in alchemy and wine, Thalia became the first real mother I ever had."

Cassia felt more connected to her mother than ever, knowing her love had been passed down through Solia.

"I'll never forget the day I met her," Solia went on. "Everyone in the royal wing was hovering at my mother's bedside, hoping to bring her through another birth. My magic responded to my fear. I slipped away in the chaos and hid in the garden, confused and ashamed by what was happening to me.

"Thalia found me in a ring of fire, trying not to scream. I don't know what terrified me more—how close I was to killing myself and everyone else in the palace, or the fact that Thalia might tell someone my secret.

"She sat down outside the ring of fire and spoke to me. You have heard her voice. You understand. All she had to do was talk to me. Her sooth-saying banished the fire and my fears."

"I'm so glad you weren't alone."

"Although Thalia didn't share my affinity, she was able to train me in magical principles and self control. She taught me magic and helped me keep my secret safe."

Cassia swallowed. "Until we both lost her."

"I tried to care for you as she would have."

"You did, even though you were still a child yourself."

"My power became stronger and more difficult to control, the older I grew." Frustration flashed on her face. "It was a threat, not an asset to our rebellion. The night of the siege, I managed to traverse Evander and me out of the fortress without disaster, but by the time we got to Cordium, my reaction to what had happened was destabilizing my magic. I left before I harmed him or his family. But I soon had a circle of war mages hunting me. I was desperate to get onto the ocean. The water would dampen my power and give me some relief, as well as interfere with their ability to sense me."

"Now I understand what Ziara and Ukocha meant when they talked about what you needed. Ziara took you to Ukocha so she could train you to use your magic."

"I wanted to come back to you, but I wasn't fit to be near you. I was a walking disaster to myself and everyone around me. The slightest thing would set me off, and my power would flare."

"Is that why Tendeso was the only one who could spar with you?"

At the mention of his name, a tendril of fire sprang to life on Solia's lips. She looked away, flexing her hand. The flame darted down her arm and into her waiting palm.

"His wind magic can rob the flames of air and put them out in a heartbeat." She closed her fist, and the fire winked out.

Cassia had seen the way Tendeso smiled for Solia. Now she saw how Solia burned for him.

"It took years of brutal training with Ukocha for me to simply live in my own skin. She said I'll never be able to make up for all the years without training. I still struggle at times. But thanks to her power and skill, I control the fire now. It doesn't control me."

Solia drew her sword and held it between them. A flame appeared and raced along the edge until the entire blade was alight. "Your mother, Ziara, Ukocha, the Empress—these great women have blessed me with their wisdom and transformed my power of destruction into a force for good. Thanks to them, I have made my power my own, and I wield it with pride. My legacy may be ill gotten, but I have freed it from the king, as surely as I have freed myself."

Cassia watched the wild element that was so balanced and beautiful in her sister's grip. "Solia, are you saying that you inherited your magic from the king?"

"Yes, Cassia. King Lucis of Tenebra is one of the most powerful fire mages ever to hide his magic from the Order of Anthros." Solia sheathed her sword.

The truth raced through Cassia's mind, setting fire to all the lies the king had made her believe.

Few witnessed the occasions when the king's veneer of strength cracked and revealed the unstable temper he never quite controlled. But Cassia had felt the effects of his inner rage.

"The day my mother died...there was no assassin, was there? The mage who killed her...was him."

"I'm so sorry, Pup."

Cassia pressed a hand to her belly, a cold sweat on her brow. "He did it with his own hands. He murdered my mother. Why?"

"His highest ambition—his lifelong delusion—is his vision of making himself the new Mage King. He, who has not a drop of that hero's blood or honor in him. He planned to use your mother for a Changing Queen and found a new dynasty. He thinks he can grow so powerful that even the Orders will not be able to stand against him."

"But he couldn't control her."

"He realized she didn't plan to wait for him to put her on the throne. She was going to take it from him. Because it belonged to her. Her triune affinity was proof of her birthright. That imposter killed her because she was the direct descendant of the Mage King and the Changing Queen."

Cassia's heart seemed to slow to a stop, even as her thoughts raced, putting the pieces together in spite of her. She had heard the voice of the first mage. She had seen the Silvicultrix and held her mother. They had revealed the truth to her across the border of death, and now Solia had brought it to life.

The Hawk of the Lustra. The Silvicultrix. She had met the Changing Queen.

"Ebah." She whispered her name in the old garden tongue. Somehow, the pendant was in her hands. When had she reached for it?

"You found your mother's secret," Solia said.

Springing to her feet, Cassia held it out to her sister. "This isn't mine. It's yours. I'm here to restore it to you."

"It's right where it belongs. It's one of your family heirlooms, Cassia.

The women of Thalia's line safeguarded it for generations. They kept it secret from the Mage Orders."

"You have always been our rightful queen."

"It was never me. The pendant was the Changing Queen's. Now it belongs to the heir to the throne—you."

Cassia clutched a hand to her diplomat's medallion, shoving the ivy pendant into her sister's hand. "That's impossible."

Solia rose to her feet and faced Cassia with the artifact in her hand. "Your magic will come. No one will be able to deny you your legacy."

"Solia, I cannot become Queen of Tenebra."

"You should have learned the truth sooner. Iris would have prepared you for your future."

"That's what she was supposed to do? Groom me to rule? This is the plot you two were working on all along?"

"Yes." Solia seemed to force the next words out of herself. "But I failed you and her. I miscalculated. I told our partisans the truth too soon. When Bellator learned it was you we intended to put on the throne, he balked. He had been willing when he thought all we would have to do was stoke the support for me that was already at hand. He deemed you an impossible candidate for the throne. But this time, I am not a girl of seventeen beholden to men."

Solia radiated the heat of her magic. Her hand came to rest on the hilt of her sword, the pendant caught in her grip. "My blade will teach Tenebra to bow before the true queen. I will forge their loyalty to you with fire."

Cassia recognized the light in her sister. It had burned inside of Cassia, too. The hope of her future queen and her love for her sister had inspired her to do impossible things. Her dream of justice and peace for Tenebrans had driven her to sacrifice almost everything.

Solia had done the same—but not for herself. For Cassia.

"I have been preparing to return to you," Solia said. "At last, I am ready. I have made myself into what you need. Not a princess. A general."

Solia had devoted her life to this. Years. Brutal training. The Battle of Souls. She had given up all her own desires and happiness. Iris had died for it. For Cassia.

How could Cassia tell Solia it had all been in vain?

WINDING JOURNEY

WHEN LIO WOKE, CASSIA'S hand was no longer in his. He worked his way out of the Slumber and unfolded himself from the chair. There had been too much sun in this room today.

The doors were open, and the balmy night breeze made the canopy flutter. From outside, he heard Cassia speaking with another woman—in Vulgus. He followed the sounds out into the Empress's cassia grove.

"Flavian?" The woman's voice rose. "Flavian will be king by midsummer? You served up the crown on a cushion to the boy who poured syrup in my shoes when we were ten?"

"He's a grown man now," Cassia objected.

"He only ever had room in his head for horses and swords. I doubt he's made room for anything else except skirts."

"I groomed him for the role myself."

"You have united the free lords and allied them with Hesperines for this? You have re-created the politics of Tenebra and Orthros to put another forgettable man on the queen's throne?"

"I did it so we could all be free!"

"Midsummer is less than two months away. We have less than two months to mobilize the plan the Empress and I have perfected for five years."

"You have a choice."

In Hesperine silence, Lio found them at the tree bench and watched.

The Golden Shield who had put Cassia in his arms now stood across from her, unmasked. The silent protector hidden in that armor had been her all along.

Solia.

Lio gazed upon the woman whose memory had first brought him and Cassia together, whose mystery had driven them on their winding journey. He listened to the priceless heartbeat of Cassia's only human family, sensing the precious mortal spirit who had survived against all odds.

The two sisters faced each other with the breadth of the tree between them.

"All I'm asking you to do is consider it," Cassia said. "Just think about letting Flavian have the throne. Think about staying here, where you were happy. You deserve that choice."

"Iris deserves for her sacrifice not to be in vain." Fresh pain seared Solia's aura.

Cassia took a step toward her. "How many more of us must die for Tenebra? Is there not victory in escaping it, too?"

Cassia sensed him then. Her aura opened to him, and she turned like a flower to the moon. "Lio."

He slipped an arm around her, and they shared a long look, at a loss for words. They had done it. They were all three standing here together.

"Lio." Her voice wavered. "This is my sister. Solia, this is my Grace."

Lio realized that through all their efforts to find Solia, he had neglected to plan his first words to her when they finally met. He didn't know what he wanted to say.

Perhaps that was for the best. This wasn't a diplomatic occasion. He was meeting his Grace-sister for the first time.

Lio started with the most important thing he and Solia shared. Cassia. "Thank you for bringing her back to us."

Solia looked him up and down. "It seems I owe you my thanks for saving her many times over."

Her aura, now unguarded by her spell armor, was pure fire. She blazed with inner light, a roar of love and anger entwined. No wonder Tendeso could not forget her.

Lio recognized the power in her aura, searing and bright. Like Xandra's. Like Ukocha's. The pieces fit together.

Well, for a Hesperine, he certainly had an abundance of fire mages among his loved ones.

But he didn't expect to win over a woman like Sunburn with any less effort than it had taken to find her.

Cassia took his hand and opened her mouth to speak, but suddenly swayed on her feet.

Lio caught her and scooped her up in his arms. "Are you all right?"

"She's been out of bed too long." Solia's voice betrayed her chagrin.

Lio strode back through the orchard, Solia marching at his side.

"We have more to say," Cassia protested.

"You're going back to bed," Solia said.

Cassia struggled to lift her head. "We can continue our discussion with me in bed."

"You're still recovering," Lio said gently. "You need rest."

"More important…things to do…than rest…" But she stopped talking and swallowed hard.

Lio carried her across her room and laid her gently in the sheets, steadying her spinning mind with his magic.

"I'll send for the healer." Solia pulled the blanket over her.

Their gazes met over Cassia. He saw it then, the accusation in her eyes.

He put a hand on hers where she still held the bedclothes. "I will never take her from you."

"You don't know what you're promising." She pulled away.

The anger in her aura was directed as much at herself as at him. He realized how much her world had changed in a matter of days. She had just gotten Cassia back and lost Iris. The Ashes had returned to her, while her throne had been handed off to another. Adding a new Grace-brother and her sister's forthcoming immortality to the mix was quite a lot for anyone, Lio had to admit. No wonder Solia felt like setting something on fire.

She didn't offend him any more than Cassia did on the occasions when her long-controlled emotions exploded. Cassia's temper was pure ice, Solia's all fire, but he found the family resemblance endearing.

Solia strode to the inner door and barked something in Dynastic at the apprentice healer in the palace corridor. Then she crossed the room again, her passage sending a current of heat through the air as she disappeared onto the terrace.

Lio slid his hand behind Cassia's neck, feeding a gentle flow of his thelemancy into her.

She squeezed his hand. "Lio, her magic runs in the family."

He sank down next to Cassia on the bed. "You mean the king."

Her mind shouted the revelation, crying out at the injustice of it with such ferocity that she didn't have to say the truth aloud to him.

King Lucis was the fire mage who had murdered her mother.

Words weren't enough. So Lio held her hand and wrapped her up in their Union, just sitting with her in her messy inner storm.

The Goddess had not given Lio his power just so he could throw it at necromancers and jinn. He was well equipped for much harder battles. Such as holding Cassia while she wrestled with a new layer of the grief she had carried all her life.

He was glad when the healers came and overrode her protests about a sleeping draught, giving her a respite.

When they departed, he sat watching her sleep for a moment, smoothing his hand over her freckled brow. Then he went to find Solia in the orchard.

She stood just under the cassia trees, out of reach of the light spilling from inside the room. She hadn't put her helmet back on, and a faint glow emanated from her skin.

"Did she tell you?" Solia asked.

"We did have some opportunity to talk before the healers arrived. She told me more about the role your magic has played in events. My respect. Your accomplishments as a woman fire mage are worthy of legend."

"I see why they call you Glasstongue."

"As you watched me in the Empress's court, I hope it was clear how I use my words. I assure you, I mean every one." He smiled. "I come from a land of powerful and volatile women."

"Cassia has lost her heart to Orthros."

"Cassia's heart is right here"—he touched his chest—"and I am portable."

"I am her immediate family," said Solia. "Per Hesperine law and custom, I can speak bluntly about this."

"Of course." He took a step closer. "You have every right to ask me any question you wish, and to show me the wrong end of that sword if you're not satisfied with my answers. I want your blessing, and I will earn it."

Lio *had* planned this conversation. He had imagined himself and Cassia giving her sister their felicitous tidings together. Why couldn't they announce their Grace bond to a single family member in peace and celebration?

"My announcement before the court, while Cassia was in such danger, was not how we wanted you to find out."

"You're the reason she nearly died in the Maaqul."

For the first time, Solia's anger burned him. He could tell himself Dakk was to blame for their separation and for much of Cassia's mental and physical suffering. But that didn't change the Craving.

"I'm sorry you had to see your little sister endure that, Solia. I won't recover from it, either. But I can make it right. If you never want to worry about her again, leave it to me and the Gift in my veins. I can make her safe from everything."

"Except yourself."

Under that golden armor, where was Sunburn, who had given bandits a scare with illusory fangs?

"You fought with Karege for years," Lio said. "You know what Hesperines are like. I thought you would take the Imperial view of our people."

"I do."

"May I ask what your objections are, in that case?"

Solia turned away from him and lifted her gaze to the sky. The air around her heated again, although no lick of fire escaped her skin. *Why?* her mind shouted to the heavens. "This is not the view I took of Cassia's destiny."

"I take it Tendeso was correct, and you remain committed to your plan to return to Tenebra."

"I haven't come this far to surrender now."

"Would not having Cassia at your side as Orthros's ambassador be as worthy of her as an appointment in your court?"

Solia faced him, flicking a finger at his chest. "You would wrap her in a medallion, when she could rise to the throne."

"You would seek to legitimize her, then, and grant her royal status?" Apprehension filled Lio. "You intend for her to be your heir?"

Solia scoffed. "As if she needs such a decree from me. My ancestors elevated themselves from pigsties to the palace with the might of their fists."

He began to realize why not even a person like Tendeso had succeeded in swaying Solia from her path all those years ago. It dawned on Lio what an uphill battle he and Cassia faced, if they were to change Solia's mind now.

Solia had not done any of this for herself. She had done it for her sister.

She studied his face. "Cassia hasn't told you."

"But you're about to, aren't you?"

ANCIENT BLOOD

WHEN CASSIA WOKE, LIO was there. His eyes gleamed with emotion and reflected light. When his mouth came down on hers, she gasped at the fervor of his kiss.

She clutched his shoulders, opening her lips for his ardent invasion. He dragged her robe up over her hips, his hands roaming her skin. She remembered a narrow soldier's bunk in a fortress in Tenebra, where he had made love to her without inhibition, and she had believed she would lose him.

He touched her body and devoured her mouth as if she were slipping from his grasp.

He knew.

She let his kiss make words impossible. He didn't want words. Only this silent declaration. She wrapped her legs around him, holding him tight.

He joined them, fangs to vein, body to body. She flowed into him as he thrust into her.

They climaxed together and spoke at last, a wordless cry to each other in the darkness. Then they lay still and would not let each other go.

"You don't have to take the throne," he said against her throat. "I won't allow anyone to push you into it. Although I cannot deny that this changes everything."

"No. Not everything."

She lay tangled with him, his braid around her ankle. The low light of the room outlined his pale shoulders, waist, and leg. She knew him. He was still Lio. He was the one person in her world who had not changed. She traced the beloved lines of his face.

"I'm your Grace," she said, "and we made an Oath to each other."

He heaved a breath. "But if this changes what you want, you know I'll always protect your freedom to choose. At any cost."

"Of course I know. You fought the Craving nearly to the death to give me a choice about staying with you. Never again!"

"I thought to save you from the throne, not to rob you of it. And yet, you are my Grace and the last surviving member of Tenebra's true royal family. I don't understand how both can be."

She touched her thumb to the smear of her blood on his lower lip. "Is it so strange, knowing how much ancient power boiled down to me? What does the blood of the Mage King and Changing Queen taste like?"

He stroked her hair back from her face. "You taste like Cassia, and I have seen you change the world with power all your own."

"That's the only power I ever really cared about. My own."

See with keen eyes. Keep our power present.

"I can't be your Grace and the Queen of Tenebra at the same time. But I can be your Grace and my mother's daughter."

"Solia says the queenship is what Thalia wanted for you."

"I know. Solia is trying to honor Iris and my mother."

Lio's smile was sad. "And do right by you."

"I understand that need. But what she doesn't understand is that taking the throne is not the only way, or even the best way."

Fight with my hands. Build our future.

"I already made my choice. I am not the one facing a decision. Solia is. She has to make room in her heart for herself—and for me. The real me, not the one she has imagined all these years. Just as I've done for her."

"If anyone can open her heart, you can. But I fear she will not let go of that vision of your future easily. Thalia's vision."

"For the first time in my life, I know my mother. She planned to take the throne from Lucis, yes. She had plans for my future. But the woman who held me in the ruins of the shattered gate would never want me to sacrifice my happiness for someone else's cause."

You will have more, and that is what's most important to me.

"She was happy as a mage of Kyria. Until the Orders forced her to give up everything she loved because of her third magic. But she didn't let them force her into a Cheran veil. Instead, she set out to seize a throne for herself. To the very last, she fought to determine her own future. And to give me a better future, too."

"You're a woman after her own heart, my rose."

"I think if I told her the throne of Tenebra is my Cheran veil, she would understand. And if I told her a greenhouse in Orthros is my temple of Kyria, she would tell me not to give it up. Not to give you up. I can have my magic and the life I want. That's what she would want for me."

"She must be so proud of you," Lio said.

"That's what she told me. Not proud of what I have yet to do, not proud if I meet certain conditions. Proud of *me*. She made me feel that I...*I* am enough."

"You are...so much, Cassia. Capable of anything. Deserving of everything. I don't want you to have any regrets."

She felt his fears in the way he held her, as if she might be torn away from him at any moment. As if they had already lost something.

Cassia sat up, cupping her hand around the back of his neck. "Look at me, Lio."

He lifted his gaze to hers. Her greatest ally. Her dearest friend. Her only love.

"Hear these words in my thoughts," she said. "Feel them in our Union."

His magic took hold of her, a desperate embrace.

"I'm a heretic," she said. "I don't bow to expectations. I don't obey. I might have been born for the throne, but Hespera and I have remade me for a much greater purpose."

He rose up on his elbow, leaning closer, hungry for her promises. "What purpose, Cassia?"

Listen to all voices. Learn from our past.

"Whatever choice Solia makes," Cassia said, "isolation is nearing its end. It cannot last. The two halves of the world that broke apart are reaching for each other."

"Yes. We can see it happening. And the consequences could be wondrous—or devastating."

"But in this era, we have a City of Hope. Orthros is the gate in our time. Hesperines are the ones standing guard at the portal. And who do you think will hold the keys?"

"Our diplomats. You saw it with your own eyes in Btana Ayal, and I felt the truth of it when I stood before the Empress with the delegations. This is about so much more than we knew."

"I was right that diplomacy is the solution. But you were also right, Lio. It is time for us to use our power. I want my magic, and I won't rest until I have it. I will reclaim the power of my ancestors...but their throne isn't big enough for what I want to do."

A slow smile came to his face, revealing his fangs. "I am not going to lose you to Tenebra."

She touched her braid at his throat and reminded him of the words she had spoken when she had made it for him. "I will never leave you, Lio. You will never go hungry another night. I love you, and I will love you for so long that I must become a Hesperine to make time for it all."

His magic surged into her like a shout of triumph, and his fangs pricked her lips as he kissed her again. She gave him her tongue, melding her mouth and hands to him to assure him that the worst had passed.

"My rebel queen," he said, his voice low and infused with mind magic, "my witch of the wilds, my blood sorceress. Praise Hespera that I am immortal and will live to see all that you will do."

"I cannot do it alone, my mind mage, my Glasstongue. We will do it all together, and the world will never be the same."

Continue Cassia and Lio's story in
Blood Grace Book 7, *Blood Gift*...
vroth.co/gift

GLOSSARY

Abroad: Hesperine term for lands outside of Orthros where Hesperines errant roam, meaning Tenebra and Cordium. See **Orthros Abroad**

acacia: see **Battle of Souls**

Accord breakers: humans who break the Desert Accord, a criminal act that threatens the Empire's treaty with the jinn.

adamas: strongest metal in the world, so heavy only Hesperines can wield it. Invented in secret by Nike.

affinity: the type of magic for which a person has an aptitude, such as light magic, warding, or healing.

affinity reading: magical test to determine a person's affinity.

Aithourian Circle: the war mages of the Order of Anthros, sworn enemies of the Hesperines, who have specialized spells for finding and destroying Hespera worshipers. Founded by Aithouros in ancient times, this circle was responsible for most of the destruction of Hespera's temples during the Last War. Oversees the training of all war mages from Tenebra and Cordium to ensure their lifelong loyalty to the Order.

Aithouros: fire mage of the Order of Anthros who personally led the persecution of Hespera worshipers during the Last War. Founder and namesake of the Aithourian Circle, who continue his teachings. Killed by Hippolyta.

Akron's Torch: an artifact of the Order of Anthros, which holds great magical power and symbolizes their authority. Prometheus stole it from the Hagion of Anthros, enraging the Aithourian Circle. It is now in the possession of his mother, Kassandra.

Alatheia: the first mage of Hespera executed for heresy by the Order of Anthros. Because she refused to recant, the inquisitors put out one of her eyes before immolating her. Known in Orthros as "the First Heretic," she is celebrated as a martyr and immortalized in a constellation. Hesperines swear sacred oaths on the star that represents her remaining eye, called the Truth Star.

Alea: one of the two Queens of Orthros, who has ruled the Hesperines for nearly sixteen hundred years with her Grace, Queen Soteira. A mage of Hespera in her mortal life, she is the only Prisma of a temple of Hespera who survived the Ordering.

Alexandra: royal firstblood and Eighth Princess of Orthros, the youngest of the Queens' family. Solaced from Tenebra as a child. She raises silkworms for her craft. Lio's childhood sweetheart.

Alkaios: one of the three Hesperines errant who saved Cassia as a child. He retrieved the ivy pendant from Solia's body for her. He and his Grace, Nephalea, recently settled in Orthros after years as Hesperines errant with his Gifter, Nike.

ancestors: forebears who have passed into the spirit phase. Imperial mages can commune with them to channel their power into spells and rituals. Hesperines cannot contact the ancestors or wield ancestral magic because their immortality prevents them from entering the spirit phase.

Ancestors' Keeping: a ritual through which the participants entrust their secrets to one another's ancestors so that this information cannot to be taken from the casters through interrogation or mind magic. The cost is that they become vulnerable to each other's ancestral magic. The secret cannot be revealed unless all participants willingly reverse the spell together.

Anastasios: Ritual Firstblood who Gifted Apollon, founder of Lio's bloodline. He was a powerful healer and Prismos of Hagia Boreia, who sacrificed his life to help Alea protect their Great Temple from the Order of Anthros's onslaught.

Anesu: the current Sandira King, brother of Prince Tendeso.

Angara: goddess in the Tenebran and Cordian pantheon who blesses warriors with morale in battle. Often portrayed wearing golden armor and bearing a sword. The second scion and eldest daughter of Kyria and Anthros, a lesser deity alongside her brothers and sisters, the Fourteen Scions.

Annassa: honorific for the Queens of Orthros.

Anthros: god of war, order, and fire. Supreme deity of the Tenebran and Cordian pantheon and ruler of summer. The sun is said to be Anthros riding his chariot across the sky. According to myth, he is the husband of Kyria and brother of Hypnos and Hespera.

Apollon: Lio's father, an elder firstblood and founder of Orthros. In his mortal life before the Ordering, he was a mage of Demergos. Transformed by Anastasios, he was the first Hesperine ever to receive the Gift from one of the Ritual firstbloods. Renowned for his powerful stone magic and prowess in battle, he once roamed Abroad as one of the Blood Errant. Known as the Lion of Orthros. Now retired to live peacefully in Orthros with his Grace, Komnena.

apostate: rogue mage who illegally practices magic outside of the Orders.

Archipelagos: land to the west of the Empire comprising a series of islands, which maintains strict isolation from the rest of the world. See **Nodora** and **Matsu**

Argyros: Lio's uncle and mentor in diplomacy and mind magic. Elder firstblood and founder of Orthros from Hagia Anatela, Gifted by Eidon. Graced to Lyta, father of Nike, Kadi, and Mak. An elder firstblood and founder of Orthros like Apollon, his brother by mortal birth. Attended the first Equinox Summit and every one since as the Queens' Master Ambassador. One of the most powerful thelemancers in history, known as Silvertongue for his legendary abilities as a negotiator.

Aromagus: agricultural mage who uses spells to assist farmers.

Ashes: band of mercenaries renowned for their great deeds in the Empire. See **Ukocha**

Athena: two-year-old Eriphite child Solaced by Javed and Kadi. Younger sister of Boskos by birth and blood. The severe case of frost fever she suffered as a mortal damaged her brain. While the Gift has healed her, she is still recovering lost development.

avowal: Hesperine ceremony in which Graces profess their bond before their people; legally binding and an occasion of great celebration.

Ayur: Azarqi goddess of the moons.

Azarqi: nomads of the Maaqul Desert who control trade routes between Vardara and the rest of the Empire. Known for their complex politics, the Azarqi were te original negotiators of the Desert Accord with the jinn.

Battle of Souls: the most prestigious tournament in the Empire, held once every eight years. The winner, known as the Victor of Souls, receives a boon from the Empress and an acacia branch, as well as the right to display the acacia symbol for the rest of their lives.

beast magic: type of Lustra magic that gives those with this affinity the power to influence animals and, if very powerful, to change into animal forms. See **changer, triune affinity**

Bellator: Tenebran free lord who kidnapped Solia and held her for ransom inside Castra Roborra. Led the short-lived rebellion that ended there with the Siege of Sovereigns.

Benedict: First Knight of Segetia, Flavian's best friend, who harbors unrequited love for Genie. Cassia trusts him and considers him a friend. Traveled to Orthros as Lord Titus's representative during the Solstice Summit.

Blood Errant: group of four ancient and powerful Hesperine warriors who went errant together for eight centuries: Apollon, Nike, Rudhira, and Methu. The only Hesperines errant who have ever carried weapons, they performed legendary but controversial deeds in Hespera's name.

blood magic: type of magic practiced by worshipers of Hespera, from which the power of the Gift stems. All Hesperines possess innate blood magic.

Blood Moon: Hesperine name for one of the two moons, which appears red with a liquid texture to the naked eye. Believed to be an eye of the Goddess Hespera, potent with her blood magic.

blood shackles: warding spell cast with blood magic, which compels a person to not take a particular action. Persists until they are released by a key, a magical condition determined by the caster.

Blood Union: magical empathic connection that allows Hesperines to sense the emotions of any living thing that has blood.

Blood-Red Prince: see **Ioustinianos**

bloodborn: Hesperine born with the Gift because their mother was transformed during pregnancy.

Bosko *or* **Boskos:** ten-year-old Eriphite child Solaced by Javed and Kadi. Elder brother of Athena by birth and blood. Zoe's best friend. Harbors anger over what the children suffered and is struggling to adjust to life in Orthros.

Broken Hands: vigilante group in the Empire who hunt down shadowlanders. Known by the tattoos on their palm, resembling a circle of broken stones.

Btana Ayal: "Shattered Hope"; the ruins of an ancient city that flourished in the Maaqul Desert during the Hulaic Epochs. Under the leadership of the Diviner Queen, the people of Btana Ayal traveled to Tenebra via a spirit gate. Their encounter with the other continent ended in tragedy, when the Diviner Queen had to collapse the gate to prevent the Old Masters from invading the Empire, destroying the city in the process.

Callen: Perita's loving husband and Cassia's bodyguard in the royal household who accompanied her to the Solstice Summit. Has since returned to Tenebra.

Capital University: university located in the capital city of the Empire, open to all Imperial citizens of any social class; known for egalitarianism and cutting-edge research.

Cassia: newgift awaiting her transformation into a Hesperine so she can spend eternity with Lio, her Grace. Once a Tenebran lady who secretly aided the Hesperines and helped Lio secure peace during the Solstice Summit. Born the illegitimate daughter of King Lucis and his concubine, Thalia.

Castra Roborra: fortress in Tenebra belonging to Lord Bellator, where he held Solia captive. Site of the Siege of Sovereigns.

Chalice of Stars: Nike's legendary round shield, which she uses along with the Stand's hand-to-hand combat techniques.

changer: practitioner of Lustra magic with the power to take on animal form.

Changing Queen: Queen Hedera of Tenebra, the Mage King's wife and co-ruler during the Last War. As a Silvicultrix, she was a powerful mage in her own right. Her own people knew her as Ebah. Also known as the Hawk of the Lustra and associated with her plant symbol, ivy.

the Charge: see **Prince's Charge**

charm: physical object imbued with a mage's spell, usually crafted of botanicals or other materials with their own magical properties. Offers a mild beneficial effect to an area or the holder of the charm, even if that person is not a mage.

Chera: goddess of rain and spinning in the Tenebran and Cordian pantheon, known as the Mourning Goddess and the Widow. According to myth, she was the Bride of Spring before Anthros destroyed her god-husband, Demergos, for disobedience.

Chief Diviner of the High Court: the highest-ranking theramancer in the Empire, who advises the Empress. See **High Court**

Chrysanthos: war mage from Cordium with an affinity for fire. As the Dexion of the Aithourian Circle, he is one of the elites in the Order of Anthros. During the Solstice Summit, he tried to sabotage peace talks with hostage negotiations.

Chuma: a Cifwani village girl to whom Monsoon is fiercely loyal. She and her family have been known to harbor shadowlanders from the Imperial authorities. Daughter of Ipika and Mumba.

Cifwani Matriarchate: powerful sister-state in the Empire bordering the Sandira Kingdom. Ruled by matriarchal clans and known for their craftswomen and warriors. The Cifwani are the present-day descendants of Queen Soteira's ancient culture.

the Collector: one of the Old Masters, both a necromancer and mage of dreams, who uses his power to possess his victims and force them to do his bidding. He has used essential displacement to amass unnatural amounts of magic of various affinities. The Gift Collectors are his willing servants, helping him carry out a far-reaching conspiracy to achieve his mysterious ends in alliance with King Lucis. With the help of Skleros and by exploiting Eudias, he entered Orthros during the Solstice Summit and would have caused terrible suffering and destruction if Lio and Cassia had not stopped him.

Cordium: land to the south of Tenebra where the Mage Orders hold sway. Its once-mighty principalities and city-states have now lost power to the magical and religious authorities. Wealthy and cultured, but prone to deadly politics. Also known as the Magelands.

Corona: capital city of Cordium and holy seat of the Mage Orders, where the main temples of each god are located, including the Hagion of Anthros.

Court of Claws: exclusive sparring area at the Sandira Court where gold roster mercenaries and royal guards challenge each other.

the Craving: a Hesperine's addiction to their Grace's blood. When deprived of each other, Graces suffer agonizing withdrawal symptoms and fatal illness.

Dakk: theramancy student from Capital University who befriended Cassia in the Sun Market on the island of Marijani.

Dawn Slumber: deep sleep Hesperines fall into when the sun rises. Although the sunlight causes them no harm, they're unable to awaken until nightfall, leaving them vulnerable during daylight hours.

Departure: contingency plan that dates from the founding of Orthros, when Hesperines feared the Last War might break out again at any time. If the Queens invoked the Departure, all Hesperines errant would return home, and the border between Orthros and Tenebra would be closed forever.

Desert Accord: treaty between the Empire and the jinn of the Maaqul Desert that ended the Thousand Fires War.

Deukalion: bloodborn firstgift of Apollon and Komnena, Ambassador in Orthros's diplomatic service who has devoted his career to improving relations between Orthros and Tenebra. Since he and Cassia, his Grace, succeeded in securing peace during the Solstice Summit, he has taken a leave of absence for her Gifting.

Desidia: the King of Tenebra's pleasure palace. Solia was traveling there when Lord Bellator and his fellow rebels waylaid and kidnapped her.

Divine Tongue: language spoken by Hesperines and mages, used for spells, rituals, and magical texts. The common tongue of Orthros, spoken freely by all Hesperines. In Tenebra and Cordium, the mages keep it a secret and disallow non-mages from learning it.

diviner: Imperial theramancer trained in ancient traditions who protects their people from necromancy and communicates with the ancestors. Their ancestral magic enables them to open passages through the spirit phase.

Diviner Queen: theramancer who founded Btana Ayal and the surrounding civilization in the Hulaic Epochs. When she led her people to the shadowlands through a spirit gate, they taught the people of what would later become Tenebra and Cordium how to use magic. When the Old Masters began to abuse the power they had learned from her, she made the ultimate sacrifice and destroyed everything she had built to contain their evil.

the Drink: when a Hesperine drinks blood from a human or animal; a nonsexual act, considered sacred, which should be carried out with respect for the donor. It's forbidden to take the Drink from an unwilling person. Or Hesperine sacred tenet, the commitment to thriving without the death of other living things.

Dynastic: mother tongue of the Owia dynasty used for all political discourse in the multilingual Empire.

Ebah: see **Changing Queen**

Eidon: Prismos of Hagia Anatela. Ritual firstblood and Gifter of Argyros.

Eighth Circle: Lio and Cassia's Trial circle. See **Alexandra, Eudokia, Lysandros, Menodora, Telemakhos**

elder firstbloods: the ancient Hesperine founders of Orthros. Gifted by the Ritual firstbloods. See **Apollon, Argyros, Hypatia, Kassandra, Kitharos**

the Empire: vast and prosperous human lands located far to the west, across an ocean from Tenebra. Comprises many different languages and cultures united under the Empress. Allied with Orthros and welcoming to Hesperines, many of whom began their mortal lives as Imperial citizens. Maintains a strict policy of isolation toward Tenebra and Cordium to guard against the Mage Orders.

the Empress: the ruler of the Empire, admired by her citizens. The Imperial throne has passed down through the female line for many generations.

the Empress's privateers: pirates who sail with the sanction of the Empress, granted by a letter of marque, which authorizes them to rob her enemies. They make voyages to Cordium to secretly pillage the Mage Orders' ships.

enchantment: a spell anchored to a power source, which can last indefinitely without a mage's attention.

errant: a Hesperine who has left Orthros to travel through Tenebra doing good deeds for mortals

Eudias: young war mage from Cordium with an affinity for weather, including lightning. Compelled to join the Aithourian circle due to his magic, he defected during the Solstice Summit, aiding the Hesperines and the Tenebran embassy against Chrysanthos and Skleros. He and Lio faced the Collector in a mage duel, in which Lio helped him free himself from the Old Master's possession.

Eudokia: Hesperine youngblood, one of Lio's Trial sisters in Orthros. Solaced from Tenebra as a child. An initiate mathematician, calligrapher, and accomplished scholar. Daughter of Hypatia.

Evander: see **Evandrus the Younger**

Evandrus the Elder: Tenebran free lord who assisted Lord Bellator in Solia's kidnapping and joined forces with him inside Castra Roborra during their rebellion.

Evandrus the Younger: son and heir of Evandrus the Elder, who was with him at Castra Roborra during the Siege of Sovereigns.

familiar: the animal companion of a Hesperine, bound to them by blood.

the Fangs: Prometheus's famous twin swords.

the Feast: Hesperine term for drinking blood while making love.

fire charm: a charm created by a fire mage that those without the affinity for fire can use to light a flame.

First Circle: Rudhira, Nike, and Methu's Trial circle. They were the first Hesperines to go through the Trial of Initiation together and founded the tradition of Trial circles.

firstblood: the first Hesperine in a bloodline, who founds the family and passes the Gift to their children.

Firstblood Circle: the governing body of Orthros. Every firstblood has a vote on behalf of their bloodline, while non-voting Hesperines can attempt to influence policy by displays of partisanship. The Queens retain veto power, but use it sparingly.

firstgift: the eldest child of a Hesperine bloodline, first to receive the gift from their parents.

Flavian: young Tenebran lord, son of Free Lord Titus and heir to Segetia's seat on the Council. Despite his family's feud with Hadria, he is admired by both sides of the conflict and is a unifying figure for the fractured nobility. Cassia has prepared the way for him to take the throne from Lucis in a peaceful transfer of power.

fortune blade: dagger issued to mercenaries by the Empress's administration, which shows they are professionally recognized and may fight for profit, and that they abide by the Empress's code of conduct.

fortune name: name given to an Imperial mercenary, by which they are professionally known. Traditionally, they take the name of something they wish to avoid in order to ward off that evil.

geomagus: mage with an affinity for geological forces, who can use their magic to conjure heat from the ground or create artifacts like warming plates for heating food and drink.

the Gift: Hesperines' immortality and magical abilities, which they regard as a blessing from the goddess Hespera. The practice of offering the Gift to all is a Hesperine sacred tenet.

Gift Collector: mage-assassin and bounty hunter who hunts down Hesperines for the Order of Hypnos using necromancy, alchemy, and fighting tactics. Known for adapting common items into weapons to skirt the Orders' religious laws against mages arming themselves.

Gift Night: the night of a person's transformation into a Hesperine, usually marked by great celebration.

Gifting: the transformation from human into Hesperine.

Glasstongue: see **Deukalion**

the Goddess's Eyes: the two moons, the red Blood Moon and the white Light Moon; associated with Hespera and regarded as her gaze by Hesperines.

gold roster: list maintained by the Empress's administrators of the mercenaries who have received the most gold in service to the Empire's interests. A measure of a mercenary's prowess, wealth, and how many contracts they have completed to benefit the common good.

Golden Shield: the Empress's personal guard, who answer only to her, an order of highly skill woman warriors with access to powerful magic. They give up their identities to devote their lives to the Empress's protection, and their families must live in seclusion so their loved ones cannot be used to gain an advantage against them.

Gomba: unscrupulous former privateer, Ziara's nemesis.

Grace: Hesperine sacred tenet, a magical bond between two Hesperine lovers. Frees them from the need for human blood and enables them to sustain each other, but comes at the cost of the Craving. A fated bond that happens when their love is true. It is believed every Hesperine has a Grace just waiting to be found. See **Craving**

Grace braids: thin braids of one another's hair that Graces exchange. They may wear them privately after professing their bond to one another, then exchange them publicly at their avowal and thereafter wear them for all to see to signify their commitment.

Grace-family (Grace-son, Grace-father, Grace-sister, etc.): the family members of a Hesperine's Grace; compare with human in-laws.

Grace Union: the particularly powerful and intimate Blood Union between two Hesperines who are Graced; enables them to communicate telepathically and empathically.

Great Temple Epoch: the historical period when the Great Temples of every cult flourished across Tenebra and Cordium, and all mages cooperated. Came to a cataclysmic end due to the Ordering and the Last War.

greater sand cat: species of large predator with special adaptations for surviving the Maaqul Desert. With specialized magic and great effort, they can be bonded to humans and ridden as mounts. See **Tilili**

Guardian of Orthros: see **Hippolyta**

Hagia Boreia: one of the four Great Temples of Hespera that flourished during the Great Temple Epoch, located in northern Tenebra. See **Alea, Anastasios**

Hagion of Anthros: the most powerful and sacred temple of Anthros in Corona, where the Akron presides over the Order of Anthros.

Haima: capital city of Orthros Notou.

Hammer of the Sun: Apollon's famous battle hammer, which he wielded while Abroad with the Blood Errant. He left it in Tenebra when he brought Komnena to Orthros.

Harkhuf Addaya Khemkare: Imperial human guest visiting Orthros to study theramancy, a cousin of the Empress. Xandra's share.

Healing Sanctuary: infirmary in Orthros founded and run by Queen Soteira, where humans are given care and Hesperines are trained in the healing arts.

heart hunters: warbands of Tenebrans who hunt down Hesperines, regarded by their countrymen as protectors of humanity. They patrol the northern borders of Tenebra with packs of liegehounds, waiting to attack Hesperines who leave Orthros.

Hedon: god of pleasure and chance in the Tenebran and Cordian pantheon, patron of sexual acts and gambling. Styled as the god of fertility and prosperity by the Order of Anthros in their attempts to promote morality.

Hespera: goddess of night cast from the Tenebran and Cordian pantheon. The Mage Orders have declared her worship heresy punishable by death. Hesperines keep her cult alive and continue to revere her as the goddess of the moons, Sanctuary, and Mercy. Associated with roses, thorns, and fanged creatures. According to myth, she is the sister of Anthros and Hypnos.

Hesperine: nocturnal immortal being with fangs who gains nourishment from drinking blood. Tenebrans and Cordians believe them to be monsters bent on humanity's destruction. In truth, they follow a strict moral code in the name of their goddess, Hespera, and wish only to ease humankind's suffering.

Hesperite: human worshiper of Hespera, persecuted as a heretic by the Orders.

High Court: council of diviners who attend the Empress during audiences. Their role is to ensure no petitioners or advisors use illicit spells to influence her decisions.

Hinan: Queen Mother who represents the Azarqi on the Empire's council, queen of an influential nomad clan with great influence on desert politics and trade. Mother of Kella.

Hippolyta: Lio's aunt, Graced to Argyros, mother of Nike, Kadi, and Mak. Greatest and most ancient Hesperine warrior, a founder of Orthros. Known as the Guardian of Orthros for her deeds in Tenebra during the Last War and for establishing the Stand.

Hippolyta's Stand: Orthros's standing army, founded by Hippolyta. Under her leadership, they patrol the border with Tenebra as Stewards of the Queens' ward. So few of the peaceful Hesperines take up the battle arts that Nike, Kadi, Mak, and Lyros are the only Stewards.

House Annassa: the residence of the Queens of Orthros, the Hesperine counterpart to a royal palace.

Hoyefe: mercenary illusionist and master fencer, member of the Ashes. Of Owia descent, he is an alumnus of Imperial University's School of Fine Arts and a playwright favored by the Empress.

Hulaic Epochs: eras of pre-history before the Great Temple Epoch, known only through oral traditions.

Huru: Ziara's first mate and lover, a knife expert and theramancer.

Hypatia: an elder firstblood and founder of Orthros from Hagia Anatela, mother of Kia. Orthros's greatest astronomer, who invented the Hesperine calendar.

Hypatia's Observatory: tower in Orthros established by Hypatia, where Hesperine astronomers study the heavens and teach their students. Every Autumn

Equinox, Orthros's diplomats watch for the Summit Beacon from here.

Hypnos: god of death and dreams in the Tenebran and Cordian pantheon. Winter is considered his season. Humans unworthy of going to Anthros's Hall are believed to spend the afterlife in Hypnos's realm of the dead. According to myth, he is the brother of Anthros and Hespera.

Imperial University: illustrious university in the Empire. Only students with wealth and the best references gain entry, usually those of noble or royal blood. Known for traditionalism and conservative approaches to research.

Ipika: Chuma's mother, who is often traveling. Her journeys to the market are suspected to be a cover for her activities smuggling innocent fugitives to safety.

Ioustin *or* **Ioustinianos:** First Prince of the Hesperines, eldest child of the Queens of Orthros. Lio's Ritual father. Solaced from Tenebra as a child. Once a warrior in the Blood Errant known as the Blood-Red Prince, he now leads the Charge. Young Hesperines call him Rudhira, an affectionate name given to him by Methu.

Iris: Tenebran lady, Solia's handmaiden and closest companion, who was with her at the Siege of Sovereigns.

ivy pendant: wooden pendant carved with a triquetra of ivy. Secretly passed down from one Tenebran queen to another and finally, from Solia to Cassia. Imbued with Lustra magic and connected to the Changing Queen in some way.

Javed: Lio's Grace-cousin, avowed to Kadi, father of Bosko and Thenie. From the Empire in his mortal life. Has an affinity for healing and now serves in Orthros's Healing Sanctuary.

Jinn: immortal beings that dwell in the Maaqul Desert. Unlike Hesperines, they were never human. Endowed with powerful magic drawn from elements of nature, they also have a connection with the spirit phase. A long history of conflict between jinn and Imperial humans culminated in the Thousand Fires War and ended with the Desert Accord.

Jua: patron goddess of the Sun Market and commerce, worshiped on the island of Marijani.

Kadi: see **Arkadia**

kaetlii: word in the tongue used by Tenebrans to train liegehounds, meaning the person the dog is bonded to and will protect until death.

Kalos: the Charge's best scout, who uses his tracking skills to find Hesperines errant who are missing in action.

kalux: Hesperine word in the Divine Tongue for clitoris.

Karege:

Kassandra: Lio's Ritual mother, an elder firstblood and founder of Orthros. Ritual sister to the Queens, who Gifted her, and mother of Prometheus. A princess in her mortal life, she became the first Hesperine from the Empire and secured her homeland's alliance with Orthros. Now the Queens' Master Economist who oversees Orthros's trade. Has the gift of foresight and as Orthros's oracle, guides the Hesperines with her prophecies.

Kella: Azarqi princess, daughter of Hinan. As second blade of the Ashes, she is a fierce warrior with a preference for daggers, as well as a water mage mage skilled at desert survival. Bonded to her greater sand cat mount, Tilili, after her legs were amputated above the knee due to a combat injury.

Kia: see **Eudokia**

King of Tenebra: see **Lucis**

Kitharos: an elder firstblood and founder of Orthros, father to Nodora. One of the Hesperines' greatest musicians.

Knight: Cassia's beloved liegehound. Solia gave him to Cassia as a puppy so Cassia would have protection and companionship.

Komnena: Lio's mother, still rather young by Hesperines standards. Fled a life of squalor as a Tenebran farmwife and ran away to Orthros with Apollon, who Gifted her while she was pregnant and raised her son as his own. Now a respected mind healer. As the Queens' Chamberlain, she is responsible for helping newcomers to Orthros settle and adjust.

Konstantina *or* **Kona:** royal firstblood, Second Princess of Orthros, the second child and eldest daughter of the Queens. From the Empire in her mortal life. As the Royal Master Magistrate, she is the author of Orthros's legal code and an influential politician who oversees the proceedings of the First-blood Circle.

krana: Hesperine term in the Divine Tongue for vagina.

Kyria: goddess of weaving and the harvest in the Tenebran and Cordian pantheon, known as the Mother Goddess or the Wife. Her season is autumn. According to myth, she is married to Anthros.

liegehound: war dogs bred and trained by Tenebrans to track, hunt, and slay Hesperines. Veil spells do not throw them off the scent, and they can leap high enough to pull a levitating Hesperine from the air. The only animals that do not trust Hesperines. They live longer than other canines and can withstand poison and disease.

Light Moon: Hesperine name for one of the two moons, which appears white with a smooth texture. Believed to be an eye of the Goddess Hespera, shining with her light.

Lio: see **Deukalion**

Lion of Orthros: see **Apollon**

lithic edges: stone weapons that allow humans to magically travel across the Maaqul, as well as banish their enemies.

lithomagus: a mage with an affinity for stone. Can manipulate stone with magic for architectural, agricultural, or battle purposes.

Lonesome: Hoyefe's fortune name.

Lucis: current King of Tenebra, who reigns with ruthlessness and brutality. Born a lord, he secured the crown by might and political schemes, and he upholds his authority by any means necessary. Cassia has never forgiven him for his cruelty to her, Solia, and Thalia.

Lustra magic: Tenebran name referring to old nature magic. Practiced in ancient times by the Changing Queen. The Orders have never been able to understand or control it, and most knowledge of it is now lost.

Lysandros *or* **Lyros:** Lio's Trial brother and Grace-cousin, avowed to Mak, Solaced as a child from Tenebra. Also a warder and warrior serving in the Stand.

Lyta: see Hippolyta

Maaqul Desert: a vast and treacherous desert the size of several states in the Empire. Few besides the jinn and the Azarqi nomads can survive here.

Mage King: King Lucian of Tenebra, who reigned sixteen hundred years ago, widely considered by Hesperines and mortals to have been a great monarch. He and his wife, the Changing Queen, made the original Equinox Oath with the Queens of Orthros. A fire mage and warrior, he ruled before the Mage Orders mandated that men must choose between wielding spells or weapons.

mage of dreams: mage of Hypnos with an affinity for thelemancy.

Mage Orders: the magical and religious authorities in Cordium, which also dictate sacred law to Tenebran temples. Responsible for training and governing mages and punishing heretics.

Magelands: see **Cordium**

Mak: see **Telemakhos**

Marijani: a wealthy, and powerful island city-state that is an important port of call for Imperial merchants, privateers, and Hesperines. See **Sun Market** and **Moon Market**

Martyrs' Pass: the only known passage to Orthros through the Umbral Mountains. When an army of heart hunters possessed by the Collector ambushed the Tenebran embassy here, Lio defeated them with his mind magic and rescued Cassia.

Master of Dreams: see the Collector

Matsu: Nodora's Ritual mother and the only other Hesperine from the Archipelagos. A beloved thespian and fashion leader in Orthros.

Menodora: Hesperine youngblood, one of Lio's Trial sisters. Daughter of Kitharos and Dakarai. An initiate musician, admired vocalist, and crafter of musical instruments. She is one of only two Hesperines from the Archipelagos and the immortal expert on the music of her mortal homeland.

Mercy: Hesperine sacred tenet, the practice of caring for dead or dying humans.

Methu: see Prometheus

Midnight Champion: see Prometheus

mind healer: see **theramancer**

mind hook: a magical artifact created by a thelemancer that grants control over others' thoughts and Will.

mind mage: see thelemancer

mind ward: mental defense cast by a thelemancer, which protects a person's mind from mages seeking to invade their thoughts or subdue their Will.

Monsoon: gold roster mercenary who defeats all challengers in the Blood Court. Known for his bad temper, he always fights alone and is said to be dangerous.

moon hours: by the Hesperine clock, the hours corresponding to night, when Hesperines pursue public activities.

Moon Market: hidden bazaar on the island of Marijani, where the Empress's privateers sell their spoils.

Mumba: Cifwani farmer, husband of Ipika and father of Chuma.

Mweya: winged Sandira deity who blessed his descendants with the ability to shapeshift.

natural phase: the physical world where living creatures exist, as opposed to the afterlife. See **spirit phase**

Nephalea: one of the three Hesperines errant who saved Cassia as a child. She and her Grace, Alkaios, recently settled in Orthros after years as Hesperines errant with his Gifter, Nike.

newgift: a newly transformed Hesperine, or a person who has decided to become immortal and awaits their Gifting.

Nike: see **Pherenike**

Nodora: see **Menodora**

Noon Watch: Karege's fortune name.

nyakimbi: means "little sister" in Sandira

Nyakou: Imperial princess, the Empress's eldest daughter and heir to her throne.

the Old Masters: the oldest known hex of necromancers in Tenebran and Cordian record. Little is known about them from legends and surviving ancient texts, but their influence is linked to catastrophic events and suffering throughout history. They extend their lives and hoard power using abusive magic such as essential displacement. See **the Collector**

ora: strong Sandira liquor

Oracle of Chera: mage with the gift of foresight, appointed by the Orders to serve in Corona. The affinity is so rare that usually only one woman is born with it in each generation.

Order of Anthros: Mage Order dedicated to the god Anthros, which holds the ultimate religious and magical authority over all other Orders and temples. Bent on destroying Hesperines. War mages, light mages, and warders serve in this Order, as do agricultural and stone mages.

Orthros: homeland of the Hesperines, ruled by the Queens. The Mage Orders describe it as a horrific place where no human can survive, but in reality, it is a land of peace, prosperity, and culture.

Orthros Abroad: the population of Hesperines who are errant in Tenebra at any given time. Under the jurisdiction of the First Prince, who is the Queens' regent outside their ward.

Orthros Boreou: Hesperine homeland in the northern hemisphere, located north of and sharing a border with Tenebra.

Orthros Notou: Hesperine homeland in the southern hemisphere, located across the sea to the southeast of the Empire.

Owia: the dynasty that currently holds the throne of the Empire.

Peanut: Tuura's fortune name.

Perita: Cassia's handmaiden and dearest friend who accompanied her to Orthros for the Solstice Summit and assisted with all her schemes. Has now returned to Tenebra with her husband, Callen.

Phaedros: mage of Hespera and brilliant scholar from ancient times. The only survivor of his Great Temple's destruction by the Aithourian Circle. After he took revenge against the mortals, he lost his status as an elder firstblood. Now lives in eternal exile under the midnight sun.

Pherenike: Lio's cousin, a warder and warrior second only to her mother Lyta in strength, a thelemancer second only to her father Argyros in power. Solaced from Tenebra as a child. Known as the Victory Star, one of the Blood Errant alongside her uncle, Apollon, and her Trial brothers Rudhira and Methu. After the surviving Blood Errant's campaign to avenge Methu, she remained Abroad alone, missing in action for over ninety years.

Prince and Diplomat: board game and beloved Hesperine pastime; requires strategy and practice to master.

Prince's Charge: the force of Hesperines errant who serve under the First Prince.

Prismos: highest ranking male mage in a temple.

privateers: see **Empress's Privateers**

Prometheus: legendary Hesperine warrior and martyr. Bloodborn to Kassandra and descendant of Imperial royalty. Known as the Midnight Champion, he was a member of the Blood Errant with his comrades Nike, Rudhira, and Apollon. Captured by the Aithourian Circle before Lio's birth. Orthros still mourns his death.

Pup: Solia's childhood nickname for Cassia.

Queen Mothers: matriarchs from each sister state within the Empire who possess the sacred artifacts that symbolize power to their particular people. Each Imperial dynasty must secure their blessings in order to reign.

the Queens: the Hesperine monarchs of Orthros. See **Alea**, **Soteira**

the Queens' Couriers: young Hesperines who serve Orthros as messengers, delivering correspondence and packages throughout Selas.

the Queens' ward: the powerful Sanctuary ward cast by the Queens, which spans the borders of Orthros, protecting Hesperines from human threats.

Rakesh: Hesperine Master Ambassador and Orthros's foremost diplomat in the Empress's court. Rumored to be Princess Nyakou's lover.

Rezayal: "Hope's Fragments"; a fanatical secret society of diviners based in the ruins of Btana Ayal, who believe only they can protect the Empire from the Old Masters. Their members are deeply embedded at every level of Imperial society and government, using any means necessary to preserve the Empire's isolation and to persecute shadowlanders. Sometimes known as the Broken Hands due to their tattoo.

rhabdos: Hesperine term in the Divine Tongue meaning penis.

rimelace: flowering herb that requires extremely cold conditions. Difficult to grow in Tenebra, even with the aid of magic, but thrives in Orthros. The only known treatment for frost fever.

Ritual: Hesperine sacred tenet. A ceremony in which Hesperines share blood, but in a broader sense, the whole of their religious beliefs.

Ritual circle: area where Hesperines gather to perform Ritual, usually marked with sacred symbols on the floor.

Ritual Drink: the Drink given by one Hesperine to another for healing or sustenance, without intimacy or invoking a family bond.

Ritual parents: Hesperines who attend a new suckling's first Ritual or who give the Gift to a mortal becoming a Hesperine as an adult. They remain mentors and trusted guides for eternity. Comparable to Tenebran temple parents.

Ritual tributary: Hesperine who establishes their own bloodline rather than joining their Gifter's family.

Rose House: the guest house on the docks of Selas where Cassia stayed during the Tenebran embassy's visit to Orthros for the Solstice Summit. Site of her and Lio's battle with the Collector.

Rudhira: see **Ioustinianos**

Sanctuary: Hesperine sacred tenet, the practice of offering refuge to anyone in need. *Or* Hesperine refuge in hostile territory, concealed and protected from humans by Sanctuary magic.

Sanctuary mage: a mage with a rare dual affinity for warding and light magic, who can create powerful protections that also conceal. Queen Alea of Orthros is the only mage with this affinity who survived the Orders' persecution of Hespera worshipers.

Sandira Court: capital city and royal seat of the Sandira Kingdom, one of the most populous cities in the world. Known for its magnificent stone architecture. Mercenaries congregate in this metropolis seeking contracts with trade caravans in need of protection.

Sandira King: eagle shifter and monarch of the Sandira Kingdom known for showing no leniency. He rules with a strong hand to meet the challenges faced by his rapidly expanding people.

Sandira Kingdom: powerful sister state that controls the flow of gold, ivory, and copper between the Kwatzi City-States and the Empire's interior. Ruled by hereditary shifters whose animal forms signify their status within the hierarchy of warriors, nobility, or royalty.

Scions: lesser deities in the Tenebran and Cordian pantheon, the fourteen children of Anthros and Kyria, comprising seven sons and seven daughters. Each has their own cult and mages. See **Angara**

Scorched Verge: region at the edge of the Maaqul where there is a major Azarqi camp that serves as a starting point for all expeditions into the desert.

Selas: capital city of Orthros Boreou.

shadowlands: Imperial term for Tenebra and Cordium, sometimes used with pity or disdain.

shadowlander: Imperial term for a person from Tenebra or Cordium

share: human or immortal with whom a Hesperine is romantically involved, sharing blood and intimacy.

shifter: a person of Sandira descent who is blessed by their ancestors with the ability to shapeshift. Sandira shifters take on the form of a particular animal with which their clan has cultivated a sacred bond over many generations.

Silklands: see **Vardara**

530 ஜ *Vela Roth*

Silvicultrix: in ancient times, a nature sorceress with command of Lustra magic. The Changing Queen was known to be a powerful Silvicultrix.

sister states: independent lands within the Empire ruled by their own monarchs, all owing allegiance to the Empress. She is seen as their eldest sister, and they are symbolically members of her clan.

Skleros: master necromancer and Gift Collector who holds the Order of Hypnos's record for completing the most bounties on Hesperines. Expert in essential displacement. Helped the Old Master known as the Collector cause devastation during the Solstice Summit.

Slumber: see **Dawn Slumber**

Solace: Hesperine sacred tenet, the practice of rescuing and Gifting abandoned children.

Solia: Princess of Tenebra, King Lucis's legitimate daughter and heir before the birth of his son. When she was seventeen, rebel lords kidnapped her. Lucis refused to ransom her and ensured all witnesses perished in the ensuing Siege of Sovereigns. Nobles and commoners alike still mourn her, not knowing she survived and escaped to the Empire.

Solstice Oath: new treaty between Orthros and the Tenebran nobility, secured thanks to Lio and Cassia's efforts during the Solstice Summit.

Solstice Summit: diplomatic negotiations between Tenebra and Orthros that marked the first time a mortal embassy from Tenebra ever entered Hesperine lands. An unprecedented event proposed by Lio in an effort to prevent war and make it possible for Cassia to stay with him.

soothsayer: Lustra mage with the affinity for soothsaying, which gives them the power to influence others' thoughts and choices with their words. See **triune affinity**

Soteira: one of the two Queens of Orthros, who has ruled the Hesperines for nearly sixteen hundred years with her Grace, Alea. Originally from the Empire, she was a powerful mortal mage with an affinity for healing before leaving to found Orthros alongside Alea.

speires: symbolic hair ties Lyta gives to trainees when they begin learning the battle arts. Stewards wear them as part of their Stand regalia.

spirit gate: a portal that allows magical travel by opening a passage through the spirit phase. Imperial diviners maintain regulated spirit gates throughout the Empire and Orthros Notou.

spirit phase: the spiritual plane of existence where the ancestors dwell, where living souls originate and to which they return in the afterlife.

spirit tear: a fleeting rip between the natural and spirit phases created by one of the lithic edges, which allows the wielder to travel in the regions of the Maaqul where stepping and traversal are impossible.

spirit walk: ability of Imperial mages, who can walk through the spirit phase to travel between locations in the natural phase. Spirit walking is only possible in the territory of their own ancestors, and they must use spirit gates in other regions.

the Stand: see **Hippolyta's Stand**

Standstill: Kella's fortune name

stepping: innate Hesperine ability to teleport instantly from one place to another with little magical effort.

Steward: see **Hippolyta's Stand**

suckling: Hesperine child.

Sun Market: bazaar on Marijani renowned for its wonders.

Sunburn: mercenary fire mage and swordswoman trained by Monsoon. The love of his life who broke his heart.

tata: Cifwani word for "father."

Telemakhos: Lio's cousin and best friend. Exposed as a child in Tenebra due to his club foot, Solaced by Argyros and Lyta. A warrior by profession and warder by affinity, he serves in the Stand. He and his Grace, Lyros, are newly avowed.

Tendeso: prince of the Sandira Court, brother of the king.

Tenebra: human kingdom south of Orthros and north of Cordium. Agrarian, feudal society ruled by a king, prone to instability due to rivalries between lords. Land of the Hesperines' origin, where they are now persecuted.

Thalia: Cassia's mother, King Lucis's concubine. Murdered the day Cassia was born by an apostate fire mage attempting to assassinate Lucis.

thelemancer: a mage with an affinity for thelemancy, or mind magic, which gives them the power to manipulate others' thoughts and control their Wills.

Thenie: see **Athena**

theramancer: a person with an affinity for theramancy, or mind healing, who can use magic to treat mental illness.

Thorn: Rudhira's two-handed sword, which he carried as one of the Blood Errant and now wields as he leads the Charge.

Thousand Fires War: devastating war between the jinn and the humans of the Empire that ended thanks to the Azarqi negotiating the Desert Accord.

Tilili: greater sand cat bonded to Kella who serves as her mount and partner in combat.

Tradewinds: mother tongue of the Kwatzi City-States, which is used to conduct all commerce across the multilingual Empire.

traversal: teleportation ability of Tenebran and Cordian mages; requires a great expense of magic and usually leaves the mortal mage seriously ill.

Trial circle: age set of Hesperines who go through the Trial of Initiation together. They consider each other Trial sisters and brothers for the rest of their immortal lives. Although not related by birth or blood, they maintain strong bonds of loyalty and friendship for eternity.

triune affinity: the combination of three powerful Lustra magics: plant magic, beast magic, and soothsaying. In ancient times, sorceresses with the triune affinity were revered as Silvicultrixes. The Mage Orders have since suppressed these gifts, and the few women who manifest the triune affinity strive to keep their power secret.

Tuura: mercenary theramancer, the Ashes' diviner and alchemist.

Ukocha: leader of the Ashes, a swordswoman and fire mage who inspires awe among mercenaries.

Union: Hesperine sacred tenet, the principle of living with empathy and compassion for all. See **Blood Union**

Vardara: now one of the mightiest sister states, once a sovereign land that fought wars with the Empire throughout history. The conflict ended sixteen hundred years ago when the Empress and a royal from the Silklands had a child together, Kassandra. Their union joined Vardara to the Empire.

veil hours: by the Hesperine clock, the hours corresponding to day, when Hesperines Slumber or devote their private time to friends, family, and lovers.

veil spell: innate Hesperine ability to cast magical concealments that hide their presence and activities from humans or fellow immortals.

veiled blood seal: Hesperine spell for securing confidential correspondence.

Victor of Souls: see **Battle of Souls**

Victory Star: see **Pherenike**

Vulgus *or* **the vulgar tongue**: common language of all non-mages in Tenebra and Cordium.

warder: mage with an affinity for warding, the power to create magical protections that block spells or physical attacks.

war mage: person with an affinity for fire, lightning, or other type of magic that can be weaponized. The Order of Anthros requires them to dedicate their lives to the Aithourian Circle.

Will: free will, willpower. *Or* Hesperine sacred tenet, the principle of guarding the sanctity of each person's freedom of choice.

Wisdom's Precipice: a tall cliff in Orthros with a treacherous drop to the rocky sea below. When Mak, Lyros, and Lio were newbloods, they jumped off in the hopes of awakening their power of levitation, only to fall and suffer painful injuries.

Xandra: see **Alexandra**

youngblood: young adult Hesperine who has recently reached their majority by passing the Trial of Initiation.

Zalele: supreme goddess of the Imperial pantheon, the deity of the sun and sky who is revered as the maker and nurturer of all creation. Believed to be too great and powerful to trouble herself with day-to-day mortal affairs, which she leaves to lesser deities and the ancestors.

Ziara: one of the most accomplished of the Empress's Privateers, famed for her powerful wind magic and daring voyages to Cordium. Captain of the *Wanted*, which she sails with Huru and their all-woman crew.

Zoe *or* **Zosime:** Lio's little sister, a seven-year-old Eriphite child Solaced by Apollon and Komnena. Loves her new family and idolizes her brother for his role in saving her from Tenebra. Has yet to heal from the emotional wounds she suffered as a mortal.

BLOOD GIFT

BLOOD GRACE BOOK VII

Can she claim her magic and her fangs?

Ancient magic is sleeping inside Cassia. Wielding it is her birthright, but her bloodright is to become an immortal Hesperine like Lio, her Grace. Until she masters her dormant magic, it's too dangerous for him to transform her. To claim both her legacies, she must return to the land that holds the secrets of her power: the mortal kingdom where she was once powerless.

Lio is ready to protect her with diplomacy, spells, or even his fists. He knows he'll need them against the lord who is still betrothed to her under human law. Most dangerous of all, the necromancer known as the Collector lies in wait, planning to use Cassia for his mysterious ends.

When the moment of Cassia's transformation arrives, there will be no turning back. Can the Gift of eternal life from Lio's blood save her from the necromancer, master of death?

Steamy romance meets classic fantasy worldbuilding in Blood Grace. Follow fated mates Lio and Cassia through their epic love story for a guaranteed series HEA.

Continue Cassia and Lio's story in
Blood Grace Book 7, *Blood Gift*...
vroth.co/gift

BLOOD DREAM

A BLOOD GRACE STORY

The nightmare is over, but can they live their dream come true?

Cassia is finally free to stay with Lio. Safe in Orthros and done with human politics, she's ready to celebrate with him and her immortal family. And yet she feels uneasy in her new home.

Lio wants the start of their life together to be everything Cassia dreamed. But he can tell something is wrong, and she's trying to hide it. Now there's nothing to keep them apart. So why is she pulling away?

They've defeated necromancers, war mages, and the tyrant king so they can be together. Can they win against the personal specters that threaten their happily ever after?

This touching and steamy Blood Grace bonus novelette is set after the events of Blood Sanctuary Part Two.

Get Blood Grace 4.5 for free!

vroth.co/dream

ABOUT THE AUTHOR

VELA ROTH grew up with female-driven fantasy books and classic epics, then grew into romance novels. She set out to write stories that blend the rich worlds of fantasy with the passion of romance.

She has pursued a career in academia, worked as a web designer and book formatter, and stayed home as a full-time caregiver for her loved ones with severe illnesses. Writing through her own grief and trauma, she created the Blood Grace series, which now offers comfort to readers around the world.

She lives in a solar-powered writer's garret in the Southwestern United States, finding inspiration in the mountains and growing roses in the desert. Her feline familiar is a rescue cat named Milly with a missing fang and a big heart.

Vela loves hearing from readers and hopes you'll visit her at velaroth.com.